"Nicole Deese will crack your heart wide open with this funny, tender, and brilliant story about a woman who finds herself forced to choose between two great loves. I could not put it down."

—Kara Isaac, RITA Award–winning author of *Then There Was You*

"*Before I Called You Mine* is Nicole's finest work yet. Thoroughly engaging with charming characters you'll want to call friends, an authentic emotional storyline that will touch every part of your heart, and, as expected, exquisite writing that will leave you captivated long after the book is finished."

—Tammy L. Gray, RITA Award–winning author

"A story about tough sacrifices, impossible choices, and the love that makes it all worthwhile, *Before I Called You Mine* is a captivating adventure of the heart that will stay with you—and maybe even change you—long after the final page."

—Bethany Turner, award-winning author of *Wooing Cadie McCaffrey*

"Beautiful, poignant, funny, and romantic—all wrapped into one heartwarming story. Deese knows how to spin a tale that makes you fall in love with the characters and feel like they're friends. *Before I Called You Mine* will stay with you long after the last page."

—Christy Barritt, *USA Today* bestselling author

"With its unique right-love-wrong-timing premise, *Before I Called You Mine* is a novel that will keep readers ignoring their chores, reaching for their tissue boxes, and sighing with contentment. It's fresh, soul-stirring, and romantic—all the things we've come to love about a Nicole Deese story."

—Connilyn Cossette, Christy and Carol Award–winning author

before
I
called
you
mine

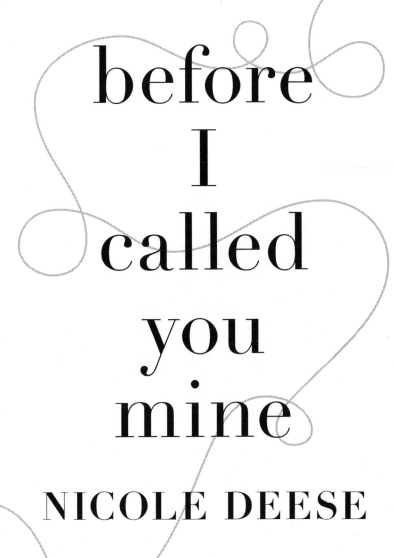

before I called you mine

NICOLE DEESE

BETHANYHOUSE
a division of Baker Publishing Group
Minneapolis, Minnesota

Published by Bethany House Publishers
11400 Hampshire Avenue South
Bloomington, Minnesota 55438
www.bethanyhouse.com

Bethany House Publishers is a division of
Baker Publishing Group, Grand Rapids, Michigan

Printed in the United States of America

Library of Congress Cataloging-in-Publication Data
Names: Deese, Nicole, author.
Title: Before I called you mine / Nicole Deese.
Description: Minneapolis, Minnesota : Bethany House Publishers, [2020] |
Identifiers: LCCN 2019040906 | ISBN 9780764234958 (trade paperback) | ISBN 9780764235580 (cloth) | ISBN 9781493422685 (ebook)
Subjects: LCSH: Single mothers—Fiction. | Man-woman relationships—Fiction.
Classification: LCC PS3604.E299 B44 2020 | DDC 813/.6—dc23
LC record available at https://lccn.loc.gov/2019040906

Cover design by Jennifer Parker

Author represented by Kirkland Media Management

20 21 22 23 24 25 26 7 6 5 4 3 2 1

To my brave warrior princess, Lucy Mei:

I am not the same daughter, wife, mother, friend,
or child of God that I was before you joined our
family. You have reshaped every crevice of my heart,
stretched the boundaries of my faith, and transformed
my once far-too-limited understanding of love.

I am exceedingly blessed to be your forever mama, and
I pray you will always remember that your heavenly
Father called you His before I called you mine.

I love you.

God places the lonely in families. . . .

Psalm 68:6

An invisible red thread connects those destined to meet, regardless of time, place, or circumstance. The thread may stretch or tangle, but it will never break.

—Ancient Chinese Proverb

chapter one

If Obsessive Email Checking Disorder were a disease, I was likely already in the final stages: trigger thumb, mindless refreshing, aimless scrolling, and, of course, an inability to focus on anything else in the entire world.

For what had to be the twentieth time in as many minutes, I paused the anxious cleaning spree of my classroom and unlocked my iPhone to check the digital envelope at the bottom of my home screen. Still nothing.

"Stop it, Lauren. You're gonna make yourself crazy." Because talking to yourself in the third person was totally rational behavior.

I stuffed the phone into the shadowy abyss of my top desk drawer and slammed it shut, cringing as broken crayons collided with last week's confiscated toys. Too bad I couldn't lock my poor self-control up in there, too. In a matter of an hour, I'd gone from promising myself I'd wait to check my phone until after school was dismissed, to caving to temptation's call at the first sight of my purse like a back-alley addict.

I stepped away from my incarcerated device and re-armed myself with lemon-scented antibacterial wipes, searching for a surface left to sanitize before my first graders arrived and happily distracted me from my spiraling restraint. I'd already fluffed the beanbag chairs in Red Rover's Reading Corner, tacked this week's favorite art projects to the craft wall, and wiped every hard-to-reach smudge off Frog and Toad's aquarium glass—all to keep my mind from wandering too far down the rabbit hole of unanswered questions.

I ran a damp wipe across the wooden date blocks displayed at the edge of my desk, pausing to update the archaic calendar system. Proclaimed there, in unapologetically red stencil paint, was last Friday's date: *November 15*. But with just three clunky turns of the last block, I fast-forwarded time.

If only I could do the same in my personal life—skip all the wait times between job interviews, blind dates, medical appointments . . . and life-changing emails. Oh, how I envied my students' ability to make the most of every moment, even the ones that seemed to last an eternity.

Or in my case, fourteen months, one week, and three days.

Not that I was keeping track.

The vibration of a door closing down the hallway, followed by the rhythmic *tap-slide-tap* of heels caused me to glance up from my clean-a-thon. I'd know those footsteps anywhere. Just like I knew exactly where they were headed.

Jenna Rosewood, my closest colleague and friend, halted in my open doorway not thirty seconds later, fisting two morning lattes wrapped in insulated sleeves. "Hey, they were all out of those blueberry muffins you like, so . . ." Her statement slid to a stop. If a pause could be considered judgy, this one had pounded the gavel and called the courtroom to attention. "Lauren," she began on a sigh, "why are you sanitizing your classroom *again* when you already did your whole deep-cleaning ritual thing before we left on Friday?"

I worked to wipe all traces of guilt from my face, but my best friend could sniff out pathetic coping mechanisms better than an AA sponsor. "There were a couple areas I missed." A lie so unconvincing not even my most gullible first grader would have believed it.

With enviable ease, Jenna wove her slender hips through my classroom's narrow rows, careful not to bump the yoga balls and balance boards tucked beneath my students' desks—four-legged chairs were overrated. Her distressed designer jeans and flouncy-tiered blouse were a perfect blend of earth tones against her Mediterranean skin. This, I knew from experience, was considered Jenna's "dressed-down" look. Seriously, the woman didn't own a single pair of elastic-waist pants, a glaring contrast in nearly every photo we took together, as *my* favorite wardrobe piece was a yoga pant that had yet to fraternize with a gym mat. But the plain truth was that no matter what Jenna wore on her svelte frame, she would always look more like a Calvin Klein mannequin come to life than a third-grade teacher in a working-class school district.

"Or perhaps," she said, assessing me as she pushed my ladybug tape dispenser aside and perched on the edge of my desk, "you sent out another email inquiry, and now you're overanalyzing life as we know it. Again."

So yeah, my best friend had both beauty and brains. Not to mention a husband who saved impossibly sick children for a living at Boise's most reputable pediatric hospital.

I paused a beat before scrubbing at a pretend ink spot near the edge of my conference table. "Maybe."

"I thought we agreed you were gonna let all this go for a while. Take a breather. Live your life and enjoy the season you're in right now. I swear you were present for that conversation, because it happened less than a week ago. In your living room." Her eyes softened to a sympathetic plea. "You have to stop trying to make it happen. You'll hear something when you're meant to."

I grabbed her caffeine offering and tried, once again, to accept her advice like a tear-off daily proverb. Immediately an image of King Solomon wearing Prada ankle boots and sipping on a skinny Americano materialized in my mind.

Jenna blew at the steam swirling out of the tiny spout in her latte lid. "Speaking of living your life, how did the recital go Saturday night with your sister? I nearly died at that pic you sent of little Iris! She had to be the prettiest ballerina on that stage."

I smiled at the memory of my niece in her pale pink tutu and tight auburn bun, fully aware of Jenna's tried-and-true diversion tactic. Bring up my niece, and I melt faster than butter on a toaster waffle. "She really was. She's making plans to spend the night at my place soon so she can have a dance-off with Skye and me again—only she made sure to tell me she won't be wearing her nice tights to my house *ever again*, since last time Skye's nails snagged them during their twirling routine."

My cocker spaniel had been named by the democracy system of my first-grade class last fall, a debate that had lasted nearly two weeks. My students had divided themselves into three potential name categories—Shopkins, PAW Patrol, and, of course, Marvel superheroes. But in the end, Skye from PAW Patrol had beaten out Black Panther and Twinky Winks. A victory as far as I was concerned. Even the most confident of women would falter at scolding a Twinky Winks in a public setting.

"S-e-r-i-o-u-s-l-y." Jenna drew out the word with all the dramatics currently available to a thirty-two-year-old. "That kid is *so* adorable. I can't believe she'll be in kindergarten next year."

My heart lurched to my throat as I brought the latte to my lips for the first time. "I know. She's growing up so quickly." How did that happen? Hadn't I only been rocking her in that swanky delivery room less than a year ago? Because five years seemed like a mathematical impossibility.

I didn't miss the way Jenna's eyes brewed with questions as she watched me take another careful sip of my coffee. "So . . . did you get a moment to talk to your sister after the performance like you'd hoped?"

Instantly, my sentimental bubble deflated. "If by *talking* you mean Lisa pointing out every available—or nearly available—man at the recital to me." I shook my head and set my cup down, fighting the urge to pace. "She does this horrible flirty thing with her voice when she does it, too, like she's talking through a cloud of helium." It was the voice she used every time she slapped on her self-appointed matchmaker badge in my presence. "I'm not joking when I say she must have introduced me to six different men over the course of two hours. And she *knows* I've taken a break from the dating scene. We've discussed it numerous times, but like usual, my sister only hears what she wants to hear."

I reached to tug another wipe from the dispenser just in time for Jenna to slide off the desk and snatch it out of my hand.

"Stop with the scrubbing already. I'm pretty sure my husband could perform surgery on your conference table."

I huffed a sigh and plopped down on little Amelia Lakier's desk, touching the scuffed toe of my navy Converse to the linoleum floor like a pointe ballerina. Ballet had been my sister's hobby, however, never mine. Just one of a thousand ways the two of us were nothing alike.

Jenna didn't need to state the obvious conclusion she'd drawn from my tirade about my sister. I could practically hear her brain connecting the dots. "So *it was your frustration over Lisa that prompted you to send out another email asking for an update. . . .*" And her assumption wouldn't be all wrong, either. Lisa might be the younger sister in our sibling duo, but she was by far the more dominant, which often left me grasping for some semblance of control whenever we parted ways.

I glanced at the clock above my door and stood to erase Friday's letter blends on the board, yet from the corner of my eye I couldn't ignore Jenna's wine-colored nail tapping her cup. "When you say you've 'taken a break from dating,' you don't mean permanently." This was how my best friend tested the waters, asking a question without actually asking it at all, though we both knew what side of the fence she leaned on when it came to the subject of my romantic life—the same side as my sister. Only Jenna's motives were honorable. I couldn't say the same about Lisa's.

I numbered the activities of the day into six parts on the left side of the whiteboard: writing, music, math, reading, STEM play, and, my personal favorite, library . . . and then turned to face my most loyal of friends.

I gave her the truest answer I could. "Possibly, yes."

She actually flinched at my words. "But, Lauren . . . it could be months and months still. Maybe even *another year* before you get the reply you're waiting for. I don't think you should limit yourself when you're not even sure what's gonna happen yet." She paused and dialed down her volume. "You know I support your decision, I just . . . I don't want you to close your heart off to the possibility of meeting someone in the meantime."

I took a breath before I spoke, not wanting to dismiss the heart behind her words. Jenna loved me. And Jenna also loved her husband. It was only natural for her to want me to experience the same kind of marital bliss she shared with Brian. Only I happened to be convinced she'd married the only Prince Charming not written into a children's storybook. "I know you support me, and I need you to trust that I've thought a lot about this. For me to even entertain the idea of a romantic relationship in this season of life doesn't make sense." Because the truth was, it wasn't my singleness that kept me awake at night. It was a yearning much, much stronger. One ingrained into the fibers of my being. "I've put myself out there, Jen. For years. I'm pretty sure I've gone out with every type of man this city has to offer, and I promise you, I'm good with being single. *Happy*, even. Truly." I gave Jenna the sincerest smile I could muster on this overly discussed topic. Between my sister, my students' parents, and the retired women at my church, I'd been on enough first dates to make a city of two hundred thousand feel like a neighborhood pond, not an ocean.

Some people had the gift of keeping their emotions in check, of not showing the world everything going on inside their head. Jenna was not one of those people. But thankfully, even though I could read every word she wasn't saying in those large, chestnut-brown eyes of hers, she had the restraint not to speak them aloud.

The morning bell chimed a familiar tune, and Jenna hooked her arm through mine as we slipped out my door. "I love you, Lauren."

"And I you, Jen."

We strode into the hall that would soon be filled with pattering feet, swishing backpacks, and excited voices, but my gaze caught on the darkened room across the hallway. Strange. Why were Mrs. Walker's lights off? She was usually here before the rooster crowed.

Jenna's eyes followed mine. "Oh—didn't you hear what happened to Mrs. Walker?"

"No?" My pulse spiked. "I didn't hear anything."

"She fell in her garage last Friday night—broke her hip in two places."

"Oh my gosh, that's horrible!" I stopped and glanced back at her locked door. "Is she okay?" As challenging as Mrs. Walker could be at times, injuries at her age could have lasting complications. She'd started as a first-grade teacher at Brighton nearly twenty-five years ago and taught for ten years before that at a school in Oregon. "Is she in the hospital now?"

"Yeah, I overheard Diana confirming her long-term sub this morning. If it's a break like my grandma had a few years ago, she'll likely need a couple surgeries and will probably be out of commission for a while."

Mrs. Walker rarely missed a day of teaching, but when she did, her short list of approved subs was well-known within the district.

"Wow . . ." An uncomfortable feeling of regret settled low in my belly. It was shameful to admit it, but I'd been avoiding Mrs. Walker for weeks, maybe even longer. It seemed no matter what idea I suggested for combining our efforts as the school's only two first-grade teachers, she always found a way to complain about something I wasn't doing right. I was either too hands-on, too unconventional, too energetic, or too lenient. Normally, I could weather her specific breed of negativity without taking it to heart; I'd had a lot of practice with her personality type over the years. But in recent months, as her rants had increased, my grace for them—and for her—had thinned considerably. Guilt wove itself around my rib cage at the thought of her awaiting surgery in the hospital. "Maybe I could organize some get well cards to send to her hospital room?"

Jenna clapped her hands together in a quick pattern of three as she approached her line leader waiting with a parent volunteer at the corner of our hallway. Seconds later her classroom answered back with a similar clap before they marched back down the hallway. "The cards are a great idea, Miss Bailey," Jenna replied over her shoulder in her most authoritative-sounding voice. "Let me know what my class can do to help."

"Hi, Miss Bailey!" Tabitha Connelly, my chosen line leader for the week, whisper-yelled at the sight of me. She held up our laminated first-grade sign as the rest of my class followed her to the corner, stopped, and waited for my clap like they'd been taught.

There was little in the world better than this moment right here—twenty-four optimistic faces, all ready to tackle a new week with contagious gusto. Not even the most mundane of Mondays could bring down this lively crowd.

I smiled at my happy crew. "Good morning, class. Let's walk."

At this point in the year, my "firsties" knew what was expected of them upon entering our classroom. The mad dash of hanging up backpacks and storing lunch boxes had calmed considerably since the start of school in September. Their voices remained in hushed tones as they took out their morning folders, set them on their desks, said the Pledge of Allegiance, and waited for me to give the go-ahead to begin their morning word scramble with their weekly partners.

Fifty minutes later, a knock on the door alerted me to the fifth-grade buddy sent to pick up my students for music class. Everyone filed into a semi-quiet line and waved good-bye. I blew them a kiss and told them we'd be working on a surprise project when they returned. That got a few fist pumps and booty shakes.

Minutes after they left, I placed a sheet of construction paper on each of their desks, preparing the guilt cards—er, get well cards—for the kids' return. Luckily, I had more than enough art supplies to share with the sub across the hall, too. I hadn't a clue where Mrs. Walker stored her own art supplies, and I wasn't about to be the one blamed for messing up her *system* whenever she did return.

Gathering up a few pairs of funky scissors, hole punchers, markers, and stickers to share, I checked the clock above my door. The sub would be releasing Walker's class for music in just a few minutes. With the exception of library, we swapped all other electives throughout the week.

Armed with the necessary supplies, I carried the art box into the hall and immediately jerked back a step at the sound of . . . a bleating animal? I glanced toward the lunchroom and then in the direction of the library. Strange. There was no sound coming from either end of the hallway. I located the alarm system above the computer lab. No flashing light to signal an emergency.

And then it happened again.

The most off-putting, ear-splitting . . . *roar*? A boisterous cheer broke out an instant later, coming from inside Mrs. Walker's classroom. I quickened my steps to cross the linoleum sea between our two rooms.

Under normal circumstances, I wouldn't dare open her door

without knocking, but instinct had me cranking the handle and throwing it open wide. And then, just like that, my feet were frozen to the floor, my jaw hanging slack at a sight that flipped my mundane Monday completely upside down.

Whoever was currently roaring at a class of six-year-olds . . . he most certainly *was not* on Mrs. Walker's approved sub list.

chapter two

Squatting on top of Mrs. Walker's oak desk was a headless man—at least I assumed he was a man. But his white undershirt, leather belt, and dark-washed jeans were all secondary details to the Kermit-green T-shirt flipped over his head and stretched tight against his face like shrink-wrap.

The lifelike screen print of a T-Rex head—complete with scary eyes and even scarier teeth—hid every trace of whatever human features were underneath. Two flailing hands sprouted directly from his short green sleeves, while his feet stomped as he projected several angry snorts.

The class hooted with laughter, some of the kids calling out for him to jump down and chase them around the room. Instead, with unnerving accuracy for a blind man, he bent his head down and picked up a stapler between his giant, cloth-covered dinosaur teeth.

For a moment I questioned the integrity of our school's security protocol.

"Awesome! Do it again!" Mason Grady cheered from the front row.

"Wanna eat my lunch?" Rosie Simons asked, holding up her princess lunchbox. "I never eat my cheese stick."

The man-saur dropped the stapler onto the desk, then proceeded to sniff the air before letting out another massive bleat.

Several of the girls covered their ears and looked around the room, spotting me near the door for the first time.

"Uh . . . Mr. Avery?" Joy Goldman hiked up her glasses and raised her hand. "Miss Bailey is—"

The T-Rex cut her off with a mighty huff.

"But, Mr. Avery! Mr. Avery!" The kids giggled and continued to point at the only teacher in the room who was not trying to reenact *Jurassic Park*.

Of all the emergency trainings we'd been given as a staff, all the lockdown drills we'd done as a school district . . . I was completely unprepared for this particular scenario. What exactly was my role here? Did I throw my box of markers at its head in an attempt to save the children? Did I distract it with the granola bar in my pocket, then rush the kids to my classroom?

"Excuse me?" I approached with caution. "Are you Mrs. Walker's sub?"

The still-blind, ready-to-charge dinosaur whipped his head in my direction, and I barely managed to bite back a scream. *Not real, Lauren. Not. Real.*

Instantly, the miniature T-Rex hands poking out the sleeve holes began to grow into two full-size, all-male arms. Ten fingers grappled at once for the hem of his T-shirt tucked unnaturally behind the nape of his neck. He gave it a sharp tug.

Fabric-ruffled hair that wasn't quite blond and wasn't quite brown stuck up in every direction. He pulled the shirt lower still, uncovering dark-lashed eyes, covetable cheekbones, and a square jawline. The shocking reveal resembled nothing of the prehistoric monster he'd portrayed.

The man blinked as if to reacquaint himself with the twenty-first century and let his *Ask Me About My T-Rex* shirt fall to his waist before he leapt off Mrs. Walker's desk. He raked a hand through his rumpled, caramelly hair and smiled a grin that had me questioning my own species at the moment. "Hi there, I'm Joshua Avery."

That was it. No explanation. No apology. No ruddy cheeks of humiliation for being caught with his shirt over his head while pretending to be a dinosaur. Just a casual greeting, as if all were perfectly normal.

I swallowed and shoved the random grouping of art supplies I was still holding in his direction, including the stamp collection my mother had found during one of her more lucrative closet-cleaning raids. "Here. This is for you—for your class, I mean. To do. If you—they—want to."

He looked down at the craft paraphernalia now in his arms and then back up to me, every student in the room focused on the two of us. "Did I miss the art lesson in Charlotte's lesson plan for today?"

Charlotte? He calls Mrs. Walker by her first name? There was something blasphemous about calling a teacher of nearly thirty-five years by her first name. "No, uh, these aren't for an art lesson. They're for making get-well-soon cards. To send to Mrs. Walker's hospital room."

"Oh, right. Sure." He nodded. "That's really cool of you. Thanks for thinking of that."

"Yeah . . . no problem." An awkward beat of I-have-no-idea-what-to-do-next loomed over me, and I hitched a thumb in the direction of the hallway. "I should get back to my room. My kids will be coming from music class in just a minute." His lack of reaction pushed me to continue. "Which means Mrs. Walker's students will have music next. They're working on a Thanksgiving program. A fifth-grade helper will be here to pick them up as soon as she walks mine back."

"Oh, great. Thanks for the heads-up." Another good-natured chuckle was followed by a gesture to the desk behind him. "I do have a schedule written down somewhere, but as you can see, we got a bit off track."

I nearly laughed at that. "Sure. Okay. Well, I'm across the hall if . . ." *If what?* "If you need anything or have any questions."

As if my arms and legs were made of metal and bolts, I took a stiff step toward the door.

"Bye, Miss Bailey," several students sang out.

I twisted slightly to wave at the class, when Joshua met my gaze with a wink.

"Yes, good-bye, Miss Bailey. Hope to see you around."

Something about the way he said my name made me want to take back the words I'd spoken to Jenna earlier this morning. Not my pledge to steer clear of the dating world, but my definitive analysis of all the men who resided in my area.

Because I'd been wrong. I hadn't met *every* type of man Idaho had to offer. And Joshua Avery was proof.

My gaze gravitated toward the half window in my classroom door more times than I cared to admit, straining to catch a glimpse of the sub across the hall. How did someone so outrageously opposite of Mrs. Walker—or Charlotte, as he'd so casually referred to her—land a teaching job in her fortress of a classroom? Had someone in the office rebelled against her wishes? Was Joshua Avery a prank sent by the school district?

Try as I might, I simply could not make sense of the situation. In this case, one plus one did not equal two. It equaled a grown man who ate staplers through his T-shirt for the amusement of children.

"Miss Bailey?" Noah Lawler's fingers wiggled in the air like worms on the end of a fishing line. "Can I get the class book bag ready? It's my turn today."

My attention snapped from the window to the clock above the door. Three minutes until library.

"Oh, yes. Thank you, Noah. All right, my little firsties," I said, addressing the room with a double clap. "Please close your folders and line up next to your buddy against the wall. We're headed to library time with Mrs. Dalton."

One by one my students closed their writing booklets as Noah practically galloped to unhook our class book bag from the hanger. Tucked inside the bag were the books we'd read together last week in Red Rover's Reading Corner. The job of bag carrier was a coveted one, which likely explained why little Caitlyn Parker's expression had morphed into a cartoonish pout. I signaled Tabitha, our line leader, to lead us onward and tapped my finger to my lips.

After the majority of my students had snaked into the hall like a slow-moving train, I took up the caboose with Caitlyn and offered her my hand. It was amazing how quickly a sour mood on a child could turn around when given a little extra attention. And with Caitlyn's mommy nearing the end of her third trimester with baby number four, extra attention was understandably more difficult for Caitlyn to come by at home these days.

I squeezed her hand after passing the computer lab and cafeteria. "So I was thinking I might need an extra helper to select a special book about Thanksgiving for our reading time this week. Would you mind checking one out for our classroom?"

Caitlyn's watery blue eyes blinked up at me. "Really, can I?"

"Absolutely," I said. "I'll tell Noah you'll be adding a book to the bag today."

"Thanks, Miss B." Her smile warmed the center of my chest as I moved to the front of the line to give another reminder to keep our lips still upon entering the library.

The instant I pulled the bulky door open, I saw him. Dinosaur man. Only this time he wasn't crouching on top of a desk, he was reaching for a book at the top of a display shelf. He handed the nonfiction hardback with a basketball on the cover to a boy with a cast on his arm. "Here you go, champ."

I blinked my attention back to my students as they filed into the large space, waving at their fellow first graders enthusiastically.

The sub shot me a conversational smile and strode toward me as if we were old acquaintances who'd had longer than a three-minute interaction.

"Hello again, Miss Bailey."

"Hello," I replied, working to mask my face into something other than the stupefaction I'd worn during our first meeting.

"I've just heard a rumor about you. Though, technically, I don't think it can still be called a rumor when I heard it from twenty-six highly reputable sources." His grin intensified. "Do you really have balance boards and yoga balls in place of chairs in your classroom?" he asked in a voice that was in no way library-friendly.

My lips twitched. "Your sources are correct."

"Incredible. I've heard of teachers shifting around their classrooms to promote better learning, but I haven't met many in person. How has it been for your students?"

"Honestly, it's been a total game-changer as far as their attention and focus goes, especially for my more sensory-seeking kids. I'm fortunate to work in a district that supports private donations and unconventional ideas."

"Unconventional ideas are often the best ideas. If more teachers were willing to step out of the box and take creative liberties within their classroom, I believe today's educational system could look vastly different."

From the kindness in his tone, I knew his statement was meant to be complimentary, but the issue he addressed shouldn't be so easily simplified. "Taking some creative liberties in the classroom definitely plays a part in bettering our educational system, but more often than not, a teacher's limitations usually begin and end with the level of support they receive from their administrating staff. Brighton isn't a wealthy school by any standard, but we're blessed with some open minds who are willing to listen to the real needs of our students. In my opinion, that's worth far more than a donation for an alternative seating method."

"Wow." The corner of his eyes crinkled appreciatively. "I can see why you were awarded a donation for your classroom. If I ever need to write a grant someday, I know who to come to."

My face heated under his scrutiny, and I could only imagine the deepening shade of crimson that splotched my neck and cheeks. My classic Scandinavian skin left little to the imagination, like a permanent mood ring I couldn't take off or even tan away. My father had never been one for handing out life advice when I was growing up, but he told me once that a blond-haired, blue-eyed girl with skin as fair as mine should stay clear from any vocations that made a profit by omitting truth. When I asked him why, he simply said, "*Because lies don't keep under skin as pale as yours.*"

"Although," the sub continued unabashedly, "take it from me, there are a few six-year-olds just across the hall from your classroom who could use some writing pointers, too."

"What?" I asked, thoroughly confused by his abrupt change in topic.

"The get-well-soon cards for Charlotte. Great idea, but I had to censor a few of my reactions while they dictated their messages to me."

I turned to face him fully. "Their messages to Mrs. Walker, you mean?"

"Oh yeah." He lowered his voice and leaned in. "One of them offered to loan Charlotte the rusty walker in her family's garage—the one that didn't sell in their annual yard sale. Another one asked if he could draw a robotic joint on her hip cast so she'd look more like a superhero. But my favorite one . . ." His pause focused my attention on his mouth. "Was regarding her undergarments."

"*What?* No way!" Three of my students who were being helped by Mrs. Dalton, Brighton's resident librarian of more than twenty years, spun to look at me from four aisles over. I clamped a hand over my mouth. *Oops.*

"Yes way," he said teasingly. "One Miss Aurora Brown mentioned how her great-grandmother had to wear special underwear for old people, kind of like her baby brother's pull-ups, but way bigger and way squishier."

A burst of giggles slipped through my lips.

"Exactly," he said through a full grin. "Now imagine if that same darling child drew a picture to match."

My shoulders continued to shake.

"*Teachers*," came Mrs. Dalton's tight voice from two shelves over. "We're ready to move to the carpet for story time now."

I nodded and tugged at the hem of my navy cardigan, trying to regain composure. What Mrs. Dalton lacked in stature, she made up for in stern scoldings. I pinched my lips together, working to erase the image Joshua had created in my mind. Quietly, I ushered my students toward the square carpet where Mrs. Dalton sat on a tall, spindly chair, her feet dangling three inches above the floor.

From the corner of my eye, I saw Joshua doing the same with his students, only where I gave light guiding touches, he gave fist bumps and high fives. Given the sour line of Mrs. Dalton's lips, she was not amused by his tactics. For some reason, this made me smile all the more. He certainly had his own way of doing things.

"Hush now, students. It's time for our weekly chapter reading of *The Boxcar Children*."

Miles Kennewick from my class waved his hand in the air, not waiting to be called on before he spoke. "Can we read something funner today?"

Oh boy. Miles was a say-it-like-it-was type of kid.

Mrs. Dalton closed the book and stared at him pointedly. "*Funner* is not a word, Miles. And we are continuing this series for the rest of the school year."

A handful of students groaned, and Miles blurted, "But your books aren't like the books Miss Bailey reads to us. Hers are funny."

This wasn't going to end well. . . . I wove my way through a sea of seated children, closing in on Miles, all the while feeling Joshua's humor-lit gaze tracking me from his side of the carpet square.

"There are millions of books," Mrs. Dalton began. "No two are the same. Just like Miss Bailey and I are not the same. Every one of us has our own unique preferences."

Five wiggly hands shot skyward, each one connected to the same question. "What does *preferences* mean?"

"It means that some of us may like scary adventure stories and others of us may like princess fairy tales—"

"Ooh, ooh!" Miles exclaimed as if he'd just had the epiphany of the century. "So *you* must like boring tales."

The deep masculine laugh of a certain substitute teacher erupted in the open yet solemn space, igniting a chorus of laughter from every corner of the carpet square. He didn't repress his amusement or even excuse himself from the room. Instead, he remained, wearing an expression that looked like an open portal to the kind of happiness most of the adult world had long ago forgotten.

As Mrs. Dalton clapped her hands and called the room back to order, foreboding pushed against the center of my chest. I worked to redirect my gaze—and my thoughts—to anything other than the distracting charms of one Joshua Avery. But like trying to calm this group of overstimulated kids, the task was proving to be impossible.

chapter three

At exactly 3:41, Jenna entered my classroom, severing my direct line of sight into Mrs. Walker's door window. "You ready to go? I told Brian I'd . . ." She stopped and glanced behind her. "What are you staring at?"

I blinked to focus. "Nothing. Just feeling a bit brain-fried today."

She hiked her Marc Jacobs handbag higher up on her shoulder. "Ah, okay. Well, Brian just called. I've got to meet him downtown to switch cars. I guess an engine light came on in my car last time he drove it, and he wants to drop it off at the mechanic before his shift at the hospital. Did you want to walk out together? Or do you need more time to . . . daydream?"

Jenna and I rarely missed a day of walking through the parking lot together. It was our thing, our slow reentry to the world of adult speak. And it was often one of the best parts of my day. There was something profoundly satisfying about sharing the inner workings of your day with someone who could truly understand, someone who'd existed in the same time and space as you. Perhaps they'd also rescued a lost tooth from the bottom of a playground slide or saved the class fish from certain death by catching that flying pink eraser pre-splash. Or maybe even had the rare honor of transcribing a get-well-soon card featuring adult diapers.

I bit back a private smile at the memory of Joshua's story. Because I shouldn't be smiling over him. Just like I shouldn't be hoping to accidently bump into him after he closed up his classroom for the day. *Ridiculous.* His position at Brighton was only for a limited time, and that was just one of a billion reasons I needed to forget all about his presence across the hall.

"Nah, I'm ready." I stepped away from my desk so I'd have no choice but to follow through. "Let's go."

I collected my purse from my cubby, then unhooked my coat from the wall before exiting my room. With admirable restraint, I did not rubberneck when we passed by Mrs. Walker's door. Instead, I chastised myself for all the mental energy I'd expended on something—*someone*—so temporary.

As we pushed out the main doors into the chilly November air, we set our pace to a casual stroll. The blue-gray sky was nearly as free of clouds as the school parking lot was of cars. I zipped up my jacket, my armor against the wind, and tried to focus on Jenna's animated story about a student bringing her father's snore plugs as her show-and-tell item.

She had just launched into the good part—the child trying to fit them inside her own too-small nostrils—when I heard the pounding of footsteps behind us. In a torturous kind of hopefulness, my stomach flipped at the thought of the potential owner of those hammering feet. I willed myself not to turn around.

Unfortunately, Jenna had no reason not to.

"Hey, um—Miss Bailey?" an unmistakably male voice called out.

As if she thought I hadn't heard him, Jenna gripped my arm and pulled me to a stop before I had time to settle on the correct expression for this, my third and final meeting of the day with Mrs. Walker's substitute.

"Sorry," Joshua said on the tail end of a cheery laugh. "I realized halfway across the lot that I still don't know your first name."

Within a single blink, my brain snapped a succession of mental pictures: tousled hair that flecked copper in the natural light, pine-green eyes with enviable lashes, and a mouth that seemed permanently curved into a smile. And there, just under his shadow-lined jaw was a tiny but angry red nick, as if he'd cut himself while shaving before showing up at school. Perhaps this clean-shaven look wasn't his usual routine? Somehow, envisioning a dusting of scruff along his jaw only added to the intellectual charm he embodied so well already.

"It's Lauren," I answered a beat past awkward.

"Lauren Bailey," he said with unexplained approval. "I imagined it would be something like that."

He'd imagined my name?

Jenna's eyes rounded to the size of her gold hoop earrings. "I'm sorry, but I don't think we've met yet. I'm Jenna Rosewood." She held out her hand in that proper I-likely-have-royalty-in-my-blood way of hers, and I prepared for an exchange I'd witnessed a thousand times.

There were certain things one got used to when selecting a former beauty contestant for a best friend. The redirection of any and all positive male attention while in her presence was one of them. But unlike every other man who appeared gut-punched by Jenna's distinctive allure, Joshua's gaze didn't linger. Nor did his handshake.

"Joshua Avery. Tech nerd. Dinosaur freak. And as of today, a first-grade sub." He glanced my way again.

"Avery . . . Avery . . . Why does your name sound so familiar?" Jenna repeated it slowly, as if his last name was the only thing she noticed about a grown man wearing an *Ask Me About My T-Rex* T-shirt. Also, where was his coat? Was he immune to the barely above freezing temperature? It wasn't as if he had extra insulation to work with, either. Joshua was made of lean muscle, long limbs, and likely the kind of metabolism that could make millions if bottled and sold on the black market.

If possible, Joshua's smile brightened several extra watts. "You might know my father, George Avery? Although sometimes he's not as eager to claim me as a son." He leaned in as if to tell us a secret. "Just don't ask him about the time I shot a weighted bottle rocket into the windshield of his Volvo. I keep waiting for him to find the humor in that one, but it's been nearly twenty years, and he still won't allow me to bring a two-liter bottle into his house."

"Hold on," I said, finding my voice and raising up a hand, as if that gesture alone might slow the world long enough for me to process the revelation unfolding in my brain. The instant he spoke his father's name, my mind rattled awake. It was a name that made my voice skip an octave and my pulse trip over itself. "Your father is *George Avery*—as in the author of *Create a Reader in 30 Days* and *Reading Express for Kids* and *Reading Express for Parents* and *Every Teacher's*—"

"*Reading Dream*," he finished with me. "Yep, that's the one."

I'd never been the fangirling type. Not even when I spotted my favorite HGTV host signing autographs at a Starbucks downtown last July. But this . . . this was different. This was personal. George Avery wasn't just a brilliant teacher-turned-author who lived somewhere in the inland northwest—he was also the reason I'd strayed from a degree in childhood psychology and ended up with a master's in early childhood development. And that was only the start of his influence on my life.

During my second week as a freshman at Boise State, I'd stumbled into what I thought was a lecture on modern psychology. Instead, I found myself mesmerized by a professor in his late-forties reading the classic children's book *Horton Hatches the Egg* to a crowd of checked-out, early-twenty-somethings. Obviously, they, too, had believed they'd entered the wrong class. But with his gentle and confident manner, Mr. Avery had continued to read about a loyal elephant who overcame every kind of hardship in order to keep his promise to sit atop a lonely egg until it hatched.

George Avery showed each illustration to the massive auditorium the way any seasoned elementary teacher would show a classroom of wiggly children. Less than five pages in, the emotionally charged tale had entranced even the most cynical of students.

By the last page, my cheeks were tear-soaked. And when he finally closed the book and fixed his gaze on his enraptured audience, his last words pierced me like a destiny-tipped arrow. *"The way to shape a child's heart is through love. And the way to shape a child's mind is through literature. When you read to a child, you accomplish both."*

With a sharp jab of her elbow, Jenna catapulted me fourteen years into the future. Back to a parking lot with the son of the living legend who'd changed my life with a children's storybook.

"Sorry, I just—I love him," I blurted without preamble. "Your dad. I've read everything he's ever written—articles, blogs, books. And his documentary series on *Little Readers Across the Nation* was absolutely fantastic. I use many of his techniques in my classroom."

"Understatement," Jenna interjected. "Lauren's responsible for overseeing the annual Reader Express Training for our entire district."

Joshua's face morphed from a delighted state of curiosity to an expression I couldn't quite determine. "Wow. I'm not sure I've ever felt as envious of my father as I do right now. Although, usually his fans are about thirty years your senior and mention 'the good old days' at least once during their praise of his accolades."

"He's a hero in education." A statement I'd said more times than I could count.

The right corner of his mouth tipped further north, revealing a deep-set dimple. "I'll make sure to tell him you said so."

"Please do," I said in reply, only because the desperate "*Please ask him to autograph my grade book?!*" seemed a little too soon considering he'd only learned my first name five minutes ago.

Out of the corner of my eye, I watched Jenna's head swivel from me to Joshua, and then back to me again. "How long do you plan to sub for Mrs. Walker, Joshua?"

His gaze didn't stray from my face for longer than the eight seconds it took him to respond. "I'm not totally sure, but my guess would be a week, possibly longer depending on what the district allows. I'm up for whatever, though. I have the time, and it's a nice change of pace to be on this side of things."

This side of things? "You don't usually work as a sub?"

"No. My degree is in education, but my career followed my minor in computer science. Charlotte allowing me to sub for her is the result of several phone calls between my father and the superintendent. He managed to convince the district that I'm in need of a refresher course inside my test market before we continue on with our project. And I'm not too proud to admit that my father and his lackeys at the district weren't wrong. I've learned a lot today."

Jenna cut in before I had the chance. "What do you mean by your *test market*?"

"First graders. I'm in tech development—educational apps and video games for early readers, primarily." His eyes found mine again and something inside me leapt at his next proclamation. "I'm working on digitizing my father's research into an administration application suitable for school districts across the nation. We hope the app will have crossover appeal. Both classroom and at-home use. Right now it's undergoing some early approvals and recommendations by higher-ups."

Jenna laughed a little too brightly, as if she, too, was experiencing the weirdest sense of déjà vu. How many times during our annual trainings had I said, "*I wish this reading program was in a more user-friendly format for our kids and their parents to use at home*"?

"What? What am I missing?" he asked, directing his question to both of us.

Jenna shook her head and began walking backward toward her Acura. "I'll let Lauren fill you in on that one. I've got to run and meet my husband downtown before he starts his shift at the hospital." Her smile was positively wicked as she eyed me from behind Joshua's back. "I'm looking forward to having you at Brighton, Joshua—for however long you're with us."

He tossed a "Thanks" over his shoulder, and Jenna held an imaginary finger phone up to her ear for me to see, mouthing the words *Call me!*

A minute later she was gone from the lot, and apart from a few black birds fighting over some smashed Cheetos on the sidewalk, Joshua and I were alone.

He scanned the remaining six vehicles parked in the rows behind us, the breeze fingering through his hair. "Are you the white Cherokee on the end there?"

"*What*?" I gasped. "How could you possibly have guessed that?"

His gaze dipped to the Jeep key fob in my right hand, giving away his tell with yet another signature wink.

"Ah. Right." I rolled my eyes and matched my stride to his. "For a second there, I was beginning to wonder if your mind-reading skills were as honed as your T-Rex impression." I couldn't help the breathy laugh that escaped me at the memory of him crouching atop Mrs. Walker's desk.

"Unfortunately, my telepathy skills still have a long way to go."

"Well, even so, I'm pretty sure you'll be every student's favorite dinner table topic tonight."

Once we reached my Jeep, I tossed my purse and book bag onto the back seat. My phone and wallet spilled to the floor, and I reached to collect the items and tuck them back inside the zippered pocket. As I turned to face him again, Joshua's forearm rested on the frame of my open driver's side door, totally relaxed, as if he was perfectly content to wait on me. *If only.*

The kindness behind such a simple gesture caused my throat to pinch.

Until that moment, I hadn't been sure there were still men in the world who took the time to open doors for women. Especially ones they hardly knew. Because if chivalry was alive in our culture today, I certainly hadn't encountered it on any of the first dates I'd been subjected to. And I wasn't sure which idea made me want to shed a tear more: the fact that chivalry wasn't dead, or the fact that my timeline for romance was.

"About dinner . . ." he started, in a voice slightly less confident than when he'd spoken of his dinosaur impressions, "I'm not exactly sure what the protocol is here, or even if there is a protocol for this, but I'll be kicking myself all the way home if I don't ask." His pause stilled my pulse. "I'd like to take you to dinner sometime, Lauren. Anytime, really. Even tonight, assuming you were planning on eating dinner tonight."

The boyish curve of his mouth intensified the tightening in my throat. Not because I wanted to say no to him, but because I couldn't remember ever wanting to say yes to a dinner date invitation more. Joshua Avery wasn't some random setup. He hadn't texted me out of the blue because a friend's brother's neighbor thought we'd have something in common. He wasn't the result of an online matchmaking site or a bribe sent by my meddling sister.

He was simply a man, asking me out the old-fashioned, face-to-face way, and everything in me wanted to melt into a sappy puddle of *Where have you been hiding these past few years?*

A light gust of wind from behind lifted my shoulder-length hair and swished the ashy blond strands across my cheek. His eyes tracked as I worked to tuck it back behind my ears. "Crazily enough, I actually *was* planning on eating dinner tonight."

"Well, would you look at us, two crazy people who planned on eating dinner on a Monday night. I knew I'd felt a connection with you—that must be it." His good-natured laugh ribboned through me, causing me to forget, or at least to pretend to forget, why dinner with him would be such a terrible, terrible idea. "Should we join our plans, then? Eat at the same place, at the same time? I promise my human table manners are superior to the manners of my T-Rex."

My cheeks actually ached from smiling so hard. "Well, when you put it like that—"

Another gust of wind cut through us. A sharp rattling sound pulled our attention away from each other and toward the windshield of my car, where a small piece of white paper flapped against the glass, the corner of it tucked under my wiper blade. Joshua barely had to extend his arm to pluck it out. The note was written on a simple piece of card stock, no preamble or privacy fold. Just bold black ink and familiar penmanship.

Don't forget about coming over tonight!
Ben

Our eyes locked on the sentence as the note became a living, breathing entity between us. I opened my mouth to explain, hoping the right words might magically appear on my tongue despite my jumbling brain cells. Because this note represented so much more than a previous commitment I'd made and nearly forgotten about. It also represented a commitment I'd made to my future, one I had no right divulging to a man I'd known for less than a day when my own family still hadn't a clue.

Joshua spoke first. "Looks like you have plans tonight."

I lifted my gaze to his. "Yes." The only word I could force to exit.

His smile retreated to half-mast. "Maybe another time, then?"

"Actually," I began with a boldness I didn't quite own, "I

don't think I can do dinner for a while." *For a while?* What was I even saying? No one mistook *a while* to mean *years*. But that was exactly what it would be for me: YEARS. And by then, Joshua Avery would have found some other woman to take to dinner on some random Monday night in the future. Heck, by the time I was eligible again, he'd likely be ready to enroll his own little caramel-headed first grader into an elementary school nearby. "My life is a bit complicated right now is all. I'm sorry."

His measured nod of understanding halted my mental spiral. "Well, then, Lauren Bailey . . ." He tapped the inside of my door with his oversize hand. I stared at his fingers, noticing his too-short nails and cracked cuticles. Someone should really tell him to put olive oil around his nail beds so they wouldn't split during winter and bleed. But that someone couldn't be me. "I hope you have a good evening. I'll see you tomorrow, bright and early."

"Thank you, yes . . . okay. I'll see you then." Feeling the bite of the wind on my face for the first time since he walked me to my Jeep, I shivered as I slid into the driver's seat and secured my seatbelt. He didn't move away after he closed my door, and for some unknown reason, the simple act of inserting my key into the ignition took four tries.

Joshua waited until my engine had fully warmed and my tires were inching away from the spot I'd parked in for the last ten years before he took a step back and tucked his hands into the front pockets of his jeans.

This time, I didn't resist the urge to look back. And when I did, his gaze was waiting for me, one that offered a wink I wished I wouldn't have to forget.

chapter four

While the majority of American women obsessed over home makeover shows, desiring crisp white shiplap walls and minimalistic living spaces to eradicate clutter, I craved something else entirely. My fingers skimmed the seam of my pocket where I'd stuffed Benny's note, giving myself an extra moment to take in the ranch home before me. The one with bicycles tossed in the yard and thirsty potted plants stationed below a porch littered with teen shoes and backpacks. But what I admired most about this house was the permanent gap in the front door, as if saying to every passerby, *Come on in! We're home!* Because the Cartwrights were *those* kinds of people. The kind who met elderly singles at the grocery store and invited them over for potato soup and card games. The kind who found pleasure in raking leaves and baking pies and taking hikes—as long as they did it together. The kind of people who believed face-to-face connection wasn't synonymous with FaceTime.

But perhaps what I admired most about them was their ability to make friends feel as close as family. Even closer, in my case.

I pushed the splintering oak door open wide with a single knock and stepped inside, carrying my gift bag. "Hello? Anybody home?" An unintentional joke, considering eight people lived inside this single-story house.

"Miss B?" a familiar voice answered back, followed by racing feet that skidded to a halt an instant before they leapt over the love seat in the living room. Benny gave me a fist bump. "Did you find my note? I made Mom pull into Brighton's parking lot so I could put it on your car."

"I sure did," I said, roughing up his silky near-black hair while pushing away the image of Joshua's hand removing the note from under my wiper blade. I held up the blue gift bag. "And I also stopped by the store. Couldn't come without it."

It was the same thing I bought him every year on this special day. Our tradition.

His braces glinted in the light as he smiled up at me. Crazy how I could still remember the first tooth he'd lost in my classroom all those years ago. How traumatic that day had been for him. Of course, back then, most things had felt traumatic to a little boy who'd lost the only world he'd ever known.

"Awesome! Thanks." He tossed the gift tissue aside and dug into the bag with the excitement of a child much younger than his twelve years. But that was exactly what made him Benny. He could be just as excited about a small, sentimental gift from an old teacher as he was about the video game he'd been saving for since Christmas. He pulled out the green container of Play-Doh and let out a whooping, "Yes!"

The glee on his face transported me back in time, back to when the young man standing before me weighed less than the average American toddler on his first day of first grade. He'd only known a handful of English phrases when he started school, but he could write most of the letters in the English alphabet and all of his numbers. That was, as long as his mama remained less than an arm's length away. Which she did for weeks . . . months, even. Gail sat with her son at his desk—writing with him, coloring with him, reading with him, and encouraging him to interact with his classmates despite the tough language barrier. And while it didn't take long for the kids in my class to win him over, Benny was less than eager to interact with me. Until the day I gave him his own container of green Play-Doh.

His need for sensory output was the olive branch that first connected us, but it was the way his little hand accepted my offering that molded my heart to his forever. As he squished that doughy substance between his fingers, something changed inside me. Something I wouldn't be brave enough to put into words until years later.

Now Ben shook the green substance, still in the shape of its container, into his palm and immediately flattened it between his hands like a pancake. Some things never changed. "I'm gonna go see if I can get Chowder to walk on it. Her paw prints would look awesome in this!"

"Eeew, Ben." The logical voice of Benny's slightly older sister, Allie, sounded as she entered the living room carrying a hardback fantasy book bearing a library code on the spine. I'd yet to see her without a novel permanently affixed to her person. "You can't let the cat walk all over that and then play with it again. That's disgusting."

"It's my Play-Doh. I can do whatever I want with it." He looked to me for approval, and I nodded affirmingly, although Allie definitely had a point.

"I bet Caleb and I can get all four of her paw prints on here! See you when Mom cuts the cake, Miss B!" And with that, he was off, bounding over furniture as if his legs were made of mattress springs.

Allie scoffed in disgust, and I couldn't help but chuckle at her look of disdain. "Hey, Allie, do you know where I might find your mama?" Gail could be any number of places. With a mix of six tween and teenage children, it was better that I ask for directions rather than wander about the house, poking my head inside bedrooms.

She pointed to the wall that separated the dining nook from the kitchen. "I think she's still baking. She'll be happy to see you."

I left my shoes and purse on the rack by the front door and strolled to the kitchen, noting and appreciating the cozy, lived-in feel of their home for the hundredth time. Two mismatched athletic socks lay on the floor near the couch next to the coffee table, where several science textbooks were stacked. Not too far away, a plate of crumbs balanced on a spiral notebook. Study food, probably. Gail often joked that her oldest boys ate a minimum of one mph—meal per hour.

Gail's back was to me as I entered the bright galley kitchen. A soft symphonic hymn played from an iPhone resting on the windowsill. She hummed along to "His Eye Is on the Sparrow," the sound barely registering above the cello's solo as she bent over Ben's cake, working her culinary magic.

Not wanting to startle her, I waited to speak until she lifted the piping bag away from the cake. "I'd offer to help, but you've seen my icing skills in action. I'm way better suited for the clean-up crew."

She turned and offered an immediate smile I couldn't help but return. "Ah, Lauren. I was just thinking about you."

"Good things, I hope." I leaned against the butcher block in the middle of the kitchen.

"Always." She laid the piping bag on the counter and wrapped me in a tight hug. "You've been missed around this house—especially by Ben." She promptly moved to pick up a barstool that weighed nearly as much as she did and placed it next to the counter, patting it twice for me to take a seat. "Here, I'm almost done with his cake, and then I'll make us both a warm cup of chai. Why don't you catch me up on your life these last couple weeks?"

I actually laughed. What did I possibly have to tell her? Nothing had changed since our last tea time chat. My life had been in a holding pattern for months now. Unbidden, Joshua's face surfaced like a distant mirage and I quickly blinked him away. There wasn't room for him here. Not in this house, and certainly not in my head, either. "I'm afraid that might be a very short conversation. Everything's pretty much the same."

She switched to her yellow piping bag and raised her petite eyebrows in a way that suggested nothing I had to say would ever be too boring for her to hear. And she meant it, too. Gail Cartwright had the kind of face Hollywood would typecast as "compassionate mother figure." Honey brown eyes, a delicate mouth framed by decades of joy, and a silver-streaked bob that curled softly under her chin.

"Let's see . . . I did find a cute note from a sixth-grade boy on my car this afternoon," I said, running the tip of my finger along the pastry knife before bringing it to my lips. Buttercream, *yum*. Gail made the best cake frosting on the planet. Sweet and dense and unbelievably creamy.

"Yes, Benny—excuse me, *Ben*—was excited to leave it for you to discover." She emphasized Ben's new name preference, and I shook my head. He might make his family call him Ben now, but I would never stray from calling him Benny. To me, he'd always be my little gap-toothed first grader. "I meant to send you a reminder text last night, but—"

"But you manage a household of eight, taxi at least four of your kids to and from their chosen extracurricular each afternoon, and co-lead a weekly support group. Really, you never have to apologize to me for missing a reminder text."

She shook her head. "You make me sound like some kind of superwoman."

"A super-saint is more like it."

"Nonsense." Gail concentrated again on the piping tip as she scripted each letter with awe-inspiring precision. Pressing, curling, breaking. Pressing, curling, breaking. Pressing, curling—"Finished."

She placed the bag in the sink, then tilted the cake stand to reveal what she'd so carefully written: *Happy Adoption Day, Ben!*

Hot tears rushed to my eyes, threatening to spill over at the slightest hint of a blink. "It's beautiful, Gail. Truly."

She laid the cake flat once again and then reached to touch my elbow. "I haven't stopped praying for the day we get to celebrate your child's homecoming. You're so close now, I can feel it."

And with those tender words, I came undone.

All the months of grueling paperwork and interviews, research and planning, and near-unbearable waiting released in a cry I hadn't allowed myself in much too long. "I'm so sorry." I buried my face in my hands, a sob-laugh bubbling up my throat. "I'm being ridiculous."

"Ah, sweetheart, don't be sorry. You're not being ridiculous. You're being a mother." She wrapped her arms around me, holding me tight as she swayed ever so gently.

I pulled back just enough to wipe my eyes on my cardigan sleeve. "Am I though? Because I don't *feel* like a mother. Most days I just feel like I'm walking through a dark tunnel with no end in sight. Like I'll be in this waiting place forever." A raw truth I'd never spoken aloud. Not even to Jenna. Because with everyone else who knew of my plans to adopt, I needed to stay strong, stay diligent in my defense of why international adoption as a single woman was the right choice for me.

Gingerly, Gail framed my face in her hands and tilted my eyes to meet hers. "Listen to me. Right now your child is sitting across the world in an orphanage, waiting for *you*, too. You may not know your child's name yet or what their face looks like when they laugh or cry, but God has already gone before you in this. He's already connected your heart to theirs in a way only He can. I know the wait can feel excruciating while on this side of things, but it's not in vain. There is purpose in the waiting, Lauren. Don't allow yourself to lose sight of that."

I nodded, trying to halt my tears by pinching the bridge of my nose. "I know you're right, I do... it's just so hard not to get discouraged when I've heard nothing new from my agency in so long—not since China gave their stamp of approval on my adoption dossier. I sent my caseworker an inquiry over the weekend, asking for an updated timeline on being matched." I shrugged, knowing I likely wouldn't hear much until the day they sent me the name and picture of a waiting child. There were no absolutes when it came to timelines, just best estimations. "I know the caseworkers have more important things to tackle than responding to another update request from an impatient woman, but . . . it's been over a year since I—" My throat constricted, my thought cutting short.

Since I took a step five sizes bigger than my savings account and ten sizes bigger than my faith and applied to be a mother of a family-less child.

"It's tough keeping our hope alive when there seems to be no end in sight. But, Lauren, there will be an end to this season. I wish I could tell you the exact date and time, but only God knows that. With Samuel, we waited nearly four years to bring him home from Haiti. Jacob was just over two. Caleb's adoption was completed after ten months of fostering him. Allie and Becca were just under a year when the judge finalized their paperwork. And our sweet Benny . . . we waited seventeen months from application to homecoming to bring him home from China. Every adoption story looks different, but every one of our children joined our family on the perfect day. God is always on time."

My heart could have sprouted wings under Gail's motherly gaze. Every time she looked at me this way, I imagined what it must feel like to be one of her children. Did they know how special they were to be on the receiving end of such focused love and attention? I could only pray my child would feel the same way about me one day. "Thank you, Gail."

After planting a firm kiss to my temple, she opened the cupboard above the sink and warmed two mugs of her homemade vanilla chai. The spicy aroma filled the room, releasing the tension in my body and bringing my emotions back to my normal baseline.

I ducked my head into her fridge and spotted the creamer, asking her what else I could do to help prep for the family party. She shook off my request and encouraged me to relax, explaining that Robert was bringing home a stack of pizzas to feed the masses any minute. Work smarter, not harder and all that. The cake was all that mattered to Benny, not Pinterest-style party appetizers.

We moved into the dining room and scooted a mountain of Allie's library books aside to set our mugs and biscotti down on the table. Everything in this adorable nook was marked by children. The pencil lines on the doorjamb declaring heights and dates, the basketball in the corner that must have rolled in from the mud room, and the gallery display of candid snapshots.

Here, in this space filled with love, the doubts that blindsided me at night were nowhere to be found. There were no whispers of "*Your faith isn't strong enough to handle this*" or "*You aren't equipped to be a mother*" or the worst one of all: "*You won't be able to do this on your own.*"

Gail noticed me staring at their most recent family picture taken just as the trees were cloaked in every shade of autumn. "How's your family doing, Lauren?"

But I knew what she was really asking: "*Have you told your family yet?*" It was the same question Jenna asked me on a regular basis—not understanding how I could keep such a huge secret from them. But where Jenna imagined cocktail celebrations full of tearful toasts, warm hugs, and promises of future adoption showers, I pictured something else entirely.

I dunked the almond biscotti into my tea, watching the crusty texture morph into a soggy sponge. "They still don't know. I'd planned to tell my sister over the weekend at Iris's dance recital, but Lisa had a different agenda she was trying to push."

"Meaning?" Gail sipped her tea as if she had all the time in the world for this story.

"Meaning the only thing she ever wants to discuss is why I'm still single at thirty-one. She's weirdly obsessed with my dating life—or lack thereof."

Gail remained quiet for a moment. "And you're still good with your decision?"

I nearly sputtered out my first sip of tea. "To adopt?"

"No, silly." She laughed. "Your decision not to date while you're waiting to be matched with a child."

I opened my mouth, ready to spout the only answer I'd ever given to this question when Jenna asked it. But the usual *yes* faltered a bit, stalling on my tongue as if it couldn't form correctly. I repeated it a second time, willing it to sound stronger, more sure of itself. Willing it to replace the *yes* I'd *almost* spoken to Joshua only a few hours ago when he'd asked me to dinner.

Gail lowered her mug, saying nothing as she studied me through her practiced mom vision.

I shifted uncomfortably in my chair, though her eyes remained approachable and soft. "I'm good with it, Gail, I really am." Finally, a sense of calm confidence strengthened my voice and encouraged my resolve. "It's not like I can go back on it now, anyway. I signed document after document stating that I'm adopting as a single woman." And we both knew the rules for international adoption from China. There were only two categories that existed in the world of Chinese adoptions. The first was to adopt as a single, unmarried woman. The second was to adopt as a married woman of two years or longer. There was no in-between. No gray area to be found. "I'm way too far into this process now to jeopardize it for a man who likely wouldn't stick around for the long haul anyway. Adopting an orphaned child is *my* calling. *My* passion. The odds of meeting a man with a similar mindset at my age are minuscule."

Her eyebrows arched ever so slightly, as if to say, "*I did.*"

"Sure, I know you and Robert are proof that it *can* happen, but statistically speaking"—not to mention what I'd witnessed firsthand as a child—"a marriage *partnership* like yours is rare. And not only because of your united stance on adoption but all your other shared values, too, like faith and parenting styles." I didn't realize how fervent my voice had become, but all of this was fact. Strong marriages and families didn't just happen. They took time, effort, work, and the kind of energy I could only imagine expending on a child destined to be mine.

I took a breath and lowered my volume. "My little family will look different than some, I know that, but I'll do everything I can to love and support my child, even if that means choosing to stay single indefinitely."

She covered my hand with hers and smiled. Its warmth checked all my neglected approval boxes, allowing me to mull over my commitment the way I'd done when I first started the process with Small Wonders International over a year ago. Nothing had changed since then. It was still the right decision. The only decision.

I would be a single mother by choice, and that relationship was the only one I needed to be focused on.

chapter five

Despite the invisible tether that linked our two first-grade classrooms, I'd managed to steer clear of any extracurricular socializing with the sub across the hall since Monday. An effort that accounted for nearly four days of not reacting when his signature laugh reverberated through the auditorium during rained-in recess. Or when he awed the students in the cafeteria with a straw trick from his college years. Or when the morning announcements came on, opening the school day with the Pledge of Allegiance, courtesy of Mr. T-Rex himself.

How Joshua could teach after such a gravelly rendition, I had no idea, but every teacher I passed seemed absolutely smitten with him. Even Mrs. Dalton had come around since he broke her quiet rule in the library. Maybe she had a secret affinity for dinosaur impersonations. Or maybe . . . maybe she saw what everybody else saw in him: a man who brought a fresh dose of cheer to every room he visited in our school.

With the weekend countdown firmly in mind, I assisted my last student into her father's SUV and closed the door, giving them a slight wave as they drove off. It was then I spotted him, my arm bent in a mid-wave, at the end of the carpool line. He was holding the gloved hand of a sobbing child. Little Mason Grady.

On instinct, I moved toward the pair, hugging my jacket tighter around my middle as a strong gust of wind stung my eyes. The weather had made a sharp turn this last week, the crisp autumn air mimicking winter's bone-chilling drop in temperature.

"Hey, Mason, what's going on, buddy?" I glanced up at Joshua before crouching to eye level with the boy.

He sniffed and wiped his snotty nose against his knit Spider-man glove. "My . . . dad . . . didn't come."

Understanding twisted my gut. Mason's parents' divorce finalized at the beginning of the school year, and the back-and-forth of rides and overnights had been taking a toll on Mason and his older sister.

I tipped his chin so his eyes met mine. "Let's go call him together, okay? I'm sure he's on his way."

A big sniffle paired with a teary nod were the precursor of Mason's arms shooting around my middle and nearly knocking me off-balance and onto my backside. Joshua placed a steadying hand on my shoulder, and the firmness of his grip created a ripple of awareness down my spine.

I patted Mason's back and spoke soothingly into his ear. "You're okay, buddy. We'll work this out. I promise."

Both his parents were good people. Stressed and burdened, yes, but hardworking and dedicated to making a new and healthy normal for their kids. Even so, Mason's emotional response to a late-arriving pickup wasn't unusual. I'd seen similar heartbreaks in dozens of children over upsets at home. I understood them well. After a shudder passed, he pulled back and wiped his eyes along his blue coat sleeve one more time.

"Okay." He reached for my hand. "Do you have any suckers in your classroom, Miss B?"

I chuckled at this quick transition. "I believe I do."

It was then I noticed Mason's other hand still latched onto Joshua's. Joshua, whose gaze was acutely affixed on my face.

Thanks, he mouthed as our eyes met.

I nodded and promptly glanced away.

Hand in hand in hand, we strolled as a trio into Brighton, Joshua opening the heavy metal door so we could enter ahead of him.

"I only like the red, orange, and blue ones," Mason said, rerouting my thoughts from the gentlemanly manners of one Mr. Avery to the prize bag in my classroom. "Not the brown ones."

"Not the brown ones, huh?" Joshua repeated. "I can't remember, are those chocolate or root beer flavored?"

"I don't know. They're just super yucky."

"Fair enough. That's how I feel about orange circus peanuts. Have you tried that candy?"

Mason shook his head.

"They look like squishy peanuts the color of peach flesh. Naturally, one would assume the flavor to be either peanut butter or fruit. But nope, it's neither. Those candies taste like chewing on a giant, flavorless foam finger." He shuddered. "It's the worst kind of false advertising."

"Gross." Mason's firm agreement as we entered my classroom had me holding in a laugh.

I retrieved my rainbow sequin prize bag from the hook above the cubbies, then held it out to Mason. He rummaged through it for several seconds until he pulled out a blue Tootsie Pop.

"Good choice!" Joshua affirmed with a pat on Mason's back as I picked up my phone and dialed the front office to let Diana know Mason was waiting in my room. She confirmed that his father had already called the school and was on his way. I relayed the news to the sweet ginger-haired boy sucking happily on a lollipop and watched from my periphery as Joshua meandered through my classroom.

"Can I have a sucker for my sister, too, Miss Bailey? She's in the sixth grade. Sometimes she pretends that she doesn't like candy anymore, but I saw her sneak a piece from the pantry last week. So she actually really *does* like it."

And this was why I adored children so much. They could flip from inconsolable to insightful in a matter of minutes. Of course, offering them sugar on a stick might have something to do with that. But still. There was nothing I loved more than the innocence of a child. I offered him another blue sucker for his sister.

Shamelessly, Joshua continued his stroll to the back half of my room. He'd peeked behind shelves and inside cubbies, perusing my classroom like an open house on the market. If he hadn't looked so darn fascinated by it all, I may have tossed my dry eraser at the back of his head for being such a snoop. Or at least, I would have threatened to. Violent acts weren't really my kind of thing.

"It appears all the rumors from Brighton's students are correct. Your classroom is totally awesome, Laur—Miss B," he corrected with a sharp glance in Mason's direction. He rolled a yoga ball out from one of the desks and bounced on it several times, right before he transitioned to a wiggle board and extended his arms like a surfer riding a wave. "I want this setup for my home office."

"She has a huge game closet, too. We got to play in here once for a pizza party." Mason popped his sucker out of his mouth and used the slobbery blue orb as a pointer. "It's over there in the corner."

Only once had Mrs. Walker allowed her class in my room for a party after one of her students won the guess-how-many-jelly-beans-are-in-the-jar contest we held the week prior to Fall Break to practice estimation. Out of a handful of prize options, the winning child chose a joint pizza party for the combined first-grade classes. Mrs. Walker spent the entire time grading papers in the corner while I refilled glasses of apple juice and handed out bowls of popcorn along with the room moms.

Joshua's gaze tracked back to the far corner closet. If eyebrows could plead a case, his would have won unanimously. I gave a single nod at his nonverbal request and he sprang into action. The instant he swung the closet door open, he released a whooshing sound through his teeth.

"Whoa." He looked as if he'd just entered the Cave of Wonders and had spotted Aladdin's golden lamp on a pedestal.

He searched the labeled game shelves. "Is this . . ." He reached inside and touched one of the faded boxes. "It *is*. This is the *original* Rock 'Em Sock 'Em Robots game. My brother and I played this so much we broke the red robot's head clean off. They started making it in the mid-sixties. Ours wasn't quite this old, but, wait—" He paused and slid his finger down a dozen more vintage board games: Scrabble, Monopoly, Clue, Candy Land, Life. "These games are all at least forty years old. This is a collector's jackpot. How do you have all these?"

"My mom."

He popped his head back out of the closet. "Please tell me she's looking for a son. Because I'm adoptable."

The irony of his statement bubbled up in my throat and exited in a choked laugh. "Honestly? I'm not even sure she wants to claim the kids she has. But to be fair, if I hadn't intervened, she would have given all those away to a thrift store."

His appalled expression sent Mason into a fit of giggles. "That's criminal."

"Probably. But she's a closet cleaner for the rich and hoardy. Nothing shocks her anymore. You wouldn't believe the stuff I've rescued from her dumpster pile."

"Where can I apply for that job—the dumpster pile sorter? Because I'd be happy to take any original Atari or Nintendo consoles off her hands. Or any vintage action figures, if we want to get super specific."

"I'm pretty sure you can find those kinds of things on eBay."

"I'm pretty sure they banned me as a bidder two years ago."

Who is this guy? "Now that sounds like a good story."

His grin reminded me of one of my more rascally male students of the past. "Not sure about *good*. But a story, no less."

The intercom shrilled with a sudden burst of static. "Miss Bailey? Mason's father is here waiting for his son in the office."

"Thanks," I said in reply while Joshua moved toward the sweet boy who was slinging his backpack over his shoulder and merrily chomping on the last bits of his lollipop.

"Guess that's our cue, Mason." Joshua directed him to my open door.

"Have a great weekend, buddy," I called. "You too, Mr. Avery."

They flashed me a return smile in tandem and exited my room with a wave.

I picked up my phone from my desk and shot Jenna a quick text, asking when she would be ready to leave for the day. It wasn't common for her to stay this late without communicating it, but she must have had a last-minute project pop up, or a phone call to make on behalf of a student. Whatever the case, I could sure use a good Jenna parking lot stroll right about now.

My screen lit up with her face and number.

I swiped to answer.

"Lauren!" The excited shriek of my best friend through the phone caused me to spin around, half expecting to find her rushing through my doorway with her arms flailing. "He did it! He totally tricked me!"

"Did what? Who? Where are you?" I pressed my finger to my ear, trying to hear over the loud staticky sound in the background. *What was that? Wind?*

"Brian!" A cascade of laughter trickled through my phone's receiver. "He bought me a car! He showed up at the end of the carpool line with a huge red bow plastered to the roof and everything! I looked for you, but I couldn't find you anywhere. It's my dream car—"

"A red Mustang convertible?" Jenna had swooned over that car for years. It was an easy guess.

"Yes! He got a great deal on it seeing as it's nearly winter, and *eeek*! I'm just so, so excited!" Another glorious round of giggles followed by the low, unmistakable murmuring of her doting husband.

"So, I take it your old Acura didn't actually need a visit to the mechanic, huh?"

"No, he was working on trade-in paperwork with the dealer. So sneaky! Anyway, we're out for a drive in it now—we have the top down, which is freezing, but our heated seats are blazing. Who says you can't own a convertible in Idaho? I can't wait to take this thing on a girls' trip with you next summer!"

"A *girls'* trip? What about me?" Brian teased in the background. "Do you hear what I have to put up with, Lauren? I buy her a new car, and she plans a vacation without me."

"Oh, you stop it," Jenna baby-voiced back. The unmistakable sound of smacking lips caused me to pull the phone away from my ear and grimace.

I spoke directly into the speaker. "Um, hello? I'm still here, and I really hope at least one of you is watching the road right now. Kissing is a known driving hazard."

"One of the best, if you ask me." Joshua's voice at my back nearly launched the phone from my hand into the closed window.

I whirled around, eyes wide. "You scared me!"

His lips curled into a smile, hands raised in surrender. "Sorry. Couldn't resist."

"Who's that?" Jenna demanded in my ear. Her lips were apparently now freed from their previous captivity. "Is that Joshua? Is he in your classroom?"

"I gotta go, Jen. Send me a pic of your new ride when you get a chance. Happy for you."

"Wait—did he ask you out again?"

"*Bye*."

"You better call me the second you leave there—"

I clicked off before she could finish her threat and cleared my throat, hoping with every cell in me that Joshua hadn't heard the last part of that conversation.

"Hey again," I said, far more breathless than was necessary at the sight of the grinning man parked on Lilly Andrew's desk. "Did everything go okay in the office with Mason?"

"Yep. His dad felt awful. Seems like a nice guy." There was something in Joshua's hand, laid across his lap. A notebook? A calendar? "But I'm actually here because I need help. And seeing as I just watched you cure an emotionally distraught six-year-old with a piece of prized candy, I'm hoping you might have a good solution for me, too."

"Well, I do happen to have the best prize bag at Brighton." Wait—who did this flirty voice belong to? It couldn't be me. *I am not a flirt.*

He handed me the spiral-bound book. "I consider myself to be a fairly intelligent guy. But I'm lost as to what all these abbreviations stand for."

"Abbreviations? What is . . . *oh.*" I flipped the rigid cover page open. "This is Mrs. Walker's planner."

"Yes. And it might as well be written in Swahili."

I focused on the shortened words and phrases written inside each calendar block. Until that moment, I'd never seen Mrs. Walker's planning system. She was a lone ranger at Brighton, refusing to attend any of the shared teaching engagements I'd invited her to. I'd asked at least a dozen times if she wanted to team up and work as partners for our students, but I was always told she was better off doing things her own way.

I turned the inked pages as if I were holding a long-lost manuscript that belonged in a museum. Would Mrs. Walker dust this for fingerprints once she was back? I wouldn't put it past her. Many of the abbreviations she used I recognized. After years of deciphering my mother's messy shorthand, these seemed fairly straightforward to me, but all pointed to worksheets and textbooks I rarely used in my own classroom.

Joshua dipped his chin, bringing his head closer to my own. "I gather you and Charlotte don't share much in common when it comes to teaching techniques."

I let out a long sigh and closed the book. "No, we really don't, I'm sorry." I bit my tongue from adding, "*She isn't exactly what you'd call a team player.*"

"So the chances of you having an abbreviation decoder in that magical prize bag of yours are . . . ?"

"Hmm . . . a decoder? Slim, I'm afraid."

"And what about the chances of you having a spare set of lesson plans you can share with me while I'm here at Brighton?" He gestured around my room. "It's easy to see you follow a much more modern and innovative approach in teaching, which is a better fit as far as my research goes." He pressed his hand to his heart. "I'd be honored if you confided some of your wisdom with me."

"My *wisdom*?" I nearly choked on the word. "But your father is—"

"A bit dated. He hasn't taught inside an elementary classroom for years, and though his theories and practices were cutting edge a decade or two ago, you've managed to merge his techniques with modern technology and STEM stations. As far as the app I've helped create, I think I could learn a lot from you." He paused and stared at me intently. "I could be free to meet up anytime tomorrow if you are. At a coffee shop maybe? I'll buy the drinks, and you bring the plans. What do you think, Lauren?"

What did I think? About meeting him for coffee, or the fact that my brain had sputtered out two seconds after he suggested it. Because neither were clear.

As we both waited for my mouth to speak a coherent response, a dangerous charge rippled between us. The proposal itself seemed harmless enough, and yet . . . and yet the idea of sharing space with this man, drinking coffee in a relaxed, non-school setting together while explaining the ins and outs of my teaching preferences, created a tension I hadn't felt in . . . maybe ever.

I hesitated for a moment, sorting through what was actually being asked of me. Not a romantic date. But a work date. A business meeting with a fellow comrade in need of what I had to offer him professionally—first-grade lesson plans. It couldn't get much more platonic than that, could it?

"I live near Porter's Coffee House on thirty-first and Bramble. I could probably meet you late morning for a bit."

"Sounds great," he said, standing up and grinning like I'd just agreed to pay off his mortgage. "Should we say ten, then?"

"Ten it is."

chapter six

"Wait, you're telling me you don't drink coffee . . . ever?" I leaned back in my chair, staring at him over our shared corner table in disbelief. I must have heard him wrong. Maybe the steam from the espresso machine had fogged over a few key words, because an admission to not being a coffee drinker was not only counter to our age group, but also to our Northwest culture.

Joshua took another easy swig of his pulp-free orange juice and tapped my purple teaching folder splayed on the table top between us. So far, we'd only managed to gloss over a few pages. "Listen, if my not drinking coffee is gonna be a deal breaker for you, then I'll stand up right now and order myself a"—he scrutinized my cinnamon dolce with extra whip and caramel drizzle—"whatever it is you're drinking there."

I stuffed down the urge to laugh, determined to get to the bottom of this new, preposterous discovery. "No, I'm just trying to understand the issue. Is it the taste? The caffeine? A personal conviction against perfection in a mug?"

The last one made him smile, and I found myself smiling right back. The same way I'd done when he'd first arrived at Porter's wearing yet another dinosaur T-shirt—this one featuring a brontosaurus with the words *All My Friends Are Dead* written in typewriter font across his chest.

"And on that note," I added before he could respond, "why would you even suggest meeting at a coffee shop if you don't drink the stuff?"

"Easy." His voice held a new layer of intrigue. "I figured going to coffee with you would feel less presumptuous than asking you out for another meal, seeing as I'd already tried that approach once. I make it a point to learn from my failures whenever possible."

Not at all what I expected him to say. Then again, most of what Joshua said wasn't expected.

"And . . ." He held up a finger. "As for not drinking coffee myself, well, that started out as a bet."

Still reeling from his previous statement, I forced my mind to pick up the pace, to quit lingering at the corner of He-Likes-Me and His-Smile-Is-Stunning and take a hard right at the stoplight of You-Are-Going-To-Be-Someone's-Mother-Soon. I took another long swig of my favorite type of caffeine, careful to check for any remnants of stray whip on my top lip. "As in someone bet you to stop drinking coffee?"

"Not just someone. Sam Pierre, my business partner." Joshua toyed with the cap of his orange juice, twisting it on and off again with his thumb. "Only at that time he was just my college roommate. We chose to build a game app for our senior project at Gonzaga, which meant pulling a lot of all-nighters. I coded until my fingers were cramped and my eyes went crossed. But every night, without fail, Sam would be unconscious by midnight. He'd just be typing away and *bam*." Joshua slapped the table. "He'd be out cold. Sitting ruler-straight at his desk and snoring like a hibernating bear." Joshua demonstrated the look, and I nearly spat out my next swallow of cinnamon goodness.

"One night I took a video of his particular brand of narcolepsy because he refused to believe me. And when I showed him, he said the only reason I could stay awake so much longer than him was due to my high caffeine consumption, so naturally . . ." He trailed off, leaving me to fill in the blanks.

"He bet that you couldn't meet your deadline without it?"

"The winner got to name the game." The corner of his mouth ticked, and his one dimple seemed to wink at me. "Ever heard of an app called Brick Builders?"

"Um, *yes*." Heard of it? Who hadn't? I wasn't even a gamer, but I'd taken care of my sister's stepsons enough times to recognize all their technology fixations. "My nephews and half of America were obsessed with that game a few years ago."

"Well, Sam wanted to name it Block Stackers."

"Brick Builders was a way better choice."

"Glad you think so, because this conversation could have just taken an awkward turn if not."

"You won the bet," I marveled.

"More important, I became a strict orange juice drinker." He raised his bottle and fake-clinked it against my latte. "Sure, some people give me a hard time about the sugar content, but I say one thing at a time. Besides, I'm pretty sure oranges were in the Garden of Eden, and it's a rare person who wants to battle that argument."

"I would think not." I shook my head at the modest way he spoke about himself. It was clear Joshua wasn't just some guy restoring broken laptops in his parents' basement. He was a visionary with a successful track record. "I'm pretty sure you did more than win a coffee bet when that game went live. For me to know about it, it had to have made a pretty big splash."

A too-humble shrug followed by another sip of his juice. "It did help jump-start my career as a tech consultant, as well as gave us a catchy company name—Wide Awake Tech Consultants."

"Clever." I laughed again. "But it also must have put a stop to your plans to teach in a classroom, right?"

"Yes, right."

There was an effortlessness in conversing with Joshua, an undeniable ease that created a mixed-bag feeling of desire and denial. I shoved the latter feeling aside and returned to a subject that had spun circles in my brain for months. "Do you mind if I ask you a personal question?"

"Is there a more personal topic than beverage preferences?"

I angled my head, pulling in my bottom lip to allow me an extra second to phrase a question I had absolutely no business in asking. "Was that difficult to tell your father? I mean, changing the trajectory of your career path after following in his footsteps all through college . . . I'd think it must have been challenging."

His eyes softened as they roved my face. "It's funny, isn't it? How much our parents can influence our choices as adults." He tapped the glass with his thumbnail. "Honestly, at first they weren't too keen on me starting a business straight out of college based on one success that felt a whole lot like roll-of-the-dice luck to them. Which, to their credit, was a valid concern. My industry is full of brilliant minds who struggle to make ends meet." He leaned back in his chair, throwing a leg over his knee and glancing at the ceiling as if trying to recall the memory in its entirety. "But no matter how much I respected my father or his chosen career path, I couldn't pretend it was the right path for me just because it had been the expected one."

Shame tiptoed through my memories—reminding me of all the opportunities I'd avoided telling my family about my own *right path*. "Were you worried about his response?"

"I figured he'd be disappointed. At least inwardly." His gaze paused on my folder. "But I remember feeling relieved more than anything else."

I leaned in, willing him to go on. "Really?"

He flicked the bottle cap back and forth on the tabletop between his hands. His brow rumpled in contemplation. "There was always this indefinable tension between my father and me growing up. We're similar in a lot of ways, my dad and I, but it wasn't until I experienced my own failures and successes that I could really appreciate our differences." He lifted his eyes to mine. "To use a construction metaphor, my dad is a master renovator. He does his best work inside a tried-and-true structure."

"And what are you?"

"An architect." He dropped a pile of sugar packets between us and started stacking them into a Jenga-like tower. A crosshatch pattern at least ten high. "If I design the building, I'm not constrained by someone else's rules or limitations." He pinched the third one from the bottom and yanked it out with a swift tug. Amazingly, the others remained standing. The brilliant flash of teeth he gave me sent a spiral of nerves to the base of my belly. "I prefer to assume both the responsibility and the risk."

"That's a lot of liability."

"But a lot of freedom, too." He flattened the tower of sugar packets. "If I make the rules, then I know which ones can be broken."

"You know," I said, giving him my most sarcastic corner-of-the-eye look, "I never would have guessed you for a rule breaker."

He chuckled. "Well, I *am* pretty timid about it."

"Timid is definitely not the word I'd use to describe you." The second I said it, I wished I could take it back. My cheeks flushed a thousand shades of foolish. "I just mean—"

He shook his head. "No disclaimers necessary. I just told you three fundamental facts about myself, so I'm pretty sure that means we're beyond the disclaimer stage now."

I scrunched up my face. "You told me *three* fundamental facts?"

He ticked off a finger as he spoke. "My coffee bet. My father-son metaphor." His eyes narrowed in that almost-a-wink way of his. "And that I've been looking for an opportunity to spend time with you outside of school since the first day we met."

His earnest tone caused something to yawn awake inside me,

like a welcome stretch after a long winter's nap. Only this wasn't the time for such an awakening. This was the time I needed to remain firmly attached to memories of singing made-up lullabies to my favorite doll before bedtime.

Yet whenever I was alone with this man, the same maternal drive that had overflowed my emotional tank for more than a year sprang a leak. It was as if my only agenda was the one sitting right in front of me, and not the one sitting three thousand miles away. In an orphanage. Waiting for me to become a mother.

I placed a hand on my folder and slowly slid it across the table toward me, warring against the newfound ache in my chest. One I couldn't afford to give attention to. "I think we should probably get back to these teaching plans before the day gets away from us."

"All right, we can do that." His words were spoken easily, as if he'd been anticipating this very reaction from me and had prepared his counter play long in advance. But there was more to the way he anchored his elbows on the tabletop and angled his head to review the handwritten outlines inside my folder. More to the way he brushed aside the muffin crumb next to my hand. More to the moon-shaped indentation that flexed in his right cheek as I stuttered through the first three activities listed in my planner for next week.

My finger underlined the words inside Monday's calendar box, but my voice faltered, stuck on the evidence my subconscious had just unearthed.

Joshua Avery wasn't the easily deterred type. Nor was he the appeasing-for-appeasing-sake type. No, Joshua was the type who designed blueprints from scratch, abandoned caffeine to test his willpower, and enjoyed a challenge even when said challenge had removed herself from the dating pool.

He was patience personified.

"You okay?" he asked, dipping his chin low to catch my eye.

I brought my cup to my lips, willing one last drop to wet my tongue and miraculously un-pause my mental stall. Please, just one more drop.

I shook it. Twice.

My cup couldn't be more empty.

"I'll go get you another one." He stood and pushed out his chair. "You want the same drink? If so, you might need to coach me through the order."

My answer crawled up my throat. "Water will be fine, thank you."

Two feet from the counter, he swiveled back. "You sure? Don't let me influence your decisions."

Interesting choice of words since that was exactly what he'd been doing since the day we met. "I'm sure."

As he waited at the counter, I slid my phone from my back pocket and tapped the screen to check the time. An email notification box surfaced to the forefront, blocking my ability to see the clock. Or anything else for that matter. Because the sender's name was the only thing I had eyes for: Small Wonders International.

The sounds in the coffee shop muted to undistinguishable white noise as I scrolled to my inbox and tapped the update I'd been waiting on.

Happy Saturday, Lauren!

First off, I apologize for the delay in responding to your request for an update, but things have been going a hundred miles an hour around our agency lately. We've been working half days on Saturdays to catch up. But I do have an update for you!

As of yesterday, your file's been moved to the top of our match pile. The Chinese government dropped the largest group of prepared orphan files into the shared agency pool about ten days ago, so that has sped things up quite a bit. I don't want to overpromise, but I think we could be sending you the big match email very soon. Keep in mind that when it arrives you'll have two weeks to accept or deny a file. We encourage all new adoptive parents to share the medical portion of the child's files with your family doctor before making a final decision. Once you accept a file, we'll submit the Letter of Intent for that child and lock them in for you as you go through the final stages of the paperwork process.

Excited to work with you more closely in the coming weeks,

Stacey Adams

My mind fumbled over the content, working in slow motion to process the phrases: *match pile, orphan files, big email, very soon.*

"Here you are. Boring old ice water with a side of this all-too-tempting cranberry almond scone." He set the chilled plastic cup and plate next to my iPhone, and I quickly darkened the screen, struggling to connect with a reality outside this latest update.

"Thank you."

He studied me. "Bad news?"

"What?"

"Your face . . . I'm trying to get a read on it. You're either in shock or upset. I can't tell which."

"Oh . . . uh." I shook my head, trying to shake a thousand jumbled thoughts into a single cohesive sentence. "I just read a surprising email—still trying to wrap my head around it."

"Well, for your sake, I hope it was surprising in the most positive of ways."

I swallowed the emotion tripping up my throat. "It is, yes. Thank you."

He slid the purple folder toward me. "I'm guessing you need to get going?"

Relief settled over me. "I probably should be, yes, but I know we didn't spend nearly enough time talking through these lesson plans and—"

"I had a great morning with you, Lauren. With or without lesson plans."

Clearly, I was too out of sorts to interpret his brand of kindness in any professional manner. "Keep it." I pushed the folder back in his direction and took out a pen from my purse, scribbling my number on the inside pocket. "Feel free to text if you need help with any of the abbreviations in there, and you're welcome to make copies of anything I have if you need to."

With the folder back in his custody, he tapped the edge of it with his forefinger and eyed me with the most pensive expression I'd ever seen him wear. "Looks like there's only one thing left for us to discuss today."

My already shaky stomach took a nosedive. "There is?"

"Yes. Which one of us gets to take home the cranberry almond scone?"

chapter seven

Two days.

Two days of not sleeping. Two days of obsessive Googling. Two days of eating cookie dough ice cream smothered in hot fudge for dinner and pretending not to think about my name sitting atop my agency's wait list.

Skye dragged her wet nose across my bare calf, and I reached down to scratch the white patch of fur behind her ears. "I know, I know. I'm pathetic."

She whined as if in confirmation. She could always tell when something was emotionally off with me. Maybe she could sense the changes in my mood, but then again, maybe she just wanted to lick the splatters of ice cream off my college sweatshirt. Either way, we were both stress eaters.

"Ugh." I set the bowl on the coffee table and watched the spoon sink low into the soupy mess. "I need to do something, Skye. Something productive. Something that . . . I don't know, feels like a step forward and doesn't add ten inches to my waistline before Thanksgiving break."

I padded across the living room in my blue-and-white striped fuzzy socks. My matching pj bottoms slipped from my hips just enough to require a cinch and tie. Skye dashed to the front door, as if I was suiting up for a run. Hardly. "It's raining outside, silly girl. I can't take you for a walk right now." Even if I could, no amount of walking would settle the adrenaline spikes Stacey's not-so-helpful email response had awakened in me.

I mean, seriously, how could that email have produced anything but anxiety in a waiting parent? It was like saying, "Hey, you over there—you who's been on the path of adoption for more than a year, you who's been trying to keep your mind occupied while still being an active member of society—well, guess what? Your wait's about to be over! Only in the meantime, you get to wait some more!"

Skye slumped onto her dog bed under the corner living room window, laying her head on her front paws. Her heavy-lidded eyes closed mere seconds before her snoring kicked in. At least one of us was able to get some good rest this week.

My text alert chimed. Four times. No, five.

Six.

Seven.

Eight.

My sister.

I hesitated before retrieving my phone off the arm of the sofa.

Between Lisa asking me what I was bringing for Thanksgiving meal and Jenna asking what happened with Joshua at the coffee shop, I was seriously considering throwing my phone into the garbage disposal. Only I couldn't. Because that would mean not being able to refresh my inbox every thirty seconds.

And that might literally kill me.

With a little too much force, I tapped the phone screen and opened up my sister's text thread. By the rapid-succession alerts, I knew she was voice-texting in her car. Lisa's favorite form of communication.

So what are you bringing to Thanksgiving?

I told Mom I'm not eating that greasy casserole thing she makes for one more holiday. If a heart attack had a face, that would be it.

I'm bringing walled-off salad.

No. Stupid voice-to-text. Not walled-off. Waldorf!

Anyway, I'm driving Iris to ballet right now. Can you believe her instructor sent out a group text informing all us parents that practice was moving from Wednesday to Thursday nights? Yeah, effective immediately. Like none of us have jobs outside of driving our kids to class.

Oh, that reminds me, Mom and I have a huge closet job coming up. Might need to use your sheep.

Deep

Jeep! I said Jeep!

I hate voice-texting! Let's talk soon. It's been forever. Love you.

I squeezed my eyes shut and counted to ten before texting back a response.

Thanks. I'll text Mom about bringing a dessert for Thanksgiving, and I'll ask about the closet job.

My finger hovered atop the alphabet pad on my phone, a cloud of guilt descending over me.

Love you. We'll talk soon.

Soon was right. Because *soon* I'd know the face of my waiting child. And if Lisa could get fired up over a schedule change on a dance-mom text thread, I didn't even want to think about the way she'd rage at me for withholding my adoption news.

I needed to make a plan. A real one this time. With people who'd been around the adoption block a time or two and had lived to tell about it.

And luckily, I knew exactly where those people would be tonight: in the basement of Calvary Community Church.

All church basements seem to share a similar vibe, and Calvary Community was no exception: geometric carpet squares, folded chairs along the back wall, a too-low ceiling with fluorescent lighting, and a foosball table waiting to be played during midweek services. But something about the familiar aroma of old hymnals and brewed coffee brought a homey kind of comfort to my anxious spirit. I never regretted making the drive to Calvary.

I noted the small circle of chairs in the center of the room and set my fruit tray beside the coffee pot. In a matter of minutes, the folding table would be filled with shared snacks and the room with animated voices—one in particular.

In the whole of the Boise-Nampa metropolitan area of nearly seven hundred thousand people, there wasn't a shortage of adoption support groups to attend, yet only one was facilitated by my favorite married couple on the planet.

"Lauren?" Gail rounded the corner, carrying a giant bowl of white cheddar popcorn. "Oh, I'm so glad you could make it tonight." She set the theater-size bucket down and pulled me into a hug.

"Me too. I would have called first, but tonight was more of a spontaneous decision." Somewhere between watching an adoption documentary on Netflix and my second pint of Ben and Jerry's.

"No apologies necessary." She gave my arm a little squeeze. "Did the agency ever get back to you?"

"Actually, yes, I got an update from them yesterday and that's actually why—"

"Hey, Gail?" Robert jogged down the staircase, his voice edged with rare urgency. "Oh, Lauren, sorry to interrupt." He focused his attention on his wife. "That new couple Pastor Todd contacted you about just arrived. They're walking in with Sara and Sam now."

The fine lines around Gail's eyes deepened. "Okay, thanks for letting me know, honey." She turned back to me and patted my arm, working to compose her face as she said, "Go ahead, Lauren. I would love to hear your news."

"No, no. I can share it later in group. Please, go and do whatever you need to. Can I help with anything?"

"I wish you could." She shook her head and gave a weighted sigh. "Truth is, some people just need a little extra grace when life's challenges fail to meet their expectations."

I didn't have time to question her theory, not when three couples entered the room all at once. The newcomers Robert had mentioned were easy to identify. And not just because I'd seen the other two couples in prior meetings, but because the husband, who could have starred in a remake of *The Great Gatsby*, stood head and shoulders above the crowd, chattering on about current weather patterns as if that were his sole reason for joining us tonight. He wore a charcoal, made-to-look-vintage bowler hat and a pair of sophisticated black glasses, neither of which hid the dark half-moons under his eyes.

When his attention drifted behind him to his wife, mine followed.

Melanie, as her name tag read, was next-door kind of pretty. Her short blond hair, trendy clothing, and matchy-matchy handbag would have warranted a second glance in any other setting, but I couldn't focus on anything other than the fury spewing from her glare. Obviously, this church basement was the last place she wanted to be tonight. I wavered between greeting her and giving her the ten-foot radius her expression demanded.

With a bravery I admired, Gail approached her, handing her a small snack plate and explaining the evening's agenda. The first fifteen minutes of group were always reserved for fellowship around the refreshments table, but by the way Melanie chucked her purse to the floor and threw her body into an empty chair, I gathered she'd rather pluck cactus barbs out of her foot than endure *fellowship* with the likes of us.

On my perusal of the snack table, I received several nice-to-see-you-again hugs, and even a compliment on my dry-shampooed hair, which had to be my favorite invention of the twenty-first century. Thankfully, along with quick-styling my hair, I'd had enough time to swap out my ice-cream-encrusted sweatshirt and sweats combo for a long sweater and boots duo.

Within ten minutes, we were all seated in the circle. I balanced a small plate of popcorn on my knee and offered a smile to the female storm cloud sitting directly across from me. Melanie did not smile back. Instead, her scowl intensified as she crossed her arms over her chest. Message received.

Robert said a quick prayer to get things rolling, and Gail went over the group guidelines, likely for the sake of Great Gatsby and his joyful bride. The rules were all common sense: no cross talking, no oversharing, no interrupting, and no advice-giving without permission. These were followed by the usual "what's said in support group stays in support group" confidentiality clause.

I was in the middle of an internal speculation of why the new couple had showed up at tonight's meeting when Gail diverted the group's attention, her eyes bright and expectant as they settled on me.

"Lauren, since it's been a few weeks since you've been back

to group, why don't you give us an update on all that's happened in your adoption journey? And if you don't mind, would you go ahead and tell us a little about yourself, too, since Peter and Melanie are joining us for the first time?"

I was fairly certain there was nothing Melanie would want to hear less, given her venomous glare, but it was clear Gail was hoping for a mood shift. I lifted the plate from my knee, crossed my opposite leg, and made a conscious effort to avoid eye contact with a certain glowering blonde. "Of course, sure."

The couple closest to me, Sam and Sara, nodded with a level of enthusiasm usually reserved for a rock concert. They were the resident head bobbers. Every group had at least one pair of those. I'd seen my fair share in the parent-teacher meetings at Brighton, too. No matter who was sharing or what was being shared, the head bobbers never stopped bobbing.

"Hey again, everyone. I'm Lauren Bailey, and I've taught first grade at Brighton Elementary on the eastside for the last ten years. I'm not married, but I do have a cocker spaniel named Skye who likes to think of herself as my better half." The head bobbers chuckled, as did Karen and Jack, a foster care couple who routinely shared their home with sick newborns in need of respite. "About six years ago, I had the privilege of teaching a little boy who changed my idea of adoption and planted a seed in my heart that grew until I was able to meet the application requirements when I turned thirty. I partnered with Small Wonders about fourteen months ago and started the process to adopt from China. There's been a lot of paper-work and appointments, but to be honest, it's all gone pretty smoothly so far." I paused. "And as of yesterday morning, I received an email from my agency telling me that I'm at the top of the wait list." Gail gasped and brought her hands up to her mouth, clapping silently in celebration. I smiled back at her. "My caseworker said my official match email would be coming soon, so of course I've been obsessively checking my email, eating ice cream for every meal, and not sleeping a wink. My true motivation in coming tonight was to give my refresh button a break."

The group laughed. Most of them, anyway.

"Oh, don't we all know that feeling!" Karen exclaimed, reaching into a plaid car seat.

"Well, it's nice to know I'm not the only one." I flicked the edge of my plate with my thumbnail. "To be honest, though, now that the *big email* could be sent out at any moment, time seems to be moving so much slower, and my patience feels much thinner."

"I'm sure many of us can relate to that feeling, too," Gail added sympathetically. "But this is wonderful news, Lauren. We'll all be ready to celebrate with you whenever that special email does show up in your inbox." She paused then, her gaze scanning the circle before coming back to me. "You made the right decision in coming tonight, no matter your motivation. The season of waiting that you're in is just one example of why we need to lean into our support systems. When life feels hard, it's imperative we reach out to our loved ones and communities and share our burdens. And in due time, those same support systems will be the people who will get to share in our blessings, too."

Even as several verbal agreements rang out around the circle, a familiar heaviness pushed against my chest. Karen patted the back of her newest pink baby bundle, and I forced my next words out before I could second-guess the level of my vulnerability. "I don't want to take up too much more group time, but I was actually hoping I could ask a few questions about all that. Is that all right, Gail?"

"Certainly, ask anything you need to, darlin'. That's why we're here." I didn't miss the way her gaze floated over to the new couple again.

"As far as support systems go, I have my best friend, Jenna, and a few women at my church, Gail and Robert, this group, as well as a few social media pages specific to China adoptions. But . . ." I hesitated, and the head bobber closest to me, Sara, picked up speed, as if to spur me on. It worked. "But I haven't told my family yet."

"About the latest news from your agency?" Karen kindly tried to clarify as shame ignited my cheeks.

"No, um, I mean, I haven't told them I'm adopting at all." Even as I said the words aloud, I knew how bad they sounded—how bad *I* must sound for admitting such a heartless truth. What kind of a woman didn't tell her own family about an adoption she'd been planning for over a year?

Every one of the well-meaning lectures Jenna had given me since last winter recycled in my mind. "I know how that sounds. It's just that things are a bit complicated with my family. They're not bad people or anything, I just . . . I don't think my decision will make sense to them."

Robert leaned forward, his salt-and-pepper eyebrows crumpling at the arch. "Lauren, what part of your decision to adopt do you think they'll struggle with the most?"

"That I'm single." Those three words hung in the silence like a dead weight, exposing me in a way I rarely allowed. Perhaps it had something to do with finding my unattached marital status at the top of my sister's New Year's Resolution list. Or how my mother constantly obsessed over my financial security like it was her part-time job. Though my father's workman's comp had run dry twenty years ago, my mother never let us forget how she'd been thrust into the workforce so her family of four could survive. She wasn't the type who called to chat or to check on me. No, her questions usually surrounded my retirement plan and low-risk stocks. I certainly wasn't looking forward to the day she found out I'd cashed in my nest egg of savings to take on a dependent.

"I think what you're doing as a single woman is really admirable,

Lauren," Sara said. "It may not be the most traditional pathway in adoption, but the world has way more orphans than it does loving parents who are willing to step up to the task."

"Exactly," Karen added with a tearful smile. "Jack and I are unlikely candidates, as well. We're in our late fifties, and while most of our friends are retiring and taking fancy vacations, we're feeding sick babies through the night. But you know, God has always provided for our needs. Saying yes to this calling has been our greatest blessing."

At this, Melanie huffed. And not the could-be-considered-a-cough kind of huff, either. It was definitely a you've-got-to-be-kidding-me huff.

"Melanie," Gail said in the same voice I used to calm an emotionally charged first grader, "do you have something you'd like to add to this discussion?"

"Yeah, I do." The hard rasp of her tone had me sliding to the back of my chair. Whatever was coming, it wasn't going to be frosted in sugary optimism.

"Mel, honey, please," her husband chided as he reached for her hand.

She jerked hers away quicker than he could make contact. "No. Don't you dare *honey* me, Peter. You were the one who dragged me here after your little chat with Pastor what's-his-name. Well, here I am. And I have something to say to uh . . ." Her eyes flashed as she read the name tag on my knit sweater. "Lauren." She bent toward the middle of the circle, targeting me directly. "Some people will tell you that adoption is a great idea, and some people will say the opposite. But I'm going to tell you the truth: None of those opinionated people are gonna be there for you when you wake up to the screams of night terrors at three in the morning. Just like none of them will be there to pick up the half-chewed food off your kitchen floor because your toddler refuses to swallow it due to his sensory issues. And not a single one of them is going to know how to stop your baby girl from banging her head against the wall because it's the only form of self-soothing she knows. You'll question your sanity a hundred times a day, asking what's real and what's just in your head. But I'll tell you what's real, Lauren. Trauma is real. And it's all-consuming. And before you know it, everyone in your life—even those Positive Pollys who patted you on the back for making such a selfless sacrifice—they'll be gone. And you'll be all alone." Her voice cracked on that last word. "Married or single, you'll be all alone." She stood, snatched her purse off the floor, and sprinted for the stairs.

Gail gave a brief yet decisive glance back at Robert before she, too, disappeared up the stairs.

Peter got to his feet, his face distorted with indecision. For a moment, I imagined him bolting after her, but instead, he looked to Robert. The helpless plea in his eyes sucked the air from the room and left a hollowness in my chest.

"I won't tell you not to go after her, Peter. But I can assure you she's in expert hands," Robert said calmly.

After a full five seconds, Peter gave a stiff nod and sat back in his chair. "I, uh, I'm really sorry about all this. We've . . . it's been a hard year for Mel and me."

"We understand trying times," Jack said. "We really do."

Peter slid his hat off his head and ran a hand through his dark wavy hair. "My youngest sister's been missing for years—living on the streets, selling her body for drugs. You name it, she's done it. None of us had any contact with her at all until a caseworker called us last summer." He took a steadying breath. "One phone call turned our whole lives upside down. Melanie was on her third round of infertility treatments while working as a sous chef at Barlow's Table downtown, so when we heard we had a niece and a nephew out there who needed a home—a family—we said yes." He chuckled sardonically. "We had no idea what we were getting ourselves into. Overnight, we became a family of four." This time, Peter let the silence linger, as if he wasn't sure how to continue. Maybe because he wasn't sure if *they* would continue.

"How old are your kids?" Even as she asked it, Sara was already nodding.

"Four and two."

"Those ages can be tough, especially because they can't verbalize their needs as well as an older child can," Robert said with an authority that brought some much-needed peace to the room. "It's a myth that babies don't remember trauma. They do—and so do the parents who care for them. Where's your head at right now, Peter?"

At that one carefully asked question, Peter broke, his words choked on a sob. "I don't know how to fix it. The kids, my marriage, any of it."

Tears gathered in my eyes and slipped down my cheeks as Sara's husband, Sam, moved to sit next to our newest member. He placed a firm hand on Peter's shoulder. "We're here for you, man. For all four of you. You don't have to walk this road alone anymore."

"I'd love to help you and Melanie," Karen said.

"Us too," Sara added.

My heart thudded in my chest. "Me too. Any way I can."

As I watched this grown man grieve for his hurting family, a sudden and convicting clarity washed over me. Whether I was single or not, my child would have needs beyond what my limited life experience could offer him or her. There would be moments I wouldn't know what to do, moments I'd need to reach past my comfort zone for help, moments that would stretch me as a mother and as a human being.

Because in the end, that's what all of us were. Human.

Just like my family.

The Bailey clan may not be known for saying all the right things at all the right times, but they were mine. Complicated as they were, they were mine. And even more important, they were my child's. If tonight was any indication, the two of us were going to need all the help we could get.

No more excuses. I would tell my family everything at Thanksgiving dinner.

chapter eight

I lay awake after the support meeting for most of the night, my subconscious mind refusing to join the slumbering sheep I'd forgotten to count. The waiting had finally caught up to me. All the stress eating and obsessive email checking. All the highlighting of must-dos and must-haves from the adoption binder I kept on my nightstand. All the late-night YouTube watching of Gotcha Day videos filmed around the world—those first face-to-face moments between adoptive parent and child. Some were seamless unions of open arms and smiling faces; others were tear-filled and tantrum-full. But it wasn't those fear and grief-based reactions that had my stomach knotting like a pretzel as the clock ticked on. Rather, it was Melanie Garrett's gut-punching statement. *"And before you know it, everyone in your life—even those Positive Pollys who patted you on the back for making such a selfless sacrifice—they'll be gone. And you'll be all alone. Married or single, you'll be all alone."*

Sometime around five-thirty, I pushed myself from the bed, padded my way down the stairs to the kitchen, and brewed my first—but far from last—cup of caffeinated confidence. I needed to pull myself together before I melted into a sappy puddle of maternal hormones. Ironically enough, I texted my mother.

Never one for pressing the snooze button, she'd likely already be mowing the lawn or hammering on a loose baseboard at this hour, but I needed to get this over with. The sooner the better.

> Good morning, Mom! What time is Thanksgiving dinner this year? Would you like me to bring a dessert and a side dish?

Spilling my secret while my mother slopped green bean casserole on our plates during a chaotic holiday meal may not be the most socially sensitive plan I'd ever devised, but it was definitely the most sensible. My mom's ears worked best when her hands were occupied.

True to form, my mother didn't text back until the afternoon school bell had rung and I was busy directing the volunteers for Wednesday's all-school Charlie Brown Thanksgiving Feast. Today and tomorrow our school would be full of volunteers, all working together to organize food, string up Thanksgiving decorations, and assist kids with their line memorizations for the gratitude portion of the event. Between handing off a stack of autumn-colored construction paper to our PTO leader and dodging eye contact with a certain male teacher across the room, I slipped my phone from my pocket and spared a half-second glance at the text screen.

> 4. Dessert. SYATD.

Unlike Lisa, my mother's replies were rarely longer than five words. And on the occasion her message was getting too lengthy, she'd just create her own unique abbreviation to sum it up. For instance, SYATD = See you at Thanksgiving dinner.

"Miss Bailey." Millie Connelly, mother to Tabitha Connelly, waved me over to the volunteers' crafting station near the bottom of the stage. She sat among eight other parent volunteers from various classes. Brighton had the best PTO on the planet.

"How many of these turkey centerpieces do you think we should make?"

I worked quick math in my head, accounting for all the classrooms between kindergarten and fifth. "There'll be eighteen groups."

"Perfect, thanks." Millie rocked her baby in his car seat carrier with the toe of her boot. Such a normal mom thing to do, and yet I couldn't take my eyes off her little guy. His dark lashes and smooth ebony skin were mesmerizing.

"How old is he now?" I asked, forcing my eyes to stop misting at the sight of his chubby cheeks and doughy fingers. His toes played peekaboo under his blanket as he blew tiny bubbles between his lips. She did a silent calculation. "Wow, it's hard to believe, but Cade will be ten months next week. He's definitely my chunkiest baby by far."

"He's adorable."

She turned back to me, gaze full of kindness. "Would you like to hold him? It's rare he'll fall asleep for me in this thing anymore. He's a bit spoiled by all the extra sets of arms in our house. You're welcome to take him—unless you have too much to do."

No amount of work would ever prohibit me from holding a sleepy baby. "I'd love to hold him."

With two quick release clicks of his car seat, Millie slipped him from the harness and handed him to me. She draped my shoulder with his fuzzy blanket. I breathed him in, unable to ignore his sweet baby smell or the way his warm squishy body snuggled into mine. His hair coiled in tight dark curls atop his head, and it took every ounce of my willpower not to plant kiss after kiss on his forehead.

How old would my child be when I finally got to snuggle him or her? Just one of a million questions I had pondered since I'd first applied. But exact age and gender would remain a mystery until that blessed match email arrived in my inbox.

Having taught both genders for nearly a decade, I truly didn't have a bias. I adored boys and girls equally and could envision either in my arms, at my table, in my heart. But the age boxes I'd checked on my application had ranged from infant up to four years old.

"If he fusses, his pacifier is attached to the corner of his blankie."

"Okay, thanks." I repositioned the sweet-smelling bundle so I could wave his pudgy hand at Millie. "Bye-bye, Mommy, I'll see you in a little bit."

He responded with a coo that made my ovaries swoon. "We're off to find Mrs. Pendleton." Luckily our school's principal adored babies as much as I did. After all, she was a grandmother four times over now.

"I think she's stuck in the middle of that huddle over there—I left when the conversation moved into political topics. I'm better at cutting leaves then debating ideals," one of the parent volunteers offered as I passed her.

Debating? Mrs. Pendleton was known for her pragmatic nature, even when those around her were sure-bent on fanning the flame of controversy—and there was loads of controversy in the public school system. I wondered which topic had taken a turn south this time. But as I approached the small mob, I realized it wasn't Mrs. Pendleton who'd captured the group's attention with her peacemaking talents.

"You can't argue with the facts. It's science," a gruff voice said as I moved to catch a view of who was speaking, only to see Joshua on the opposite side of the semicircle.

"But that's the thing, Don," Joshua offered in a respectful tone, addressing a man I recognized as the grandfather of one of Jenna's third graders. "Our education system has often linked the study of paleontology to the teachings of evolution, but there are actually plenty of profound archeological findings to confirm the claims of intelligent design. It's not nearly as one-sided an argument as you—or today's educational system—might believe. New discoveries are happening all the time. I'd be happy to share my research on the matter with you and anyone else who's interested." He spoke with contagious charisma, and I found myself, once again, marveling at his confidence. This time for sharing his opinion on such a widely disputed subject with a group of strangers.

Perhaps I admired that quality most in Joshua because it was an attribute I greatly lacked. I often struggled to state my personal convictions with the people who shared my DNA, much less people I hardly knew.

"Once again, you've wowed us, Mr. Avery. I'd sit in a lecture of yours any day. You're definitely an apple who didn't fall far from the tree." Mrs. Pendleton patted him on the back and spotted me several feet out from the circle. "Miss Bailey, please tell me you've come over to bring me that handsome baby."

I snuggled him closer, brushing my cheek over his curls. "Will I be let go if I don't give him up? Because if so, it's been really nice working at Brighton."

She laughed, and so did most of her companions. Everyone except Joshua, who watched me with unnerving quiet. I tore my eyes away from him and studied the baby in my arms instead, tucking the blanket more securely around his solid form. Mrs. Pendleton broke away from the group to join me.

Purposefully, I kept my feet moving, fighting the pull of a man I wished I could dislike. Or at the very least, feel indifferent toward. But neither could be further from the truth.

"Does everything look to be running smoothly for Wednesday's program?" she asked. "Our volunteer turnout is incredible this year."

"Yes, it really is. Most have committed to staying after school tomorrow, as well, to help with setup." I switched the baby to my other side, his head burrowing under my left collarbone. "And apart from the select readings from each classroom, your role will be the same as last year—to emcee between groups. I'll email the rundown tomorrow morning."

"Excellent, I'll look for it—although there's one surprise that won't be listed on your agenda, but it will be great." She tilted her head and smiled. "Thanks for heading this up again. You're a superstar teacher." She paused, and I knew with eerie certainty where her line of thought had drifted. Other than Jenna, Mrs. Pendleton was the only soul in our school who knew about my future plans—mostly because she'd be the one needing to approve my leave of absence after the adoption.

"You'll be a superstar mother, too." She squeezed my shoulder and grinned at my sweet-smelling arm cargo. "You look good with a baby, Lauren."

I gave a shallow nod, not wanting to encourage the conversation further for fear of being overheard. But Mrs. Pendleton needed little encouragement to continue speaking. "When my Minnie couldn't get pregnant for the first five years of her marriage, I just kept encouraging her to protect her hope. Without hope, life feels so empty."

I didn't exactly know where my boss stood on issues of faith and God, but she certainly believed in inspirational quotes. She drew from a deep well of them. None were exactly scriptural, but all were thought-provoking. And all were offered with the best of intention and heart.

With a light touch on my arm, she excused herself to extend her gratitude to the craft table workers, currently tracing a huge batch of pumpkins on orange construction paper.

"I see you've got the rock down."

I squeezed my eyes closed for half a second at the sound of Joshua's voice at my back, unwilling to acknowledge the spike in my pulse at his nearness. Having coffee with him had not helped put him in the box marked "professional colleague only." It had done just the opposite—broken down walls that were meant to be firmly in place.

"The rock?" I asked with a brief glance.

"Yes, the baby rock." Joshua demonstrated the side-to-side hip motion I wasn't even aware I'd been doing. "My brother and his wife had their second baby last year. I've seen *the rock* a lot. Rebekah does it even when someone else is holding Calvin. Although she doesn't seem to be a fan of me pointing that out to her."

"I can't imagine why not."

Laughing off my sarcasm, he bent low, lifting the edge of the blanket from my arm to peek at the precious face underneath. The action sent goose bumps scattering along my bicep. "Yep, you're definitely an expert at the rock."

"Is he asleep?" The thrill that I could put a baby to sleep flooded my brain with the kind of serotonin I wished I could package in a bottle and sell.

"Either that or he's mastered the art of drooling with his eyes closed."

In that moment, it didn't matter that my lower back had started to ache or that my forearms were stiff and cramped from maintaining this position. Because right here, cradled against my chest, was *my hope*. My purpose. It was more than a feeling, it was a conviction. One I couldn't deny or excuse or replace. I was made for this, to be a mother to a motherless child. I knew it in the same way I knew God was still in the business of answering the prayers of His children.

Although the irony of this confirmation happening while sandwiched between Joshua and a borrowed baby . . . well, that I couldn't explain. Apparently God had an epic sense of humor.

chapter nine

Early release days were always chaotic, but early release days before an extended holiday break? Absolute insanity. Kids were pumped full of extra excitement and often extra sugar, too. But the multicultural Thanksgiving program was proving to be a big success.

All Brighton students had been seated in mixed-grade groupings on autumn-colored leaf cutouts, feasting on the Charlie Brown Thanksgiving foods: popcorn, buttered toast, jelly beans, and pretzel sticks. Adults filled the chairs in the back, grinning and videoing while elected students shared their gratitude essays in front of an audience of their family, friends, and peers. Some were sweet and sentimental, others funny and winsome, but all helped to create a warm and inviting spirit of love and community. An atmosphere, I couldn't help but note, far from the one I'd be experiencing with my own family tomorrow.

From under the felt pilgrim hat I wore, I peered out at the full auditorium from my place near the front of the stage, my eyes continuously scanning for the one face I hadn't seen since the program began. The last class was reciting their poems, and any minute now Joshua was supposed to give our closeout speech and dismiss the students to their parents. Where was he?

My concentrated stare caught the attention of a few older girls who waved and gestured at my *Have A Happy Gobble Day* sweatshirt and turkey earrings, giving me an approving thumbs-up, which I returned with a festive smile, one quickly replaced with concern as the final applause broke out.

I cleared my throat and smoothed the front of my sweater, preparing to take Joshua's place on stage to conclude the program, when giggles erupted toward the back of the room. Like watching thousands of ecstatic fans participate in the wave at a crowded football stadium, every head and body turned in rapid succession from back to front.

My attention shot to the double doors, where a giant apricot-colored orb worked to heave itself through the too-tight opening. The crowd cheered on, counting to three as the sphere pushed and pushed and then . . . catapulted inside. Head over end, it rolled like a catawampus bowling ball, nearly taking out a group of students refilling popcorn bowls. After several seconds, it self-corrected, bouncing back on its feet once more and confirming its true identity for the first time.

It was not, as I'd first assumed, a mammoth piece of overripe fruit but a massive sumo-turkey. Specifically, the already-been-plucked-and-ready-to-be-carved kind of turkey. Bloated with air, the dinner entree lumbered down the center of the room, waddling like a pregnant woman due any moment with quintuplets.

And suddenly the question of Joshua's whereabouts had become crystal clear.

Though he couldn't bend without losing his balance, he parted the hysterical crowd like a rock star, waving and giving out fist bumps—or, rather, wing bumps. Parents scrambled to take out the phones they'd already tucked away as staff refereed the younger, more excitable children.

"He certainly knows how to make an entrance, doesn't he?" I hadn't noticed when Jenna had moved to stand beside me, but she was here now, nudging me with her shoulder.

"He certainly does."

I glanced up at Mrs. Pendleton, who waved him toward the stage through gut-splitting laughter of her own. She beamed as if he were the lifeblood of Brighton Elementary and not a fill-in teacher wearing a blow-up poultry costume.

The instant she stepped away from the microphone, I realized that *this* was the surprise she'd been referring to on Monday. The two of them had planned it together. For the children. And by the looks of it, Joshua couldn't have been happier to have obliged her wishes.

It took several dads to hoist him onto the stage, and when he got there, his wings lacked the proper extension to hold the microphone to his mouth, so Mrs. Pendleton held it for him. Without breaking character—if one could call an air-filled dinner entree a character—he delivered a Thanksgiving message to every kid in the room that had parents applauding and kids cackling. As a last reminder, he encouraged the students to limit their screen time during the break and engage in the real-life relationships around them instead. A noteworthy proclamation coming from a man who made a living as an app developer. When he'd finished speaking, Mrs. Pendleton invited the audience to take pictures with Mr. Gobble inside the PTO-made photo booth near the front office.

Seeing as Joshua's fate was sealed as a photo prop for the remainder of the event, I headed to the student pickup area and assumed the release responsibilities for both of our classrooms. After sending each child off with their correct guardian—and a reminder to read over the holiday weekend—I was thankful my last activity of the day was introvert-approved: clean-up crew of one.

After tossing all the dirty plates and recycling all the used construction paper, I surveyed the auditorium floor, currently undergoing a much-needed mopping from our stellar facilities team. Taking a turn at the lobby, I noted the photo line that had once snaked down two hallways had finally cleared. However, the photo area itself, a five-by-seven carpet space that had been gussied up in all the festive flair of fall, was getting plenty of good use from Brighton's staff. Several teachers bunched together, all vying for their place in a group selfie with today's mascot.

"I'll take it for you," I offered.

Jenna, who was likely the instigator of said group selfie, shook her head. "No way. You need to be in it, too, Lauren. We can squish."

Laughable, since there were at least eight adults and a turkey trying to squeeze in the frame of a cell phone screen. "That's okay, really. I'm much better at taking the pictures than being in them." I held out my hand to collect the various phones from teachers and administrators alike. "I don't mind at all."

Thankfully, they obliged me. I stood back, taking photo after photo until all the phones in my hand had a post-worthy picture to share on social media. All the while, Joshua's smile game had remained strong. How he wasn't dying to get out of that ridiculous getup, I had no idea.

"And now it's your turn, Lauren," Jenna insisted. "Come on. Your Gobble Day shirt and pilgrim hat beg to be commemorated, too."

Despite my protests, Jenna didn't take no for an answer this time. She gripped my elbow with the strength of someone four times her size and pulled me over to the photo site, smashing me between one of Joshua's drumstick thighs and a decorated apple crate. "Ah, there. This is going to be super cute!"

It was Jenna's turn to stand back with an iPhone, only she didn't just one-two-three *snap* like a normal person. Nope, that would have been much too simple for my best friend. Instead, she insisted Joshua scoot in closer and put his wing around me. You know, for the sake of the holiday spirit and all that jazz. I glanced down at the petite pumpkins surrounding our feet and wondered if my aim would be good enough to knock the phone from her hands on my first pitch.

"Perfect. You both look great. Now say *Turkey Butt*!"

"Turkey Butt," we mocked.

"And . . . done. Okay, I'll text it to you both later."

Oh, I'm sure she would.

After I gave her a quick hug good-bye, I began turning over the stacked apple crates and filling them with the loose decorations around the carpet. Although this wasn't my designated clean-up area, I didn't mind taking it on. Most of my co-workers still had pumpkin pies and casseroles to bake, tables for twenty to set, families to get home to. My forty-five minute out-of-the-box Thanksgiving brownies could wait until tomorrow morning, and Skye was likely on her third nap of the day.

"Is there a secret storage closet for holiday paraphernalia?" Joshua asked as he located the release valve under his left wing to deflate himself. Within seconds, he was buried under mounds of flabby peach plastic. He reached behind his neck and fished for the pull tab.

I continued collecting ribbon, burlap, and twine from the floor. "Yeah, it's at the end of the fifth-grade hall. There's all kinds of randomness stored back in there."

He hopped a little, trying to get a grip on the slippery fabric.

"Um . . . do you need help?"

Still engulfed inside a silicone turkey head, he flashed me a semi-embarrassed grin. "I won't turn you down if you're offering. I'd really rather not show up at my parents' house looking like a sumo wrestler who lost three hundred pounds overnight."

I laughed and moved toward him to help. "I agree that it's probably a sight you should spare your loved ones."

The teeth of the cheap zipper snagged several times on its way down his back, forcing me to use my other hand to pinch the plastic beneath it to act as a guide. I worked it lower, uncovering the full length of his damp white undershirt. The fabric seemed to breathe with him, exposing every ripple and muscle beneath it. And suddenly my own oxygen intake seemed at risk. I swallowed, tugging the zipper lower still, until the tines jammed at the top of his waistband.

"Okay." My voice felt sluggish, my mouth not quite in sync with my thoughts. "You're in the clear now."

I took several steps back, allowing space for him to take over. Making quick work with my hands, I gathered the rest of the decorative apples from a wicker basket on the floor.

"Thanks. Gosh, the fresh air feels good. It was hot in there."

Out here, too. "I bet it was."

From the corner of my eye, I watched as he peeled away the silicone cap suctioned around his neck and head and allowed the fleshy layers of plastic to fall in a heap at his feet. He stepped out of the costume and raked a hand through his sweat-slicked hair. Soft curls curved above the tips of his ears and at the nape of his neck while the rest of his hair stood at attention. An apple dropped from my hand and bounced on the linoleum.

He bent to pick it up, tossed it into my collection basket, then reached for the stack of crates beside me. "How about I carry these babies to the storage room for you?"

"Oh . . . uh . . ." *Words, Lauren. Speak words now.* "You don't have to do that. I can totally handle it on my own."

He gripped the bottom crates and hefted them up. "I'm sure you could," he said. "But why not split the load with a guy who needs to earn back a hefty dose of masculinity after identifying as naked poultry for the last two hours?"

He didn't need to earn anything back in my book, but arguing with him would be as pointless as the hollow fruit in my arms. "Okay, thanks." I lifted the basket filled with pumpkins and all things fake and draped the Thanksgiving banner and the emerald, orange, and gold tablecloth used as a backdrop around my neck like a scarf.

"That's a good look for you," he said, appraisingly. "Not many people can pull off holiday plaid."

"Says the man who just took off a turkey suit."

"Touché."

We made the trek down the fifth-grade hall and took a hard right at the backstage door, which led to an even narrower passageway crammed with miscellaneous fundraiser signs, art supplies, and auction materials. I stopped in front of a black door and reached for the keys in my back pocket. Once unlocked, I propped the door open for Joshua to set his load down inside first before I did the same.

"So what's on the docket for you tomorrow?" He dusted off his hands with a hard clap and swipe. "Do you do the whole extended family thing? Or are you more of the immediate family gathering type?"

The mention of my family brought the mental jolt I needed to keep my thoughts focused. I relocked the closet, then twisted the knob to double check it. "Let's see, it will just be my parents, my sister, Lisa, and her husband, her stepsons, and my niece, Iris."

"Sounds like a manageable size."

I shot him a loaded grin. "You might not say that if you met them."

"Why not?" He laughed. "They a tough crowd?"

"They're just . . ." What were they exactly? "Really different from me." I stopped, shook my head. "That sounds stuck up. I didn't mean it to come out like that."

His gaze rested on mine, his hands finding the pockets of his shorts as if he had all the time in the world for a pre-holiday therapy session. "How do you mean it, then?"

I released a nervous laugh, wishing I'd just kept my mouth shut. "You really don't want to hear about the Bailey drama."

He glanced behind him and pulled up the half bookshelf someone once painted into a fake fireplace for a play. "Actually, I do."

He gestured for me to have a seat while he moved a rickety stepladder over for himself in a passageway half the width of a mining tunnel.

"Really?" I looked around at the tight quarters. "You just want me to sit here and talk about all the dysfunction in my family?"

"Do you have somewhere else to be?" he asked, as if this were a totally normal thing to do in a musty storage space, in an empty school building, on the day before a major holiday.

"Well, no, but—"

"Perfect."

I laughed and shook my head, giving in and arranging myself on the faux-fireplace-bookshelf combo across from him. And maybe the strangeness of it all—the isolated quiet in the middle of a school day, the upcoming four-day holiday weekend, the fact that tomorrow I'd be spending the day with people who likely wouldn't support my future life decisions—was the exact reason I found myself providing an answer I hadn't fully shared with anyone outside of Gail.

"For various reasons, my family has always struggled to be close, but about five years ago, things between us all got even more distant after I . . . after I made some changes in my life."

He remained quiet, but his eyes shone with interest, compelling me to go on.

Why was this so hard for me? Gail never seemed hesitant when it came to sharing about her faith. "My parents didn't raise my sister and me to believe in organized religion of any kind. I never went to Sunday school or attended church camps or any of that. And honestly, that was all totally okay with me. I wasn't against church or God exactly, I just couldn't imagine any of that being a part of my life."

"So what changed?" A simple, straightforward question that revealed little of his own convictions or feelings.

"I was given an invitation to go to a Christmas play at a student's church, with a family I'd come to love during that school year." I smiled at the memory of Benny handing me a beautifully embroidered card with red and green holly on the corners. A ticket to the play was tucked inside. "I went with them that night, and afterward they invited me back to their house for hot cider and cookies. We talked until late in the evening, mostly just get-to-know-you type conversation, but at one point, I remember telling them that I wanted to know more about what they believed and what they shared together as a family. Over the next few weeks they answered dozens of my questions, and shortly after the new year, I accepted Christ as my Savior." I blinked away the moisture building behind my eyes. "I felt like I had purpose for the first time in my adult life."

He sat quietly for several seconds. "I couldn't agree more. Faith in God is what gives our lives purpose." A response that matched what I'd believed to be true about him for some time. "So . . ." He hedged, clasping his hands together with a slight frown on his face. "I'm gonna go out on a limb here and guess that when you told your family all that, it didn't go so well?"

"Understatement," I said, plucking invisible lint off my turkey sweatshirt. "After I told them that my previous misconceptions about God and the church weren't how I believed anymore, the wheels on our family wagon fell off . . . and we'd only been operating with three to begin with. In the beginning they asked some questions, but mostly to debate their own views and opinions. Now it just feels like my 'weird convictions' are the elephant in every room we're in together, which makes conversing about anything that matters . . . challenging." To say the least. Especially when those conversations would soon revolve around a life change that would affect them all.

"So you're the only believer in your family. That's tough." He seemed to mull the statement over. "My brother was on the fence for a lot of years, nearly tore us apart with his anger over an offense that happened inside his home church. He told me once that if God and church were a package deal, he didn't want any part of either of them."

"What happened with him?"

"He met Rebekah." He chuckled. "And she wouldn't give him the time of day until he made a complete U-turn with his life, a one-eighty we'd been praying he'd make for a long time. After they married, my dad started referring to her as Saint Rebekah."

I smiled at the sweetness of such a nickname. I could hardly imagine such an alternate reality. Me as a wayward prodigal, my parents as the faithful prayer warriors who prayed me home. "You're really blessed to have a family like that, you know."

He dipped his head, pinching his mouth to one side in contemplation until his eyes found mine again. "Sometimes that's easy to forget. But you're right. They are a blessing." His lips parted into his signature expression once again. "What's your game plan for surviving tomorrow?"

"Hot fudge brownies."

Joshua busted out a laugh that melted the remaining tension in my chest. But the truth was, hot fudge brownies did have a way of making everything better. Even ridiculously hard conversations with the Bailey family.

chapter ten

I placed my Jeep in park and something like reflux flared in my chest. My parents' three-story, craftsman-style home loomed before me, confirming the never-judge-a-book-by-its-cover sentiment of old. Where the exterior might be polished and pristine, the reality of the dysfunction inside was . . . well, not.

Was it too late to ask Jesus to take the wheel now that I was no longer driving? Surely there was some catchy country song about entering the lion's den on Thanksgiving Day. Where was Jenna when I needed her? She was a walking Spotify channel, always at the ready to throw out a symbolic lyric or show tune.

I stepped out of the car and opened the door to the back seat, grateful I'd gone the extra mile and frosted my out-of-the-box brownies. Double-fudge with chocolate icing might be my only ally for the next three hours. Two, if luck were on my side.

An expletive soared through the crisp afternoon air, and I turned in time to see two teen boys rounding the corner of my parents' garage. A pair of glowing embers crashed to the ground. In an instant, the light was snuffed out completely on the paved driveway. Cigarettes. Of the many things my stepnephews had been caught doing since gaining my sister as a stepmom six years ago, this one fell somewhere in the middle. At fifteen and thirteen, Austin and Andrew Metzer walked through life with the maturity of toddlers in adolescent packages.

Neither of the boys moved an inch as I approached. Maybe, like several of my first graders, they believed if they stood still long enough, they'd simply acquire invisibility superpowers. Or perhaps they just hoped my eyesight was too poor to have seen the cancer sticks hanging from their mouths.

Unfortunately for them, neither was true.

"Happy Thanksgiving, boys." Balancing the brownies on top of my mostly apple and grape fruit salad, I headed for the porch steps. "Would one of you mind holding the door for me, please?"

At my casual tone, the boys looked momentarily dumbstruck. Austin, the older of the two, elbowed his younger brother in the ribs as if he'd just tagged him in a game, then hightailed it around the side of the house.

The thirteen-year-old jogged toward me, bounding up the short flight of stairs in pants I suspected weren't nearly as flexible as he made them look. How much longer would the super-skinny jean trend survive?

"Thank you, Andrew. How very gentlemanly of you."

He refused to make eye contact. "Uh-huh."

"Andrew?" Somehow, he managed to shove the tips of fingers into his too-tight pockets. Really, that should be a universal requirement for all pants: pockets made to fit an entire hand. "Smoker's lung won't get you a girlfriend."

Eyes still averted, he mumbled, "I didn't even inhale."

"Okay," I said, in an I-wasn't-born-yesterday tone.

He stared out at the spot his older brother had occupied moments ago. "Just, please don't tell Lisa, okay? She's super pis—I mean, she's really ticked at me—about my grades. I already lost my phone for a week."

I smiled and touched his shoulder. I didn't have it in me to rat either of them out tonight. Not when the holiday agenda would soon be overthrown by judgmental commentary over my reckless decision: a.k.a. adopting a child as a single woman on a teacher's salary. A decision that would not align well with my mother's "security first" life mantra.

But neither of my nephews needed to know all that.

"I'll tell you what, if you and Austin handle dish duty for Grandma after dinner *without complaining*, I'll forget what I saw."

Relief flooded his acne-pocked face. "Wait—seriously?"

"Seriously, but you're going to go tell Austin to put that stolen pack back in his dad's truck, right?"

He swallowed. "Right."

"And you'll never touch them again? Because if I find out otherwise, I can pretty much guarantee your phone will be confiscated for a lot longer than a week."

"Yes. Promise."

"Perfect." We reached the top step together. "I'm so glad we had this little chat."

"Yeah . . . me too." He gave me an almost-smile that, on any other day, would have made me laugh. But my brownies were sliding into my fruit salad bowl, and the purse on my shoulder had slipped down to the crook of my elbow, and I really just needed to get this holiday meal over with.

Andrew twisted the knob and popped the door open for me.

My plank-walk awaited.

Andrew slipped behind me, fading into the background of privileged suburbia with ease, while the smell of reheated turkey breast and overdone stuffing saturated the air. For a moment, the familiar aroma took me back to the days of my childhood home—one I hadn't been inside for over a decade. Funny, because that robin's-egg blue 1970s split-level resembled absolutely nothing of this custom-built three-story house with hardwood floors and granite countertops. But I supposed that was the thing about moving: A person could upgrade their location, their appliances, and even their tax bracket . . . and still find room to unpack their old habits.

I stepped through the entryway into the spacious and modern floorplan decked with neutral paint and thick white baseboards my mom had chosen to finish herself.

"Dad?" I didn't know why I called it out. I knew exactly where he'd be—the same place he was every time I came over. Recliner by the window, overlooking two acres of a well-groomed lawn. A new crime novel rested on the sofa table beside him—different title and author, same CSI-looking cover, bookmarked with a Juicy Fruit gum wrapper. His aluminum walker and cane resided in the corner, half hidden by the afghan he refused to use.

"Ren?" My father was the only person who called me by a nickname. "That you?"

"Sure is. Happy Thanksgiving, Dad." I crossed the room toward his chair. "Guess what! I baked your favorite dessert." And hopefully said dessert would sweeten him up to the idea of becoming a surprise grandfather to a child unknown . . . even to the mother.

"Please tell me it's brownies. I hate all that mushy canned pumpkin stuff your sister tries to pass off as pie."

"Good guess. It is." I bent to kiss his temple. "How are you today?"

"As good as any other day, I suppose." A nonanswer. My father's favorite kind.

Distracted by the lack of swirling voices in the house, I glanced toward the kitchen and scanned the empty dining room. "Where is everybody?"

"Lisa and Trent went to the only open store on the other side of town to get more rolls or something. They took Iris with them."

"Ah." That explained why the boys were wandering around outside unsupervised. "And Mom?" I ventured cautiously.

"Putting together some new closet hack downstairs."

"Gotcha." Because, naturally, Thanksgiving dinner was the best time to assemble an organizational unit for her business. I shoved the thought down and worked to re-engage my happy face.

"You cut your hair?" he asked unexpectedly.

I fingered the ashy blond ends of hair resting on my shoulders. "Not recently, no. You probably just haven't seen me wear it down in a while."

"You should wear it like that more often. It's nice." A high-level compliment coming from him.

"Thanks, Dad."

"When you were little, I used to tell you it was like corn silk. So pretty and soft." His eyes glazed over, and I wondered what had inspired this rare stroll down memory lane.

I leaned against the arm of his chair, wishing I could stretch this rare moment out for forever. "I remember that, too."

"It was a long time ago."

A lifetime ago, really. And yet my heart couldn't forget that old version of my daddy, even though I hadn't seen him that way in so many, many years.

He cleared his throat and the spell was over.

"You should put that fruit salad in the fridge before it gets warm." He pointed to the bowl I'd placed on the side table near him.

"I will." I straightened out my spine and my sentimentalities. "How can I help out with dinner . . . or with anything, really?"

He snorted. "Your mother already has everything figured out, Lauren. You might as well just take a seat in here and wait." He pointed to the sofa across the room. "I'm sure she'll let you know *if* you're needed. But don't hold your breath." Years ago, after his accident, his resentful comments about my mother's take-charge personality would barely scrape off his tongue, like the dull blade on a butter knife. But now his razor tone held a serrated edge, sharp enough to draw blood.

My father turned his face back to the window.

Conversation over.

"Um, I think I'll go let her know I'm here."

In another life, his grunt could have been taken for a chuckle. But that life had ended the day he fell three stories from a rooftop, busted his pelvis into three parts, and nearly died from loss of blood. Most days, he acted as though death would have been the better fate.

I set the pan of brownies next to the kitchen sink and placed my fruit salad in the fridge before trekking down the carpeted staircase, so unlike the stairs Lisa and I had grown up with that belched and creaked if breathed on the wrong way.

"Mom?"

"Down here."

I followed the zippy sound of a power drill into an open area to the left of the laundry room. Kneeling before a large plastic structure, with several loose screws and instructional diagrams surrounding her, was the owner of Closet Queens. Mom bit her lip in concentration as she connected a corner piece to a middle shelf.

"That looks good, Mom." I skimmed a freshly screwed slab with my fingertip. "Very versatile." High praise in the closet industry.

My mother spared me an impatient glance. "What time is it?"

"A quarter after four."

She sighed heavily and clapped her hands hard before pushing herself to her feet. Her knees popped and cracked like an amplified version of Rice Krispies cereal. "You're late."

What did that matter? She was the one building a closet while cooking—and likely burning—a turkey breast she got on special during Thrifty Tuesdays. "I brought a fruit salad and brownies for the people who may want an alternative to pumpkin pie."

She huffed. "You didn't need to do that. You know I always have Grandma's Cookies on hand." As in the individually packaged treats she bought in bulk from Sam's Club, not a recipe sourced from a blood relation. That would require communication with her extended family members. "Did Lisa tell you we could use you in the field soon? The Roth family over on Franklin Hill are downsizing. We could use another transport vehicle to haul some loads to the thrift store."

"*In the field*" was mom-speak for cleaning out closets. Literally. That's what she did for a living. But though she spoke like a commanding officer, throwing down military jargon the way a millennial abused emojis in a text thread, her family knew otherwise. At the end of the day, her arsenal included nothing more than dirty dustrags, flexible clothing cubes, and the occasional back-of-the-door shoe rack. But by the way she talked, she and my sister were in the trenches together every day. Saving lives one dirty undergarment at a time.

"When are you thinking? I could help after church on Sunday," I began, keeping my tone light and unbothered by the inevitable eye roll that was coming. "I'd just need to run home and change and let Skye out for a bit, but I could be out there by two if that works?"

My mother's harried expression locked onto my face. "You're still doing that, then."

"What? Going to church?" I asked, trying and failing to pull the same levity into my tone as before. "I try to go every Sunday, yes. I really enjoy the people, and my pastor is so friendly and down-to-earth. It's a refreshing way to start off the week."

She waved her hand. "I didn't ask for a three-point lecture, Lauren. I get enough of those from your sister. I'll let you know when we need you—likely won't be till next week."

I clamped my mouth shut. The postmenopausal sheen on my mother's forehead glistened as she spoke. It seemed ever present these days. Much like the *Closet Queens* tank top she layered under the thin, knit-blend cardigan she usually discarded within minutes of putting on.

Mom's cropped hair had thinned around the crown and

silvered above her temples, an aging effect that drove Lisa crazy. "*A bottle of hair dye could take twenty years off you, Mom. You can afford to go to a salon every few months, you know.*" But like all things vanity-driven, our mother refused. Nina Bailey was too practical for such fanciful living like root touch-ups by a stylist. To our mother, there was always, always a reason to save for the worst-case scenario.

A door slammed somewhere above us, and the ceiling creaked in steady increments.

"Lauren? Mom? What are you two doing down there? The green bean casserole's smoking," Lisa called from somewhere upstairs.

Little did she know the casserole wasn't the only thing smoking today, but that conversation would have to wait for another time, because tonight was about announcing my adoption. And if I didn't say something soon, reserving a placeholder for an after-dinner conversation, the evening would pass us by the same way it had the last several times I'd planned to tell them.

Instinct took over as my mother trudged toward the stairs, passing in front of me. I whipped out a hand and gripped her forearm, nearly knocking her off her feet.

"For crying out loud, Lauren." She swung around, and I had the impulse to duck, even though my mother had never once laid a hand on either of her children. "What is wrong with—"

"There's something important I need to share with the family tonight." There, I'd done it. I'd just taken the first step. I was basically Neil Armstrong all over again.

My mother's eyes held a glimmer of . . . what was that look exactly? Excitement? Hope? "Have you put in for an administrator position yet?"

Much too late, I realized my mistake. "Oh no, Mom. It's not job-related. I'm really happy teaching first grade at Brighton. I don't have any plans to leave my classroom." At least, not long-term. My adoption leave would fall under the umbrella of maternity leave in my school district, but after the benefit of those months ran out, I'd go back to teaching again.

My mother's gaze chilled to suspicion in record time. "Then what is it? What's wrong?"

"Nothing's wrong. It's something good, actually. Positive." At least, I would choose to see it that way. "But, um, I would really rather wait till we're all together before I say anything more. Maybe before we serve dessert—"

"Lauren? Where are you?" Lisa called down the stairs, only this time, her voice held the air of a Disney princess, not an overdramatic sister. "Come up and meet our dinner guest."

My mother cursed under her breath and shook her head. "When will that girl start minding her own business?"

"Wait, what guest? Lisa invited someone to Thanksgiving?" An eerie premonition soured my gut as my mother tromped on ahead without another word. In that one regard, my parents were quite similar. Silence had always been their weapon of choice.

My baby sister waited at the top of the stairwell, motioning me forward with Oscar-worthy flair. "Hey, Lauren, this is Marcus. You remember him, don't you?"

Panic pulsed through my head as I followed my sister's pointer finger to a man wearing a fuzzy, milk-white sweater. He shuffled to stand beside her, his receding hairline glistening an oily sheen as he rotated toward the light. "Hello, Lauren. It's nice to see you again."

Without so much as a grunted greeting, my mother pushed past our odd grouping in the foyer on her way in to the kitchen. She didn't have the social graces for awkward meet-and-greets. I wished I could play the same card.

"Oh, uh . . . hello." My gaze flicked from my sister to the Gollum-eyed man with the shedding sweater. "We've met before?" For the life of me, I couldn't place him. He didn't have a look I'd easily forget.

"You remember, don't you, Lauren? You two met at that cute

little farmers' market in Hillsboro last summer," Lisa offered unhelpfully. "The one with that goat's milk booth you loved so much."

I vaguely remembered choking down a mini sample of the milk and stating it was better than I'd anticipated. A reaction that wouldn't be considered noteworthy to anybody besides my sister.

I tried to connect the dots back to Marcus, who was picking at a piece of lint on his sleeve. "So you're a goat's milk vendor, Marcus?"

"No, actually." He blinked upward. "I was in the booth next to the goat-milk guy. I farm alpacas."

And just like that, my well of shallow conversational skills ran dry. I opened my mouth and immediately closed it again. As somewhat of an expert in surface-level niceties, considering all the blind dates my sister had arranged over the years, drawing a complete blank was rare for me. But alpaca farming might take the prize for the oddest occupation I'd encountered from one of my sister's male acquaintances. And I once endured a two-hour wine tasting event with a taxidermist.

I blinked and tried again. "Alpacas? Wow, that's . . . really unique." My only reference for the hairy mammal stemmed from the book *Is Your Mama a Llama?* But something told me Marcus wouldn't care for that comparison or my childlike recitation.

"Many people aren't aware of this, but alpacas are some of the most harmonious creatures living on our planet today. I consider myself lucky to work with them."

Harmonious creatures? But wasn't YouTube full of spitting alpaca videos? Or was that llamas? And what was the difference between them anyway? Whatever the answer, this was certainly not the conversation I'd planned on this evening.

Leave it to Lisa to destroy my agenda by making one of her own.

"That's lovely. I wish you well with all your alpaca farming endeavors." Because what else could I say, really?

"Dinner's ready!" Mom bellowed from the kitchen.

I pinned my sister with a look that said, *Whatever you've done, undo it. Now.*

Lisa patted Marcus on the back, and a cloud of microscopic white hairs puffed into the air. "I invited Marcus to join us for Thanksgiving. I figured it would be the most convenient way for the two of you to get to know each other, considering how busy you've been lately, Lauren."

But we both knew this little stunt had nothing to do with convenience. It was punishment, payback for my lack of engagement in Lisa's primary communication style lately. Unlike normal people who texted in short paragraph form, my sister texted like a woodpecker after too many margaritas. I simply didn't possess the supernatural ability to respond to every whim and thought she sent off into oblivion.

Sweat gathered under my arms and at the nape of my neck as the herd of my family—and one stray alpaca farmer—migrated toward the dining room. I shot Lisa a glare that would translate in every language and clasped my hand around her skinny arm. No way was she getting out of this that easily. I squeezed, and she jolted to a stop before rising up on her toes to call into the next room over. "We'll just be a second, Marcus. Find a seat anywhere. *Trent!* Help Marcus find a seat. And not the one nearest the window, that chair leg is wobbly. Mom needs to fix it."

"Am I the only one capable of working a screwdriver around here?" Mom grumbled.

I yanked my sister into the alcove between the pantry and the hall closet, planting my hands firmly on my hips so I wouldn't throttle her. "What do you think you're doing? Why would you invite a stranger to Thanksgiving dinner to 'get to know me better'?"

Lisa had the audacity to quirk her microbladed eyebrow into an arch. "I'm helping my big sister out."

I pinched my lips tight to hold in a string of words I hadn't used since eleventh grade. "Helping me? No, Lisa. This is *not* helping me. I've told you at least a dozen times: I'm not interested in dating. I'm happy with the single life. *I want to be single!*"

She actually laughed. "That's ridiculous, Lauren. You're not happy, you're just way too set in your ways. And you're wasting precious time. You may not know this, but there's an expiration date on finding a decent man—preferably one without a trunk load of baggage." She pointed in the direction of the dining room. "Marcus has a lot going for him." She ticked off her fingers one by one. "He's in his early forties, he's never been married, no kids, has a steady career—albeit an unusual one. But still, that package is hard to find at your age."

"At my age? You're only *two years* younger than me."

"Yes, but I'm married. *With* a family."

Twice. My sister had been married twice. And before her twenty-fourth birthday, no less. And her *family* often looked more like a leaky rowboat than the fancy cruise liner she pretended they were on social media. But those contrary details were never mentioned during these get-married-or-rot-to-death lectures of hers. Most of the time I wondered if the only reason Lisa was so desperate to see me married was to prove the old adage that misery really does love company.

"I want different things for my life, Lisa." Things I'd hoped to share with the family before my sister had invited Old MacDonald to dinner. "Please stop with the matchmaking stuff already. If it ever does happen for me, it won't happen like this."

I blinked away a sudden image of Joshua's smiling eyes as Lisa's expression pinched into suspicion. "What's going on with you?"

I exhaled a courageous breath, ready to launch the proclamation like the firing of a cannon. "Well, a lot actually. I've decided to—"

"*Girls!* Stop gabbing over there and come to the table already! Thanksgiving only lasts for a day. I can't reheat the turkey a second time."

Lisa huffed and rolled her eyes at our mother's beckoning. "Come on. But this isn't over."

No, it isn't. Far from it, actually.

Together we moved toward the insanity of Thanksgiving with the Baileys.

Austin and Andrew shoved their way in through the back door, selecting the seats farthest away from their father, Trent, who was heavily engaged in some kind of war game on his iPhone. Marcus sat beside him, his ice water halfway guzzled—likely an attempt to stop from overheating under the polar-bear pelt he wore as a sweater.

Lisa called for her daughter, Iris, who, like usual, was in the living room trying to coax the geriatric cat from under the sofa. So far, she was zero for a thousand.

"Iris, I said *right now*," Lisa repeated sternly.

My sister's cherub-faced preschooler, with strawberry blond pigtails braided on either side of her head, begrudgingly obeyed. She was promptly positioned in the chair between her father and mother, her bottom lip pushed out in a weighty pout.

"Art," my mother hissed through clamped teeth. "Did you not hear me? I said dinner was ready."

"I think I'll take it out here tonight."

No matter what the occasion, major holiday or a random Wednesday night, this conversation never failed to be the opener of every Bailey mealtime.

"No, you'll take your seat in *here*. At the table. With your family. On Thanksgiving." My mother clunked down a bowl of soggy-looking green beans with a crusty top layer. "Lauren has something she wants to say to us."

Every noise in the house seemed to fizzle out at once.

Trent cut his gaze away from his iPhone, both boys stopped adding rolls to their plates, and Lisa paused filling Iris's glass with milk mid-pour to stare at me.

Every part of my body blushed with the kind of prickling heat that could set a person aflame.

The only sound in the room was the hollow drag of my father's cane working its way to the table. The *tap-slide-tap* sounded ten times louder than usual. My mother reached over my place setting and planted a steaming pan of freezer-aisle cheesy potatoes in front of her granddaughter.

Iris crinkled her nose. "But I don't like yellow cheese, Mommy."

Lisa pinched her daughter's upper arm and leaned in close, though her voice could have been heard outside. "Hush, your aunt is talking."

Confused, Iris looked up from her oozing plate and met my gaze. "No, she's not. She's just standing there. Her mouth isn't even moving. See?"

My niece, the only sane member of my entire family.

"Well, she's about to talk. Go ahead, Lauren. What is it? What do you want to say to us? Now that you have everybody's undivided attention." Lisa had been fluent in snarky remarks since the age of eight.

My father continued his slow shuffle to the opposite end of the table.

Sweat prickled the length of my spine. Why was it ten thousand degrees in this dining room? And why did it feel like my throat was closing in on itself? "Actually, um . . . well, I wanted to . . . um . . ."

And then, as if he could sense my silent mortification, Alpaca Man, who up to this point had done nothing more than observe my circus of a family, stood and pulled out a chair for me. One point to the farmer. Could farmers sense fear in people the same way animals could?

"Do you need to sit down? You look pale. Here." He gestured to the empty seat, and I didn't hesitate to sit in it. For his kindness, I'd willingly purchase a lifetime supply of whatever alpaca goods he sold on his farm.

Ironic that my only allies at this dinner table were a stranger and a five-year-old.

The wrinkle between my mother's eyebrows pulsed with impatience as she took her seat at the head of the table and placed a paper towel over her lap. "Well? What is it, Lauren? We'd all like to eat before Christmas."

"Right, exactly . . ." I said with a forced chuckle as sweat adhered my shirt to my back like glue. "I realize we're all super hungry, but I just thought it was important, on this day of gratitude, to thank Mom for taking time to put together this delicious Thanksgiving meal for us. Way to go, Mom." And then I gave my mother a thumbs-up. My mother. A woman who frowned at every cheer routine my sister had ever performed in high school. "Anybody else have anything they'd like to add?"

It looked like the tell-them-sometime-before-my-kid-graduated-from-college plan was what I was going with now.

A mumbling of awkward thank-yous ensued around the table as I scooped a big helping of greasy potatoes onto my plate and passed the tray to my left. The orange and yellow oils pooled around the white rim, nearly splashing onto my mother's white tablecloth. Lisa's suspicious gaze was still trained on my face.

I ignored her and smiled at Marcus instead. "Marcus, maybe you can tell us a few facts about alpacas? I bet Iris has some questions she'd love to ask you."

New plan: Keep the farmer talking until my dad asked for his second beer and my mom started throwing dishes into the sink like Frisbees.

My niece chewed thoughtfully, careful to keep her lips closed before swallowing. "What *is* an alpaca? Are they the same as llamas? Like in your funny book, Aunt Lauren?"

"No," Marcus said dryly. "Alpacas are superior to llamas in nearly every way." He reached for a few leaves of lettuce and a scoop of my fruit salad, avoiding the turkey altogether. "Although the majority of the world thinks they are synonymous with each other, they most definitely are not."

Strike one: weird sweater. Strike two: not good with kids. Strike three: vegetarian.

Sometimes I wondered if my sister's only criteria for matchmaking was male and breathing.

"I'll admit, I've wondered the same thing." As in ten minutes ago. "Would you mind enlightening us on their differences?"

"Llamas are isolated creatures," he said with the same disdain I'd use to describe a bloated dead rat. "But alpacas have been known to die of loneliness. They need friends and social communities. Similar to humans."

Austin coughed out a short laugh. "You're kidding, right? You think they're like humans?"

Based solely on the pinched look of Marcus's face, there wasn't a kidding bone in his body. "They are *better* than most humans I've met, actually. They have a gentle nature and are extremely sensitive to their surroundings. People could learn a lot from their peaceful existence."

Austin and Andrew exchanged a look that failed to conceal their amusement.

"Boys," Lisa reprimanded while Trent shoved a loaded bite of stuffing into his mouth. "Don't be rude."

Iris reached toward Marcus, her wiggling fingers outstretched. "Can I pet your sweater? The white fur looks just like my grandma's cat."

Marcus jumped back, nearly toppling his chair to the floor. "Whoa, absolutely not! This sweater is *not* made of fur! It's made of *fiber*. From my prize-winning alpaca, Herbert. And it's too delicate to be washed."

Game. Over.

The boys exploded with gut-shaking laughter, rocking the table and completely annihilating what was left of my sister's short fuse. No matter how she tried to regain control over the evening or how many compliments she gave his prize-winning fiber sweater, Marcus wasn't going to be reeled back into her matchmaking scheme. He tossed his napkin to his plate and excused himself, which only caused my nephews to laugh harder.

And as I observed the chaos before me—Lisa stumbling over herself to walk Marcus to the door, my mother shaking her head and shoveling another scoop of green beans onto her plate, my father complaining about his dry slab of turkey breast—I couldn't help but wonder what a certain dinosaur-loving substitute would have done given the same situation. If a five-year-old girl had reached across the table to pet *his* much-too-delicate-for-real-life sweater, how would he have responded? I smiled as the answer materialized in my mind.

He would have let her—but only *after* he'd roughed up his hair and gotten down on all fours to do a full impression of the chosen animal, of course. But still, he would have let her pet his sweater. And I would have loved watching every minute of it.

chapter eleven

Skye followed me up the stairs, her favorite bone sticking halfway out of her mouth as she escorted me into my bedroom. I flipped on the light and gave her a brief report on the Thanksgiving shenanigans that occurred at my parents' house. She lived for dramatic stories, especially ones involving her favorite person in the world, my niece, Iris.

"But unlike you, Skye, Marcus wasn't into being petted by a five-year-old. I know, so weird, huh?" Skye brushed her side against my pant leg, leaving a trail of black fur. She was hoping for a rubdown of her own. And, naturally, I obliged.

After Skye's love tank was significantly filled by belly rubs, I changed into my flannel pjs and finished up my nightly routine in the bathroom. Skye trotted to the corner of my room, performing her usual circling routine before finally slumping onto her fluffy bed. Though my eyelids felt heavy from exhaustion the way they did every time I was with my family, I was determined to finish at least three chapters of *Yours In China, An Adoption Guide for the Single Mother.* Penance for my cowardice tonight.

"Night, sweetie," I yawned-talked to Skye, picking up my phone to turn off my morning alarm. There would be no Black

Friday shopping for me this year. Apart from the annual tree lighting tomorrow night with Jenna and Brian, I'd be staying home to organize my office into a child's bedroom. *My child's bedroom.*

At my touch, my phone screen brightened with a text box hovering in the center, as if suspended there by a magical force.

So did your brownies save the day at Thanksgiving like you hoped?

A local number with no assigned contact, yet I knew without a flicker of doubt who the sender was. I jerked upright and immediately set Skye on high alert. She shot across the room to stand at my bedside, tail wagging at full speed.

"It's okay, girl. It's okay." Who was I really trying to calm? My dog or myself?

I edited the contact info to add Joshua to my phone, then texted him back.

Not exactly. But please tell me yours was wonderful?

You'll never hear me complain about buttery mashed potatoes and apple crumble . . . although I can't say the same for my waistline.

I laughed, and Skye jumped onto my bed, nudging my elbow with her nose so she could lay her head on my lap.

Yum. Sounds delicious. My family isn't exactly known for their culinary skills.

Or their tact.

There had to be at least one noteworthy dish at your table . . . ?

I batted at the pillow behind my back, sliding it up my headboard, a ridiculous smile plastered on my face.

Not really, but does a noteworthy guest count?

?

My sister showed up to Thanksgiving with a blind date for me. An alpaca farmer.

Why is there no emoji option for this?

I bit my bottom lip.

My thoughts exactly.

So was Ben there, too?

I scrunched my face up. *Ben?* I didn't know a Ben, other than Benny Cartwright. But Joshua wouldn't know him; he'd graduated from Brighton Elementary last year and was now in middle school.

I started a text, deleted it, and then started again, opting for a single question mark.

?

Is there more than one Ben who leaves notes on your Jeep while you're at work?

As his words registered, I laughed so loudly I scared an almost-asleep Skye. I'd barely calmed her when Joshua texted again. He was a quick draw.

I figured he was probably someone you had a past history with . . . maybe part of the whole life complication matter you mentioned before?

Joshua thought my *life complication matter* was an ex-boyfriend? I'd never once considered how that note had looked on the hood of my Jeep through his eyes . . . but I suppose that option made sense. In a hilarious kind of way.

Well, to be fair, Ben and I do have a long history together. Five years, in fact.

I chuckled to myself as I sent it, letting it hang there for just a second longer than needed.

But it's not the kind of history you're referencing. Benny is a former student of mine. He's twelve. And his idea of a date would be videoing a round of BeanBoozled until someone tossed their cookies.

BeanBoozled . . . is that those nasty flavored jelly beans? Like grass and booger and vomit?

Yes.

😫

Exactly. So, no. Ben wasn't at Thanksgiving. It was just my family and a random alpaca farmer. Honestly, it was a pretty brutal evening. I hope not to repeat it anytime soon.

Only, as I typed it, regret settled low in my belly. I would have to repeat it soon—not with Marcus, but with the rest of them. I'd failed my mission. Again.

Does that mean you don't have an ex-boyfriend who wants to come back? 🤨

I read his text and then read it a second time.

Three dots appeared at the bottom of our message thread, indicating he was typing something new.

I do realize this is none of my business.

And yet, he didn't retract his question. I rubbed my fuzzy-socked feet together and watched the conversation dots appear again. I waited.

But I've run through several scenarios in my head, and that one fit best. The I-have-a-very-attached-ex-boyfriend complication. Was I wrong?

Again, I pinched my lips together, this time ignoring the forbearance of getting too close to the water's edge without wearing a life preserver.

No pining ex-boyfriends here.

What about current boyfriends? (Excluding 12-year-old former students named Ben, of course.)

I hesitated. How far should I allow this conversation to go?

No. (But thank you for making Benny an exception.)

So, you're not dating anyone?

I feel like this is a poorly written multiple choice test. My answer continues to be D. None of the above.

I released a breath and lightly tapped my head against the solid headboard at my back. We needed a subject change. And quick.

Have you heard how much longer you'll be subbing at Brighton?

Will my answer hold any bearing on our previous conversation? Because if it's a matter of biding my time until I'm no longer the teacher across the hall then . . . 😊 Unless, of course, your life complication issue falls under my one deal-breaker scenario.

And what scenario is that?

That you're a dinosaur hater. I'm not sure I'd be able to look past that kind of admission, Lauren. Don't be cruel. Put me out of my misery now if so.

I laughed again, bit my lip.

Who could hate dinosaurs? 🦖

😅

Good. Now that we have that out of the way, I spoke with the district yesterday. They've asked me to stay until Christmas break.

I did a quick calculation of the weeks he'd be at Brighton if he stayed that long: just over four. Which meant a month more of working side-by-side with him—field trips and Christmas parties and holiday performances. Something like panic ricocheted in my chest. If he'd managed to get under my skin the way he had in only a couple of weeks, then what on earth would I be like by the end of December?

But what about your real job? And the reading app? What's happening with all that?

Reading app is still caught in the red tape of approvals. The holidays always slow everything down. Generally speaking, this is usually the season I work with my team to generate new ideas.

I started four texts and deleted them all.

But if that was your way of hinting for me to go back to my real job, then you're gonna have to spell it out. I'm dense when I want to be.

I made an aggravated sound and tossed my phone toward the end of my bed, staring at it for several minutes as if it were a loaded weapon. Then I sighed, repositioned until I was flat on my stomach, and retrieved my phone.

That said, I haven't given the district an answer yet.

Several emotions warred in my gut at once.

Why not?

Ah, you're back. Thought you might have lost your phone.

Nope. Had to tend to my dog.

I side-eyed the snoring Skye beside me and felt a twinge of guilt at my white lie. Nearly a minute passed, and I wondered if Joshua had sensed my dishonesty.

But then . . . a picture surfaced.

Though I couldn't tell what breed he was, the dog had markings like a black lab, with soulful eyes and a graying muzzle. His head was propped on Joshua's lap. From the looks of his outstretched legs, Joshua was lying on his bed, too. The realization sent a shock of delight through me.

So he was a dog person, too.

He's really cute. What's his name?

Joshua

🙄 The. Dog.

Brach. He's a gentle giant with an old soul.

My grin spread wider at the realization of his name.

Is that short for Brachiosaurus?

You just earned a thousand bonus points. Show me yours . . . ?

Refusing several possible retorts to that loaded lead-in, I simply snapped a picture of Skye, who looked rather lovely as she slept, and sent it to him.

Meet Skye, short for nothing, but chosen by the PAW Patrol lovers in my first-grade class.

She's a beauty. Must take after her owner.

The compliment wove around my ribs, making it difficult to take in a full breath.

You're not one of those crazy Black Friday shoppers, are you?

No. I hold out on the crazy crowds until tomorrow night.

?

The lighting ceremony at Grove Plaza. It's crowded and cold and my nose is usually on the verge of frostbite, but it's tradition. And it's wonderful. I haven't missed in years.

Who do you go with?

Usually with Jenna, depending on where her and Brian spend their Thanksgiving. It's my favorite night of the year.

Wow. That's quite the endorsement.

Wait—have you never been?

The thought seemed absurd. Everyone who had lived anywhere near our city had attended the Grove Plaza lighting ceremony at least once.

Nope.

😫

Are you kicking me off the island now?

Seriously? The ceremony is like a rite of passage. What could be more important on the night after Thanksgiving than the tree lighting ceremony?

Leftovers.

Now I'm the one with a lack of emoji choices.

He replied with a picture of a fridge stocked full of Rubbermaid containers.

That's impressive, but it's no twenty-five foot Christmas tree.

Sounds like a challenge. I accept.

?

My leftovers vs. your tree lighting event.

. . .

This is the part where you say, "That's a great idea! We should totally watch the tree lighting together. Why didn't I think of that?"

Nothing. I literally had nothing to say back.

. . .

I know you're there, Lauren. I can see your thinking dots.

Just tell me where and when to meet you.

You're relentless.

😂 Have you been talking to my mom?

If I say yes, I want to be perfectly clear that this can't be a date date. It would just be a friend thing.

Fine with me.

. . .

I smashed my head in the pillow, hoping logic or reason would choke me out before I had to respond to him again. I couldn't do this. I shouldn't do this. And yet there was no way on this earth I was going to *not* do this.

I still see you, Lauren.

I released a slow breath and typed a sentence I knew I'd likely regret in a matter of minutes.

I'll meet you by the fountain at four thirty.

I'll bring you a slice of apple crumble.

chapter twelve

Like all the years before, my nose was the first to freeze, and I'd only been waiting in the cold for Joshua for five minutes. With my coat buttoned to my chin and an extra-thick scarf wrapped around my neck, I stomped the frosty grass below my boots, desperately trying to warm up the stiffening muscles in my calves—or maybe I was preparing to make a run for it and call this whole thing off. What had I been thinking, saying yes to a nostalgic evening with him and my closest friends on my favorite night of the year?

I tried to breathe out the tension in my chest, but all that did was make me cough and shiver. I glanced at the clock on my phone. Three minutes past. The dense parade crowd made spotting a newcomer difficult. There were hundreds, maybe even thousands of people gathered around the plaza so far, and the tree christening didn't officially begin for another two hours. But by the way I was sandwiched in by other winter-clad bodies, I feared I hadn't been the only one to name the frozen fountain as a meeting place.

How will we ever find each other?

My phone buzzed in my gloved hand, and I suppressed a smile at the name that appeared on my screen. "Hello?"

"Next time I think I'll choose the place we meet. It's insane out here!"

I laughed. "I know, sorry. I didn't really think this part through very well." Not that he'd given me a chance to do so last night. I lifted up on my tiptoes, searching for him through the masses. "What are you wearing?"

A pause. "That question seems a little out of line for this not-a-date date."

I rolled my eyes and looked for him in the opposite direction, noting every male I spotted had some shade of navy, charcoal, or black adorning their head. The season of knitted hats was officially upon us. "It would be a lot easier to find you in your turkey costume."

"And yet . . . I still managed to find you just fine."

"What?" I did a full pirouette, and all the oxygen in my lungs crystalized at once. Phone still pressed to his ear, he stood directly in front of me, his grin far too reckless to be considered platonic. "Your nose is quite pink, Lauren Bailey."

"I told you I suffer from tree-lighting frostbite. It's a temporary condition."

His expression managed to warm even the chilliest parts of me. We ended the call at the same time and slipped our phones back into our jacket pockets.

I tipped my gaze upwards. "You could have told me you were wearing a red hat."

Joshua's crimson stocking hat accentuated his ruddy cheeks and the mossy flecks in his eyes. "Nah. That would have been too easy."

A couple of teenage boys shoved past us, knocking into Joshua's shoulder and unknowingly into me, as well. "Whoa there." As the back of my heel made contact with the base of the cement fountain, Joshua braced a firm hand on my forearm, steadying me with ease. "It's probably time we find a place to park ourselves for the evening, unless fountain skating was on your agenda tonight?"

"Think I'm good, thanks."

Securing his other hand at the small of my back, he guided me away from the swarm of people loitering near the fountain and into a field littered with blankets and lawn chairs. The moment we were past the crowds, I sidestepped my way out of the intimate connection.

He didn't seem to notice. "Do you know where your friends are?"

"Yes, Jenna texted me earlier. They saved a place for us." For *us*, as if Joshua and I had become a unit that deserved a title—but we weren't a unit, and there was no titling necessary. We were simply two people who happened to work together. Two people who loved kids. And dogs. And reading. And George Avery. Although, as his son, Joshua held the corner on that commonality. Nonetheless, I couldn't think of him and me as an *us*. We were simply Joshua and Lauren, colleagues who sometimes met up at random social outings.

End of story.

"I think they're over that way, on this side of The Grove Hotel."

Jenna had sworn she'd be on her best behavior tonight, which, naturally, I had to outline for her: One, no suspect eyebrow waggling. Two, no insinuating comments.

The good seven or eight inches of height Joshua had on my five-foot-five frame offered him a vantage point far superior to my own, but also an ability to cut through the immovable forms who made no allowances for me whatsoever. After I'd become tangled in a web of wool scarves and puffy coats for the third time, he finally reached back, took hold of my gloved hand, and pulled me through the crowd without a single misstep.

The late-November air stung my eyes as we careened around fir trees and street lamps, past pre-parade vehicles tossing candy to children, and individual vendors capitalizing on glow-in-the-dark swords and snowflake wands. The instant we rounded the edge of the hotel, my mouth watered as a sweet and familiar aroma captured my senses. As a general rule of thumb, I rarely purchased event food. But goodness did I love toasted almonds encrusted in a buttery blend of cinnamon and sugar.

Joshua tugged on my hand and halted us in front of the cart. "Please tell me these are a part of your tree lighting tradition?"

I nodded once. "I'd say they're a must."

He turned to the vendor wearing a Santa hat and asked for two bags.

"Oh, I didn't mean for you to buy me a—"

He shook his head before I could finish. "Rest easy. Buying toasted almonds from a food cart on Lighting Night is actually a standard practice for a not-a-date date."

Joshua paid, and the vendor handed each of us a miniature white bag of steaming almonds. I couldn't help but sigh as the spicy warmth wrapped itself around me.

"Thank you," I said.

"Anytime." And something about the way he said it, with his soft-focused eyes shimmering in the winter light of the setting sun, made my insides yearn to step closer to him.

"Lauren! Joshua!" Jenna's voice broke through my haze of cinnamon delight. I spotted her atop Brian's shoulders, waving a crystal-blue snowflake wand in the air like Queen Elsa herself.

"Perfect timing." He took my hand again, though my need for a guide was now obsolete.

I should have broken free from the grasp immediately, as there was little argument over which side of the relationship fence hand-holding belonged to, but for some reason, I didn't let go. I just . . . didn't. That was, until Brian lowered Jenna to the ground. Her dismount was a spectacular show of flexibility and athleticism. And a perfect distraction for my stealthy hand-holding removal maneuver, in which I clutched both my hands around my bag of toasted almonds as if they weighed fifty pounds and I wasn't quite sure how to carry them *and walk* at the same time.

"Hey, you two! So glad I spotted you. I swear the festival must have doubled in attendance this year."

She drew me in for a hug as Brian stepped up to do the same as soon as she let go. Brian wasn't quite as tall as Joshua, but apart from being four shades darker in complexion, their lean builds and broad shoulders were quite similar. "Hey, Bailey. It's good to see you, girl. Jenna told me you were bringing a friend from work tonight."

Brian extended a friendly hand to Joshua, though he was clearly waiting on me to make the official introduction between them.

I looked to Joshua first. "Joshua, this is Brian Rosewood. He's a pediatric surgeon at Boise Pediatrics Hospital. And Brian," I began, observing the quick male handshake between my best friend's husband and my . . . uh . . . "this is Joshua Avery. . . ." And then my mind just sort of blacked out, like a plug that had been aggressively disconnected from its power source.

The two men continued to stare at me, and I quickly shoved the prongs back into the socket and spewed out the first thing that came to mind. "He's the sub across the hall from me." The moment it was out of my mouth, I wanted to reel the words back in and start over. But much like the older brother I never had, Brian rarely missed an opportunity to highlight my verbal blunders.

"Well, it's nice to meet you, Joshua From Across The Hall."

I waited for Joshua to step in and correct my minimal definition of his occupation and list off his ridiculously impressive résumé to the slightly cocky, slightly overeducated medical professional in our mix, but no such thing happened. Apparently, Joshua was more interested in watching me flounder than he was in repairing his reputation.

"Actually . . ." I shook my head, flustered. "What I meant to say was that being a substitute teacher isn't his full-time career." I felt the shift in Joshua's focus, and my half-frozen cheeks began to thaw under his intrigue.

"Oh? What field are you in?" Brian asked him.

"Educational technology."

My mouth gaped at his too-simple answer. "Actually, Joshua *owns* a tech consulting company with an emphasis on education. He has several employees, but he's the visionary behind creating the apps and games. They market to large-scale, kid-focused organizations. Right now he's waiting on a big approval from the Board of Education that would integrate his app-based reading program into school districts across the country."

Brian's eyebrows rose a full inch. "Wow. You're a tech head? Now there's a field with a promise for long-term job security."

"I'm sure the same can be said about yours," Joshua said with an infectious grin.

Jenna looped her arm through Brian's and looked at him adoringly. "He's a gifted surgeon."

Brian bent to kiss his wife square on the lips. The two never shied away from physical displays of affection. When they were first married, I blamed it on the newlywed factor. But three years later, I doubted that excuse still applied. They were just *that* type of couple. The super handsy, super cuddly, super oblivious-to-the-public-eye type of couple. I couldn't imagine losing my social awareness the way they seemed to. Then again, I'd never been close to sharing a relationship like the one they had together either.

Brian straightened, something sparking in his gaze as he turned to address Joshua again. "It's actually ironic I met you tonight. I wonder if you might have some insight on a project I've been mulling over with a few of my colleagues at the hospital."

"Yeah? What kind of project?"

"We're hoping for some kind of digital tour geared for anxious kids who might have upcoming surgeries and long-term stays to feel more comfortable while inside the hospital. We've been given some grant money to work with, but so far our pitches to the board haven't had a whole lot of traction."

Joshua seemed to lock into the idea instantly. He had that deep-thinking way about him that I'd come to admire over the past couple of weeks, the one where he scrunched his chin upward, pushed his lips into a duckbill, and let his gaze travel from left to right. "Hmm. So perhaps an app that offered a choice of avatars resembling the child's specific medical need or ailment? And maybe a talking animal of some kind who could act as the tour guide. He could take them step by step through things like getting an IV and whatever other preparation they might need for their specific procedure."

"Yeah, exactly," Brian encouraged, his smile becoming wider by the second. "What else?"

"Maybe a virtual challenge or obstacle course for the patients to pass, earning points as they go that they can cash in for special privileges or prizes at the hospital? You could do a lot with the incentive aspect." His eyes snapped back to Brian's. "You could even create a connected space for doctors and nurses to comment on their patients' virtual progress, as well."

"Seriously? This is genius, more than we've come up with in weeks of brainstorming meetings." And then to me he said, "He's really good at this." Like I had anything to do with Joshua Avery's brain power.

Brian's eyes narrowed. "What do you think about meeting with my colleagues? See if we can get enough ideas circulating for a board presentation?"

"Sure. Just let me know when you're thinking, and I'll see if I can work it in." Joshua nudged my shoulder with his. "But only if Lauren can introduce me again."

"Done," Brian said with a laugh, and I covered my cheeks with my gloved hands. "But seriously, I'll be in touch about this soon. The timing of all this feels more than a little coincidental."

An ear-crackling rendition of "Santa Claus Is Coming to Town" pulled at our attention as a fire truck decked out with lights and garland kicked off the parade. The attendees smashed together, all vying for the best possible view. I lifted up on my tiptoes, wishing the giant man in front of me would take a step to his left, when Joshua's warm breath caressed my ear.

"I'm not even sure my mother could explain what I do in such detail. I think I need to hire you to give some pointers to my new marketing manager."

I kept my focus straight ahead, yet the ticking pulse in my throat made my words sound strained. "I'm just a good listener."

A bold smile was his only reply as a group of carolers tossed candy into the crowd and several floats moseyed by us. Children danced and giggled on either side of the main street, causing the drivers and spectators to wave and laugh. Their wonderment was as contagious as their joyful spirits.

"I'm growing increasingly concerned about your nose." Joshua's chin brushed the top of my ear as he spoke, setting free a series of flutters in my lower abdomen. "The color has changed from watermelon pink to eggplant purple within the last hour."

I brought a hand up to my face. "I honestly can't even feel it anymore."

He pulled off his glove and touched the tip of my nose with his toasty finger. I couldn't inhale for nearly half a minute. "Yeah, I'm no doctor, but I'm pretty sure if we don't do something for it soon, you won't have anything left to hang your sunglasses on next summer."

"I don't think they make nose muffs."

With that endearing look firmly affixed to his face again, he placed his hands on my shoulders and turned me to face him fully. "I'm gonna fix you."

"I'm fine, really. It's always this way when—"

"Shhh." He lifted the softest of my two scarves away from my coat and began to wrap it around the back of my head, as if he'd done this maneuver a million times before. I studied his face, only inches away from my own, as he made a crisscross pattern with the excess fabric. Taking care to cover my nose and chin as if I were made of the most delicate porcelain, he left a small gap for my mouth before he tucked the two loose ends under my knit cap. "There, that's better."

"Totally." The scarf puffed a bit as I chuckled. "Because this isn't awkward at all."

"Better awkward than amputated, I always say." He angled his head, as if to get a better view of his handiwork. "You actually look kind of . . . exotic."

"Mummy exotic or bank robber exotic?"

At his hard laugh, Jenna and Brian turned their attention from the parade's finale float to us.

"What are you two doing over there?" Jenna peeked around Joshua's back to make eye contact with me. Her eyebrows shot up. "Wow, Lauren. That's quite the fashion statement."

"Thank you." I curtsied. "I'm hoping to start a new winter trend."

Joshua's grin intensified. Yet as crazy as I may look to the public, his scarf trick had actually helped. Considerably. My nose no longer felt like a frozen carrot attached to the center of my face.

"Ooh! Here we go!" Jenna clapped her hands as Brian stepped behind her, cradling her against his chest. "The countdown's about to start!"

In a beautiful display of unity, our entire city cheered as the countdown board lit up on the tree's platform. Every patron in attendance gazed upon the unlit tree standing tall in the middle of the square with giddy expectation. It was nearly impossible to see the top of the branches from where we stood, but everything surrounding the wide base was picturesque: wreath-wrapped lampposts, miniature towns set in storefront windows, and "O

Christmas Tree" playing from the unseen speakers tucked throughout the winter wonderland.

"Ten . . . nine . . . eight . . ." Forgetting my mummified face, I clasped my hands at my chin the way I'd done long before I'd started driving myself here each year. There had been so many traditions lost to the Bailey household the day my father had slipped off that roof. So many holidays spoiled by the bitter taste of resentment, marital discord, and the eventual foreclosure auction that would unravel us all. Yet somehow, despite it all, I'd managed to preserve a single magical memory of my family during the holidays. And it was right here. At this tree. A tradition I planned to carry down to my own little family one day.

I'll be a mother next Christmas. The thought wrapped itself around me like a long-awaited hug, and for a moment, I allowed myself to imagine what it would feel like to wake up on Christmas morning with a child in my arms. *Lord, please, let me hear something soon.*

". . . six . . . five . . ." The rumble of Joshua's voice beside me broke through my future ponderings. Though his mouth moved at the appropriate time, his gaze was unfocused, his thoughts seemingly far away from the here and now.

"Three . . . two . . . one!"

The awed gasp that seized the crowd the instant the tree's lights illuminated the plaza for the first time never failed to stir my emotions. Better than a million brilliant twinkle lights was the breathless hush that managed to capture the voices of a thousand-plus people. It was *this* moment, this purity and reverence, that broke me every time—not only for a tree, but for the true beauty of all that Christmas represented to a broken world in need of hope.

The nostalgic glow from the lights radiated off the faces of the countless admirers, and I couldn't help but glance at Joshua once more, expecting him to be as captivated as all those around us. But Joshua's gaze wasn't locked on the tree. Instead, it was locked on me.

"Did you like it—the ceremony?" I lowered the scarf away from my face and tucked it below my chin so I could speak freely. "I'm always in awe of how quiet our city can get in those first few seconds when the lights come on. I think that's my favorite part."

His throat bobbed once before he answered. "It was beautiful."

Joshua wasn't a man of few words. Whenever I didn't know what to say next, he never failed to chime in with some witty quip or comment. And yet right now, he seemed content to just be . . . quiet. Still.

The crowd around us began to disperse, mothers and fathers pushing strollers with sleeping infants and lovers old and young snuggled tight. But the two of us simply remained where we were, allowing the world to pass us by. No longer were we the ones barreling through the masses looking for the world to make space for us. We'd found it. Right here, beneath the branches of a Christmas tree.

I didn't know how many minutes passed or how many people had exited the plaza, but by the time Brian and Jenna said their good-byes and traded contact information with Joshua, more litter than attendees remained on the streets.

"Where'd you park?" he asked as we strolled down the quieting sidewalks of downtown.

"In the parking garage. You?"

"By the old Mexican restaurant on Sixth."

I stopped. "That's nowhere near the garage."

He shrugged and shot me a smile that could have been a tripping hazard if I'd still been walking. "I've never been great with directions."

I didn't believe that for a second. He was simply a gentleman who didn't want me to walk to my car alone at night. "Well, I'll be happy to give you a ride over there."

"I don't mind the walk. Fresh air is good for the brain."

"According to the reader board up there on the bank, it's twenty-eight degrees outside. I don't think that's good for anybody's brain."

He chuckled and knocked his shoulder into mine. "Hey, thanks for letting me tag along tonight. It was really great."

"Wait—does that mean my Christmas tree lighting was better than your usual day-after-Thanksgiving leftover buffet?"

Another deep rumble reverberated from his chest. "I don't think you can have an honest appreciation for my grandmother's holiday baklava until you've tried it, but yes, you won the challenge tonight for sure."

"I won? *Yes!*" I beamed at him under the warm halo of street lights as we entered the parking garage and suppressed the urge to do a victory dance on the corner of Ninth and Front Street. "If you can't tell, I never win anything. I actually might need you to put this moment in writing for Brian, because I've lost every game tournament the Rosewoods have hosted for the last three years. Like, dead last kind of losing. I'm pretty sure Brian doesn't even mark my points down anymore."

Joshua laughed. "You can't be that bad."

"I really am, which is why I should have insisted on a prize for tonight's winner, because I knew the tree lighting festival wouldn't disappoint. It never does."

His stride slowed. "Okay, so what kind of prize would you have chosen?"

I glanced at him from the corner of my eye, our footsteps echoing off the walls in the tomblike space. "Oh, I don't know. I'm not actually being serious."

"Well, now curious minds want to know: What kind of prize would Lauren Bailey want if she could win anything in the world? No limitations."

"Goodness." My eyebrows spiked. "No limitations at all? That's more like a genie-in-a-bottle wish."

"What would your wish be, then?"

We approached my Jeep at the far end of the garage, but instead of unlocking my doors and slipping inside to crank up my heater, I pursed my lips and leaned against the hood, thinking. "Hmm. That's hard. I suddenly have empathy for all the beauty pageant contestants who answer 'world peace' as their big platform goal."

He smiled in response to my nervous chatter. "It's not nearly as hard as you're making it. What do you want most?"

But wasn't that a different question altogether? "Hmm." I closed my eyes, allowing my imagination to run wild as it leapt over physical obstacles like mortgage payments and early retirement to a realm where my fantasy bordered on reality. And there it stopped, in the same place it always did when I gave myself permission to desire something outside the lines of my control. Something that had turned the corner of want and need and had merged into a substance as vital as the blood pumping through my veins. Only motherhood wasn't a prize to be won. Adoption was a privilege, a blessing, a responsibility so much greater than myself.

"There. You have it, don't you?" His question sounded far too certain to be a guess.

I opened my eyes to find him peering steadily at my face. "What?"

His gaze reflected the confident tenor in his voice. "You wore that same expression earlier tonight, too. During the lighting. You definitely have something in mind."

The air between us thinned, as if our altitude had skyrocketed to thousands of feet above sea level in a matter of seconds, leaving my lungs burning for oxygen. How had he been able to discern my mental track so easily? Even if I had the most readable face on the planet, I'd still managed to keep this child-size secret from my family members for over a year. And yet this man I'd known for only a matter of weeks was on the verge of cracking it wide open.

I rubbed my lips together, willing my brain to skirt around the obvious in search of the abstract. "I just want what everybody wants, I suppose."

He'd moved in closer, his breath a white pocket of cinnamony air between us. "And what's that?"

"To bring a little bit more hope to the world, in whatever way I can."

He didn't speak, and yet his eyes roved my face as if he had, as if he'd asked a hundred questions only to receive the one answer he hadn't expected.

"You do that, daily. In your classroom." His statement resonated all the way to my bones. "Those kids adore you."

"Not nearly as much as I adore them."

He studied me in the orange-tinted light of the near-empty parking garage. "The way you teach . . . it's inspiring. *You're* inspiring. It's obvious to everyone who sees you in your classroom that you do what you do out of love, not out of obligation."

The pause that followed his declaration had me assessing him again. Every time I looked at him I uncovered something new, something more insightful and profound than the time before. And no matter where I was or how I'd coached myself beforehand, I never wanted to walk away from him. Even when I needed to.

"What about you? What would you wish for?"

His gaze slid down my face and lingered on my mouth. "Something I hadn't planned on wanting again."

The tick of his pulse against the base of his throat awakened my own, and somehow in that one sentence we'd switched from hypotheticals to something much more specific. Something that made my ribs ache and my toes tingle, and suddenly the only thing I could focus on was how close our noses were to touching.

As he closed the gap between us, my frozen lips had already begun to part, already begun to imagine the warmth that would envelop them, when he changed course and pressed a soft kiss to my cheek instead.

"Good night, Lauren."

Three simple words that pulled me from the swirling chaos in my head and haunted me all the way home. Whatever rules I'd dictated before the start of our non-date had been completely nullified by the wanting I was certain Joshua had seen in my eyes as I'd stood before him like a homeless puppy. And yet . . . and yet he hadn't acted on it. Instead, he'd done the one thing I'd been too weak to do: walk away.

chapter thirteen

There was no better cure for a clouded mind than fuzzy socks, hot chocolate, and a Christmas movie on a weeknight. I knew this well, because it was the only remedy that distracted me from thinking about what had *almost* happened in a dimly lit parking garage last Friday night. I still couldn't understand how I'd been so careless.

While I scrolled through Pinterest, pinning crafty gift ideas for my students to make for their parents, Jenna continued her running commentary on the scruffy-looking love interest starring in tonight's holiday romance. She dug to the bottom of her popcorn bowl, where her half-popped salty kernels lived, and tossed several in her mouth at once. Cringing slightly at what sounded like a person chewing on gravel, I pinned both a popsicle stick photo ornament and a mason jar snow globe to my virtual board.

When the camera crew did a close-up on the hero's unshaven jawline, Jenna nearly slid off the sofa cushion. "I mean, look, seriously, what was that casting director thinking? He's *so* shaggy! Who's in charge of those awful sideburns?"

I glanced up long enough to see a man with a rugged beard and plaid sweater removing a wax snowflake from the eyebrow of the actress playing Holly. Or maybe it was Merry. Or Joy. It had to be one of those, right?

"Yeah, it's not so great."

"*Not so great?* Lauren. Come on. Close your laptop and get into the movie criticizing spirit with me. It's what we do."

I pinned a few more ideas to my board labeled *No-Mess Christmas Projects*. "I think you're doing pretty well on your own."

"*No*," she whined in that this-is-how-I-got-my-way-as-a-teenager voice of hers. "I need you."

"And I need to figure out what we're doing with our students so they have something to give their parents. Christmas break is just around the corner."

She chucked a pillow at me, but I blocked it before it made contact with my head. As usual, Skye rushed to my rescue *after* the fact, and Jenna tossed a piece of popcorn for her to snatch midair. No wonder she loved coming to Jenna's house.

My pouty friend readjusted herself in the overstuffed loveseat, crossing her perfectly toned calves underneath her. She muted the cliché plot on the TV and switched her focus entirely to me.

"What?" I asked, not bothering to glance up from reading the directions on a very impressive ornament frame made from pinecones. "Why did you stop ogling your favorite nineties hair model?"

"Because I'd rather hear about my best friend's real-life romance. I'm due for an honest update on you and Joshua."

At his name, my stomach plummeted twenty floors. "*What?* Jenna, there is no 'me and Joshua.'"

"There is so! I saw the way you two were *making eyes* at each other in the lunchroom today." She flicked her pointer finger at me. "And don't try and tell me it was because of the pumpkin loaf Annette brought in to the staff lounge. Something's going on, I know it. So tell me what really happened between you two after Brian and I left the tree lighting."

For once in my life, I wished I could tell a believable lie. Instead, I accepted my handicap and tried to think of a suitable explanation that might throw her off this track forever. I couldn't exactly say nothing had happened between us, but then again, nothing *had* actually happened, right? I mean, for a blink of a second I'd considered what it would be like to feel his lips brush against mine, but . . . no. I hadn't kissed Joshua. Because that could never, ever happen.

"Oh my gosh. Something really *did* happen." Jenna actually hopped while still seated in that lotus flower yoga position of hers. "Tell me everything. Brian loved him, by the way. Not that he used the word *love*, of course, but you know what I mean. I could totally see the four of us hanging out and doing couple things together and—"

"No."

"Going on vacations and maybe even—"

"No. *Stop*." I fought the urge to plug my fingers in my ears and sing the ABCs, if only to drown out her squealy inflections.

I shut my laptop and set it aside so I could focus all my energy on de-escalating Jenna. "You are getting way too—"

"Lauren, he *likes* you. Like really, really *likes you*. Can't you see that?"

Why did that statement alone make me want to listen to a nineties boy band and dance on the sofa while using my hairbrush as a microphone? "That doesn't matter." It *couldn't* matter.

"It absolutely does matter. He's a good one, Lauren. Joshua Avery is a fantastic guy who loves God and his family and likes you a whole, whole lot. What more do you need?" She flung her hand toward the television. "He's ten times better than anything we've watched on these cheesy movies lately. I know you have to see that, too. And I also know from the way you're acting that the two of you must have made some kind of connection—whether or not you set out to do so. You might be able to fool everybody else, but you're not fooling me. Not for a single second."

I picked up one of Jenna's fur pillows and smashed it against my abdomen, needing a buffer from her romanticism of reality. "Jen . . ."

She softened her approach, this time playing the part of Sincere and Loyal Friend. I honestly liked this version of her best. "Just tell me what happened."

"Nothing." The truth. Thankfully.

"That *nothing* doesn't sound like a complete sentence."

I paused, rubbed my lips together, and then carefully crafted the rest of the sentence. "We didn't kiss but . . ."

She clasped her hands, eyes wide. "But . . . ?"

"But . . . I don't know. We did have a moment, I guess."

"A *moment*!" A whisper yell if ever there was one. In Jenna's world, I'd just announced a five-star proposal.

"Relax. It wasn't even a full sixty seconds. Probably more like ten seconds, tops," I explained. "But yes, there was a very brief, very hormone-driven moment where I thought that maybe . . ."

"Yeah?"

"That maybe he might kiss me." My cheeks flamed at the admission like I was a nerdy bookworm freshman all over again and had finally been asked to a dance by an upperclassman.

"So what happened?"

"He said . . ." I held it out, trying to see if Jenna might actually fall off the couch the longer I made her wait. "'*Good night, Lauren.*'"

"Wait . . . I'm sorry. *What?*" She shook her head. "You said you two had a moment? That's an ending."

"I know." I'd analyzed and rehearsed those tension-filled seconds at least a dozen times over the weekend. "Which was exactly what I needed him to do—to say. And he did it. Because I asked him to. Because when he invited himself to the lighting festival with us, I told him we could only attend as friends."

She threw her back against the sofa cushion. "Wow."

I nodded, picking at my nails. "So you're right. Joshua *is* a good man. But he's not *my good man*, Jen. He can't be. It wouldn't be right for me to start something with him now when I'm so close to being matched. And it certainly wouldn't be in the best interest of my future child, who will need all my focus and attention." And then, of course, there was the pesky little issue of all the paperwork I'd signed in my adoption dossier stating that I would be adopting as a single woman. But Jenna looked about as interested in rehashing China's marital status rules for adoption as I felt about repeating them.

I needed a cold drink, something to wash down the disappointment building in my throat. I'd fought so hard against the hope of *maybe if* . . . and yet here I stood, thinking about him, talking about him, wanting to forget about him. Because if Joshua had been sent as a test from God, then I hadn't been faring too well at all. Maybe that's what it had all been about, me not selling out. Me not giving in. Me not growing winded before the race had actually begun.

I reached inside Jenna's oversize fridge for a sparkling water, popped the tab, and guzzled it down until the carbonation burned my throat and rinsed away my wavering resolve.

"What's that sound?" Jenna called to me from the other room.

I swallowed, hoping she hadn't heard me drinking like a cavewoman all the way in the kitchen. "What sound?"

"A muffled buzzing or . . . wait—I think it's your phone?"

I patted my hips, realizing too late that I was wearing my pocketless pjs and my phone was still stuffed in the bottom of my work bag on the couch. Yet another sign of my distracted life as of late.

I set my can on the countertop, then unzipped a series of pouches, reaching my phone on the last ring.

"Hello?" My chest pounded as the contact name registered.

"Lauren?"

"Yes." A breath more than a word.

"This is Stacey with Small Wonders. Did I catch you at a bad time?"

Was there ever a bad time for my adoption agency to be calling? Not in my book. "No, no. This is fine. How are you?" I said, remembering my manners at the last possible second. It was hard to think with my heartbeat drumming against my skull.

"I'm doing quite well, thank you. These are actually my very favorite calls to make. Lauren, we're just minutes away from sending you a possible match, but we always like to touch base by phone first."

"*Really?* You . . . you have a match for me?" Tears sprung to my eyes immediately. I reached out for the sofa, missing it altogether before I slumped onto the arm like a boneless jellyfish.

Jenna moved down the length of her sofa until her knees brushed mine and she could cover my hand with hers. Somehow her best friend spidey sense had clued in on exactly what I needed before I had a chance to voice it aloud.

"Yes. He's an adorable baby boy. Only ten months old, and he comes from an orphanage partnership we've worked with for quite some time in a province near Guangzhou, China."

Tears streamed down my cheeks uncontrollably now. "Oh my gosh. Wow. A *boy*."

No, a *son*.

I glanced at Jenna. Tears streaked her cheeks as well, making mine come all the quicker.

"You'll have two weeks to make a decision on moving forward with him after reviewing his file, of course. There are several pictures and also a video of his nanny holding him. His medical needs appear to be very manageable, minor. But you'll still want to have a medical professional look them over with you." She paused. "If you decide you'd like to move forward with him, you'll just need to submit a Letter of Intent that we'll send on to our partners in China."

"Yes, the LOI. Right." My brain was starting to click now,

starting to comprehend that this was, indeed, the phone call I'd been waiting on for nearly fifteen months. And perhaps a lifetime before that. This was the phone call that would make me a mother. To a baby boy.

Stacey's patient voice reeled in my thoughts. "Yes. If you have any questions, please don't hesitate to reach out to me." She paused a second time, apparently conferring with someone in the office. "All right, Lauren, the file has just been sent to you."

"Okay," I said. "Okay." I pointed to my laptop and Jenna seemed to know exactly what I was asking of her.

She retrieved it from the end of the couch and opened the lid, waiting for me to take over.

"Blessings to you, Lauren. All of us here at Small Wonders are thrilled to be a part of your child's story."

"Thank you. Thank you so much."

After I hung up the phone, Jenna pushed the laptop aside and tackled me with a hug that made me break into a sob. "It's a boy? You're going to have a son?"

All I could do was nod into her shoulder and tell myself to keep breathing.

"Lauren, oh, Lauren . . ."

"I know." There weren't words for this. There were barely even thoughts.

After another few minutes of ugly crying, we finally broke apart.

I needed to see his face. My son's face.

Jenna swiped under her eyes, then backed away. "I feel like I should give you a few minutes, let you see him for the first time on your own?"

I shook my head and held out my hand to her. "No, please stay. I want you here with me."

Unshed tears glittered in her eyes, and she took the seat beside me without another word.

We both seemed to be lacking sufficient oxygen, as there were no exhales to be heard when I clicked into my Gmail account.

Sure enough, just as promised, there was a waiting email from Small Wonders International, linked to a large attachment file.

"Okay," I said, releasing the breath I'd been holding. "Okay."

My shaky fingers hovered over the mouse. *This is really it.*

I clicked into the email.

The eight attachments took nearly two minutes to load and then . . .

I scrolled down the screen to find the JPEG files first. I couldn't wait a single minute longer to see his sweet face. No matter what his paperwork said or what his medical information contained, none of it mattered as much as seeing his long-awaited picture for the first time.

The instant the first photo came into focus, I started to weep.

Jenna saved my laptop from slipping off my kneecaps as I cupped both my hands over my mouth and stared into the eyes of my son. Dark chocolate, almond-shaped eyes full of curiosity stared back at me. He sucked on three fingers as he sat in the center of a red carpet, a plastic teething toy gripped in his opposite hand. Under mile-long lashes, he gazed directly into the camera as if to say, *"Here I am, Mama."* His cheeks were pudgy and round, his skin baby-smooth and flawless . . . except for a single pink scar that trailed from his right nostril to the soft peak of his upper lip.

I never wanted to stop looking at him. Ever.

"He's beautiful, Lauren," Jenna whispered reverently. "He's so, so beautiful."

"He is." *And he's mine.* The thought cinched around my heart and pulled tight. This child was *my child.* My baby boy.

We clicked through the next three photos—one of him lying in a wooden crib, one of him sitting in a makeshift highchair drinking a bottle, and one of him . . . smiling. Jenna and I both swooned hard over his gummy expression. Had I ever seen anything more breathtaking in all my life? No. Certainly not.

By the time we played the video, my chest felt like it couldn't hold even one more ounce of happiness inside it without combusting. I *felt* every coo, every babbling word, every rattle of his toy as he shook it. Completely captivated, we watched those twenty-six seconds over and over before Jenna reminded me that there were other attachments still waiting to be viewed in the email.

I chose the translated document first, labeled *Wang Yong*.

It was the name he'd been given the day he'd been found abandoned on the front steps of a bicycle shop and turned over to the welfare department by the shop's owner. He'd only been a few days old. Sick, hungry, and needing proper medical attention for his cleft lip.

I read through all the notes regarding his Finding Day twice. There weren't many details outside the name and location of the shop, along with a tiny newspaper clipping of him with his newborn picture, which had been used to search for any living blood relatives. He was taken to the hospital to treat his dehydration and then again for a surgery that took place two months later on his upper lip.

There was a long document charting his routine at the orphanage, his sleep schedule, his eating schedule, things he enjoyed, nannies he was attached to, and toys he enjoyed playing with.

All of it surreal. Because all of it meant that *he was so real*.

We scanned the X-rays and medical jargon—most of which I didn't understand, with the exception of one line: *He has recovered fully from his surgery*.

"Hello, hello? You two get sucked into another Netflix binge or—"

We jumped at the sound of Brian's voice. We'd been so wrapped up in reading that we hadn't heard him come in.

"Brian!" Jenna practically leapt off the sofa, running to him and smashing headfirst into his chest. "Lauren got it!"

"Got what?"

"The call! There's a baby boy, and he's everything—he's like, the most precious thing I've ever seen and you need to go over his medical files right now because she can't say yes until she has a professional look them over and—"

He silenced her run-on sentence with a kiss, and I couldn't help but smile. When he finally pulled away, he said, "Of course I'll look it over, babe. I'll do whatever I can to help." And then to me he said, "Congratulations, Lauren."

"Thank you."

He set his bag on the counter, then turned to open the fridge. "Let me just grab a quick snack and then I'm all yours."

I'd never loved my best friend's husband more than I did in this moment. "Thank you, Brian."

Snack in hand, Brian made his way over to the sofa. I opened the translated medical document and scans, handed him my computer, and gave in to my body's need to stand and stretch and breathe.

Just breathe.

I paced the length of their dining room as Brian read. And studied. And read some more. A smear of pale blue scrubs pulled at my peripheral vision as his leg bobbed up and down.

After an eternity of silence, he finally said, "Honestly, his case looks great. There are a few different techniques to repair a cleft lip and palate, and it's possible he'll need a follow-up procedure once the plates in his mouth mature, but based on all the notes, he looks to be in really good shape. I have a friend I can refer you to once you're settled back home in the States."

If I'd been aware of any hesitations before, there wasn't a single one left now. "Really? Wow, okay. Thank you."

Overcome with delirious happiness, Jenna threw her arms around me again, and we laughed until our sides ached. It was the kind of happiness that stuck to your bones and pumped through your heart and made you undoubtedly aware that you'd never actually known the true meaning of the word until right then.

Because I, Lauren Bailey, was going to be a mother.

chapter fourteen

Undeterred by the sun's groggy display of dawn outside my living room windows, I stepped into my rubber boots, threw on a heavy fleece jacket, and retrieved my extra change of clothes from the sofa. As trendy as the flannel and leggings look might be for women my age, muddy work boots paired with the paint-smattered button-up I'd owned since high school weren't Brighton-approved classroom wear.

The clock on the microwave read a quarter after five when I opened my front door and trekked to my Jeep. But not even the super early morning, the ice-slicked streets, or the storm clouds brewing overhead could burst my happiness bubble today.

For the first time in over a year, I was actually *eager* to tell my family about my adoption. No longer was I filled with the cowardly ways of Old Lauren, a woman who often reserved a pocketful of doubt that maybe God wouldn't come through for her or that maybe she'd heard Him incorrectly or that maybe there was another woman, a wiser, better-equipped woman suited for such a calling. But last night Old Lauren had been replaced by an emboldened, ready-to-face-her-giants-and-tackle-the-world New Lauren.

Because little Noah Yong Bailey—yes, I'd named him in

the wee hours of the morning!—deserved to be known and loved by everyone who had the privilege of seeing his precious, toothless smile.

I'd spent hours printing out his baby photos from the email files last night and saving them to my desktop, phone screen, and even in a few frames around my house. I also forwarded all the attachments to Gail, crying with her on the phone as she exclaimed God's faithfulness over and over. I prayed that same faithfulness would shelter me during the upcoming conversation with my mom and sister.

"You have arrived," my phone announced as I made the final turn into my mother's job site. I'd texted her last night, asking if we could get together this morning before the start of school. Her reply had been the Roths' address.

No matter. Today wasn't about my mom's poor communication skills.

Today was about Noah.

My mother's Closet Queens pickup was parked in the center of a U-shaped driveway in front of an estate four times the size of my townhouse. How long had she been working?

No sooner had I popped my driver's side door open did I hear my mother shout, "Head's up, Lauren."

I barely registered her words before she flung a giant black-and-white panda bear off the front porch. At my head. Good thing my mother's pitching arm was not what it used to be. The bear smacked into my chest, then slumped to the ground, face-planting onto my boots. I stared down at the oversized stuffed animal, wondering if any other thirty-one-year-old women were spending their morning being assaulted by carnival toys. "Your reflexes aren't as good as they used to be, Lauren."

"I haven't had a whole lot of opportunities to catch flying panda bears lately. Will there be any other airborne mammals coming my way, or should I head up there?"

My mother almost smiled. "Can't promise there won't be,

but you can throw that one in the back of your Jeep. Your job will be thrift store duty. There are a few piles started inside for you already."

"Sure, I can take it all after school." I bent to grab the panda's paw and it slipped through my grasp. The sucker was heavier than I thought. What was it stuffed with? Pea gravel? "What time did you start this morning?"

"Five." She put her hands on her hips, stretched her back. Her white Reeboks were looking dingier than usual for this time in her tennis shoe rotation. She only purchased a new pair once a year. During the after-Easter sale at Fred Meyer's. "We have another big one lined up after this, so we need to get it finished."

"Ah, okay," I said, hugging the bear around the middle and hefting it toward the back of my Jeep with a grunt that reminded me of my unused gym membership. "How's it been going in there?"

"Not too bad." Code for a better-than-normal job. Good, then she'd be in a decent mood. Strangely enough, my mother was at her best when she was organizing piles of other people's junk. She was an expert at establishing control in chaotic situations. "We finished two storage closets, a linen closet, and the walk-in pantry yesterday. Finishing up the master now so the movers can come in the morning."

I hurled the panda into the back of my vehicle and shut the trunk door. "Wait—that thing came out of a master closet?"

My mother's eyes lit with uncommon amusement. She turned back to the front door, calling over her shoulder, "Come inside. I'm sure your sister could use a hand before you have to leave."

Pleading silently for a double helping of grace and patience, I took the porch stairs two at a time, racing to keep up with my mom's rigid pace. I gasped as I entered the massive house lined with moving boxes and furniture coverings. "Wow, where are these people moving to—the family who lived here, I mean?"

By the looks of all the cardboard marked *FOR DONATION* in big black letters, they were obviously downsizing. A lot.

"They're overseas someplace," my mother said, clipping about, her stride rivaling that of an Olympic speed walker.

The cathedral ceilings and expansive rooms disoriented me as I followed her through a maze of organized chaos.

"Overseas?" My interest heightened. "Why? For a job?"

She halted at the door at the end of a marbled hallway. "I'm their closet cleaner, Lauren, not their life coach. I didn't ask, and they didn't tell."

My mother had a knack for killing curiosity before it could even muster a breath in her presence. She'd always been a firm believer in keeping her business to herself and letting the rest of the world do the same. Funny how my sister held the exact opposite life philosophy.

We entered a bedroom at the far end of the hall, although *bedroom* wasn't exactly the term I would have used to describe it. My childhood Barbie DreamHouse didn't begin to compare to the extravagance of this space. A chandelier hung from the ceiling on a long, ornate chain surrounded by faux copper tiles that looked like something straight out of Queen Elizabeth's bedchamber. I glanced around for a snooty butler who would banish me and my rubber boots from such a classy residence. Why would anybody leave such a spectacular house?

"You gonna gawk at that ridiculous ceiling all morning? Or are you gonna help us out before you have to go?"

My attention snapped back to my mother's irked expression, and I followed her the rest of the way into the master closet, patting the pocket of my coat for reassurance that I had my iPhone, where Noah's sweet face lived. I smiled at the thought of him so close to me.

Floor-to-ceiling shelves lined three of the four walls. Cabinets, drawers, and shiny metal hooks were placed in just the right order to make organizing a dream. Yet stuff was stacked and crammed everywhere the eye could see, and probably a lot of places it couldn't, too. An avalanche of wigs, hats, belts, costume jewelry, and shoes towered near a mirror that resembled the magical one from *Snow White*.

"Yeah, this is what we call the catch-all closet." Lisa stretched tall, shaking out her quads and then pressing a hand to her lower back. "I just found a wrapped Christmas present in a padded envelope dated six years ago. Hope Great-Grandma Betty wasn't expecting a thank-you card before she bit the dust."

"Lisa." Mom groaned. She also wasn't a fan of death commentary.

My sister threw up her hands. "What? Snooping is a part of the job, Mom."

"What can I do to help?" I interjected, noting how my mother looked ready to clobber Lisa with a soccer cleat. How the two of them had managed to work in close proximity for so many years and not end up in a state penitentiary . . . I truly had no idea. "Besides taking that load to the thrift store." I glanced at my watch. "I'm yours for another hour and fifteen minutes."

Lisa nodded toward Accessory Mountain. "You can toss that entire pile over there in a box. It's all donation, too."

"No problem." The toe of my boot hooked around a gold belt, and I teetered, reaching out for the sturdiest surface nearest me. Thankful I hadn't fallen face-first into a glass jar of pennies, I read the bold print on the sealed cardboard box tucked under a long dress coat. *FOR UGANDA*. "Uganda?"

Lisa's long blond ponytail flicked over her opposite shoulder as she looked back at me. "What? Oh yeah. They must have forgotten that one when they left. Hopefully it wasn't too vital."

"Who?"

"The people who lived here. They all up and moved to Uganda a couple weeks ago. They were totally the religious, save-the-world types. Gave up this beautiful place to go live in a village with no running water or stores or even schools." She shook her head. "I so don't get people like that."

People like that. Her words jabbed into my gut, refusing to settle as I thought of the kind of family who would say yes to the sacrifices involved in such a calling. A missionary calling. I immediately wished I could have heard their whole story . . . from them, not my sister.

Lisa tossed several warm sweaters into my working pile. "I mean, what difference could five white people who obviously haven't lacked a day in their lives make to an impoverished African village?"

And just like that, I had my in. I recognized it immediately—the moment I'd asked God to give me as I bowed my head last night before drifting off to sleep.

"I don't think it's possible for us to measure the impact one person can have on another, but I do believe that offering hope to someone without it is invaluable."

Lisa whipped her head around, obviously not expecting me to comment. "Uh, okay. Were you listening to a Tony Robbins podcast on the way over here or something?"

"No," I said with a calm not my own. "But I have given a lot of thought to how I might help the poor and vulnerable in our world. There are so many problems—poverty, hunger, abuse, war. And if I turned a blind eye, claiming 'It's too overwhelming,' then you're right—no impact would ever be made at all. But making a difference starts with being willing to help where and how we can right now." Something I'd heard Gail say many times over.

My mom continued to pack the books in the corner, but Lisa's hands had stilled along with her gaze, as if daring me to continue so she could come up with a cutting counterattack.

But I wasn't going to back down this time.

"Actually," I said, flinging a pair of nude pantyhose into the box behind me. "That's one of the reasons I wanted to come out here this morning. I have something I'd like to share with you both—and with Dad, too, of course." It was then my mother halted her task, her expression skeptical yet focused. "I should have told you sooner, and I'm sorry I waited longer than I should have, but I'm excited to tell you—show you—now. And for you to be involved." I fought to hear my voice over the *ba-bump, ba-bump, ba-bump* thudding in my ears.

No, I won't be afraid. Noah deserves a strong mother. "In just a few months, I'm going to be adopting a baby boy from a Chinese orphanage."

Unbelieving stares followed by heavy mouth breathing was the only response in the room.

I rushed on, hoping to fill the silence with information that might supersede whatever negativity might be brewing. "I received an email last night with his pictures and medical records and, he's, well, I'll show you—" I pulled my phone from my pocket, but as I tapped on the virtual photo album, a flood of comments and questions launched from them at once. Most of them were indecipherable, with the exception of two phrases that pegged me straight in the heart: "You can't afford to adopt a child" and "You don't know the first thing about being a parent."

My arm dropped to my side. The picture of Noah's smiling face remained pressed against the inside of my palm like a treasure I vowed to protect. I pleaded for God to help me, for His grace and compassion and every other available fruit of the Spirit to intervene and make them see, make them understand. "I realize this probably feels like a shock to you, but I've actually been in the process to adopt for over a year and—"

"Lauren, this is ridiculous. You can't be serious right now." A haughty sound escaped Lisa's throat. "I mean, what are you thinking? You can't just . . . just . . . adopt a kid from some orphanage across the world and suddenly expect to know how to be its parent. It doesn't work like that." She kicked a random pair of black high heels out of her warpath. "How will you even take care of it while you're at work? You aren't Angelina Jolie. Adoption isn't the fairy tale all those rich celebrities make it out to be with their full-time nannies, cooks, and housekeepers. You'll have to be all that *and more*." *Because you're single* were the words her eyes added as her ponytail swooshed from left to right. "Mom, say something here."

But then I saw my mother's eyes. They were the same eyes that told my father he was worth nothing to our family after his workman's comp ran out and we lost my childhood home to the bank. The same eyes that announced she would be taking over the household finances and paying off my father's debts by starting a business of her own. Even if it broke her. And her marriage. And her children. Yes, those were the same hardened, bitter eyes that took my measure now and left me to bleed before she even spoke a word.

"Are those churchy friends of yours behind this? Filling your brain with all that nonsense about saving people who are too broken to be saved? You're a single first-grade teacher, Lauren. You cannot afford this."

"What? No, my friends haven't put me up to anything. And neither has my church—" was all I could get out before she came at me again.

"I don't believe that for a minute. The daughter I raised would never make such a reckless decision about her future. This sounds a lot like religious brainwashing." The word spit from her mouth like venom.

"Mom, stop. *Please*. I haven't been brainwashed by anyone, but I do want my life to matter, and I do want to make a difference on this earth in whatever capacity I can. There are *millions* of children in our world who have no family, no parent figure at all to guide them, nurture them, love them." I laid a hand over my heart as a sudden clarity rushed over me. "I can do something about that, and truthfully, I believe I'm *supposed* to do something about it. Not because my church told me to, and not because I think I'm ready for all the things motherhood will throw at me, but because I trust that adoption is a part of God's plan for my life."

"Adoption will bankrupt you."

The hot coals simmering low in my belly caught fire in my chest and spread to each of my limbs. "No, it won't! I've saved, Mom—for *years*. I've pinched every penny and budgeted for the costs involved, but since we're on this subject, I've actually received two different grants from nonprofit organizations who support single women in the adoption community—"

"Please don't tell me you threw your life's savings away on this? Lauren!" Her voice cracked, but I doubted she was capable of shedding a single tear over me. "Has my life taught you *nothing*?"

"*I don't want your life!*" The words punched out of my mouth before they even had a chance to register in my brain. "I'm going to adopt this baby, hold him in my arms, and give him everything I never had as a child—starting with love!"

Shock and hurt flickered across her face, and some detached part of me asked, *What did I just say?*

She slashed a finger in the air, and I swore I could feel it slice me in two. "Don't come asking me for money when this thing implodes your life. I didn't raise you to be such a fool."

"He's not a *thing*! *He's my son!*" I yelled after her as she pushed out of the closet.

Lisa stood opposite me, her face slack with the same stunned panic I felt in every cell of my being. "What. Just. Happened."

Shame nibbled away at my insides. "I didn't mean . . . I didn't think. . . ." I closed my mouth, not willing to add to my list of growing regrets. Because I had meant what I said to my mother. Perhaps that was the ugliest part of all. I'd meant every single word.

Lisa remained silent for a few seconds more before pulling herself onto a free-standing cabinet and exhaling deeply.

"So this was the big secret you've been keeping from us." She chuckled humorlessly. "I can honestly say I never would have guessed you'd be hiding a baby." She considered me a minute more. "And I'm guessing this is also why you've cut yourself off from the opposite sex?"

I gave a single nod, unwilling to share any more of the specifics. "I've chosen to adopt as a single mother. It's what's best."

"Listen," she said, sighing again, "I get that you're all full of maternal feelings right now. Those hormones are crazy strong. Believe me, it's why Iris is here."

I glanced up to watch her nip at a nonexistent hangnail on her thumb, realizing that whatever she was about to admit wasn't something I'd heard before. Come to think of it, this was all new—a complete role reversal. I was the peacemaker in our family. Never Lisa. "After step-momming the boys and dealing with Trent's psycho ex, I wanted my own child, a child that came from my body, my blood. I was sick of Brenda barking orders at me—telling me everything I wasn't doing right to care for their sons." She paused again. "So I got pregnant with Iris, and I honestly believed that having her would help me love Trent's boys more. Because maybe whatever was wrong with me for not being able to love them the way I knew I was supposed to would correct itself with her birth."

She shook her head, gently kicking the heel of her boot against the cabinet door. "But having my own baby didn't fix anything. Motherhood is a tough job, but mothering children that aren't my own . . . well, it's the hardest thing I've ever had to do." In a rare show of vulnerability, her eyes met mine, tears dangling from her bottom lashes. "Saying yes to a baby won't fix what's messed up in you or your family. Take it from me."

I extinguished her words the instant she spoke them. I wasn't the same kind of broken as my sister. Our lives couldn't be more different. I had faith, a relationship with God, and a calling on my life to follow and obey. She had years of rebellious living, a suffering marriage, and a home life that mirrored little of the convictions I knew to be right.

"I didn't come here to ask your permission, Lisa, or even to gain your acceptance. I've already said yes to Noah." His name empowered me to continue. "I'm going to be his mother, and you're going to be his aunt. I just thought you'd want to know."

chapter fifteen

Like a grouping of cancerous cells, my family's cynicism had slithered into my subconscious and infected my thoughts with their poison. No matter how hard I tried to return to the blissful state of a woman who'd just glimpsed the face of her baby for the first time, I had barely been able to manage a smile since returning to my classroom over eight hours ago.

Once again, I'd entrusted them with a tender piece of my heart, and once again they'd tossed it back in my face like in a violent game of hot potato. Heat flared in my chest at the remembrance of my mother's words to me: "*Don't come asking me for money when this thing implodes your life. I didn't raise you to be such a fool.*"

Why should I feel bad for what I said to her? Nobody ever stood up to my mother. I'd spoken the truth.

Too agitated to grade papers or decorate my classroom with the box of snowflakes I'd pulled out of the game closet yesterday, I dumped a large tub of colorful counting cubes onto my conference table to give my hands something to do, something to fix. I broke the colorful mismatched squares apart, finding satisfaction in the *pop-snap* sound they made as they disconnected from each other.

"Knock, knock. Lauren?"

My hands stilled. I wasn't ready to face the man who belonged to that voice, and yet in he came.

"Hey." I chucked a stack of red cubes into the tub and kept my gaze on the mess in front of me.

"Yikes." Joshua scanned the sea of snap cubes. "I feel like I just walked back into my childhood bedroom. Only that mound would have been Legos, not math cubes, and they would have been scattered all over my carpet like tiny spikes of death."

Without an invitation, he plunked himself down opposite me. "Here, I'll help."

Sorting through another pile, I flicked my gaze north. "You don't have to. It won't take me long." And even if it did, that was the whole point. I didn't want to take this negativity home with me, not when my home would soon be Noah's home, too. It felt wrong to taint the space he'd soon be crawling around in with this foul mood.

"I want to," Joshua said in that flirtatious tone of his, which I was beginning to realize was actually just his normal tone. As if he didn't know how to be anything other than ridiculously charming all the time.

He unsnapped several rows of cubes. "I didn't see you in the lunchroom today. Or at recess."

"I had some grading to catch up on." The lie sizzled on my tongue like Pop Rocks.

"Huh, strange. 'Cause I don't think I've handed out a single worksheet since before Thanksgiving break."

"Yeah, I don't know." I shrugged. "Guess I just got behind somehow."

And this, ladies and gentlemen, was exactly why you should never tell a lie. Joshua had been using my planner—teaching his class using *my* lesson plans—so he knew better than anybody else that I hadn't been grading today.

He placed a set of ten on the table and searched into my

deepest soul with those mossy green eyes of his. "Are you okay, Lauren? You don't seem like yourself."

I scooted away from the table and reached for the plastic container on the floor. I couldn't have *the conversation* with him right now. Not like this, anyway. Joshua deserved more than my leftover frustration at my family.

"I just have a bit of a headache is all."

Container propped on my lap, I prepared to sweep the cubes haphazardly into the bin, but Joshua stopped my arm and chuckled, as if my dramatics were solely for his amusement. "Wait a minute, what's happening here? Weren't we supposed to be organizing these by colors?"

Trapped beneath his hand, I met his gaze, a rabid fear rising in my chest. This couldn't happen like this. I couldn't allow him to lure his way into my mushy center. "I think I need to leave it for another day."

His eyes darkened with concern as he removed his hand from my arm. "You do? Because I've never seen you put away anything in your classroom half finished like this."

I cut my gaze from his face and stood, picking up the plastic tub. "Well, it's late. We both should get going and allow the maintenance team a chance to do their job."

"So we're back to this again, are we?" He made a throaty sound I couldn't quite decipher, but knew I didn't care for. At all. He laced his fingers behind his head and lounged back.

"What's that supposed to mean?"

A contemplative smile curved his mouth. "It's what you do—whenever you don't want to talk to me. You escape."

"I do not *escape*."

"You do, actually." A matter-of-fact statement. "I guess I was hoping after the lighting festival that I'd finally gained some ground, that you might be starting to trust my intentions a bit more. . . ." He shrugged, not finishing his thought. I'd never done well with fragments. Maybe because I'd grown up in a home where there was little left to the imagination on where someone stood relationally with anybody else in the family. I wasn't used to filling in the gaps when it came to statements of approval. It had always been feast or famine. All or nothing.

"Trust your intentions? Joshua, I told you from the beginning how it had to be between us, and you seemed to understand."

Without taking his eyes off me, he stood, his steps as sure and measured as his voice. "How can I understand when you won't let your guard down long enough to have a real conversation about the possibility of you and me? When you won't tell me why I can't take you out on a real date?" He paused long enough to disarm me, taking the tub from my hands and setting it down on a desk. "Because that's what I want, Lauren. I want to take you out. I want to eat with you, laugh with you, and spend time with you in whatever capacity you'll give me. And sometimes I think you might want the same thing, and then other times—" He pointed to Exhibit A again on the desk. "Other times I'm not sure what to think."

His shockingly male scent made thinking about *anything* difficult at the moment, yet I knew he wasn't wrong. I knew I'd done a terrible job at keeping him strictly in the friend zone. Of living within the boundaries set for platonic male and female co-workers. I searched for words and came up with nothing more than a squeak before his much-too-tender eyes locked onto mine, and I was immediately transported back to Old Lauren. The one who teetered between present and future. Between reality and hope. I allowed her one last second to linger, one last second to bathe in a moment of possibility, before I broke the spell and spoke the words that had circled around my heart for well over a year.

"I'm going to be a mother."

Through the window of his eyes, I watched his thoughts swirl and swirl and then finally sputter to a stop. "A . . . a mother?"

In any other situation, the southern flick of his gaze to my abdomen might have been comical. But there was nothing even remotely funny about this moment. And I doubted there ever would be—not five years from now. Not even ten.

"No, Joshua, I'm not . . ." I shook my head softly. "I'm adopting a baby. Soon."

The words settled between us, and I saw the exact instant he understood the full weight of my meaning. My heart wasn't his to win because it had already been won by a little boy with wanting eyes and a winsome smile.

He said nothing for the longest time, continuing to stare and work out a calculation he didn't seem willing to share. "A baby."

"Yes, his name is Noah. I saw his pictures for the first time last night. He's ten months old and lives in China, in an orphanage. I've been waiting to be matched with a child for a long time—nearly a year and a half. And there are certain requirements I've agreed to, commitments that are best for Noah in the long run."

A single nod followed by an exhale. "I assume not dating is one of those requirements."

For the billionth time in the last twelve hours, my eyes grew damp. I nodded. "I didn't even tell my family members about the adoption until today." I pushed the memory of that brutal conversation away and worked to keep myself present in this one.

Joshua's eyebrows seemed to be having an entire conversation without him ever opening his mouth.

"I know this is a surprise . . ." I hedged.

"A surprise?" He laughed at that, raking a hand through his hair like he wasn't quite sure what else to do. "Lauren, prior to last week I couldn't imagine a scenario more touchy than having to navigate through a regretful ex-boyfriend. But a . . . a baby." He seemed to recall something else, taking an extra second to shape his mouth around the word. "Noah."

Somehow, Joshua saying his name was a deeper level of real than when I'd watched my baby's video on my laptop for the first time.

"I wasn't trying to mislead you. I promise, I wasn't."

He nodded, then looked away from me. "You told me you were in a complicated life stage, I just . . . I didn't realize how complicated."

I swallowed, refusing to release the apology that tiptoed up my throat. Because I wouldn't apologize about Noah. I would never be sorry I chose him first, because if I had to do it all over again, even knowing a man like Joshua could walk into my life at any moment and threaten the desires of my heart, I would choose him still.

I would choose Noah.

In all the weeks I'd known Joshua, I'd rarely seen him wear anything but his faithful, hope-springs-eternal expression. But not now.

Defeat shadowed his gaze and dimmed his once-constant smile. It was the face of a man who engineered solutions for a living and yet couldn't work out the problem in front of him. Because this equation had already been solved, and there was simply no factor that could involve the two of us together.

chapter sixteen

According to the Crayola color wheel, there were exactly nineteen distinctly different shades of blue. Add too much yellow, you get green. Too much red, and you risked falling into the violet and purple range. Somewhere between breakfast and a trip to the home improvement store, I'd become somewhat of an expert on *blue*.

I stood back, tilting my head to the left and right, squinting at the crudely painted swatches on Noah's nursery room wall, hoping one might call out to me. But so far the only thing that had called out to me was Skye when she needed a potty break, and Jenna, trying to pin me down with her let's-set-a-date-for-your-adoption-shower texts every five minutes.

Swiping my phone off the desk that still needed to be moved from this room, I snapped another pic of the most indecisive wall in America and sent it off to my best friend with nothing but a question mark. When I'd first visited the paint section four hours ago, I was set on a shade in the classic denim range, but instead, I'd come out more confused than ever, holding sample quarts in aqua, cobalt, and navy.

My phone dinged with Jenna's response.

No, this is not a movie theater. It's a nursery. That paint is WAY too dark.

Sigh. You know when you go into a perfume store and the sales people bring you a bowl of coffee beans to sniff before you try out another scent? I think I need coffee beans for my eyes.

It's called blinking. And I'm sure you have at least one color swatch on that wall that will work.

HELP!

How about the one second to the left. What's that called? Also, how does a New Year's Day shower sound? I think it could be totally cute! I just found these darling decorations on Etsy. Look.

A pic of blue and silver plates, banners, and giant confetti balloons downloaded to my screen.

New Year's? I can't imagine people wanting to spend their holiday that way. Second one is called Cadet Blue. I'll paint more of it and send you another pic to confirm.

LAUREN, seriously? People want to be a part of this with you! Yes, send pic after you paint more.

I laughed and set the phone down so I could grab a fresh foam brush from my supply bag, then poured the correct paint into the disposable tray. One could never have too many throw-away brushes or plastic paint trays, in my opinion. Because if there was a worse job than cleaning paint supplies, I didn't know what it was.

Once the brush was sufficiently drenched in paint, I swiped it across the wall. My phone dinged again. And again. Jenna's harassment would have to wait until I finished forming this sadly misshapen rectangle. I quickly reconfigured it into a heart. There. That was better—much happier, the way a nursery should be. Lifting my brush away from the wall, I took a step back and reevaluated the color. It was definitely growing on me. Cadet might just be the one.

Hastily, I snapped another pic while trying not to drench my screen in latex paint. With a tap-swipe-tap of my knuckle, I clicked on the picture and selected Jenna's contact, asking her if this one could work as a nursery color.

Gingerly, I tucked the phone back into the waistband of my work sweats—yes, that's a real thing—and prepared to tape off the large window that overlooked the snow-capped mountain range. It was this view that had inspired me to buy this place years ago, back before any housing inflation and when the banks only required a minimal down payment. It wasn't large by any means: just a townhouse with two standard bedrooms, two full baths, and one sufficient living area on the main floor. But the view . . . goodness, I loved it. Just over a year ago, sitting at my desk, right under this window, I'd submitted my adoption application to Small Wonders. And soon enough, these same magnanimous mountains would watch over my sweet Noah as he slept.

A text alert snapped my attention away from the scenery and back to my phone. I pulled it out and nearly dropped it into an open paint can.

> Can't say I'm known for my decor advice, but
> I'm rooting that Noah will love it.

My entire body prickled with goose bumps as I swiped up on my screen, trying to make sense of why Joshua was replying to a text I'd sent to—*oh.* I'd sent him the picture, not Jenna. How had I never noticed they were neighbors in my contact list?

Heat crept up my neck, radiating from my cheeks and ears.

What do I even say to him? Sorry, I'm an idiot? Sorry, I just sent you a picture of my future nursery? Sorry that my subconscious mind doesn't quite understand the new rules of engagement between us?

Another text chimed.

If you're freaking out that you accidentally texted me a picture of your wall . . . don't. I've been trying to find a reason to text you for days. So can I?

I bit my bottom lip, letting the soggy paintbrush slip back into the pan, drowning a slow death of thick blue paint.

Can you what?

Text you.

The soft sound that escaped me was almost a laugh, yet like all things Joshua, the unexpected message had tugged a little too close to my heart to be met with any kind of flippancy. Because there was nothing flippant about whatever we'd become to each other in such a short period of time.

Yes, of course.

Hi.

Hi.

I slid down the wall opposite my Cadet Blue handiwork and held my breath as I waited for Joshua's thinking dots to materialize into words. I was certain that whatever he was typing deserved my undivided attention. It had been nearly a week since we'd spoken, nearly a week since those heartbreaking eyes of his had arrested my ability to breathe.

After I told him what was really going on, I'd half expected him to ignore me, to withdraw the way . . . well, the way other men in my life had withdrawn when disappointment knocked. But Joshua hadn't dismissed me. In fact, yesterday I'd been almost certain he was waiting around to say something to me after the all-staff meeting, but then I got caught in a discussion with Mrs. Pendleton, and the next thing I knew he was gone.

And maybe that was the most noticeable change between us. Though Joshua still smiled at me in the hallways and had even winked at me from across the lunchroom two days ago while we directed kids to the correct food lines, there was an unspoken tension between us now that I simply didn't know how to navigate.

I'd witnessed Joshua's ability to create common ground in a dozen different social situations. He never lacked for conversation and was well versed in how to put the other party at ease. It was his gift.

In only a matter of a few weeks, he'd shifted the equilibrium in our entire school. And yet, between us, the familiar rhythm we'd once found now felt disjointed. Achingly so. The truth was, I simply didn't know how to be uncomfortable with Joshua.

> I need to apologize. And before you tell me not to, please hear me out. Deal?

I skimmed my index finger over his text box before typing a single *okay* in reply.

> I haven't known what to say since you told me. It's not often I'm at a loss for words, either. 😊 But while your news came as a surprise, I need you to know I'm happy for you. Noah couldn't ask for a better mother.

Despite my resolution to stop tearing up every time somebody mentioned my son's name, there was no chance I could blink the moisture away now. I typed four different responses, all working to embody what his support meant to me. But it proved an impossible task. *Thank you* was my reply, and I hoped it would be enough.

Jenna texted again, asking if I wanted baby shower games or if I'd rather have something more sophisticated like champagne and appetizers. I dismissed her questions for now, focusing all my energy on Joshua's incoming message.

My last day at Brighton will be December 20th.

In theory I knew this, yet disappointment flooded me to see it typed out in stark reality. I knew he couldn't remain there forever, but my heart grieved for his absence just the same. How could one man have made such an impact on so many people in such a short time?

Brighton will miss you.

I sent it before I could edit the most obvious omission in the world—that I would miss him, too.

And I'll miss Brighton.

Can I ask you something?

My stomach clenched tight, anticipating the next ding.

I'm not exactly sure how to phrase this, since this is brand-new territory for me, but if there's ever anything I can do to help in bringing Noah home, would you tell me? Please?

The question pushed into my diaphragm, cutting off my air supply as I held in a sob. Sending in my Letter of Intent for Noah had made me the weepiest person on the planet.

Yes, I will. And thank you. That means so much to me.

More than I could even express. God had given me Gail and Robert, and Jenna and Brian, and though my heart knew that keeping Joshua in my life at any capacity was a risk, kindness was a commodity I couldn't easily turn away. I didn't know when—*or if*—my family would choose to be involved in Noah's life, so support mattered now more than ever. Of the many stories I'd heard in the Cartwrights' weekly adoption meetings, the topic almost always circled back to strong support systems.

Bottom line—the adoption families with an invested community of friends and family struggled far less than the families who went at it alone. I may be single, but I had no desire to be an island. Not after I'd heard what Melanie and her husband had been going through—were still going through, from what Gail had told me. No, I wouldn't turn down help. Especially not from a man like Joshua Avery.

I know things have to be different now, but I hope you know I'm still your friend.

Are you trying to make me cry? Because if so, you're doing a really good job.

Sorry. 🤪 Oh, before I forget, I left something for you in your mailbox in the office.

Okay, thanks. I always forget to check that box.

I tapped the toe of my Converse on the carpet. Five, ten, twenty times. And then I asked.

Would you like to see his picture?

Is that a trick question?

Less than thirty seconds later, I sent him every photo I had of my precious boy across the world.

Anxiety clutched at my insides as I waited for his response.

He's perfect.

☺ I think so, too.

Also, the blue you picked for his wall is definitely the right choice.

I laughed this time, for real, ease and comfort slowly inflating the space between our communication once again.

You think so?

Yeah, look at his pic again. I can practically hear him saying, "I prefer Cadet Blue to all others."

Ha. Yes, silly me. I've been agonizing over it for hours, but all along the answer was right there. In his eyes.

They are the window to the soul. Or at least, that's what I've read. Send me a picture when it's all finished, okay?

I will.

One last thing.

I doubt that.

I suddenly felt elated by this new equilibrium we seemed to have found tonight.

Why is there a computer desk in his nursery? He seems a little young to be gaming. But then again . . .

This room used to be my office. I'll move it down the hall at some point.

When I had a friend here to help me, is what I didn't add, but Joshua filled in the gap anyway.

Let me know when you need it out of there, and I'll move it for you.

Thanks, that'd be awesome. I'll let you know.

I'm counting on that.

I stared at his last text, and for only an instant, I allowed myself to imagine what life would have been like if I'd met Joshua two years from now. Noah, of course, would be running—possibly streaking—through the house like a toddler with something to prove, and I'd be . . . well, I'd be somewhat of an expert on middle-of-the-night diaper changes and a master at hiding peas and spinach in every finger food possible. And Joshua would be . . . Joshua would be himself. And then upon meeting my little family of two, he'd fall desperately in love with us both, putting all the warnings about the stresses of insta-families to shame because love would be enough to fill every need and hole.

A ridiculous fantasy that would never—*could never*—be a reality.

Joshua would be my friend, for however long it made sense, and maybe someday far down the road, he'd become Noah's friend, too. And that would be a gift I'd never take for granted.

chapter seventeen

The second Sunday in December was Baking Day at the Cartwright house, an event I'd been participating in since Benny's first Christmas season at home. Each year after attending the early service at church, we'd dedicate an entire afternoon to baking holiday treats for different organizations and foster/adoption families in our community. Trading in a week's worth of paint fumes for the delectable aroma of Gail's homemade gingerbread had been a major upgrade to my routine.

With a holiday basket filled with a variety of yummy treats on my lap, I navigated us to Melanie and Peter Garrett's house for a special delivery from the front seat of Gail's van. Though there were piles of treats back in Gail's kitchen waiting to be packaged for delivery, she'd heard the Garretts were leaving on an emergency road trip later this evening with their two children, and she didn't want to miss a chance to bless them, even in the smallest of ways.

I'd muted Siri's voice on my phone's map and simply gave directions as needed so we could still have a conversation without the constant interruption of a robot. "Once we get off Thirty-Second Street, you'll take a right on Spruce and then a left at Black Briar Estates."

“Got it. Thanks,” she said, setting her cruise control on the two-lane highway. “I just love seeing all the lights and holiday decorations up, don’t you?”

“Absolutely.” Everything about this year’s holiday season felt more intense somehow, like each of my five senses had heightened to a new level. The pine trees were more fragrant, the twinkle lights glowed brighter, and everything from melt-in-your-mouth sugar cookies to my late-night hot cocoa ritual, while finishing the trim in Noah’s nursery, tasted richer than I’d remembered in years past.

Thankfully, my to-do list in the nursery was nearing the finish line. Joshua had agreed to move the clunky work desk out of the room tomorrow after school, and I couldn’t be more grateful for his help. Things weren’t completely back to normal yet with him, but there had been a concerted effort on both our parts to funnel whatever romantic feelings had developed between us into Noah-oriented feelings. My son had become the subject of approximately ninety percent of our communication—a safe, platonic topic for us to discuss at school or via text threads in the evenings. And Joshua had no shortage of questions, either. *How did you decide on international adoption? What made you choose China? Have you always wanted to adopt? What are you most excited for? What are your fears?*

Our discussions had been lengthy at times, ending well after Cinderella’s curfew, but his questions never failed to make me dig deep. For a man like Joshua, a man who’d grown up with a church family and with parents much like the Cartwrights, these kinds of exchanges came easily to him. But in many ways, when I spoke on matters of faith, I felt like a child playing dress-up in a closet made for mature believers only. Though Joshua was always quick to swap my timidity out for truth.

As Gail turned onto Spruce, my insides fluttered with nerves. I hadn’t seen the Garretts since their first night at group, though I’d wondered about them often.

"How are they doing—Melanie and Peter?"

Gail's pitying smile was answer enough. "A little better. They say they're committed to staying in the group, though, and they've recently started working with an attachment therapist. Our hope is that with time they might let us help." She flicked on her left blinker. "People have to want to be helped. And while I'm proud of them for taking the first steps, there's a long path ahead of them. True attachment is rarely easy or convenient. It can be exhausting work, but it's also the most rewarding work I've ever done."

"Did *you* struggle with attachment?"

Gail's laugh was light, kind even. "Yes. Every one of our children required something a little different when it came to bonding with us as parents. Even the babies. Some of our kids needed a more hands-on approach, and some needed a bit more space to process, but all of them needed to be shown we were trustworthy. That we would meet their needs. That we were theirs forever."

Forever. The word rang bright in my ears. I'd done a lot of research on attachment, even taken some online classes by the renowned Trust-Based Parenting Institute of Texas. But hearing it from Gail was far more impactful. She'd told me stories of the early days, of course, but the difficult days she spoke of seemed light-years away from the family she had now. I tucked that nugget of wisdom in my heart and studied the newer subdivision of single-family homes in Black Briar Estates, searching for the Garretts' address.

"They're just up there on the left. Three-nine-one."

Gail parked in their driveway, and in a matter of moments, we were ringing their doorbell, both our faces holding an extra dollop of holiday cheer as the door swung open to reveal a worn-looking Melanie with a chubby, near-naked toddler on her hip.

"Oh . . . um, hello." Melanie took us in with equal parts shock and surprise.

"Merry Christmas!" we replied in unison.

Gail stepped forward. "Lauren and I made you some special treats to take on your road trip."

"You'll love Gail's gingerbread—it's everybody's favorite," I added. "And the peanut butter balls are better than any you could buy at a bakery."

"Uh . . . thank you?" Melanie took the outstretched basket and gave the now-whining toddler a bounce on her hip. Another nearly naked child raced through the house in the background while Peter's voice rang out from somewhere out of sight for them to come and get in the bathtub.

Immediately a tiny voice yelled back, "But I hate taking baths!"

Melanie closed her eyes, her cheeks flushing as she breathed slowly through her nose. "Sorry, it takes both of us to do bath time with these two. But I'll let Peter know you stopped by. We . . . we really appreciate this. Peter's grandpa is in hospice, and we're hoping we can say good-bye before he passes. . . . He's over in Missoula. I've been trying to pack up, but as you can see . . ."

"Lauren and I would love to help you get ready, Melanie," Gail interjected in a most unlike-Gail tone as she peered around Melanie's slight figure and pointed to the leather sofa overburdened with three full laundry baskets. "Why don't you and Peter tackle bath time with the kids, and we will tackle your clean laundry so it will be easier for you to pack up."

I worked to rein in my surprise at Gail's assertive suggestion, then quickly nodded my head in agreement. "Absolutely. You won't even notice we're here. We are certified laundry ninjas."

"Oh no, that's—I could never ask anybody to—"

"*Mel?* Do you have Aubrey out there? I could really use a hand!"

"It sounds like Peter needs you," Gail prodded in that therapist-like way of hers. "You wouldn't have to worry about us at all. We'll be quick and quiet, and we can leave as soon as we're finished folding. It would certainly make your packing easier." She smiled, paused. "Just say the word and we'll get started."

I wondered if Melanie was aware of the test she'd just been given by Gail. Her answer determined so many things about their future . . . and yet, we couldn't force the help on her. She had to choose it. To want it.

A brisk wind blew past us, causing Aubrey to wail.

Melanie rubbed the sweet girl's plump leg, her moment of indecisiveness suddenly cleared. "Okay," she said. "Yes, but I don't understand why you'd even want to do this for us."

"It's simple," Gail said, taking a step inside the modern home and wrapping her arms around Melanie and the baby. "Because folding your laundry is how we can love you best today."

Later, after leaving the Garretts' house on a cloud of euphoria, we returned to Gail's kitchen to assemble another dozen or so baskets. I couldn't wait to bless other families. Melanie was shocked when she'd come out of the bathroom to find piles of folded clothing sorted by age group and ready to be tucked inside a suitcase. Her once-hardened exterior had begun to crack . . . and all it had taken was a few extra minutes on our part and a willingness to meet a need.

Kindness wasn't overrated.

I stretched my back from side to side as Benny and his older sister fought over whose turn it was to find a new holiday playlist on my phone for our last few basket assembles.

"Miss B, can you tell Allie it's *my* turn now?"

"No way. I only got to choose two songs so far because you played the entire *Avengers* soundtrack—which isn't even Christmas music!"

"Kids," Gail practically sang. "If we can't figure it out without fighting, then I'll gladly choose the next songs. There's a new hymns instrumental album I've been waiting to hear for some time."

Both children groaned, and I took that moment to head to the restroom.

The hallway bathroom had a beach theme to it—handpicked seashells and dried starfish resting on the shelf above the toilet. A sand bucket filled with fresh washcloths and a framed picture of a young Benny and Allie building a sandcastle sat on the counter near the faucet. Benny's cheeky expression, like his personality, was big and bright. Would Noah's be like that, too? Or would he be more reserved like Allie?

I turned on the tap, washing the chocolate down the drain and taking in the hot mess that now adorned my apron.

A knock sounded on the bathroom door. Benny. "Miss Lauren, you had a call on your phone. Actually, two calls."

"Oh, okay. Thanks, bud." I quickly patted my hands dry on the towel hanging by the mirror, then cracked open the door to take the phone from my favorite twelve-year-old.

I expected to see Jenna's name on the missed call list since she was likely still out bargain shopping with her mother. Between the two of them, they'd already purchased a complete wardrobe for Noah, including shoes and clip-on ties.

But it wasn't Jenna's name in the notification box. It was Small Wonders adoption agency.

I tapped on the voicemail, trying to fight the building anxiety over why they'd be calling me on a Sunday afternoon. Were they even open on the weekends? I didn't think so.

I closed the bathroom door to block the Jonas Brothers' rendition of "White Christmas" and cupped the phone to my ear to listen to the message.

"Hi, Lauren, this is Stacey at Small Wonders. I'm sorry to call you on a Sunday, but I just heard from our office staff in China and, well, I need you to call me back as soon as possible. Call me on my personal cell. It's . . ."

I repeated the number out loud and immediately dialed, telling myself all the while that everything was fine. Nothing to worry about. It was probably just regarding the next stage in the paperwork process. Visa applications could be tricky.

But the instant Stacey answered and spoke my name, all my positive thinking died.

From somewhere outside my body, I heard it. A rhythmic knocking. A doorknob jiggling. A voice calling.

"Lauren, is everything okay?"

Gail's muffled words waned in and out of focus like a child playing with the volume on a TV remote. Up and down. In and out. On and off.

"Lauren . . . sweetie, can you let me in? Tell me what's happened."

A part of me wished I could answer her, wished I could reach up, unlock the door, and let her inside this small space with me.

But I couldn't do that. Because if I did, it would all be real.

And it couldn't be real.

Please, God, don't let it be real.

Another twist of the doorknob, another light knocking sound, and then several hushed voices seeped beneath the hollow door.

"Is Miss Lauren all right, Mom?"

A pause.

"I don't think so, honey. Why don't you and your sister go put a movie on in the family room, okay?"

Two metal clicks of a turning lock later, and Gail was inside the bathroom, closing the door behind her and settling down beside me on the ocean-blue rug. Or maybe it was Cadet Blue?

"I have a key," she said. "As a mom of a herd of teenagers, it's essential."

I managed to nod as disjointed thoughts clogged the space between my ears. I stared at the hand still clutching the phone, wondering when my fingers had stopped tingling. They'd gone numb.

Like my heart.

Like me.

Gail remained silent for so long that when she finally did speak, her voice sounded too loud for such a tiny space. Too nice for the nightmare closing in on every side.

"What did they say, Lauren?"

I shook my head. How could I ever say it?

She wrapped an arm around my shoulders, pulling me close, asking again. My body remained stiff and unyielding. I didn't want to be hugged. I didn't want to be anything. Anywhere.

"Did something happen to Noah?"

Reflex had me squeezing my eyes shut as nausea churned in my belly. The overpowering scent of gingerbread and freshly whipped frosting made me want to retch, to strip myself of everything sweet and good and right.

Because that's exactly what has been done to me.

"He's not . . . he's not mine." The words tasted metallic.

"What? No." Gail's shocked reply was more than I'd been able to articulate to Stacey. More than I'd been able to comprehend. "That's not—no. How can that be?"

"A glitch. In China's orphan assigning system. He was matched with a different family before I was . . . in Connecticut. He's not mine."

He's not mine. Noah's not mine.

"Oh, Lauren." As if I weighed nothing, she pulled my head against her chest and let her tears wet my cheeks while my own eyes remained dry.

For the first time since being matched to Noah, I had no tears left to cry.

I had nothing left at all.

Not even the title of *mother*.

chapter eighteen

Monday, December 9. 7:45 a.m. Text from Jenna.

Hey, the office said you're getting a sub today. Are you sick?

Monday, December 9. 10:04 a.m.

Lauren, I'm getting worried that I haven't heard from you. Is it the flu? I hope you're not texting back because you're sound asleep. Let me know when you wake up.

Monday, December 9. 11:37 a.m. Text from Joshua.

Sure, sleep the day away so you don't have to deal with the lunch line. I see how it is. J/K. Jenna says you have the flu? Guess we should reschedule the desk moving this afternoon? Unless you need some chicken noodle soup? Ben and Jerry's? Whiskey?

Monday, December 9. 1:21 p.m. Text from Jenna.

I'm officially freaked out. I checked with the office again and they said you aren't coming in tomorrow either. What's going on, Lauren??? I'm headed to your house the minute school is out.

Monday, December 9. 2:06 p.m.

I just spoke with Gail. Oh Lauren . . . I don't even know what to say. Can I come over? What can I do?

Monday, December 9. 2:08 p.m.

I'm not ready to see anyone yet. Soon though.

Monday, December 9. 2:08 p.m.

Okay. I love you, Lauren. Whatever you need . . . I'm here for you. Always.

Monday, December 9. 2:10 p.m.

I know. <3

Tuesday, December 10. 7:55 a.m. Text from Joshua.

I popped in to your classroom to say good morning to you . . . but unless you've aged about thirty years, started wearing bifocals, and changed your ethnicity to Hispanic, it probably wasn't you. Sorry you're still feeling lousy. I'll live text all today's big happenings. Wouldn't want you to miss out on a riveting day at Brighton.

Tuesday, December 10. 9:29 a.m.

> Scarlet Peters just asked if I'm old enough to remember a time before cell phones. I assured her that I am, indeed, a survivor of the dreaded BT (before technology) era. I'm fairly sure she—and the rest of her classmates—think that screen time was invented with electricity. Godspeed, history teachers of America!

Tuesday, December 10. 11:15 a.m.

> STEM time. Donovan just chucked a hundreds block at Mason R's back. That kid needs to try out for the majors. Willing to take a 60/40 cut for scouting him. Fine, I'll do 70/30. Final offer.

Tuesday, December 10. 12:59 p.m. Link to a video of class singing "We Wish You a Merry Christmas."

> Sorry, but it's the only song they know all the words to from music class. Hope it cheered you up.

Tuesday, December 10. 2:34 p.m. Text from Jenna.

> Can't stop thinking about you. I'm so, so sorry.

Tuesday, December 10. 2:39 p.m. Text from Joshua.

> Less than thirty minutes to go and Violet tosses her cookies all over Mason R's backpack. It's not that kid's day. Probably should let him pick from your magical prize bag. If I don't hear back from you in two minutes, I'll consider that consent.

Tuesday, December 10. 2:55 p.m.

> Will you grace us with your presence

tomorrow? Crossing my fingers you say yes. Not sure I can hold down the fort without you much longer.

I powered off my phone, clutched it to my chest, and tried to pretend the world was as simple as Joshua had made it out to be.

chapter nineteen

As a young girl, I remembered questioning my dad about the four bedridden grandparents in the original *Charlie and the Chocolate Factory* movie. My youthful body and active mind couldn't grasp the concept of living in bed, eating nothing but boiled cabbage, and wearing only threadbare nightgowns—not to mention staring at the same three faces all day long. Like usual, I'd asked far more questions than my father was willing to construct answers for. An ironic exchange, considering only a few years later, he would choose a similar path after his fall.

But unlike my father, I refused to give up on life the way he had.

With shaky arms, I shoved the hundred-pound comforter off my weary body and found my footing on the icy floor below. As cold seeped into my bones, I repeated the mantra I'd been saying to myself since deciding to go in to work tomorrow morning. "Just one day at a time."

Gail had advised me—numerous times—to use my three personal days and two of my stored-up sick days and take the week off. But I couldn't do that to my students. They didn't deserve a bedridden-by-choice teacher. They deserved the Miss Bailey before the call. The naïve first-grade teacher ignorant of soul-crushing computer glitches that stole children from the hearts of the mothers who loved them.

I'd give anything to be her again.

And yet, even as I thought it, shame descended over me like a storm cloud. Wishing I could be her again meant never having laid eyes on Noah's sweet face. Never knowing the hope of motherhood to come. *Is that really what I want?*

Too afraid to wait for the answer, I headed for the shower and tried to will energy into my body. I needed to see what condition today's sub had left my classroom in and read through any notes before I showed up to school tomorrow morning.

I'd never been a fan of coming to Brighton at night. It was too dark, too cold, too empty without the children who gave it purpose. Though I'd only been absent from this place for two school days, I felt like a foreigner visiting an unknown land the moment I entered the shadowy lobby and switched on the main lights.

At least there was nobody here to give me an awkward hope-you're-feeling-better pat on the shoulder—or worse, a probing stare while asking about the symptoms of my rumored flu bug. I knew Mrs. Pendleton and Jenna would never break my confidence about the truth of my absence to the staff, but even still, I simply didn't have the energy to answer twenty questions about body chills and fevers or be told which homeopathic tincture I should take the next time a virus tried to take me down. All I wanted—*needed*—was time in my classroom with my kids so I could forget everything having to do with babies. Or adoption. Or shattered future dreams.

Tomorrow morning couldn't come soon enough.

I shoved my key into the glass office door and sailed past the secretary's desk. It was a blessing not to have to stop for chitchat with Diana about all the social happenings at Brighton before I could gather the sub's notes from my mailbox. But as I rounded the corner to the mail station wall, my eyes wouldn't believe the sight in front of them. My box, the second from the left on the top row, was stuffed to overflowing. I grabbed an empty box from the stack near the copy machine and began scooping get-well-soon cards, letters, and drawings—so many precious drawings—into it. Unfolding one such piece of art, my chest knocked twice at the smiley-face balloons colored across the page with the words *Feel Better!* scrawled along the bottom in red crayon.

Still in search of the sub notes, I spotted a small blue gift bag smashed in the back of the four-by-ten rectangle. I tugged it out, a mixture of dread and anticipation causing my fingers to trip over themselves as I freed the package and pried it open. With a single peek under the tissue paper, my heart lurched to a stop.

A plush blue-and-green T-Rex stared up at me with big oval eyes.

I pinched the red tag around his neck to read the words penned there.

How could I resist?
—Joshua

Joshua bought Noah a present. I clutched the dinosaur to my chest as tears climbed my throat, creating the first fracture in my carefully constructed dam of denial. Days of bottled-up emotion now threatened the integrity of a structure that only a few minutes before had felt solid and secure.

A single tear trailed the length of my cheek and dripped off my chin. And then another rolled down after it.

Stop it. Don't do this here. Not now.

But my chastisement was immediately combated with the recycling of Gail's compassionate rebuke. "*You need time to grieve, Lauren. Your heart grew attached to a little boy it believed would become your son . . . and now it needs time to let that same little boy go. Be gentle with yourself.*"

Only, I didn't want to be gentle with myself.

I wanted to be a mother. I wanted Noah.

And right now . . . I desperately wanted to sleep.

In less than ten minutes, I scribbled out a new lesson plan for tomorrow's sub, left a message on the school district's sub line, attached a note for Diana, and hoofed it out of the office.

Back to the parking lot.

Back to my townhouse.

Back to my bed.

As it turned out, I'd been unfair to criticize Charlie's relatives. Because sometimes going back to bed was the only option a broken heart could handle.

chapter twenty

The doorbell might be the worst invention of its century. Why anyone would devise something so profoundly irritating, I couldn't possibly understand. Nor could I understand the people who buzzed it like they were seeking asylum from a zombie attack.

Skye barked relentlessly at the sound. "Hush, Skye. They'll go away." I rolled over, my face brushing against Joshua's stuffed T-Rex as I pulled the blankets over my ears, my eyes, my broken heart.

The doorbell continued.

So did Skye.

My phone pinged a text alert.

I slashed an arm out from under my cave of covers and ripped the device off my nightstand. It was Jenna.

Not leaving till you open the door.

Pretending to sleep was so much easier than trying to hold a conversation—text or otherwise—but the doorbell had now taken on a melody. Was that . . . "Stayin' Alive"?

I'm serious. Not leaving.

Ugh. The second my socked feet touched the floor, Skye was up off her bed and darting past me on my hike down the stairs to the front door. I hastily punched my arms through a worn-out cardigan hanging on my banister, unlocked the deadbolt, and opened the door to reveal my best friend . . . and Joshua? A pang of guilt resounded in my hollowed heart at the sight of them bundled to their chins as if they'd planned to do a winter sit-in if necessary. And apparently they'd each come bearing gifts. Jenna: a bucket of cleaning supplies. Joshua: two armloads of groceries.

Before I could register what was happening, Jenna hurled herself into my unyielding body. Her arms tightened around my waist as her wool-mittened hands caused a fire-starting friction on my upper back.

"What are you two doing here?" The sleepy rasp of my voice betrayed my silent alibi, and alarm sparked in Jenna's eyes as she pulled back to assess me.

"Were you just . . . sleeping?" For the first time, she seemed to take in my rumpled appearance, assessing the state of my hair far too long to be considered complimentary. I touched my ponytail, willing my flyaways to tuck themselves back into my hairband and go along with the charade that I'd only been reading. With my eyes closed. Since about noon.

"Think I'm gonna go with a yes on that one," Joshua said, without a hint of judgment. "Mind if I bring these bags inside for you?" He made a move toward the door, and Skye gave a warning bark, still standing guard at my side as she waited for a command I wasn't sure I would give.

Joshua knelt and set the bags down beside him on the porch. He offered his hand for Skye to sniff, saying her name and sweet-talking her as if they'd been great friends in a past life. After only a second of hesitation, she went to him, rubbing her nose against his open palm.

Traitor.

"My house isn't exactly company-ready." Understatement.

Jenna raised her bucket-o-clean as the mop handle drooped to one side. "Figured you'd say that, which is why I came prepared. I'm gonna clean and Joshua's gonna cook."

"What? No. That's not . . . that's not necessary."

Joshua patted Skye's head, then hefted the bulging bags to his chest once again. "If you want to get technical about what's *unnecessary*, then I think you should probably evaluate all the cold air you're letting into your warm house by continuing this conversation with us on your front porch." He inclined his head toward Jenna. "Besides, it's like she said. We're not going anywhere."

"Come on, Lauren. Just let us inside. We want to help. *Please*," Jenna begged, stomping her fur-lined boots on my welcome mat.

Defeated and chilled, I double-tapped my outer thigh to signal Skye to move aside so they could pass. She obeyed.

"Thank you." Jenna kissed my cheek on her way in, keeping any comments about the way I'd let my house go these last few days to herself. She climbed my stairs, dictating where Joshua could set the groceries down in my kitchen. "And don't forget to put the milk products in the fridge," she bossed. As if I weren't standing there at all. As if I were caught in a Dickens drama, playing the part of the Ghost of Christmas Past while I observed the interactions of a life that no longer felt like mine.

I waited for the mortification of such an untimely visit to sink in, for a reminder of why I should be rushing to assist them with their self-assigned pity tasks. Shouldn't I be scrambling to take out the trash or unloading the dishes that had been trapped inside the dishwasher since Sunday? Because strangely enough, I simply couldn't dredge up enough energy to feel anything but tired.

So, so tired.

My body craved the solace of my down comforter and the peace of my bedroom.

". . . pantry or cupboard?"

I blinked to refocus. "What?"

Concern edged Joshua's gaze as his eyes found mine. He held up a box of Raisin Bran. "Cereal. Where do you keep it?"

"Oh, um . . . the tall cupboard. To the left of the fridge."

"Great."

Another few cabinets banged open and closed, taunting me to move. To do *something*. But not even the fact that Joshua Avery himself was standing in the middle of my unclean kitchen, becoming far too acquainted with my half-eaten take-out containers and unwashed dishes, could make me do anything but slump onto my sofa and wait for it all to be over.

Minutes later, he strode back into my living room and sat on the coffee table directly across from me. Our knees bumped and my gaze trailed the length of his dark-wash jeans. They were a good fit for him. The tailored hem brushed the top of his canvas shoes. Not too short. Not too long. But just right. Like him.

"Hey," he said, softly. Invitingly. "We missed you today. At school."

My focus remained on his perfectly shaped kneecaps.

"I heard you came in to the office last night. Left your sub notes on Diana's desk."

Was that really last night? Why did that feel like a week ago . . . or longer?

"Uh-huh, I did," I answered.

He touched my hand, causing my gaze to lift to his. "I'm sorry I didn't know, Lauren."

I didn't want you to know. I wanted you to stay the same. To be the one person who still sent me ridiculous texts and made me feel like everything could be . . . normal again.

"Who told you?" I asked.

He looked momentarily conflicted. "I don't want you to hold it against her. In truth, I didn't give her much of a choice. I found your address in the staff directory and planned to check on you after school today—with or without an explanation."

It had been Jenna, then.

I nodded. I didn't blame her. I couldn't.

"I've been worried about you," he continued.

I dropped my gaze to the carpet. "I'm okay."

"I think our definitions of that word aren't the same." His light chuckle sobered quickly.

"I thought I was ready to go back today, but I wasn't." I shrugged. "I did bring all the get-well-soon cards home though. Thank you for those. And thank you for . . . the gift. I'm sure Noah would have loved it."

A momentary hesitation was followed by a hard exhale as he raked both hands down his face. "Oh, Lauren. I'm . . . I'm sorry. If I'd known what had happened before today, I would have taken that out of your box and—"

"It's fine. Turns out, stuffed T-Rexes are really good listeners." My attempt at humor failed, but I couldn't handle anybody else feeling sorry for me.

Especially him.

He lifted his hand to the side of my face to brush the stray bedraggled hair off my cheek. He tucked the loose strands behind my ear. "I can be, too."

I closed my eyes and expelled a truth I hadn't yet articulated, not even to Gail. "I don't know if I can do it again."

Bits and pieces of Stacey's phone call had started to come back. Her telling me to take some time to recover, along with a reassurance that I'd be first in line whenever I was ready to be matched again. *If I'd be ready again . . .*

"All you can do is take it one day at a time, Lauren. That's all any of us can do."

I looked up then, staring into his eyes.

His sad smile had me wanting to reach out and tap the corners of his lips, to change his frown into an expression that suited him far better. Because sorrow wasn't a match for him.

Perhaps he was thinking something similar about me as he touched my trembling chin.

"Hey." Joshua's tender voice melted my insides. "You're gonna make it through this."

Was I? Because I wasn't so sure. I squeezed my damp eyes closed and willed my tears away. "I don't want to cry another tear. I'm done crying."

He searched my face for understanding. "Then what do you want?"

"To laugh again." I squared my shoulders and worked to sit up straighter on the slouchy sofa. "Tell me something funny."

"Lauren . . ." My name sounded strained, pain-filled even, but I shook my head to cut off whatever sympathy Concerned Joshua was about to deliver. I didn't want another drawn-out conversation about the stages of grief. I'd had enough of those from Gail. Right now I needed Carefree Joshua.

"Your texts were the only thing I looked forward to over the last few days." I let out a shaky breath. "They made me feel normal again. Like, I don't know, like maybe I don't have to be stuck here forever." In this sadness. In this heartache.

He nodded once and cleared his throat. "So one time, when I was much younger, I wanted to experiment with my mother's traditional strawberry Jell-O salad, so I opened the lid of her Tupperware container and shoved a handful of tiny plastic dinosaurs down through the Cool Whip layer and into the red gelatin. But unfortunately for me, I didn't realize my mom was taking that salad to a big women's event at our church. And unfortunately for her, she didn't notice my, uh, culinary addition until the ladies began commenting on the surprises inside their desserts."

And just like that, my face cracked into my first real smile in days. "Didn't you realize plastic dinosaurs were a choking hazard?"

"I was seven. Easily forgiven for my boyish ways, but I guess even then I had a thing about making my mark on the world. One dinosaur at a time."

"I think you've succeeded."

His smile broadened. "I've been a nerd since the day I was born. Just ask my family."

The comfort I found in his presence made me yearn to soak up every second of it that I could.

"I don't want to interrupt, but Brian's on his way over," Jenna said, coming down the stairs and then finding a place beside me on the sofa.

"He is?" I asked.

"Yep, and he's bringing a hot loaf of French bread and a bottle of red to go with our pasta. Oh, and he's chosen a board game, too. Sorry, we'll be stuck with whatever he's picked out, so tonight could get interesting."

"Uh, you do realize my pasta-making skills are limited to spaghetti, right?" Joshua asked.

Jenna laughed. "Spaghetti's perfect. It's all comfort carbs in the end, anyway. If Lauren's up for it, she makes a killer meat sauce."

Joshua playfully tapped my knee. "What do you say? Wanna be my sous chef for the night?"

I couldn't formulate an appropriately cheeky response. I was too distracted by the thought that my friends were staying. Not for an afternoon, but for an entire evening.

For me.

"Thank you both. For doing this." I rubbed my temples. "Even though I'm such a—"

"A wonderful person who would do the same for either of us?" Jenna cut in. "Can we at least all agree now that your days of shutting us out are over? Because I don't think I can handle going three days without you ever again."

Acutely aware of Joshua's presence across from me, I fixed my attention on Jenna. "Agreed."

"Good. And now that that's settled"—she stood and looked pointedly at Joshua—"do you mind if I get your help moving a certain *something* from a room upstairs?"

He gave a brisk nod as a new kind of pain punched through my chest wall. By the expression on her face, I knew exactly what she was hinting at—the desk in the nursery.

"Leave it," I said. "Let's just leave that room alone for now." *For now, or forever?* That was still to be determined.

"But wouldn't it be better if we just moved it out to the end of the hallway and—"

Joshua studied me as he replied. "I'm sure there'll be plenty of time to make those kinds of decisions later. Let's just leave it be for now."

She looked between us and relented with a sigh. "Sure, okay. Then I'll just bring down the clean towels from the laundry room and put them away in the linen closet."

A compromise I could grant. Folding laundry was one thing, but rearranging the nursery? Not a chance.

Skye pattered up the stairs after her, leaving me alone with Joshua.

"I better go boil some water for the pasta," he said, standing to his full height and giving my shoulder a light squeeze.

"Do you mind if I run upstairs for a minute? I'd like to freshen up a bit before we make dinner."

He winked at me, yet I couldn't help but note how contrary it was to the concern that still edged his gaze. "No problem."

Heart pumping from all the extra exertion, I climbed the stairs two at a time. But before I made a dash for my hairbrush, I reached out and closed the nursery door, banishing my view of the Cadet Blue walls and the half-assembled crib for the foreseeable future.

Spaghetti sauce I could manage, but I wasn't sure when, or if, the door to the nursery would ever be opened again.

chapter twenty-one

People often complain about the busyness that surrounds the Christmas season. Always too much to do and never enough time to accomplish it all. But embracing the chaos had somehow become my latest coping mechanism in life. I'd accepted all the mental distractions provided by classroom parties, crafting sessions, and staff gift exchanges that helped one day bleed right into the next.

And if not for the hours between midnight and six in the morning, I could have easily fooled myself into *being fine*. After all, I'd managed to do that with almost everybody who passed me in the hall or conversed with me in the break room. But, of course, not everybody was fooled by my freshly showered, mascara-wearing self. The J-gang, made up of Jenna and Joshua, hovered worse than a helicopter parent during the first week of kindergarten.

Even now a prickle of awareness breathed down my neck as Joshua's eyes met mine from across the staff lounge. Inches taller than the rest of our male staff, the tips of his hair brushed the green and red streamers hanging above the cake table. Mrs. Pendleton had already given her good-bye, thanks-for-making-our-school-a-better-place speech to Joshua after she provided an update on Mrs. Walker's expected return at the first of the year.

Clapping, cheering, and gluttonous sheet cake consuming had ensued, though I hadn't so much as touched the slice I'd been handed nearly ten minutes ago. The festive sprinkles adorning a thick layer of waxy frosting were just too much. Or maybe it was Joshua leaving Brighton that was the *too much*. I'd known this day was coming—for weeks now. The going-away party had been listed on every office memo and staff calendar since Thanksgiving break. Yet somehow the day had still snuck up on me like a surprise attack in a dark alley.

Joshua held his paper cup filled with punch and saluted the staff for making him feel so welcome. He complimented the school as a whole, throwing in a few well-placed jokes, as well as an announcement that his reading app had just been given full clearance to launch sometime early next spring.

Again, the teachers applauded him. Truly, the man couldn't make an enemy if he tried.

". . . so as great as this good-bye cake tastes," he continued, "I'm afraid you'll be getting a lot more of me at Brighton—just in digital form."

I tried to join in on all the back-patting and lighthearted jokes, but I simply couldn't think of anything funny about Joshua leaving Brighton. Not one single thing. Gaining him in digital form was hardly a consolation prize.

After another few minutes of mingling with the masses, I tossed my uneaten cake into the trash and headed back to my room to close up for the coming holiday break. There would be no point in taking down the handmade snowflakes pressed to the wall of windows overlooking the parking lot, not when an epic storm was predicted to blanket our city in white over the days to come. A few inches had fallen last week, but most had been slushed away by the indecision of December's highs and lows. I could relate.

Not four steps inside my room, I saw them. Two tiny plastic dinosaurs propped on my desk near my coat and purse, as if they'd been waiting on me to return from the party and take them home. Joshua had been leaving these little trinkets around the school for me to find since the day I'd returned, his version of Elf on the Shelf. Sometimes they had a funny joke or quote attached to their necks; other times he left a piece of candy with them or a pack of gum. His hiding places had become a game for my students each morning as they'd found them stuck inside cubbies, coat pockets, library books, and once inside Frog and Toad's aquarium.

But today's miniature dinos weren't actually hiding at all. They were simply out in the open, placed on top of a package, waiting for me.

I slid my fingertip down the long, curved neck of the brontosaurus and over the spiked scales of a green Stegosaurus. A tiny smile slipped through my mask of melancholy as I thought of the hands that had placed them here on his last day at Brighton.

"You found them." There, framed in my doorway and backlit by the fluorescent lights of a hallway he'd never have reason to walk again, was a man who'd come to mean far too much to me in the past six weeks.

"They sure didn't make me work very hard today."

He shrugged. "We figured we'd go easy on you since it is the start of Christmas break, which is basically a holiday in itself."

No teacher in their right mind would argue with that. "True."

He crossed the room and slid the gift closer to me. "Go ahead."

"I'm the one who should be giving you a—"

He shook his head. "This is a guilt-free zone. There are no *should haves* allowed here."

I clamped my mouth shut and reached for the package on my desk. It was obvious by the shape and weight of the gift in my hands what lay beneath the reindeer-printed paper . . . but that made the effort he'd taken to wrap it even more thoughtful.

With two good rips, I uncovered a familiar hardback I'd read cover-to-cover multiple times over the last decade. I'd loaned out my personal copy of George Avery's award-winning textbook *The Art of Teaching Kids to Read* to many a teacher throughout the years. I'd earmarked, highlighted, and underscored my favorite passages from front to back, sharing it at conferences across the Northwest. But the copy in my hands now had an updated cover, all shiny and new, the pages crisp and bright. A gold sticker on the front proclaimed *Revised and Updated Edition!*

Of all of George Avery's published works, this one had always been my favorite.

"Joshua . . . thank you. I—"

"Open it," Joshua prompted.

I shot him a quizzical look, then lifted the cover to reveal an inscription. I sucked in a breath.

Lauren,

My favorite son (adjective added only because said son is hovering close by) has asked me to sign a copy of this newly revised copy to a friend he insists, "makes a difference every day." I have less guilt retiring from the classroom knowing there are teachers like you in our world. May God bless you for your sacrifice and love.

Please stop in for a cup of cocoa. I make the best in the Northwest . . . or at least, the best in my house.

George Avery

I continued to stare at the words printed there, failing to come up with any adequate ones of my own. George Avery had signed a book to me.

Because of Joshua.

"You're happy, right?" His worrisome question broke my trance. "I should have clarified that this was also a cry-free zone."

I shook my head, refusing the exit of my happy tears, and hugged the book to my chest. "Yes, I'm happy. Thank you so much for this."

Reassured, his smile brightened. "He means it, you know. The invitation for cocoa. It's basically a summons."

"Oh, gosh . . ." A nervous laugh bubbled up my throat. "I can't imagine actually doing that."

"Well, I can, because we also want you to come for Christmas."

The book slipped down to my abdomen as my glance snapped up to his. "*What?*"

"Christmas. You know, it's that little holiday sandwiched between Thanksgiving and New Year's. And don't try to tell me you can't come, because Jenna already told me about your promise. And to be honest, I'm a little scared of what she'll do to me if I don't follow through on my end."

I sighed. *Jenna.*

Jenna had called last night as she was packing for the trip she and Brian were bound for right after school let out. Ten whole days she'd be away, skiing with her in-laws in Tahoe—a trip she was now considering canceling because of me. It was the first time in our friendship I'd been legitimately angry at her selflessness. But missing a holiday vacation because I was a little more Eeyore than I was Buddy the Elf was absolutely unacceptable.

"I'm not getting on that plane tomorrow if you tell me you're just gonna stay home, Lauren. Why won't you accept Gail's invitation for Christmas dinner? You've always split the day between the Cartwrights and your family."

It wasn't the first time she'd asked that question. And she

wasn't wrong; I had been following that schedule for years. But I just couldn't do it this Christmas. I wasn't ready to be back in Gail's house or to smell the fresh loaf of gingerbread she would make on Christmas morning. I simply couldn't trust myself not to fall apart at the familiar scent or worse, at the sight of Benny. I might be able to suppress the memory of the awful phone call I'd taken in their bathroom while I was at home or in my classroom, but not even my best distraction tactics could keep it from my mind while back in the Cartwrights' home. And I refused to ruin anybody's Christmas.

"I just can't," I nearly whispered into my phone. "Trust me."

"Then what about going to your sister's house or stopping in at your parents'? I know they're not the best company to be around right now, but . . ."

"Believe me, being home alone on Christmas is a better alternative than being at either of their houses." I'd planned to drop off gifts for the kids, but there'd been no apology for what my mother had said to me regarding my decision to adopt. We hadn't spoken in nearly a month. And Lisa's texts had been absent of anything having to do with the adoption conversation, as if by not talking about it, I might have changed my mind. How exactly was I supposed to handle them now? What would I even say? *"Oh, actually, never mind about what we discussed in that messy closet. The baby boy I was going to adopt . . . yeah, well, he belongs to someone else now."*

"Okay." Jenna's determined tone alarmed me. "Then it's settled. Brian and I are staying home. We'll do Christmas with you this year."

"No, you will not! I'll be totally fine. I'm not a depressed teenager. I'm an adult. I don't need a babysitter."

"Lauren."

"What do you need me to say to convince you, Jenna?"

"Say you won't be alone." Her voice snagged on the last word, and I could picture the tears flooding her fiery eyes. "You can't expect me to go off and have a good time knowing you're here alone, trying to heal from a broken heart."

I sighed into the phone, searching for a compromise we could both live with.

"Okay," I said quietly. "I'll find somewhere to go on Christmas Day."

"You promise?" She sniffed.

I hesitated, racking my brain for how to go about keeping such a promise. "Yes, I promise."

"Lauren?" Joshua asked, pulling my mind back to the present. "Spend Christmas with me. Please."

I glanced out the window nearest my desk. "You don't have to invite me to your family's Christmas, Joshua. Jenna really shouldn't have said anything to you. I'll be fine. I have options."

"I'm sure you do, but I hope you'll choose this one. My family will be honored to have you join us—they're counting on it, in fact." He touched my shoulder, the tips of his long fingers grazing the naked skin at the base of my neck. "Plus, the crab legs are out of this world."

"I'm sorry . . . did you just say *crab legs*?"

"Yep. Why?" Panic masked his face. "You're not allergic to shellfish, are you?"

"No . . . but what does any of that have to do with Christmas?"

He smiled. "Quite a bit, actually. But I'm not going to spoil the surprise. You'll just have to experience it for yourself."

He laughed at whatever confused expression stared back at him. "Trust me, as long as you're a fan of crustaceans, you'll love it."

I gave him a slow nod and felt myself caving to the idea of Christmas with the Avery family. "Are you positive I won't be an imposition on your parents?"

"One hundred percent. They'll love you."

I swallowed, trying not to read into such a kind statement. "Okay."

"Great, then I'll pick you up tomorrow. After four."

"Uh, tomorrow is only December twenty-first."

"I know, but I need you to help me shop. I drew Rebekah's name and I'm clueless."

I thought back to our previous conversations involving his family members. "She's your brother's wife?"

"Yep. And if you don't help me she'll end up with a holiday-scented car air freshener and a gift card, and there's a strict no-gift-card policy in the Avery household. Plus, I know for a fact that you haven't purchased anything for your nephews yet. I saw the list on your desk."

I scoffed and crossed my arms over the hardback book on my chest. "And how do you know I haven't already ordered them something off Amazon?"

"Did you?" He arched an eyebrow.

"No, but my point is, I *could* have."

"And *my point* is that after four tomorrow, I'm all yours."

"Um . . ." I laughed, wondering how he'd managed to twist this entire conversation around, as if I'd been the one begging for his gift-giving advice. "I think you mean *I'm* all yours. You're the one who needs the shopping help, remember?"

His smile lit a match in the base of my abdomen. "That works even better."

chapter twenty-two

I'd read about wedding festivities in Asian countries, where the bride and groom partake in a week's worth of detailed events before they exchange vows. Apparently Christmas with the Averys was much the same. The list of holiday activities I was expected to participate in had grown exponentially since accepting Joshua's original invitation. So far he'd mentioned caroling, ice-skating, a candlelight service at his parents' church, and something about seafood. And that was all before Christmas Day.

Joshua slid his gooey cinnamon roll across the table top at the food court. "Time's up. Trade."

"What? But I've only taken one bite of this one—"

"You obviously did not grow up with a brother."

He swapped our plates and took a giant bite of my maple and pecan roll. I frowned and cut the corner off his original deluxe with extra cream cheese frosting. "Nope. Can't say Lisa and I ever fought about food."

He chewed and pointed the end of his fork at me. "So what do sisters fight about, then?"

I rolled my eyes good-naturedly and combed through my memories for a theme. "Hmm . . ."

Joshua switched our plates and immediately stabbed the frosted roll once again.

"Hey!" I tugged the plate back from him. "Was that some kind of diversion tactic?"

He swallowed and laughed. "You're catching on. But I actually am curious."

I held up a finger and took a small bite of the maple variety. It melted on my tongue, and I couldn't help the tiny sound of pleasure that vibrated in my throat.

Amused, he leaned back in his chair, watching me. "That good, huh?"

I nodded and wiped the corner of my mouth with my napkin. "You've got to admit that my pick was way better than yours."

"Happily. The original is always good, but yours is better. Let's hope Rebekah feels the same about your picks for her, too."

"Oh, she will." I'd stalked her social media pages before we shopped at the department stores. It was easy to figure out her fashion likes and dislikes by the pictures she'd posted.

"Whoa . . . such confidence," he teased.

"I can say the same about your little victory dance in the toy store over that robot ball thingy you found for my nephews."

"It's called a Sphero Bolt, Lauren. And they're awesome."

I gave him an exaggerated eye roll. "Please don't go into all the engineering mechanics again. You might as well ask me to translate hieroglyphics."

He chuckled and gestured for me to continue. "Anyway, go on. Your sister fights. What were they about? Stolen clothes and boyfriends?"

"Oh my gosh." I wadded up my napkin and threw it at his chest. "That is such a guy thing to say."

"Well? Then what?"

My cheeks heated as I realized that his guess really was what most of our arguments had been over. "Well . . ."

"Ha! I was right?"

"Stop gloating. You have no idea how annoying it is to go into your closet and have nothing to wear because everything you own is in your sister's dirty hamper."

His laughing continued, and I took the opportunity to have another bite. I wouldn't have to guess where the extra five pounds had come from this holiday season.

"And what about the boyfriend fights?"

"I don't want to talk to you anymore." I fake pouted.

"What if I promise not to laugh?"

"I wouldn't believe you."

"Okay, then what if I promise *to try* not to laugh?"

Giving in to his puppy eyes, I rubbed my lips together and tried to recall the details. "Once there was this neighbor boy who was exactly a year younger than me and a year older than Lisa."

His eyebrows hiked a half inch, but he made a show of saying nothing.

"Anyway, we both liked him, so we both wrote him notes asking which one of us he liked more."

"Really?" Joshua inched the maple roll in his direction once again, never breaking eye contact with me. Sneaky man. "How did he respond?"

"He wrote a note back to each of us, explaining that he preferred the other sister more, only Lisa and I never shared his response with each other, so each of us just went on believing he'd chosen the other sister. We spent an entire summer trying to one-up each other to win over his affection. Only all the while he was secretly going out with Megan Floyd from two blocks over."

"No way!" Joshua smacked the table. "What happened when you finally found out?"

"We burned his letters and then TP'd his house four weekends in a row."

"Ha. Brilliant!"

"We laughed at him from our window as his parents made him clean it up every time. He never did find out it was us." It was a rare moment of sisterly collaboration. If only we had more to collaborate on these days.

"Are you two still close?"

I took a long sip of ice water, deciding how best to answer that. I'd shared bits and pieces with Joshua about my family, about the disconnection that had started around my sixth-grade year and continued on into adulthood. But in many ways, Lisa was in her own boat when it came to the dysfunction of our parents. "I wish we were closer." The truth.

He tipped his head as if waiting for more.

"Lisa has always been a strong-willed, leader-type personality, which can be awesome depending on what—or who—she's trying to lead. But it can also be . . . well, alienating if you don't align with her causes."

"Ah, right. You've mentioned her interesting matchmaking tactics before."

"Those are hardly her worst offenses," I mumbled before drinking some more water.

His next bite stalled midair, and instead of shoving it into his mouth, he lowered it back down to his plate. "Have you talked with her much since . . ." In his prolonged hesitation, I heard his unasked question.

"No." I shook my head. "Nobody in my family knows the adoption fell through yet."

I cringed at my use of the phrase *fell through*. Adoption shouldn't be categorized in the same vein as a failed business transaction.

"Why not?" Joshua had an innocent way of inquiring about the deep, personal stuff without seeming judgmental or critical.

"Because if I tell her what happened, it will only fuel her arguments against me adopting in the future." And lately I had enough doubts of my own to sort through.

"So, she feels the same way your mom does?"

I remembered the text thread Joshua and I shared a few nights before all my hopes had come crashing down, one of our many midnight conversations when my inhibitions had been low and my vulnerability high. It was one thing to discuss my family's negative views on God and the church, but quite another to pinpoint my most painful moments of rejection as a daughter.

"Similar enough, yes." Though Lisa had her own reasons to think I was being reckless and irresponsible.

"Which likely plays into why you don't want to spend Christmas with them." A statement underlined in empathy.

Again, I nodded. "Yeah, but I do plan to drop off my gifts for my sister's kids." Though the thought of facing Lisa again so soon was enough to make the doughy goodness in my stomach rebound.

Joshua scraped the last bite off his plate. "Speaking of kids . . . I do have one more present I need to search for if you're up for it today. I'm hoping you might have some ideas for a four-year-old girl?"

"Your niece?"

"Yep. Four going on fourteen."

"Aren't they all." I smiled, thinking of my own niece and wishing the emotional climate was better between Iris's mother and me. It'd been way too long since she'd slept over and begged to do my hair in what she called a snake braid—code for tangled mess. "Sure, I still need to get Iris something, too." I scooted my chair and hooked my purse over my shoulder. "And I know just the place."

"This is insane." Joshua stood in the center of the Build-A-Bear store, surrounded by every kind of stuffed creature imaginable and several dozen harried parents all vying for the perfect accessory for their child's newest fluff-filled toy. His eyes widened like a soon-to-be roadkill victim.

"More insane than usual, yes. It is Christmastime."

"Still." He wiped a hand down his face, and I fought the urge to laugh at his bewilderment. "How do we even go about . . . doing this?"

I nudged him and pointed to the far left of the store. "We start over there at the choosing station. You first have to pick a shell."

"A shell?"

I took pity on his confused state and pulled him toward the selection line. "Yes, we'll pick out the shell of the animal you think Emma would enjoy most, and then we'll fill it with stuffing and a heart. Iris has a cute little puppy she got here a couple years ago on her birthday. Right now, though, she adores unicorns—like every other little girl in the universe—so that's what I'm going to get her for Christmas."

He reached for the one and only dinosaur shell left on the shelf.

"Um, do you really think *Emma* would choose a dinosaur over a sparkly pink unicorn?"

He paused, looking down at his selection as if considering this idea for the first time. "Hmm, you might be right."

"I mean, to a four-year-old girl, a dinosaur and a unicorn are likely in the same general category—but one is definitely prettier than the other."

He spun around so quickly I nearly tripped into a pile of empty panda skins.

"Did you just compare a mythical creature to one of the greatest wonders to ever walk our planet?"

Feeling more ornery than usual, I smirked and selected our two limp unicorn forms from the shelf. "You mean, one of the greatest *extinct* wonders? Yes, I did. Because I'm sure you can see how a child could easily confuse extinction and mythology."

His eyes narrowed on me, causing a bout of suppressed laughter to expand my chest, a feeling as foreign as it was rare these days. "You just declared war, Lauren Bailey."

Exhilarated by the challenge in his tone, I practically skipped to the fluff tank line. With quick, long strides, he followed after me.

As we waited to fill our multicolored unicorns with batting, Joshua used the time to inform me of all things dinosaur, as if he were debating a hot topic at a political rally.

"Did you know a single T-Rex tooth was over a foot long?"

"Can't say that I did."

His grin broadened. "And did you know the Dromiceiomimus could run up to forty miles an hour?"

"Nope," I said as snottily as possible while the grandmother in front of us filled four black-and-white puppy dogs to maximum capacity.

"And it's currently under debate by paleontologists, but it's believed that the Stegosaurus could actually sing through the crests on its head."

That one stopped my charade cold as my mind tried to make sense of a singing dinosaur the size of a school bus. "Did you just say *sing*?"

"Yes." Joshua was loving this impromptu trivia game. "Sometimes as a warning for predators but also for romantic encounters."

My jaw slacked just enough at his explanation that Joshua reached out and gently tapped the underside of my chin to close my gaping mouth.

"See? So much better than a myth." He spoke in such an intimately quiet voice that I nearly forgot I was in the middle of a toy store days before Christmas. And suddenly I wanted nothing more than to hear him speak that way to me again. To hold me close and whisper against my mouth and—

"Miss? Miss?"

Joshua placed his hands on my shoulders and spun me to face the exasperated Build-A-Bear employee waiting to fill my droopy unstuffed creature.

"Oh, sorry. Here you go." I handed her the lifeless unicorn and tried not to react to the loss of Joshua's touch.

"Just tell me when," the clerk said, pumping the fluff pedal with her foot.

The velvety unicorn expanded to life.

"That's good," I said, making sure the neck was still floppy enough to be snuggled by a child.

"And what would you like to add inside it?" she asked.

"Oh . . . uh . . ." With all of the dinosaur talk, I'd forgotten about this part. The specialty add-ins.

The young woman, who looked to be in her last year of high school, began listing off our choices with about as much enthusiasm as the stuffed animals she filled. "A fabric heart, a beating heart, a fruity fragrance, a sound machine, a voice recorder . . ."

Joshua's breath on my cheek sent a shock wave of tingles up my spine. "That's more choices than I give myself in an entire day."

I laughed and then spoke to—I searched for her name tag—Kelsey. "I think we'll just do the fabric heart option today, thanks."

Kelsey nodded and reached into the bin of flimsy, satin-red hearts. She handed them over to us with instructions to make a wish before she sewed them inside our chosen creatures.

And just like that, as I brought the silky heart to my lips, the obnoxious organ in the center of my own chest began to knock.

What should I wish for? The question flitted through my mind, yet the gravity of it took root.

Without hesitation, Joshua handed his wished-on heart over, as if it was the easiest thing in the world to do. As if giving it away didn't have lasting, eternal implications or consequences. As if simply believing in happily-ever-afters was enough to make them a reality.

Why can't I be the same way?

As if sensing the struggle going on in my head, Joshua stepped in to me and placed his hand on my upper back. "You need more time?"

Something about the patient way he asked, warming my face with his gaze and my ears with the timbre of his voice, prevented me from retreating behind my crumbling wall of self-protection. Because I was beyond exhausted from reinforcing the boundary between Joshua and my heart. What exactly was the point of blocking him out now anyway? It wasn't like I was actively pursuing a child to bring home at the moment. As far as Small Wonders was concerned, I was on hiatus until . . . until I didn't know when.

What if losing Noah was the big neon sign confirming that adoption wasn't meant to be my path? That no matter how much I'd prayed it into being, the adoption door, just like the nursery door in my home, was supposed to remain closed. What if . . . what if Joshua had been the door I'd been meant to open from the very beginning?

He searched my profile now, waiting for an answer as I closed my eyes and braved a new wish before I planted it deep inside the batting.

"Make the right wish?" he asked as we stepped out of line with our finished Christmas gifts.

"Yes, I believe I did."

The crease between his eyebrows deepened, as if he was trying to solve a crossword with one too many blanks.

"Come on," I said, ready to push through the crowd even though my heart, like the one in Iris's unicorn, continued to buck under muted layers of half-processed thoughts. "We're not even close to finished yet. We still have to choose the outfits."

"Wait—outfits? But they're unicorns." He gestured widely with his arms, nearly smacking an older man carrying a pile of sequin dresses across the store to his wife. Joshua apologized before catching up to me. He softened his voice. "I haven't the first clue about any of this stuff."

"And that's why you have me." I smiled up at him, testing it out, this new feeling of letting go, of giving in to the attraction I'd been denying myself for weeks. I was done pretending that Joshua didn't stir up every romantic ideal I'd ever had. Because he did. And more.

Again, he eyed me, like he wasn't quite sure what was happening, but also like he wasn't about to turn this new, enthusiastic-about-everything Lauren down.

"Look up there." I pointed at a crowded shelf where every kind of glittery outfit, hair bow, and custom shoe awaited. I didn't step out of the way as Joshua reached past me. "Those princess dresses are adorable, but if Emma would rather have something more casual or sporty, they have a ton of more options near the front."

"Um . . . . well . . ." I couldn't get enough of this off-kilter Joshua. "Considering Emma makes me drink from a tea set plastered with crowned ladies in ball gowns, I'm gonna go with princess on this one."

Seriously, he has princess tea with his niece? What had I ever been thinking to push this man away like he was a piece of forbidden fruit?

"What?" he asked. "Why are you looking at me like that?"

"I just really want to see that, you drinking from a princess teacup."

"You're welcome to join us anytime."

"I might just take you up on that." I tipped my head and used a tool from his favorite flirtatious tool box—a wink. "Now, which color dress do you want?"

Briefly, his gaze dipped from my eyes to my mouth as several harried customers pushed past us on their way to the cash registers. Neither of us moved until I blinked.

"Blue," he said finally. "Definitely blue."

I secured the sparkly, periwinkle gown at the top of the display. "See? You're better at this than you thought."

Our fingers brushed slightly as he took the miniature hanger from my hand. "You make it easy."

But wasn't that how it was supposed to be? Because I was certain that falling in love with Joshua Avery would be exactly that—the easiest thing I'd ever done.

chapter twenty-three

I anchored my hip against my bathroom vanity and willed my hand to steady as I applied onyx liquid liner to my upper eyelid. My third attempt. Seriously though, who had time for this on a daily basis? It was usually around this point in the beautification process that I'd call Jenna and ask for a step-by-step tutorial on how to create a proper "smoky eye" look, preferably one that wouldn't land me in the center of a sarcastic meme with the hashtags *#nailedit* and *#failed*. But seeing as Jenna's cell coverage was spotty in the mountains—and also how I wasn't quite ready to divulge my current mental standing with All Things Joshua—our limited communication was probably for the best. All she really needed to know was that I was keeping my promise: I wouldn't be alone on Christmas. Other details, like how I was meeting Joshua's family tonight for caroling, cider, and a stroll through the Winter Gardens . . . well, I'd catch her up later on all that.

My phone buzzed with a text from Joshua.

When should I pick you up?

I rubbed my freshly glossed lips together.

I didn't realize going to the gardens meant getting a chauffeur, too?

It's too bad my horse-drawn carriage is still in the shop. Hope you're okay with a Ford Explorer.

Sigh. Guess it will have to do. 😉

Thanks for compromising. Also, my mom wanted me to tell you to dress w-a-r-m. (In case you weren't aware that it is winter. In Idaho.)

Butterflies pinged off my abdomen wall as I imagined meeting Joshua's parents for the first time.

Are you POSITIVE it's okay for me to intrude on your family time tonight? I'm feeling a little weird.

Sorry to break it to you sweetheart, but you ARE weird.

You're not helping.

Are you asking me to spike your cup of apple cider?

No. 🙄 But seriously, you're 100% sure?

You've exceeded the statute of limitations on that particular question. See you in fifteen minutes.

I set my phone back on the counter and tapped my thumbnail against the porcelain sink basin. This was really happening. I was spending an evening with Joshua and his family. I was actually going to meet George Avery. Tonight.

The next fifteen minutes were spent pulling on an extra pair of socks and trying on three different tunic-length sweaters—none of which would even be seen under the twenty-pound sleeping bag of a jacket I'd be wearing. I unearthed the deeply discounted mid-calf, fur-lined snow boots I'd purchased last spring but never worn. I quickly removed the tags, but unfortunately for me, these babies still needed to be laced. I carried them downstairs, secured a place on the middle of my sofa, and began the tedious task.

Joshua knocked twice, and I hollered over Skye's frantic barking for him to come inside since my fingers were currently tangled in a set of bootlaces I was ready to burn.

Joshua paused in the entryway to pet Skye's head. "Hey there, Skye. I brought you something. Look!" He reached into his coat and pulled out a Milk-Bone the size of my forearm. Eyes wide, she stilled immediately. "First you need to sit." She obeyed with excited panting. "Ah, what a good girl. Here you go." Gently, she bit the edge of his offering and padded off to her doggie bed in the corner of the living room to feast upon his gift.

"You realize that bone just earned you a million brownie points in doggie currency, right?"

"Too bad, my goal was two million. Guess I'll have to bring better treats next time." He made his way over to the sofa, where I fumbled with the ends of my laces, pulling hard as I crisscrossed them under another set of stiff metal pegs. Where was good old Velcro when you needed it?

"Wow," he said, eyeing my boots. "Those look like . . . a process."

As if on cue, the laces snapped away from my thumb and forefingers. The once-taut cords went slack, releasing all the ground I'd gained in the last four crisscross passes. I let out an exasperated cry and fell back against the couch cushions like one of Skye's flimsy rubber toys. "I hope your parents are okay with me showing up in my Cat in the Hat slippers, because that's about all I have energy to wear at this point."

He laughed. "Here, let me have a go."

Before I could stop him, he knelt in front of me and placed my foot between his knees. My next breath stalled out as he pinched each shoelace and started to thread. Through one hole, and out the other, he climbed his way up my calf, weaving with a precision that made me question his true calling in life.

"Were you a cobbler in a past life?"

"No, but I was a Boy Scout."

"Of course you were."

He finished crossing the last three X's on my right boot with enviable ease before tying the laces at the top. "The trick is not to release the tension as you lace."

"Right." And what of the tension in my abdomen that was near combustion level?

He double-knotted the bow he'd just tied and took care to tuck the excess string behind the tongue of my boot. My gaze refused to stray from the deftness of his fingers as he worked the same kind of voodoo on my left boot. Women all around the world would pay good money for Joshua Avery to assist them with their shoe-lacing needs. Jealousy licked up my spine at the mere thought of him doing this for any other female under the age of eighty-five.

"See?" He patted the side of my leg before pushing up to full height from his squatted position on the floor and offering me his hand. "You just needed a little help." I accepted his hand, allowing the warmth to envelop me like a fleece blanket on a snowy evening.

"A little?" My voice sounded surprisingly hoarse. "The only thing I did was put them on my feet."

"And what a fine job you did at that," Joshua said, pulling me up to standing position. The rubber toes of our snow boots bumped as the ghost of his hand grazed my waist. Our eyes held for a full three seconds before he cleared his throat and inclined his head toward the front door. "We should probably get going. Do you have everything you need? Coat, gloves, hat, scarf? My mom is the designated Winter Police in our family. She can't relax if she even *thinks* about someone shivering. She's the worst with my nephew."

"Calvin," I recalled easily, mentally reciting the facts he'd told me on the phone last night as I reached for my coat on the couch. Emma and Calvin were his niece and nephew. Four years old and eighteen months. Emma was extroverted, sassy, and totally smitten by what she called "the Mary Poppins accent." Calvin was her opposite. Reserved and reluctant to leave his mama's shadow. I ignored the pinch in my chest as such an image came to life in my mind.

"Good job remembering his name." Joshua took the puffy black coat from my hands and held it open for me to slide into easily. I zipped it up and tied the sash at my waist. "Although I'm pretty sure being great with names is a teacher's gift. My dad has that ability, too. He can still remember the names of kids he taught in his class twenty-five years ago." At the mention of his highly esteemed father, an echo of insecurity resounded inside my head.

My family wasn't like the Averys. A fact I knew implicitly, even without having met them yet. The contrast of our vastly different upbringings was as obvious as the star that led the wise men to baby Jesus. The Baileys didn't have lighthearted inside jokes or sweet nicknames for each other, and the number of family outings we'd planned in public since my middle school years amounted to exactly none. At best, my family tolerated each other. Although recently that practiced tolerance had been stretched to a new breaking point.

As if he could hear the doubts fogging up my brain, Joshua took my hand and pulled me to the front door. "Stop overthinking whatever it is you're overthinking about tonight. They're going to love you, Lauren. You'll see."

We'd only been at the Winter Gardens for a few minutes, yet I was certain I never wanted to leave, no matter the massive drop in temperature expected later tonight. The light displays along the main cobblestone path were pure magic, embodying the Christmas spirit with twinkling movement and sentimental holiday music piped in by underground speakers.

I spotted Joshua's father easily. He was lifting his granddaughter to point out an angel hidden on the highest branch of a barren dogwood tree. George was tall like Joshua, his hair more silver than brown, and his midsection a bit more filled out, but their smiles were a carbon copy of each other. How had I not seen the stark resemblance the first time I'd met his youngest son at Brighton?

Joshua was speaking to me as we approached the Avery clan, but I couldn't focus on anything but my fangirling thoughts. I was about to meet *the* George Avery. And his wife, Elizabeth, and his older son, Joel, and his daughter-in-law, Rebekah, and his two precious grandbabies, who were currently digging through his popcorn bag with bulky gloved hands. He laughed as a pile of kernels fell to the sidewalk, the sight only adding to the surrealism of the moment. What was the appropriate response for meeting a man who'd shaped and challenged your entire career path . . . and so many other life choices, as well?

"Hey, hey now, you two! You better save some of that popcorn for me!" Joshua hollered seconds before sweeping his well-bundled niece into his arms and spinning her around like he was a carousel ride.

Several pieces of popcorn escaped her clutches mid-flight as she squealed, "Uncle Joshua!"

I giggled at the sight of them, unable to stop the flare of desire that settled in my chest.

He placed her feet back on the ground, but Emma immediately clung to his side, wrapping her arms around his leg and begging for him to do it again, all while speaking in the best pretend English accent I'd ever heard. He set one hand on her puffy hat and held his other one out to me. Nerves churning, I stepped up to his side and stared into the eyes of a family I'd been idolizing for years.

"Everyone, this is my good friend Lauren Bailey. World's most dedicated first-grade teacher, epic spaghetti-sauce maker, and a talented Christmas-gift supplier."

"Hello," I said. "Thanks for letting me join your family tonight."

"Well, with an introduction like that, we should be the ones thanking you for joining our ragtag crew." George Avery was talking to me. Actually speaking and walking and holding out his hand to—*Oh my gosh!* I was shaking his hand.

"Joshua's told us quite a bit about you. I'd love to pick your brain about a few things for my next book when you come over to the house—I'll give your ideas full credit, of course."

I blinked. Maybe twice. Or maybe a hundred times. I couldn't be sure about my blinking because I wasn't even sure I was taking in oxygen. "*You* want to pick *my* brain?" I shot a questioning glance in Joshua's direction. What exactly had he been saying about me? "Why? Almost everything I've learned is from you—your books and lectures. I owe so much to you. This is . . . it's an honor to meet you, sir."

If possible, his smile stretched even farther up his cheeks. He turned to his wife, who had just finished securing a tiny blue mitten onto Calvin's little hand. "Elizabeth, are you hearing this? I have a fan who's not even old enough to be an AARP member."

"Ha, and that's quite the ego boost at our age." Elizabeth, a classy, petite woman wearing red cat-eye glasses and a purple parka placed a hand on her husband's back and extended the other to me. "It's so nice to meet you, Lauren. We're happy you can join us for Christmas, too. And I'd love to get your red-sauce recipe. Joshua told me it was better than my mother's." She looked admiringly at her son, warmth and pride shimmering in her eyes. "A revered compliment."

"Oh, I'm sure it's not nearly as good your mother's, but—"

Joshua cut me off by draping his arm around my shoulders and tucking me in to his side. "Hey, nothing against Me-maw, but you all know I call a spade a spade. And Lauren's is better. Plain and simple."

His parents laughed as Joshua rotated us a full hundred and eighty degrees to introduce me to Joel—a slightly trendier, slightly shorter version of Joshua—and then to Rebekah, Joel's wife. Decked out in matching black Columbia jackets and buffalo-plaid winter hats, they could have graced the cover of a J. Crew catalog—the holiday edition. Especially with that handsome toddler boy strapped to her back. Rebekah had obviously given her children her gorgeous Mediterranean complexion and slender build, while their big eyes and Avery smiles were one hundred percent Joel's contribution.

A slight tap on my hip diverted my attention to the darling dark-haired girl blinking up at me. "And I'm Emma Elizabeth Avery."

I curtsied low and replied in kind, using my best Downton Abbey–worthy impression. "It's lovely to meet you Emma Elizabeth. I'm Lauren Delane Bailey."

Her eyes twinkled as she gave me a curtsy of her own, causing the entire group to stifle their amusement. "It's lovely to meet you, too. Do you like peppermint candy canes?"

"I do, indeed," I said, keeping up the ruse.

Emma twisted toward her mama, and in a sweet all-American accent she asked, "Can I share mine with Lauren, Mom?"

"Of course, honey."

The little girl beamed as she flitted off to unhook a candy cane from the strap of Calvin's baby carrier to bring it back to me with a heart-melting grin. The generous gesture clouded my vision as I thanked her for her kindness. Rebekah smiled in a way that suggested she was accustomed to such spontaneous sweetness from her daughter, and I couldn't help but wonder at the pride she felt over her child. The faint echo of a yearning I hadn't quite managed to mute taunted me with wants and hopes I wished I could temporarily sever from my heart.

After a casual conversation regarding the dropping temperatures and approaching snowstorm headed our way within the next few days, we migrated up the path as a singular unit. Joshua jogged away momentarily to secure us each a cup of hot apple cider. We remained at the rear of the group, though I could still hear the easy banter of his parents and the *oohs* and *aahs* regarding the elegance of the Winter Gardens.

We slowed our pace as a seasoned group of carolers ended a pop version of "It Came Upon a Midnight Clear" and transitioned into a hallowed rendition of "O Holy Night" next to a gorgeously elaborate Nativity scene. There had to be ten thousand twinkle lights outlining the stable-like structure, all of them reflecting the truest meaning of Christmas inside, a babe swaddled in muslin and lying in a manger. Emotion thrummed in my throat as the chorus broke into multiple layers of harmony, the high notes pricking my eyes with tears that froze on my lower lashes.

My gaze traveled from the carefully carved infant snuggled on a mound of hay to the statue-still face of his mother, Mary. Her expression, etched in eternal awe, beckoned to me, as if daring me to consider the questions I'd never been brave enough to ponder in years before. But as I held her divine gaze, I wondered at the God who'd destined this young woman for such a high calling. How had her faith been strong enough to handle such a daunting task? How had she been ready for such an unconventional journey to motherhood? For all the heartache and struggle ahead of her?

I fought to break the tangled web of thoughts before they

could take me somewhere I couldn't afford to go. Somewhere too raw and untouchable. Because if my calling was even a shadow of Mary's, then why hadn't God offered me the same strength to endure my trial? Where was the faith I'd been promised? The unshakable peace?

How had I gotten it so, so wrong?

I twisted my body away from the holy family just in time to catch Joshua's father circling his arms around his wife, nuzzling her neck until she gave in to his efforts. She rewarded him with a tender kiss on the mouth. And in that one affectionate act, shared between an adoring husband and wife, the contrast between my childhood and Joshua's was made perfectly clear. If my parents had ever kissed that way, it hadn't happened for many, many years. And wasn't that what a child deserved? Two loving parents who were *in love with each other*? Had I really been so blinded by my own selfish desires, my own intention to erase the past and start again on my own, that I'd neglected to account for the role of a father? And the role of a devoted husband? Had my yearning to adopt stemmed from my own brokenness or from God's heart?

Joshua's voice warmed the wool headband covering my ears and redirected my focus. "I'm glad you decided to come tonight."

His words stoked an internal fire that had no business burning, especially with the promise of snow in the air. Yet defying the odds proved to be what Joshua did best.

I tipped my chin to face him. "Me too."

Without another word, he reached for my hand and tucked it inside his own, squeezing it as his full baritone sang out the end of a chorus I would never listen to the same way again.

"O night divine, O night, O night divine."

chapter twenty-four

The snowstorm the newscasters had been predicting for Christmas week hit sometime between midnight and eight in the morning. I couldn't be sure of the exact time, of course, since I cared more about sleep accumulation than snow accumulation, but apparently not everybody felt the same way. My missed texts from Joshua—time stamp starting around 5:00 a.m.—were proof enough.

Are you awake yet? Have you looked outside? Six inches and counting.

Also, you should check your power. Nearly half the city is out. You doing okay? Need rescuing? I might know a guy.

If you've been carried off by an overweight snowman smoking a corncob pipe, please reply with #1. Stuck inside a snow berm #2. Frozen into an ice sculpture for the viewing pleasure of many #3.

Or none of the above because you're STILL ASLEEP . . . #4.

I squinted at the too-bright screen and tapped out a reply, one eye refusing to stay open.

#4. Ignorance is bliss.

Until your nose catches frostbite.

I can live without a nose.

Check your lights.

But that requires getting out of bed . . .

So does everything else we have planned for today.

I huffed as I exited the sanctuary of my warm cocoon and darted to the light switch—yep. Dead.

I scrambled back in bed, a tiny rush of adrenaline shooting up my spine.

No power. ☹

Your rescuer says to stay put because the roads are getting slick. He's out running errands for his erratic mother at the moment but can be there in 45 minutes. Pack an overnight bag.

I may have jolted upright at that last comment.

??

An overnight bag? To what, stay at his parents' house? On Christmas Eve? No way. This wasn't some made-for-TV holiday movie premise. This was real life. And in real life, the I-only-met-you-yesterday types of acquaintances didn't offer invitations for sleepovers on the biggest holiday of the year.

The roads won't be safe to drive tonight. My parents have a guest room with your name on it. Already checked with them. Go pack your bags.

Snow makes you bossy.

No, it makes me grateful for studded tires and a wood stove.

I heaved a deep sigh. He made a good point. I wouldn't want him out driving on the roads tonight, either.

And then I remembered. Lisa.

I'd finally texted my sister last night, asking if I could stop by her place sometime this afternoon to drop off the packages for her kids before heading to Joshua's parents' house.

I actually have an errand I need to run.

Good thing my holiday rates are very reasonable then.

Hang on. Let me text my sister again.

I shot Lisa a text, asking if I could stop by this morning instead of this afternoon. She replied immediately.

We're packing up now to head to Mom and Dad's. They still have power and a big generator. Is your power out, too?

Yes, but I'm heading to a friend's house in a bit.

Can you take the gifts to Mom and Dad's?

Nausea swirled in my gut at the possibility of seeing my mom, followed closely by an even stronger emotion at the thought of not being with my family at all on Christmas Day. How long would this estrangement between us last?

My phone buzzed in my hand. Joshua was calling me.

"Hello?"

"Hey there." He sounded out of breath.

"Hey," I said, concern edging its way into my own voice. "Why do you sound like you're running track? Are you okay?"

"If you call hiking through a parking lot in a snowstorm on Christmas Eve with four dozen eggs and eight pounds of butter *okay*, then yes. I'm totally okay."

I threw my blankets off my bare legs as if declaring some kind of weird solidarity with him and yanked my carry-on suitcase out from underneath my bed. If Joshua was willing to run errands in a blizzard, then I wasn't going to make him wait on me for a single extra minute. "That sounds horrible. Also, side note: What does your mom need that much butter for?"

"Do you really want me to answer that?"

"Hmm. Probably not."

"That's the right answer." I heard a car door slam and then a shuddering exhale.

"You sound like you're freezing!"

"I can't say I'm a candidate for heatstroke."

Were his teeth chattering? "Crank your heater up! Right now! I'm shivering just listening to you." And also because I was beginning to feel the slow temperature drop of a house without a heat source. Heat was the one true luxury I afforded myself in winter—keeping the thermostat at a constant 73 degrees, even on the frostiest of days.

"Look who's bossy now." He half chuckled, half chattered. "But I didn't call to talk about my numb face. I called to tell you to get Skye ready to stay, as well. She can hang out with Brach. I'll make sure he's a gentleman."

"Really?" I stared down at my Oreo-colored dog currently snoozing away on her princess bed as if snowpocalypse wasn't happening on the other side of my bedroom walls. Who were these generous people anyway? "That's so . . . I mean, your parents don't even know me, Joshua. This feels like way too much to ask."

"They know enough. And you didn't ask. I did. I'll be there soon, and then are we heading to your sister's?"

I swallowed, partially dreading my next words. "No, actually. To my mom and dad's. That okay?"

"Of course. Whatever you need to do. As long as we're back home before four."

The words *back home* rang in my head over and over like a malfunctioning doorbell. What would it be like to make a home with Joshua?

"Okay," I agreed. "I'll see you in a bit."

I attempted to lower the phone and click off, but before I did, I heard his voice again.

"Hey, Lauren?"

"Yeah?"

"I'm glad you weren't kidnapped by a snowman with a corncob pipe." And with that, he was gone.

Goose bumps traveled up my arms, granting me all the motivation I needed to pack for two and be ready and waiting for my knight in snow-studded armor to arrive.

Joshua's black Explorer idled across the street from my parents' house, our easygoing banter falling flat as soon as I saw their parked vehicles in the driveway.

"It's that one there?" He inclined his head to their house.

I made a small grunt of confirmation, and he placed a hand on my bouncing knee.

"What do you need from me, Lauren?" His soft question provided both a comfort and a confidence I'd been lacking.

"I'll be okay." I rotated in my seat to face him. "But I think it's best if I go to the door alone. I just don't want you to feel like—"

He shook his head, cutting my guilt in half. "*I feel* like I want to be a help to you in whatever way I can. If you think it's best for me to stay in the car, then that's what I'll do. No questions asked."

I studied his face, wishing I could be half as selfless and kindhearted a friend to him as he was to me.

"I should go," I whispered a bit more huskily than intended.

"I'll be here."

It was that statement that carried me across a mostly snow-free driveway likely due to my mother's strict plowing schedule at the first sight of a flurry. I shifted the packages in my arms so I could swipe my frozen hair off my face. The snowfall had slowed considerably, but the consistency of the dense flakes had morphed into more of a hard ice pellet, one that clung to my hair as if made of Velcro. The tinny *rat-tat-tat* sound pinging against my parents' front window to my left became the soundtrack of my momentary boost of bravery.

I knocked. Twice.

Nothing.

Shivering, I gave in and rang the doorbell.

Lisa pulled the door open a few seconds later, her red cowl-neck sweater and black jeans accentuating the most feminine parts of her figure. You'd never know her house didn't have power this morning, since she looked as polished as ever, regardless of her lack of a blow dryer and vanity mirror lights.

The familiarity of Lisa's presence brought an unexpected surge of nostalgia, and for half a heartbeat I wished we were the hugging type of sisters, the kind who settled their differences with a warm embrace and a handful of compliments. But the Baileys weren't known for their affection—such a contrast to the Cartwright and Avery families, who handed out hugs like they were free mints from their favorite Mexican restaurant.

"Merry Christmas, Lisa." My first spoken words to my sister in nearly a month. "I hope the kids enjoy these gifts—I had some extra help on the boys' present this year. Should be a hit. Or at least, that's what I've been told." Yep, my nervous rambling was back with a vengeance.

"Thanks," she said a bit flatly, taking the packages from my arms and setting them next to the shoe rack in the entryway two steps inside.

"Oh, and the bag there has all the ugly socks in it. For the stockings." I'd started the tradition as a broke college student in my early twenties: buy the most hideous pair of socks possible and stuff them deep inside the toe of the hanging stocking. My family always laughed at the weird design or theme I chose for them. But I wouldn't hear their thoughts on what I'd picked out for them this year.

I worked up the best Christmas cheer of a smile I could muster. My sister was obviously not in the mood to reciprocate.

Despite the biting wind and Lisa's dead-eyed stare, the start of a nervous sweat broke out all over my body. Her not-so-subliminal message of blocking the entire doorway declared *You shall not pass.*

"Well, I should probably get going. My friend's waiting for me in the car." I hitched a thumb toward Joshua. "Please tell everybody I said Merry Christmas, okay? I hope Mom's ham turns out and that Dad enjoys his new slippers. And I hope . . ." *We can be sisters again, the kind who talk and laugh and enjoy life together, because I miss you. And I miss Mom and Dad, too.* My temples throbbed from the cold as I secured a hand on the banister and placed my snow boot square on the first porch step. "I hope tomorrow is everything you want it to be. Bye." It was then my sister shot a verbal dagger into my back.

"So that's it? You don't talk to us for a month, make my work life a living hell with Mom after your outburst, and then leave me to wonder about the new nephew I'm supposedly getting from . . ." She thought for several seconds as if trying to come up with the country. "China?"

So this was happening. Right now. I glanced at Joshua's car

parked along the curb, wishing I could evaporate like the cloud of exhaust puffing out from under his back bumper, but that would be too easy. And nothing involving my family was ever easy.

Slowly, I turned back around, willing patience into my tone as I pushed the painful words out. "He wasn't . . . there was a computer glitch. He wasn't available for me to adopt after all."

A beat. And then two. "What does that mean—for you?"

Heat flared in my cheeks at her audacity to make me spell it out for her, as if the words didn't splice my heart open every time I repeated them. "Exactly what I just said. I won't be adopting him." *Easy, Lauren. Your job was to deliver Christmas gifts, not add insult to injury.* "He already has a family in process."

"But what about all the other orphaned children in the world? The poor and vulnerable you lectured us about? Aren't there others in need of a family? Isn't that your way to *make a difference?*"

I stared at her, anger simmering in my gut as she threw my words back in my face. My sister was a lot of things, but ignorant wasn't one of them. She wanted me to attack, to prove her right. "I'm not sure what I'll do next."

A laugh—measured and cruel. "I could have guessed that."

"*What?*"

She gestured to me. "You. This. It's what you do—what you've always done. When things get too hard, you're ready to throw your hands up and walk away from the whole thing. Just like you did to us when you became all religious and we didn't want to jump on that wagon with you. Well, news flash: The parenthood wagon isn't a six-hour day of craft and carpet time like in your classroom. It's painful. It's messy. It's freaking hard work."

And just like that, I'd reached my boiling point. "You don't know anything about—"

"Adoption? Maybe not. But I do know something about parenting kids with a history I knew little about. But like usual, you don't ask for anything I have to offer. Instead, you ride off on your Debbie Do-Gooder high horse, pegging us as your unsupportive, uncaring family. Oh, wait, no. I believe the phrase you used was *unloving*."

I gaped at her. In all of our past disagreements, Lisa had never spoken to me with such hostility. "I don't have a high horse, and I never said that!"

"You're right." Her gaze grew unfocused, as if trying to recall a memory. "You just told our mom that you wanted to be nothing like her—that you wanted a child of your own so you could love them better than she was able to love you. Believe me, I remember every word of that speech, because I've heard it. Multiple times. By the woman who sacrificed everything so you could have a roof over your head and food on your plate." She peered off into the distance. "She wasn't perfect. I know it, and so does she. But she's our mother and you have *no right* to point your self-righteous finger at her."

"I'm not doing this with you, Lisa. Not on Christmas Eve." Shame pricked my conscience. Or maybe it was the conviction of the *honor thy mother and father* passage scrolling through my mind. I stomped down the steps, slipping on the last one and landing hard on a snow-dusted shrub.

I heard Joshua's car door open and immediately slam shut as I righted myself from the ground, conscious of his waiting presence at the edge of the driveway in my peripheral. I started toward him, a warning on my tongue to stay clear of my sister's sticky web.

"Well, this just seals the deal nicely, doesn't it? I guess you really have made up your mind to call it quits, then."

I shouldn't have stopped, shouldn't have engaged, shouldn't have taken a big, juicy bite out of the poisonous apple she dangled in front of me. But that's exactly what I did. "What are you talking about?"

Her gaze veered away from me to the man trudging up the

driveway behind me. I turned quickly and held up my palm to halt his steps.

"Your whole no-dating-because-you're-going-to-adopt mandate." She shook her head, only it wasn't disgust I saw on her face, but . . . pity. "Unless, of course, you're gonna try to convince me that spending Christmas Eve with a man and his family doesn't mean anything."

Another wave of shame washed over me.

"Joshua's a good friend," I said as if I'd rehearsed the phrase multiple times in front of a mirror, keeping my inflection mild and unassuming. But Lisa picked up nuances in tone and expressions on a face like she worked full-time doing FBI surveillance.

"The intense way he's watching us right now would say he's much more than that."

"I don't have to justify anything to you. That's not why I came here today."

"No, you just came to drop off your guilt gifts and check off the box labeled *family*. Don't worry. We're all used to that from you by now."

And then Joshua's hand was on my back, speaking to me in a tone that suggested urgency, only I couldn't hear his words over my rage.

Clenching my fists, I stared my sister down, a forbidden sob hanging on the edge of my voice. "You're right, Lisa. I don't know how I could ever feel unsupported by this family. You're just the warmest, most hospitable, accepting bunch of people out there."

"*Lauren*." And within that one firm yet tender word, I knew exactly what my sister would hear in Joshua's voice—the unapologetic concern of a man whose feelings for me exceeded the friend title I'd attached to him. "It's time to leave."

Joshua secured an arm around my shoulders, steering us away from my parents' home.

"It's Joshua, right?" Lisa's question echoed in the wintery stillness.

He paused our trek to meet my sister's inflexible gaze. "That's right. And you're Lisa, Lauren's sister."

Her quivering lips nearly lifted into a flattered expression. "My big sis hates eggnog. And also that awful 'Christmas Shoes' song they play at the top of every hour on 106.5. It always makes her cry. Oh, and fair warning, she hoards her Draw Four cards during UNO but is always willing to share her dessert, even if it's her favorite."

What was she doing?

He nodded. "Good to know. Thanks for the heads-up. Merry Christmas to you all."

She sniffed, and for a moment, I could have sworn I saw tears leak from her eyes. "Merry Christmas." She dusted the snowflakes from her sweater and ducked back inside the house. The slam of the door rattled through my frozen bones.

Joshua didn't speak as he opened my car door for me or even after he climbed inside the driver's seat. He simply exhaled, turned the key in the ignition, placed his hands on the steering wheel, and accelerated to the end of the street . . . all while humiliation burned a hole in my gut at the dysfunction he'd just witnessed.

Despite the dash vents pumping out hot air at maximum capacity, I shook more than I had moments ago in the December cold.

"Joshua, I'm really sorry you had to—"

"No," he cut me off, pulling over to the curb. "Please don't apologize to me. You asked me not to get out of the car, but I couldn't just sit in here and watch you . . ." The tendons in his neck tensed and relaxed, tensed and relaxed. "I'm sorry, Lauren."

An apology I felt had little to do with him exiting the car without my permission and everything to do with my screwed-up family life. Even still, Joshua had come after me because . . . because he'd been worried. About me.

The revelation urged me to give in to the impulse my entire being craved: to lean forward and press my mouth to his, to feel the heat of his breath mingle with mine, and to allow him full access into the mess and pain and all the unsightly places I'd tried and failed to bury over the last two decades.

His gaze trailed my face, warming my lips with the idea that he might be thinking something similar. That maybe he, too, had thoughts that leapt over the friendship fence into this new, undefined territory we found ourselves in now.

"I need you to know that I didn't invite you to Christmas because I have expectations of you—or us."

Humiliation pinched my throat. "Of course. I know that—"

"Because I support you. In whatever you decide to do, not that you have to decide anything at all right now, but I would never want to be the reason you didn't . . . I couldn't be that guy, the one who pulled you away from God's plans for you."

All the things he didn't ask circled around my mind the way my sister's hostile questions had, like hungry vultures waiting to attack: "*But what about all the other orphaned children in the world? Aren't there others in need of a family?*"

"Please don't let what my sister said get to you. She doesn't know what she's talking about." And yet even as I said those words, desperate to believe they were true, my pulse whooshed harder in my ears.

He nodded, yet remained otherwise unmoved as he searched my face for several more seconds. "I don't want to make things any more complicated for you."

"You haven't. You've only made things better." I touched his hand. "Which is why we should be driving to your parents' house right now and not stuck here talking about my sister or her theories for another second."

I straightened in my seat, deciding we needed a major morale boost if we had any hope of celebrating Christmas Eve the way it should be celebrated. I turned on his radio and found the round-the-clock holiday station, hoping against hope that it wasn't the infamous "Christmas Shoes" song. Thankfully, it was "Rudolph the Red-Nosed Reindeer."

I cranked it up and began to hum along. "Have you ever been through Cherry Lane? The neighborhood is all decorated like gingerbread houses. It's not too far from here, and I'm sure that street's been plowed by now since it's a major attraction."

The concern on his face began to thaw. "It's on our way."

"Great, because I think we could both use a helping of holiday spirit right about now."

"Couldn't agree more."

And then Joshua was driving our all-wheel-drive sleigh to the Avery house—save for one tiny, but necessary, holiday spirit detour.

chapter twenty-five

Joshua's childhood home smelled of burning firewood and cinnamon sticks, the kind left to simmer on a stovetop for hours on end so that even your lungs were infused with holiday warmth. Much like everything in the Averys' tidy Tudor-style home.

Unlike Robert and Gail's house, stocked full of sentimental knickknacks, art projects, and sports equipment, Elizabeth and George Averys' minimalistic approach to home decor and furniture still managed to be invitingly cozy.

After changing out of my snow-soaked clothing, I set my carry-on inside the guest room closet and appreciated the harmony of the soft gray duvet cover and cream-colored walls. An ivory poinsettia on the dresser was the only decoration outside of the rustic frame above the bed that read *Bind My Wandering Heart to Thee.*

I padded back down the hall in the direction I'd seen Joshua take Skye when we'd first arrived. He'd given me a brief verbal tour, highlighting the location of my room, the restroom, and the kitchen as he'd held on to Skye's collar to lead her out back to meet up with Brach.

Taking a right at the first corner, I entered a quaint living area with a love seat and two classy wingback chairs before my gaze settled on a tiny Christmas tree perched on a table near the hearth. I moved toward it, feeling every bit the sneaky intruder rather than an invited guest. Still, the unique tree pulled me toward it. Adorned with miniature white lights and a couple dozen heart-shaped ornaments—most with four-digit years engraved or painted on them—the tree told a story I wished I could hear.

"Lauren? Is that you out there?" As if I had been caught with my hand in the cookie jar, my spine snapped straight, and I spun around to face . . . nobody. The room was empty.

"I'm in the kitchen . . . it's just past the bookshelf on the left there with the oversize glass jar collection my wife insists matches her motif. Call me old-fashioned, but I believe bookshelves should be reserved solely for books."

I stifled a laugh and made my way past the shelf in question and into the kitchen nook, where George Avery stood at the white marble kitchen counter, bent over a bag of . . . crab? He pulled out a bundle, the smell of fresh seafood quickly filling up the small space. He must have just arrived home, too.

The instant he saw me, his face lit up with a familiar grin, putting my earlier imposter-like feelings to ease—an ability that must be a special gene in the Avery family line. "Sorry for hollering at you from across the house like that, but as you can see, my hands are full of crab legs"—on cue, he lifted a handful of legs from the grocery bag and placed them in a bucket of icy water—"and as good as these suckers will taste tonight all smothered in garlic butter, they're too stinky to go on a walk through the living room."

That time I did laugh. "That's more than okay. I was actually just admiring the little Christmas tree out there. It's beautiful."

"That's our anniversary tree. Thirty-four years today."

I moved in closer, leaning my hip against the counter. "Your anniversary is on Christmas Eve?"

"Sure is. Our first date was at a little crab shack downtown. It's why we eat this meal together with our family every year."

"That's a lovely tradition." Several seams around my heart may have snapped at his sweet tale. "Can I help with something?"

"As a matter of fact, I could use an extra set of hands. Mind grabbing a towel from the top drawer next to the sink there?" He dipped his head to indicate direction. "If you could toss it over my shoulder, that'd be great."

Jenna wouldn't even believe this right now. Me, opening drawers in George Avery's kitchen and draping a towel over his shoulder like an old family friend. Oh, how my life had changed in these past few months. Joshua had tilted my whole world on its axis, which led me back to why I was even here. "Have you seen Joshua? I wonder if I should go check on how the dogs are getting along."

"Oh yes. Sorry." He chuckled. "I saw him as I was on my way inside. I'm supposed to tell you the doggie introduction went great and that he's down helping his mom with something in the basement for a minute. I can tell you where the stairs are if you'd like, but you're welcome to stay here if you don't mind listening to an old man's corny jokes."

"Not at all, I'm happy to help. I'll wash up." I turned on the tap, pumping the lemon-scented soap onto my palms.

"Great. Joel's family should be here anytime. They only live a few houses over."

"Oh, really? I didn't know they lived so close."

My comment seemed to surprise him. "Yep. Elizabeth has been harping on Joshua to buy a place in our neighborhood, as well, since he spends so much time with Joel's kids. But between me and you, I think his real reason for not wanting to sell his condo is because he's collected way too much tech junk over the years and doesn't want to face the limitations of a moving truck. But we'll see." He shrugged. "Miracles happen, and my wife usually gets what she prays for."

I smiled politely while my mind wandered through this conversation like the outsider I was. What would that be like? To have parents who begged me to live closer, much less *choosing* to live on their street and seeking their involvement in my everyday life and not just at random. My being here for Christmas had to seem very odd to the Avery family. "I'm sure living close has a lot of perks."

He dumped another handful of legs into the bucket, then covered them up with another big dump of ice. "I'm fairly sure babysitting would be the top perk for both Joel and my Elizabeth. We love living near our grandkids." His words swelled in my chest, creating a mini tidal wave of desire, followed by an instantaneous wake of regret. I might never know the blessing of doting grandparents, even if Noah had been mine to mother.

He shoved the bucket to the side of the counter and slung the towel from his shoulder to wipe away the moisture residue. Then he pointed to the fridge, as if I was supposed to know exactly what he wanted me to grab from inside. But I opened it anyway, because when George Avery pointed, you didn't hesitate to obey.

"How are you at making coleslaw, Lauren?"

"I've never made it before."

"Then you'll be perfect."

I laughed. "I'm happy to give it a try."

I collected several ingredients from the shelves and drawers, at his request, and then he slapped a wooden cutting board in front of me. "If you can chop cabbage and spoon mayo from the jar, then you can master coleslaw."

"I don't know, those are some pretty high expectations. I once struggled to spread peanut butter on toast." I'd been five, but still, it was the truth.

His eyes crinkled a breath before a belly laugh burst from his throat. "I knew I liked you."

A compliment I'd hang on to forever.

Much like Joshua, George was the type of person you wanted

to be around, the kind you wanted to collect inside jokes with and prepare a meal alongside in a kitchen on a holiday afternoon.

He gave me a quick rundown on what to chop and provided me a bowl to "dump it all into" so that I could start the mayo-spooning part of the recipe instructions. While I chopped and dumped, he asked me about my teaching experience at Brighton—how long I'd been there, what the school's atmosphere was like, what I enjoyed most, and if I had any plans to move beyond first grade. I told him I didn't, a response that caused him to pause his potato peeling and give me an approving nod.

"I miss it—teaching that age. First grade was always my favorite. A big part of me wanted to show up at Brighton with Joshua on that first day." He chuckled to himself. "But it was more important for him to get a feel for the kids without me there. And from the sounds of it, I'd say you helped him out a lot. He thinks highly of what you've accomplished in your classroom."

The tips of my ears grew hot. "He didn't need much help. He's a natural with the kids."

"Pretty sure he told me the same about you."

Several seconds of silent cabbage-staring later, after my cheeks had finally started to cool, I switched the subject of questions to him. "How many years did you teach in the classroom?" If I remembered right from all the training documentaries, it was somewhere close to the thirty-year mark.

"The first time? Just three years. And then back for another twenty-six."

"Oh?" I scooped up more chopped cabbage and dropped it into the bowl. "I don't think I knew you took a break after the first three years. Did you switch schools? I thought I remembered you saying you were in the same district for the duration of your classroom time."

His eyebrows revealed his surprise at my knowledge. "I didn't switch schools, I actually quit teaching after that third year. I'd convinced myself it wasn't my calling, or rather, my wallet had convinced me."

The knife stilled in my hand, the blade halfway through the onion he'd given me. "You quit teaching?" I'd definitely never heard this story before, and I'd heard dozens of stories about his early teaching days on documentaries and simulcasts at teacher conferences, sharing his failed attempts at helping kids connect to literature. I simply couldn't imagine him as anything but George Avery, Teacher Extraordinaire.

He rinsed several potatoes in a strainer, then selected one to peel. "Elizabeth and I were struggling to make ends meet, so much so that we'd actually considered moving into her parents' attic." He shook his head and plopped a naked potato on the counter. "Elizabeth was newly pregnant with Joel, and her morning sickness was something terrible. Should have been called all-day sickness. She couldn't work for months, and our bills were piling up. A newly hired resource-room teacher in a district where thirty percent of my kids' parents were either incarcerated or on parole definitely didn't come with a shiny paycheck."

I'd stopped cutting now, watching him intently.

"I left work one afternoon and made a few calls to some buddies, asking them for any job leads. One of my buddies had lined up a managerial position for me at a local hardware store. I knew how to structure teams and schedules and enjoyed working with my hands, so it felt like a good enough fit. Plus, with the overtime they promised, I would practically double my teacher's salary. It all made sense on paper, and yet . . . when I walked out of my principal's office that day . . ." A frown tugged at the corners of his mouth. "There are some days you'll remember for the rest of your life, and the day I quit Lincoln Elementary is near the top of my list."

The sinking statement pulled at my insides. "But you still went to work for the hardware store?"

"Yes." The word dripped with regret. "It was easy to justify why *my way* was better. After all, God wouldn't want us to struggle, right?" An uncomfortable chill crawled up my spine at his sarcasm. "There had to be someone else meant to teach those kids, someone more qualified than I was, because trying to get those kids to connect to the alphabet seemed like a foolish effort when their worlds had been shattered over and over again."

I pictured the faces of a few of my past students, the ones from less-than-desirable home lives. *Much like my waiting child across the world.* I immediately redirected my focus to the coleslaw carnage around me. "What changed your mind? What made you go back to teaching?"

"We had Joel, and as my wife likes to say, he removed the scales from our eyes. All those things we thought we needed, we thought life owed to us, maybe even that God himself owed to us . . . were actually just wants. Not needs. Joel brought us a lot of sleepless nights, but he also brought us perspective. The extra money had been nice but . . . there was this missing peace. That's p-e-a-c-e. So Elizabeth and I started praying together in the evenings. And after about a year, I went back to the school and asked for my old job back. Five years later, after working up a thousand failed plans for connected reading and starting an after-school club for safe adults to read to kids in need, Reading Connection Express was born. My testimony can be summed up in one phrase: God's way is rarely easy, but it's always better than mine."

Though I knew the end of his story—published books, reputable documentaries, national conferences, college commencement speeches—my throat still tightened with emotion. Hearing the personal details, the struggle, the regret, the victory . . . it turned on a faucet of feelings I hadn't realized I'd shut off until now.

"There you two are." Joshua strode into the kitchen, placing a hand on my back as I blinked away the moisture in my eyes. "Sorry I abandoned you to this guy—he can be unruly."

"Nonsense. She's enjoyed hearing all about your embarrassing childhood moments. I made sure to tell her about the time you used your Superman underwear for a surrender flag in the front yard." George winked at me before adding, "But I better pick up the pace in here before Mom sees that the potatoes aren't ready."

A commotion in the other room distracted me. Joel's family had arrived.

"That story is inaccurate," Joshua said matter-of-factly. "They were *Lego* underwear. And I've already told Mom that no one cares about the side dishes served with this meal. We're here for the crab legs. And the butter."

"No, silly head," a cute female voice exclaimed. "We're here for Christmas Eve!" Emma, decked out in a darling red and gold holiday dress, tapped her way across the kitchen in shiny black shoes.

"But mostly for the crab," Joshua mumbled under his breath with a wink shared only with me a second before his mom entered the kitchen, carrying a giant stainless steel pot. "You'll see."

Joshua wasn't wrong. He wasn't even in the same stratosphere as wrong. The Avery Family Anniversary Christmas Eve Crab Feed could easily be considered last-meal-on-earth material. I'd never buy crab in a can again.

Sometime between Joshua tying a plastic bib around my neck and Emma singing "Jingle Bells" while using the shelled crab legs as her instrument of choice . . . I'd completely fallen in love with the lot of them. I'd laughed my oxygen supply out more than once, sucking wind so badly that my sides ached, especially after Joshua intentionally bumped my shoulder at the exact moment I finally got the perfect grip on the cracking tool. After such an unfair move, I shoved my entire pile of crab legs in front of him, declaring his punishment was to crack them *all*. He agreed without a fight, and his mother and Rebekah applauded my sass. "Good one, Lauren," Elizabeth affirmed. "Don't you let him get away with that."

Stuffed to the point of not even wanting to discuss dessert, we concluded our evening with George reading us the first chapter of Luke. I could listen to his storytelling voice every day of the week and never tire of it. His baritone was as deep and distinguished as an Oscar-winning actor. Emma interrupted the passage multiple times, fluffing the ruffly skirt of her dress and asking questions like "Where did the wise men buy their gifts, Papa?" and "What kind of wood was the manger made out of—did it have splinters in it?" and "How could a star shine so brightly for all that time?" All the while, her baby brother slept soundly on his mother's lap, instinctively sucking his fingers every few seconds. The scene burrowed deep into my subconscious.

Even now, hours after the last dish had been washed, dried, and stacked, and long after the fireplace had stopped crackling, I could still see them snuggled together, the image of mother and child. Why wouldn't God just take my desire away already? If I was supposed to wait, supposed to press pause on my adoption plans, then why did I still feel like my lungs were being pummeled by an iron fist every time I saw a woman around my age with a child?

I changed into my pajamas, blue-and-white flannel pants and a matching *Let It Snow* thermal top—the only set I owned appropriate enough for staying with non-family members. Joshua was busy stoking the wood stove when I came out of the guest room. Firelight danced across the back of his snug shirt, shadowing his muscles and highlighting his tapered waist and strong legs. He prodded at the fire, reconfiguring the logs while his biceps flexed and tightened in sync with my growing attraction.

He latched the stove door closed before he pushed off the

ground and saw me resting my hip against the sofa, watching him, like a pathetic Christmas Eve Stalker.

"Hey," I said after an awkward pause.

His amused smile only increased my sudden onset of insecurity. "Nice pj's. And it looks like you got your wish."

I glanced down at my socked feet, unsure of his meaning.

"The snow. There's over twelve inches outside now. Joel said he had to plow his driveway for the second time tonight just to get his car back inside the garage when they got home."

My eyebrows shot up as I went to the living room's darkened bay window. "Seriously? That's insane! I can't remember the last time we got this much snow in a single twenty-four-hour period." I cupped my hands around my eyes, pressing my forehead to the glass to peer into the yard. A streetlight a few houses down cast a beam of light onto the quiet road.

"The porch light is on the right of the front door if you want to turn it on."

"That's okay, I don't want the light to disturb your parents."

"They're on the opposite side of the house. Plus, my dad sleeps like the dead and my mom uses some kind of white-noise app she swears by. '*Joshua, I'm telling you, this app even drowns out your father's elk-call snore! Where has this been for the last thirty-four years?*'"

I laughed at his spot-on impersonation of his mother and flicked the light on.

"Wow." Amber light illuminated the snow-covered walkway and a generous portion of the Averys' property. I leaned my head against the cool windowpane, losing myself in the tranquil beauty from my toasty place indoors. My gaze roved past the covered porch swing to the bushes near the back fence that now resembled fluffy white cotton balls. "Have you ever wondered about the magic of snow—I mean, how transformative it is to nature, how beautiful it makes everything look? I think I could stare at this scene for hours."

After several beats of no response from Joshua, I'd begun to think he'd stepped out of the room without me knowing. I pushed away from the window, rotating to see if—but Joshua was standing right where I'd left him, his gaze fixed on me.

"Yes," he said, his voice a heart-stopping rumble. "I know the feeling well."

I waited for him to say more, to add another sentence that might complete his thought. Something about nature or winter or *anything* other than his unending stare, because . . . because he didn't say things like that to me anymore. He hadn't since the day I told him about Noah. It'd been weeks of careful conversations, careful touches, careful moments alone together.

But he didn't disqualify anything, he simply allowed his words to steam up the windows of my heart even more. Careful Joshua had been challenging enough to be around, but if he continued to look at me like this . . .

He broke the spell, lifting a delicate glass container with snowflakes etched into the sides of the crystal that I hadn't even noticed he'd been holding. "Can I interest you in my grandmother's baklava?"

A soft laugh tumbled from my lips. "Baklava? This couldn't be the same baklava you've mentioned once or twice or, I don't know, four thousand times since Thanksgiving, is it?"

"The one and only. Consider this the holy grail of all baklavas." He smiled in a way that made me wonder for the hundredth time why he hadn't walked down the aisle with a lucky bride ten years ago. It was interesting that out of all the family stories and co-worker stories and business stories he'd shared with me during our nightly phone calls, he'd never once offered any information about his past romantic endeavors. But to be fair, I'd also never asked.

"If you're nice, I'll share this forbidden fruit with you. But if my mom asks . . . you never saw this, deal?" He detached a blue sticky note from the foil on top and wadded it up in his hand.

"Wait, let me see that."

He shook his head.

Aghast that he would crumple a note from sweet Elizabeth Avery, I strode toward him. "What did that say? Let me read it."

"Why?" He held his clenched fist above his head, making me jump on my tippy toes. I still couldn't reach it. I'd never felt so short before Joshua entered my life.

"Seriously, how old are you?" I asked between failed swipes.

He pretended to yawn, obviously enjoying my moment of struggle immensely. "Thirty-two going on eleven."

I jabbed my finger into his ribs, and immediately he crumpled. I ripped the paper from his grasp and unfurled it quickly, reading it out loud as I speed-walked around the sofa before falling onto the corner seat of the couch: "'Joshua, I didn't bother trying to hide Grandma's special stash this year, BUT THIS IS FOR OUR CHRISTMAS PLATTER. DO NOT EAT IT OR YOU WILL GET COAL. Mom.'"

I gaped at him as he plopped down beside me, planting his feet on the coffee table without a care. I swatted at his leg. "You're stealing your grandma's baklava from your mom's Christmas platter? Joshua, that's horrible!"

"My mother's Christmas platter has plenty on it already. Don't worry." He opened the lid, selected a honey-glazed triangle, and chomped down on it. "She doesn't really mean it anyway."

I referred back to the all-cap letters on the note. "Her note seems pretty straightforward to me—"

And then he shoved a triangle into my mouth. *Whoa.* The combination of crispy, gooey, nutty, and delectable was downright otherworldly. I might have moaned before I cupped a hand under my chin to catch the walnut crumbles trying to escape.

"This is . . ." But I couldn't finish because I was too busy chewing. Experiencing. Joshua was absolutely right. This baklava had Holy Grail status.

"Is it worth getting coal in my stocking for?"

I nodded and pulled my legs up underneath me, grateful our nightly phone call routine had taken the form of a face-to-face conversation tonight.

As I adjusted to get comfortable, my leg brushed his.

"Right there's good. Thanks." He set the baklava container on my knee.

"So first I'm an accomplice, and now I'm a table?"

He caught my eye and our smiles matched.

While he finished off a bite, I took advantage of his full mouth and asked a question I'd never dared to ask before. Maybe because I wasn't sure I wanted to hear the answer, or maybe because I knew whatever answer he gave wouldn't change my circumstances.

"Can I ask you something?"

"Sounds like you just did."

I nudged his leg with mine again. "Have you ever been in a serious relationship?"

He stilled, swallowed, and then met my eyes with humor-filled surprise. "Well, that's quite a big leap from baklava."

I shrugged. "You've just never talked about it."

"I could say the same thing about you."

"There's nothing to tell for me, really." I released a self-deprecating laugh. "A lot of first dates that rarely made it past date number five for some reason or another. A few of them were blind dates, but most were setups from well-meaning people who just wanted to see me happily married before I entered my thirties." I shrugged. "Obviously, I stopped dating altogether after I submitted my application to Small Wonders. . . ." I threw the emergency brake on that runaway thought before it could travel any further. "Anyway, that's the skinny on my sordid relationship past. Now you get to tell me about yours."

"Isn't there something way more interesting we should be talking about on Christmas Eve than past relationships?"

I cozied deeper into the cushion. "Absolutely not."

The fire crackled and popped, as if it, too, was eager for Joshua's response.

He released a long exhale, then threaded his fingers behind his head, settling in as if this were a pay-by-the-hour therapy session. "I met Chrissy at a party for Brick Builders. She was one of the sponsors and . . ." He thought for a moment. "We seemed to have a lot in common. She was a self-starter, too, and had launched a commission-based business that was becoming quite successful. She traveled a lot, so our first year together was mostly long-distance."

The words *first year* stood out, plucking a chord of jealousy that hummed inside me long after he started talking again. "The second year was . . . well, I was starting to think more seriously about us." His eyes flickered back to the container of baklava, as if needing a neutral place to land. "We put off a lot of important conversations due to the demands of our growing clienteles and business opportunities, and neither of us wanted to sacrifice the little face-to-face time we did have on potential disagreements." He chuckled lightly. "That should have been my first clue. Honestly, our relationship didn't make sense to anyone else in our lives, but we just kept saying that if it worked for us, then that was all that mattered."

"So, what happened?" I asked softly, sensing pain underneath his quiet reply.

"In Hollywood our breakup would fall under the category of *irreconcilable differences*. Because when we finally did have those big talks, the ones we'd put off for nearly two years, we couldn't agree on something pretty important."

It felt like an invasion of privacy to poke at the disagreement he referred to, but Joshua quenched my curiosity on his next breath.

"It was simple, really. Chrissy couldn't imagine being a parent, and I couldn't imagine not being one."

"Oh . . ." I hadn't been expecting that. Not even close.

His eyes returned to mine. "Yeah. There's not really a happy medium to be found in that one."

"No," I said under my breath. "There's really not."

Several beats of silence passed before a sudden fist of irony punched through my heart. Joshua's last relationship had failed because she didn't want kids. And ours hadn't had a chance to begin because I did.

"I'm sorry." An apology I'd spoken for more reasons than I could name.

"That was four years ago," he went on smoothly, oblivious to the unjust conclusions I'd just drawn about his romantic life. It wasn't fair. None of it. "And I've honestly been so busy with work these last few years that I haven't really slowed down long enough to think that way again until . . ."

And this time, *this time* I didn't wish for him to disqualify his unfinished thought. I didn't want him to switch gears or fill in the blank with anything but me. And whatever was happening between us.

"Until . . . ?" I barely breathed.

"Until you."

The admission cut the final thread between holding on to what was and embracing what could be. I didn't give him time to second-guess our proximity, or the fact that I was making the first move. I slid my palm over the dime-size dimple in his cheek, my fingers parting through the waves of hair just above his ear as I eased myself closer, so close that I could see the individual cords in his neck tense and his thick eyelashes double-blink before they slammed closed.

"Lauren." He spoke my name as if those six inconsequential letters could have formed a paragraph all on their own. But I heard the unspoken desire in them just as clearly, just as profoundly as the heartbeat pounding against my eardrums.

We both wanted *this*—a next step, a new beginning, a new

kind of us. We'd grown weary of existing in the space between co-workers and more. Friends and more. Hope and more.

I didn't speak as my wandering fingers skimmed his ear, his jaw, his temporarily stilled mouth. And then I let my lips do the skimming. I touched my mouth to his and one tentative kiss led to two. Two to three. And three to—

"*Lauren.*" Firm hands bracketed the sides of my face, forcing me to stop my exploration of his mouth and take in his pleading, desperate eyes instead. "Tell me what this is."

Only I didn't want to supply answers about our future. I only wanted this moment right now. I only wanted him.

But the intensity of his gaze made the price of admission clear: If we did this, if we stepped onto this moving conveyor belt, there would be no reverse, no U-turns back to a destination marked *Friendship Only*.

"What do *you* want?" I whispered a breath from his lips.

The wince that vibrated his throat made my own ache with need. "You know what I want. But this isn't about me."

"So make it about you. What do *you* want, Joshua?" A foreign kind of recklessness crashed through the walls of my subconscious, demanding I ignore the convicting knock somewhere in the depths of my being.

"You," he said. "I want *you, Lauren.*"

Hot and sure, his lips found mine again. Fire danced across my mouth, spreading into my bloodstream and igniting all the lonely and forgotten places. Every past memory marked by neglect and abandonment scrambled to the sidelines, forced to make room for the one thing I'd desired above all else—*love*. The kind that cheered. The kind that stayed. The kind that fought and protected and endured.

And yet even as his mouth moved in time with mine and his fingers pushed through my hair to cradle the back of my head, a cloud of doubt descended over my heart.

This isn't right.

I shoved the uninvited thought away, pressing into Joshua and losing myself all the more in his kiss. I wasn't willing to surrender a single inch of the emotional territory I'd just given to him tonight. Because being with Joshua *felt right and good*. He was everything stable, safe, secure. With him there were no agonizing waits or pointless heartaches. He was real, tangible, and right here in my arms.

Something weighted slipped from my knee and clattered to the hardwood at our feet, breaking the spell of our kiss and pulling us apart. With dazed expressions, we located the source of the interruption at the same time.

"Uh-oh . . ."

It took Joshua a few seconds more to articulate a coherent thought as we stared at his grandmother's scattered baklava on the living room floor.

He swiped a rough hand down his face. "Guess this confirms what I'll be getting in my stocking tomorrow." A sly smile sneaked onto his mouth. "But I'll take coal every year if it means kissing you again."

chapter twenty-six

And kiss again we did—all through Christmas Day and into the week following. Joshua had made up an excuse to see me at least once a day, knowing my holiday vacation time would soon be coming to an end. We'd eaten at new-to-us restaurants, enjoyed a few favorite childhood movies together, and worked on a one-thousand-piece jelly bean puzzle—which remained unfinished due to Joshua's boycott over not having an actual bowl of jelly beans to eat while we slaved away.

This morning we'd taken our furry friends to an indoor dog park to play. And by the way Skye whined whenever it was time to say good-bye to her favorite pooch pal, it was obvious she'd grown just as attached to Brach as I'd grown to Joshua in these last few weeks. I smiled at the heap of multicolored fur snuggled together in my living room, Skye's nose and Brach's giant paws hanging off the sides of the doggie bed.

My gaze drifted over to Joshua again, the way it had a dozen-plus times this afternoon. His feet were propped on the edge of my coffee table, his fingers typing furiously on the keys of his laptop while a slight crease crinkled his brow. He'd been like this for the past two hours, working on a digital storyboard for his upcoming presentation at Brian's hospital after the New Year.

I was also supposed to be working—going over my lesson plans for next week and readying my mind to be back in my classroom, but as usual, Joshua proved a distraction I couldn't resist. He bit the corner of his lip in concentration, my favorite of all his nerdy expressions.

"Why do I get the feeling you're secretly mocking me right now?" he asked without breaking cadence in whatever nerd code he was typing.

"Not mocking—just admiring your discipline."

He laughed. "Well, staying up till two and three in the morning every night this week is probably not discipline as much as it's succumbing to the pressure cooker of panic that I won't get this storyboard finished in time. I still need to send it all over to Sam for a final test before the presentation." He lifted his gaze from his screen. "But it was either work at home and not get to see you on New Year's Eve—which was completely out of the question—or bring my work to you. Sorry I haven't been the best company today," he added with the most endearing of smiles.

I hugged a throw pillow to my chest. "You won't hear me complaining. It's nice to spend a day together like this—relaxing, even. Also, I can't wait to hear what happens at that meeting. Brian thinks you're a shoo-in." I still couldn't believe how quickly Brian had set up a meeting with the board of pediatrics, or perhaps I couldn't quite believe how quickly Joshua had been able to translate Brian's big-picture vision into a detailed, animated proposal. Whatever the case, the two of them had been on the phone more than Jenna and I had been during the winter break.

"You feel ready to get back to reality on Monday?" he asked.

I blinked, trying to center my brain around the word *reality*.

"Teaching? Kids? Brighton Elementary?" he prompted teasingly. "Has the extended break made you forget your real life?"

My brain refused to move past the words *extended break* and *real life*. Each of them triggered an entirely different meaning that had nothing to do with school and everything to do with a future I'd been trying to avoid. "Oh. Ha. No, I haven't forgotten, but I won't pretend the early wake-up calls won't be brutal."

"I can relate. If I don't get to the halfway point by tomorrow afternoon, I'll likely be heading to bed when you're getting ready for school next week."

I rested my head on the back of the sofa. "It's gonna be weird, going back to school without you there." And then because I didn't want to come off as an overly needy female, I added, "Don't get me wrong, I really am thrilled for your contract with the hospital. It will open up a whole new world for you in consulting, won't it?"

He reached over, covering my socked foot with his hand and giving it a squeeze. "It's only a *potential* contract for now—a lot has to happen for it to move past these initial stages. But yes, it will be an expansion into a whole new territory. That said, it's not uncommon for something this big to take upwards of a year, with all the trial and error and waiting on the legal teams to sign off on this or that. The timing is rarely ever quick." He slid me toward him and kissed the top of my head. "But if God does allow this thing to move forward, I'm confident it still won't top my time with you at Brighton."

We shared a ridiculously sappy grin, and I wondered, not for the first time, if we were headed in the same direction as those overly mushy couples I'd often accused Brian and Jenna of being.

I snuck a glance at the clock on the bottom of his screen. "You sure you're still up for going to Jenna and Brian's tonight? Because if you'd rather just stay here and work—"

He silenced me with a kiss. "I have five more days to work on this before my deadline. We're going over there. Brian owes me another game of Risk."

I rolled my eyes. "Jenna and I are probably better off in

another room, watching a movie. I doubt either of you would notice we were missing." The last time we played, the night they'd come over to . . . to visit after my time off from work, their strategy planning had been all-consuming.

After setting his laptop on the coffee table, he wrapped an arm around me and pulled me into his side. "I'd notice." He rested his chin on top of my head. "Believe me, I notice every time you're not around. That's part of how I knew."

"Knew what?" I coiled one of the strings from the neck of his hoodie around my finger.

"That you were it for me." He shifted and smoothed down my hair. "When you didn't come to school in the days following all that happened with . . ." When he didn't continue the statement, the breath I'd been holding released. "I thought I was gonna lose my mind if I didn't see you, Lauren. I've never felt like that before, about anything or anyone."

His thudding heartbeat pressed against my ear, steady and secure. "I feel that way about you, too."

He tilted my face up to his, kissing me with a tenderness that begged for tears. Because I'd fallen in love with him. There was no other way to spin it. No other way to write this story. I was in love with Joshua Avery, and everything in me wanted that to be enough.

Our evening with the Rosewoods was going exactly as I'd predicted: Brian and Joshua were huddled over the official Risk handbook, researching obscure plays, while Jenna and I shared several how-do-we-get-out-of-this glances over the top of their heads.

She lightly cleared her throat and then mouthed, "Cookies?"

Careful not to draw attention to myself, I slid my chair out from the table and slinked away to the kitchen. Jenna opened a narrow cupboard near her spice cabinet, rose up on her tippy-toes, and reached way into the back to pull out a box of Samoa Girl Scout cookies.

My eyes rounded at the sight of her holding a treat made with actual cane sugar.

"What is even happening right now? I figured we were coming in here for one of your sweetened-with-date-juice energy balls," I teased.

She wiggled her eyebrows conspiratorially. "Nope. Technically it's not New Year's yet, so I'm still eating whatever I want. Brian's mom actually gave me two boxes of these in my stocking. I'm pretty sure she thinks supplying me with Girl Scout cookies means I owe her a grandchild now, though." The minute her joke was out, she slapped a hand to her mouth. "Oh, gosh, I'm sorry, Lauren. That was insensitive—"

"No, it's fine. I'm sure she does want grandkids. And you and Brian will make some beautiful babies together someday."

"Don't say that too loudly," she rebuked with a smile. "We're not quite ready to be parents yet. We still have some traveling we want to do, and Brian's plotted out this whole financial graph thing he wants us to follow. All I know is that we're currently on the green dot and we have to get to the blue before any mini Rosewoods can be made."

"Ha, sure," I said, though I hadn't a clue what wanting to wait for children felt like. I'd dreamed of becoming a mother since before I graduated from high school.

Jenna hopped up on the counter, prying open the bottom of the cookie box. "So what about . . ." She ticked her head toward the room where the guys were still nose-deep in the Risk rule book. "What does *he* think about adopting?"

The phrasing of her question threw me for a minute. Not *What does Joshua think about you adopting*—but *adopting*. Period. As in a process that might involve him. I knew Joshua wanted to be a father. He'd told me as much, and I also knew he'd been ultra-supportive of my plans to bring Noah home, but

. . . but I hadn't asked him about his thoughts regarding adoption directly. It had become one of the many hot topics I'd avoided when we talked about the future.

"What?" she asked, pulling out a cookie and holding it between her fingers. "What's that face . . . you *have* talked with him about it, right?"

My spastic breathing was probably Morse code for *I'm a coward. I'm a coward. I'm a coward.* "Not specifically, no."

"Not specifically?" Jenna's head jerked back. "What do you mean *not specifically*? Lauren, it's all you've talked about with me for the last *two years*. How have you not mentioned it to each other? I mean—" she paused to release a deep breath—"I understand that this last month was tough, but your dossier is still over there . . . just waiting for you to say you're ready to be matched again. What has Stacey said about all that? How long can you be 'on hold' with the agency before your documentation expires?"

Truth? I had no idea. I knew there were expiration dates, yes, but if I asked my agency about the specifics, then I'd have concrete answers. And if I had concrete answers, then I would have to make concrete decisions, and that seemed far too . . . concrete.

"I haven't had much contact with Stacey." Or any contact since asking to be placed on hold. I reached for the box of cookies even though I had zero appetite in light of this conversation. My stomach always seemed to knot when I thought about the future these days.

"So . . . you're not talking to your agency, either?" Jenna's restraint to keep her inside voice intact was impressive. "Help me understand this, because I'm super confused right now."

That made two of us. "I'm on hold. Till after the New Year."

"Well that's *tomorrow*." She lowered her voice again, nearly hissing. "When you said things had progressed between Joshua and you, I assumed that meant vital conversations were happening about the future. It's not like he doesn't know you're a half step away from becoming a mother. I'd think he'd at least ask some questions about what— "

"Don't put this on him." Defensiveness crept up inside me. "He's always willing to talk about anything I'm willing to talk about."

"So it's you who's shut him out, then." Her on-target chastisement hit the mark.

"It's not exactly a first-week-of-dating kind of conversation. It's hard and complicated." Words I didn't want anywhere near my relationship with him.

She shook her head, staring down at the stylish holes in the knees of her jeans. "I guess I just really hoped the two of you had discovered a loophole together. Like . . . like sometime during the holiday break you called the agency and figured out how you could be in a healthy romantic relationship *while still* moving forward with your plan to adopt from China. I just never would have guessed . . ." She shook her head, and I braced for her next words. "That you would give up on something you've been so passionate about for so long. Something you're only a few steps away from now."

"I never said I was giving up. I simply haven't made a decision yet." And yet even as I spoke it, my heart bucked in rebuke.

Joshua's deep laugh sailed through the dining room and into the kitchen, where Jenna's gaze remained trained on me.

"No," I said, shaking my head. "You don't get to look at me like that. Don't pretend you weren't the one who pushed me toward him every chance you got or that you didn't purposefully arrange for me to spend Christmas with his entire family before you flew off to Tahoe."

"I did, yes, but my hope was that you'd get to have *both* your dreams come true, Lauren—the adopted child you've been praying for as a single woman *and* an awesome guy who wants to be a part of your future."

I caught myself a half second before I rolled my eyes at her naïveté. "Well, it doesn't work that way." At least, not as things were now. If I was willing to wait a full two years after the day I married—*if I married*—then I could reapply to adopt from China, which then would mean starting the long wait to be matched to a child all over again. So sure, could I potentially have both dreams come true at once? Yes. In a minimum of four-plus years.

All the information on my application was legally binding, an oath designed to give a vulnerable child the most stable home life possible. If I continued with a match, I'd have to do so as a single woman.

Jenna jammed the cookie from her hand back inside the crinkly plastic tray and shoved the package closed. Apparently, this conversation had soured Jenna's sweet tooth, as well.

"I'm sorry," she said with a shake of her head. "But I think you're wrong for not at least involving him in this conversation—hard as it may be. If he's going to be a part of your future, then you have to discuss the whole picture with him."

I knew she was right, especially after what Joshua had disclosed to me about his last relationship. But how could I talk to him when I was still so confused myself?

Jenna's eyes turned glassy. "I may not be the most faithful churchgoer around, but I saw your face when you got that first picture of Noah. . . ." Her voice hitched half an octave. "And I told Brian after you left that night that watching you walk this journey over the past two years has changed something in me. I've always believed God was real, but I . . ." As she searched for the right words, the faint knock in my chest strengthened. "I hadn't understood how much He cared about all the personal details in my life until I saw you open that little boy's file. It was like all your struggle and sacrifice to get to that point was nothing in comparison to the reward of your faith in Him. It made me believe that He might have a plan for my life, too. That maybe the very things I've been so afraid to say yes to all these years are the very things He wants me to trust Him with."

At her vulnerability, I swallowed down the bitter truth that rose like bile. A truth I hadn't trusted myself to speak aloud to any person. But here it was: That little boy hadn't been God's plan for me. He'd been a mistake, a neon sign stating that all my struggle and sacrifice had been in vain. That my deepest desires hadn't mattered much after all.

"I love you, Lauren." Jenna slipped off the counter and wrapped me in a hug I was too detached to feel. "And that won't change, no matter what you decide to do."

"Ah . . . there you two are," Brian said, walking into the kitchen and swiping the box of Girl Scout cookies off the counter. "I don't want to interrupt whatever girl-power conversation is happening in here, but in the dining room I'm dominating poor Joshua, and he could use a boost of moral support."

"Afraid it's the other way around, bro," Joshua said as Jenna released me from her embrace.

I met his eyes for the briefest of moments to see a flicker of worry cross his features.

"Unhand my cookies or you will lose far more than the territory you've conquered on a board game." Jenna jabbed a pointed finger at Brian.

He dropped the box to the counter immediately, raising his palms in surrender. "Man. Where can a guy find a good snack around here?"

"There's some guacamole in the fridge and your favorite chips in the pantry. But if you touch my cookies again, you'll be the one on the surgeon's table."

Brian kissed her on the cheek before rummaging through the fridge.

Jenna looked from me to Joshua. "I'll grab the chips and bring them to the dining room."

"Thanks," Brian said as he swung the fridge door closed.

"Oh, babe, you'll have to hear Joshua's latest ideas on the app he's been working on for the hospital. I think the board's gonna be blown away by the new options he's come up with. I don't know of anything like it."

"Cool, yeah. I want to hear all about it," Jenna said, prodding Brian out of their kitchen and glancing back at me with a look that said *talk to him.*

As if we could have a big-picture conversation in the middle of my best friend's kitchen on New Year's Eve. Sure, I hadn't been totally open with him, but this wasn't the time or place for that to change.

"Everything good?" Joshua asked, coming to stand in front of me.

"Of course, we just had a lot to catch up on."

He nodded but in no way looked convinced. "You know you can talk to me, too, right? About anything." He scanned my face. "You're a tricky balance for me sometimes. I'm torn between thinking I need to give you space to process and wanting to be in your head with you. I know I came into your life in the middle of a big journey, but I'm here now, and I don't plan on being anywhere else."

Guilt chomped on the soft spot in my conscience, and once again, I felt an almost reckless desire to pull him close and hold on to him with every morsel of strength I possessed. I snaked my arms around his waist. "And I don't want you to be anywhere else."

We'd managed to finish over half a game of Risk without Brian threatening to overthrow Joshua and his strategies from the Rosewood Kingdom. They did, however, start a Risk winner's graph. My hope of transitioning to simpler—and quicker—games like Yahtzee or UNO had become a moot point.

The purse I'd left hanging on the back of my chair vibrated

during yet another lengthy discussion, this time involving an illegal play by Jenna. I reached into the inside pocket and glanced at the voicemail notification waiting there for me: Stacey—Small Wonders.

What? Why was she calling me on New Year's Eve?

Somehow, I managed to slip the ticking time bomb back into my purse for the remainder of the game, assuring myself every few minutes that my curiosity could wait, that Stacey's message was probably just a routine check-up since we hadn't spoken in a while. But as soon as Jenna tuned the television to the ball drop at Times Square, I snuck away to the restroom so I could listen in private. No small irony that the last time I'd received a voicemail from Stacey I was also standing in a friend's bathroom.

I locked the door, swiped through my recent call list, and tapped on the voicemail play icon. Holding the phone to my ear, I clenched my teeth so hard my jaw began to ache.

"Lauren, hey . . . it's Stacey at Small Wonders. I've been wanting to check up on you and see how your Christmas was and how the last few weeks have been."

Okay. It's just a check-in. Nothing more.

"And I know you asked to be placed on hold until after New Year's, but a really special file came across my desk this morning, and I believe you could be her perfect match. I'd love to send her information over to you. I'm leaving here in the next hour, but I have everything uploaded and ready to send to you. We're closed tomorrow for the holiday, so I'll leave my personal cell number for you—just call or shoot me a text if you're open to reviewing it, and I'll send it right over." Stacey paused. "She's a little older than the age window you originally provided us, but I'm telling you, this is a very special little girl who deserves a special mama. You'll have forty-eight hours to place her file on hold if you're interested in pursuing her. Happy New Year, Lauren. I hope to talk to you soon."

I listened to the message a second time, trying to convince

myself I'd misheard her. Because she couldn't possibly have a child in mind for me. A name. A face. A little girl.

A daughter.

Turning the faucet on high to drown out my thoughts with white noise, I leaned against the counter and stared at the pale-faced woman in the mirror. The one who had no earthly idea how she was going to live through the next two minutes, much less the next two days.

God, what are you doing to my heart?

chapter twenty-seven

The email came at 8:44 a.m. on New Year's Day.

And by 9:44 a.m. I was sitting in Gail Cartwright's driveway.

Are you home? I really need to talk to you.

Yes! Kids are still at the youth group all-nighter from last night. Wanna come over?

I'm already here.

Not thirty seconds after I sent the text, Gail opened her front door with a smile on her face, as if it was totally acceptable that I drove all the way across town and didn't think to call her first. But Gail had never been one to bother with social norms.

Laptop in hand, I exited my Jeep and trudged up her slushy walkway and porch steps.

"Happy New Year," she said, opening the door wider for me to enter.

"Happy New Year." My response sounded as remote as my current grip on reality.

"Coffee or tea?"

I shook my head, setting my laptop on the end table. I was jittery enough without an added caffeine boost. "No thanks."

"You can take a seat on the couch—just excuse the pile of clean laundry there. I haven't gotten to it yet."

I hadn't even noticed the white basket overflowing with clothes and likely wouldn't have, if not for her pointing it out. "Actually, I think I need to stand. I don't think . . . I don't think I can sit right now."

"Sure," she said. "Whatever you need. Are you okay if I sit?"

I nodded while Gail, a vision of serenity and calm, took a seat in the recliner, her gaze tracking me as I paced her entryway like an agitated zoo animal. In true Gail form, she didn't bother with questions like *Can you tell me what's happening?* or *Are you okay?* because clearly, I was not okay. She simply waited for me to be ready.

"I got another match. This morning."

Her expression shifted ever so slightly, but likely due to my unenthusiastic demeanor, she remained poised like a certified crisis counselor. Raising six teenagers should earn her some sort of insta-certification.

"How do you feel about that?"

I stopped pacing. "I have no idea."

"It looks like you have lots of ideas."

I slammed my eyes closed. "Yes . . . I do. But none of them are coherent. This . . . everything is different now."

"Since Noah?"

Since Joshua. I shook my head and tears tumbled down my cheeks. "Yes and no."

A delicate lift of her eyebrow was the only response to my double-mindedness.

"I met somebody."

"Since Noah?" Same question with a completely different meaning.

"No, before Noah. In November, actually. I didn't tell you because . . . because he wasn't supposed to mean anything to me. He wasn't supposed to matter. I'd been so sure, so dead set on not letting my heart feel anything for him other than friendship, but then when everything fell through with the adoption, I just . . . I gave in." My voice broke. "And now I'm in love with him."

Her eyes rounded, unblinking. "And he . . ."

"Joshua." Just his name made my insides ache with longing. "I'm pretty sure he feels the same about me. He's wonderful, Gail, the kind of man you pray your daughters will marry one day. He's kind and compassionate, and he loves children." I swallowed back a sob. "He has a strong faith in God and strong family values—I spent Christmas with his whole family and they're, well, they're a lot like you guys."

She set her coffee mug on the coaster beside her, and I expected her next question to be about Joshua—about my spastic profession of love or at least an explanation of how we met.

Instead she asked, "And how do you think a relationship with Joshua fits in with your calling to adopt?"

Her question gutted me. "I don't know. To be honest, I've spent more time lately doubting that calling than chasing after it." The truth caused my chest to heave as if in search of air, more air than I could inhale in ten breaths. "Because what if I got it wrong—backwards? Maybe losing Noah was my wake-up call, you know? Maybe I took the hard way when all along God was telling me to wait for a different path—for Joshua."

"Do you think that's what God is saying to you—to take a different path?"

"I have no idea what He's saying to me anymore! Everything is so . . . so not the way I thought it was going to be!" I threw my arms up, feeling something between delirium at my lack of sleep and hysteria at the utter absurdity of the last month and a half.

"Have you asked Him? Have you asked God what He thinks about all this? About Joshua and this new match?"

I twisted back, my gaze finding hers briefly before falling

away again. "No." Pinpricks of heat crept up my neck and into my cheeks. "I haven't."

No trace of judgment shadowed her face. "In my experience, it's really difficult to hear God's voice when my ears aren't tuned in. But I can tell you one thing, Lauren." And even as she spoke my name, my bottom lip began to quiver. "God doesn't trick His children. He loves us, and everything He asks of us, or allows us to walk through, has a purpose."

"So what was the purpose in me getting attached to a baby who was never meant to be mine? Or in allowing an incredible man like Joshua to take the sub job across the hall if he was supposed to remain off-limits to me?" My tone was clipped, desperate. "Because I don't get it."

"Ask Him those questions. He's big enough to handle your anger, your confusion. Your hurt."

An answer that sent me spinning in a new direction.

"It's a girl—the match they sent me." I swiped at my eyes, the words rushing out without filters. "She's five, and she's been living at a children's facility in China sponsored by an influential couple here in the states for orphans with heart conditions. Hers was discovered at sixteen months. She'll need a surgery once she's adopted, but she's been receiving basic medical treatment since she's been at The Heart House. There are dozens of pictures of her, maybe thirty? I don't even know. But her smile is huge and her eyes always seem to be laughing and there's even a video of her singing 'Jesus Loves Me' in broken English. And"—I suddenly couldn't even get the words out fast enough—"she loves books. Like sleeps with a pile of them on her bed every night. She's holding one in almost every picture I've seen of her." I sucked in a breath. "Gail, they're the same books I read to my class—all translated into Chinese: *The Story of Peppa Pig, If You Give a Mouse a Cookie, Chicka Chicka Boom Boom*, and . . ." A sob washed away the completion of that sentence. Because there were some things too sacred to share openly. Too vulnerable and raw. But there was also no doubt in my mind as to why Stacey had felt so compelled to send the little girl's file to me—all my credentials were in teaching and working with her age group. Still, not even Stacey could have known the connection I'd uncovered.

Gail stood, taking me in her arms without speaking a word.

"What do I do? Tell me what to do."

She rubbed my back as I wept on her shoulder.

After a few minutes, she led me to the sofa, my puffy eyes still tender and sore from all the tears I'd cried.

"I can't lose him—I can't lose Joshua. Not now."

Gail's hand stilled on my knee. "Does that mean you're willing to say no to this little girl?"

I squeezed my eyes shut once again, tears leaking out of the corners. *No*, my heart wailed. *I'm meant to be her mother!*

"Why does it have to be either or?" I lifted my head as my emotions flailed in search of the impossible. "Why can't the answer be an *and* instead of an *or*? Because maybe there is a way I can have them both." I'd suddenly morphed into Jenna, grasping for a perfect scenario that would involve everyone getting a happily-ever-after. I faced Gail fully, my mind high-jumping over every hurdle that popped up on this mental track. "What if—what if Joshua and I dated in secret? Like, after we were home from China and had settled in to a routine." I breezed past the part where I'd said *we*—as in the little orphan girl and me. "And maybe Joshua and I can wait a few weeks—months even—before we introduce him to her. We'd take everything slow. I mean, that could work, couldn't it? The only regulations regarding my marital status are about everything leading up to the adoption process. But there's no hard rules about what happens after, right?"

"As far as legal ramifications that would disrupt your adoption? No. The second your plane touches down on American soil, that child is under your authority and is no longer bound to any international adoption requirements. You'd be free to do what you think is best for you and your child."

My quick-lived feeling of euphoria faded as Gail's expression remained unchanged. "But?"

"Do you really think that being in a new dating relationship during your child's first year home is in the best interest of your child?"

A single question that provided answers for so many others. I'd attended two attachment seminars in the last couple of years, I'd read the books on connection and bonding, heard the stories about how important cocooning an adopted child was during their first year home, building trust, building security, building true attachment. And I'd seen Gail and Robert's real-life testimonials as they parented their adopted children . . . and yet still, my heart craved another way. A different way.

She went on. "That first year is the most crucial, especially when adopting an older child. She'll be grieving—no matter how well cared for she is at that children's home. Leaving the only place she's ever called home, and the only people who've ever cared for her, is a traumatic event. That's a fact, not an opinion. Navigating life in this new world will require your undivided attention—and your undivided heart. She won't know the language, the food, the sounds, the smells. Everything will be uncharted. Adoption is beautiful, Lauren . . . but it's not part-time. We often say in group that parenthood is a hamster wheel of self-denial, sacrifice, and unconditional love."

Melanie's rant from the adoption group months ago scrolled through my mind: *"You'll be alone. Married or single—you'll be all alone."*

"What if I can't do it, Gail?" The near-silent admission slipped through my lips. "What if my fears are right and I'm not strong enough or capable enough to do this on my own? I've made such a mess of everything. . . ."

She slid her hand over mine. "None of us are strong enough

to handle the hard apart from God. But you don't have to fear being alone, sweet girl. He's asking for a partnership with us. Can you see how He's already given you a wonderful community of trusted friends and loved ones—that's just one of the many ways He's been preparing and providing for you since this journey began. We aren't powerful enough to mess up God's plan. Can we deny it? Yes. Can we delay it while we chase our own way? Absolutely. But sometimes our character needs time to catch up to our calling." She stroked my arm. "The Bible says God pursues us with unfailing kindness. And it's that same undeserved kindness that leads us to repentance."

Repentance. A three-syllable word that clanged in my ears and reverberated through my bones. When our eyes met again, I knew what had to be done.

Even the most committed boyfriend on the planet wasn't a husband. There was a reason behind the adoption rules, and whether I liked them or not, they were the right reasons, because they put the needs of the vulnerable child *first.* Something I'd been failing to do for quite some time.

"I think I need to go."

Gail nodded as if she'd been expecting me to say exactly that. But before I could stand, she pulled me in, wrapped her arms around me, and prayed.

For me.

For Joshua.

For a little orphan girl far, far away.

chapter twenty-eight

Of all the moments for Joshua to be waiting on my doorstep, holding a carton of eggs and a to-go cup of coffee, his timing couldn't have been worse. I wasn't ready to see him yet. I'd barely had time to examine my own fragmented heart, much less add Joshua's into the mix. Why was God forcing my hand? Wasn't it enough that I needed to have the conversation within the next two days? I at least needed a few more hours to sort out the details.

My gait slowed as I approached him from behind. The back of his puffy jacket and crimson beanie sparked a memory of the first night we'd spent together outside of school at the tree lighting festival. Just one of many moments circling my heart over these last two months.

Skye barked from behind the front door as Joshua rang the bell for a second time. Every part of me prickled with an urge to slink away like the coward I'd become, and if not for the crunching ice under my boot, I might have caved.

He twisted around to face me, his work satchel banging against his hip. "Oh, hey there, beautiful. I didn't realize you were going out this morning."

Obviously, the sweatshirt hood I'd tightened around my face

had masked my red-rimmed eyes from his assessment. There was little beautiful about me today—inside or out. His eyes glanced to the laptop peeking from the tote hanging off my shoulder.

"Yeah, I . . . had some errands to run." The lie soured on my tongue.

"Oh?" His eyebrows spiked. "Nearly every store I tried this morning was closed for the holiday. It's the first time I've had to shop at a gas station for breakfast items, but I didn't want to chance you not having enough."

"Enough . . . ?"

"Eggs." He eyed me comically, holding up the bounty in his hands. "I hear they're pretty critical for making omelets."

Omelets.

Bits and pieces of a half-heard conversation drifted back to me from the car ride last night. Joshua wasn't here for a surprise drop-in this morning; we'd made plans to make omelets together on New Year's Day. Joshua had gloated about some secret method Sam—his business partner—had showed him years ago, and I'd nodded along, agreeing to whatever would distract him from asking too many questions about my extended visit to the bathroom during a mediocre ball-drop performance.

"Ah, right, yes." I shoved my house key into the lock and pushed inside, holding the door open for him to follow.

"Lucky for you, though, Coffee Hut was open." He handed me the steaming to-go cup. It was then I noticed Joshua's restless eyes looked eerily similar to my own, minus last night's mascara residue, of course.

"Did you not sleep last night?" I asked, averting my attention to my ridiculous dog, who was currently whining at Joshua's feet—or rather, at the lack of Joshua's canine companion.

"Sorry, Skye. Brach's at home today." He patted her head as I shooed her from the entryway and pointed at her corner.

"Is it that obvious? My lack of sleep?" He huffed a laugh and shucked off his coat, plopping his satchel onto my side table—as if it were the most natural thing in the world for him to do. As if, in such a short period of time, our lives had melded into a singular rhythm, a unified motion of existence. "Guess that's what turning thirty does to a guy: ruins his ability to pull off an all-nighter without notice."

"You pulled an all-nighter? Why?"

Chances were high our reasons for staying up all night weren't the same. He likely hadn't been wrestling with God over whether or not to send an email to a certain adoption agency first thing this morning.

I took the gas station eggs from him and noticed he was wearing the T-shirt I'd bought him for Christmas: *If you love something set it free . . . unless it's a T-Rex.*

I started for the sink to wash my hands as he anchored himself in the middle of my kitchen, his arms extended wide as if he was about to make a global announcement. "I finished it, Lauren."

The words were spoken with such triumph that I broke my concerted effort to avoid eye contact with him. "You finished . . . ? Wait, you finished the storyboard for the presentation? But I thought you still had several days of work to do on it?"

He carried on as if I hadn't even spoken, his adrenaline like a pulsating aura of energy around him. "Something happened to me last night, something I haven't experienced in *years*. Not since the creation of Brick Builders." An animated grin spread across his face as he plucked the whisk out of my utensil jar and tossed it in the air, catching and releasing it several times over. "Sam's already texted me to say he thinks the layout is killer—like nothing he's ever worked on before."

"Really? Wow." A thought tugged at the back of my mind. "And you'll still be able to keep up with the demands of the reading app if this one takes off, too?" I set the mixing bowl next to the carton and prepared to crack the eggs.

"Absolutely. We'll continue to stay the course with the educational apps for school districts nationwide, but at this point, the work left to do on that project is minimal, which feels even more divine considering I had the distinct impression—sometime around three in the morning—that this hospital project is the next big step for Wide Awake Consulting."

"Wow, Joshua. That's just . . . incredible." *And I'm going to miss all of it.* I bit the insides of my cheeks to keep the sadness in my voice from leaking out my eyes. "I'm proud of you."

He dropped the whisk next to the empty bowl and snaked his arms around my middle from behind me. Placing his chin on my shoulder, he spoke in such a low tenor my insides hummed to life. "And do you know what I kept thinking about as I burned the midnight oil?"

Likely not what I'd been thinking about all night. Not trusting myself to speak, I shook my head.

"That none of this would have happened without you." He pressed a warm kiss to the sensitive spot below my right ear. "Somehow, in just a couple of months, you've managed to make every aspect of my life better."

Too much. It was all too, too much. The egg slipped from my grasp and broke against the glass rim of the bowl, the shell and yolk mixing into an inseparable mess. Much like my entire life.

"I'm sorry," I barely choked out before I rushed to the sink, bowl in hand.

"Hey, it's fine. It's just one egg. We have eleven more."

Despite my best efforts to shield my face from him as I rinsed the contents down the drain, Joshua placed a hand on my back and steered me toward him. "Are you all right this morning?"

Not even a little bit. "Honestly, no." The only full truth I could offer at the moment. "I feel bad to admit this, but I lost track of time when I was out this morning, and I was hoping I might take a shower before . . . before we have breakfast together. I'm feeling a bit self-conscious." *And if I don't leave this instant, the last fraying thread holding my sanity together will snap.* "Would you mind if I ran upstairs for a few minutes? I won't be long."

"Self-conscious?" His thoughtful, tender gaze roved my face. "Lauren, I've never once looked at you and found you lacking in any way. This morning included."

Stop, please just stop. He moved in close, leaned down, and pressed a soft, distracting kiss to my lips, and I silently begged him not to ask anything more, not to force his way inside my scattered mind. I needed time to figure out how to defuse the ticking clock that had become the background noise to my every thought.

I broke away, our lips a mere breath from touching again when I offered, "Ten minutes, okay?" Though not even my most optimistic self believed it would be nearly enough time.

Before I could walk away, he caught my hand and tugged me back to him. "My manners really want to tell you to take your time getting ready, but I'm afraid my stomach isn't going to survive much longer without food." He patted his flat belly as if to prove a point. "Mind if I eat a bowl of cereal before we make our omelets?"

I bobbed my head once and slipped my hand out of his warm grasp. "Help yourself."

The instant I ducked around the corner, nausea brewed in the base of my abdomen. I took the stairs quickly, the feeling intensifying as the distance between Joshua and me grew.

As if on their own volition, my steps slowed just one stair away from the landing, and the hard knock against my rib cage increased to a staccato-like thud. A pull I couldn't explain drew my gaze from the entrance to my bedroom to a new target: the closed door I'd avoided for nearly a month.

No! my mind screamed. *Do not open that door.*

Yet the insistent prompt inside me would not be convinced.

My chest heaved as I took a step toward the nursery and lowered my hand to grip the cold metal doorknob.

As if to prove that whatever lay inside this space couldn't hurt me any worse than my current heartache, I cranked the knob hard and shot inside the room like the snap of a rubber band. But the acrid odor of freshly painted walls that had been trapped behind a closed door for weeks smacked against my senses and silenced whatever mental mantra I'd so foolishly believed would keep me strong.

My focus sharpened on the mini baby sanctuary I'd created months ago for a child I'd hoped would be in my arms by the turn of spring, and slowly but surely, all the air squeezed from my lungs. Searching for warmth, I wrapped those same baby-less arms around my chest as my gaze found the only piece of art I'd purchased before that devastating phone call.

"For this child I have prayed."—1 Samuel 1:27

The verse sparked a rush of hot indignation through my blood.

Because *prayed* I had—every single day and over every piece of paperwork and payment. Only where had God been when I'd begged Him to guide my path during all those months—*years*? Where had He been when I'd scrimped and saved and sent off the bulk of my retirement account in a single check? Or when I'd taken Gail's recommendation and attended those three-day attachment seminars, using my personal days? Or when I'd driven forty minutes to the adoption group nearly weekly for the past eight months?

And where had He been when Noah's file had been mistakenly sent to me when he clearly belonged to someone else?

But perhaps my biggest question, the one nipping at my spirit since I'd left Gail's house was simply this: If God wanted me to adopt as a single woman, then why did He allow me to meet Joshua when I did?

I lifted my eyes to the unmoving ceiling fan and spewed the raw and indignant prayer churning inside me. "I was willing, God. I was open to whatever you asked of me, ready to bring that baby boy home and make him my son and never look back. But you took him away. And now you want me to just . . . to what?" I flung my arms away from my body. "To pretend like Joshua never existed, either? I can't do that!" *I won't do that.* "He's . . ." A dry sob broke my rant. "I love him. *I love him.*"

From somewhere deep inside me, a response surfaced, an impression so intense I pressed the heel of my hand to the left side of my chest.

Trust me.

But how? *How do I even do that now?* There were too many variables, too many hearts at stake. Pressure built behind my eyes again. Why wasn't there a snooze button I could press on my life? I needed more time!

I shook my head, over and over, unable to imagine facing a single day without Joshua, much less an unknown future. Because if I did this, if I said *yes* to the little girl with a broken heart and a bed full of books, I couldn't possibly ask Joshua to wait for me. I couldn't possibly expect him to step aside while I devoted every waking moment of my time, energy, and affection to a child—*my child.*

Needing space from the framed verse, I took a step back, my heel colliding with the paw of the overstuffed panda I'd taken from my mom's job site a month ago—the last time I'd seen my mother face-to-face. One more relationship casualty at the hand of my adoption journey. And the tally wasn't even in yet.

I scowled at the black-and-white stuffed animal, and then at the children's book resting against its paw. The book George Avery had read aloud to my college class more than a decade ago, a book that had steered me in the direction of children and education and to the start of my teaching career. The book I could quote by heart as I turned the illustrated pages for my first graders at the beginning of every new school year.

And it was the same book I saw stacked on the tiny mattress of Ting Fei's bed a million miles away.

I'd once deemed *Horton Hatches the Egg* a providential God whisper, a divine tool He'd used to point me in the next right direction and onto the next right path. But today, instead of this representing the beauty of faithfulness and unconditional love, it felt like a cruel, heart-stopping joke. Swiping the classic piece of literature away from the pudgy panda, I spun around, ready to bury it in the bottom of my desk when Joshua's voice startled it out of my hand.

"Lauren?"

The book arched across the carpet, a flurry of colorful pages and typed narrative landing in a heap at his feet.

"I thought I heard a . . ." The statement fell away as his gaze roamed the inside of a room I'd never once invited him into. "Cadet Blue," he muttered while taking in the walls.

Panic seized me at the sight of him standing at the threshold of the place where my confusion and doubt mingled.

I wasn't ready for this. *We* weren't ready for this.

But again, the words ribboned through the hollows of my soul, a whisper that caused the tightness in my chest to momentarily subside.

Trust me.

Joshua bent and reached for the book at his feet, turning it over in his palm and reciting Horton's motto with a reverence that caused my throat to constrict. "'I meant what I said, and I said what I meant. An elephant's faithful one hundred percent.' This is one of my dad's favorites." When his eyes met mine, his smile sobered. "But something tells me you already knew that."

"Yes," I said on the end of a shallow exhale. "It was the first children's book I heard him read aloud, actually, as a freshman in college. It's the story that got me into teaching, into believing that reading to a child could shape their future. And it's . . . it's followed me ever since." In more ways than one.

As if respecting a boundary line I'd never actually verbalized, he seemed to hesitate before asking, "May I come in?"

Every cell in my body wanted to reject his request, yet somehow my mouth said, "Yes."

With a contemplative perusal, Joshua explored the nursery, pausing every so often, as if he could hear all the secrets my heart had spoken in this space. Though there wasn't much to see in way of decor—blue painted walls, an unhung picture, a crib still waiting to be fully assembled—his gaze locked on the glittery party invitation sitting on the rocking chair by the window.

I barely refrained from crying out when he lifted it to read. His back was to me as he skimmed the words Jenna had so perfectly inked with her calligraphy pen.

You're Invited to a New Year's Adoption Shower
For: Lauren Bailey and her baby boy, Noah Yong!
Where: 4459 Carriage Trail Loop, Boise ID
When: January 1st at 1:00 p.m.
Note: Please see insert for Lauren's registry needs

Today was certainly not the New Year's Day I'd planned on.

Joshua set the card down as gently as if he were handling a newborn babe, then rotated to face me. In a matter of seconds, the ten-foot gap between us had stretched to ten thousand. "What's going on, Lauren? Something's changed, hasn't it?"

"Yes." The word burst from my mouth, as if to relieve the pressing ache behind my ribs. But I couldn't hold back for another second. Joshua deserved better than a cat-and-mouse game from me. He deserved the truth and all the messy details that came along with it. "Small Wonders called with a new match for me. Last night, while we were at Jenna's house." I took a breath. "She's a five-year-old girl in need of a heart surgery, and she's been living in a sponsored children's home in China for the majority of her life. They sent her file to me this morning."

His shoulders stiffened. "Wait—but I thought you were on hold? I thought that meant you weren't receiving matches until . . . until you told them you were ready to again."

"I was on hold, but . . ." The dryness in my throat made swallowing impossible. "Stacey—my social worker at the agency—asked me to take a look at this file because . . . because she thinks I'd be a good fit for this little girl."

The three seconds it took for him to speak could have been a year. A century, even.

"And what do *you* think?"

I pushed away my conflicting emotions. "My mind's been all over the place since I left Gail's house this morning."

A flicker of hurt flashed across Joshua's face, and stupidly, I attempted to explain it away—the hiding, the avoiding, the deceiving. "Gail's been a part of my journey from the start—from before the start, actually. I needed to talk to her first, to get her insight and advice because she knows this world so well." I rushed on. "I was planning on asking you to come over after I got back home and had some time to sort out my thoughts a bit more, but when I arrived, you were already here. I'd completely forgotten about the omelets."

"Okay." Only, it was obvious it wasn't. Nothing was okay.

"I'm really sorry."

He raised his eyes to mine again, and the impact was enough to force me off center. "For not telling me about this last night? Or for putting me off yet again this morning when I got here?"

The hungry hand of shame groped for a hold on me. "Both."

Though his tone quieted, the accusation in his voice was far from tender. "Why is it so difficult to tell me things—*important* things, no less? Have I given you some reason not to trust me?"

An emphatic "No, of course not!" rushed from my lips as I moved toward him, yet despite being close enough to touch, neither of us reached for the other.

"Then why? Why do you insist on keeping everything to

yourself when I'm right here—when I'm asking for you to let me in and give me a chance?"

"Because . . ." The sensation of oncoming tears tingled the tip of my nose.

"Because?"

"Because telling you everything means I'll lose you."

He grabbed hold of me then and pulled me close. "No, you won't. I told you, I'm not going anywhere, Lauren."

But you have to. I closed my eyes, clinging to Joshua's embrace as if my desire to keep him near could change the conviction now rooted deep in my soul.

"Tell me about her," he whispered into my hair. "I want to know everything you read in her file."

Everything I knew about Ting Fei could be summed up in a matter of minutes, yet I stretched it out, hoping to paint the fullest picture I could for him. And for myself.

I told him about her abandonment at four months old, how she was left in a laundry basket outside of a grocery store, how she was placed in an orphanage just south of Beijing, how her first heart surgery was a success at sixteen months, and then finally, I told him what I knew about her transfer to The Heart House around eighteen months old.

"She's waiting on another surgery, hopefully her last, but the cardiologists there say she'll have a better chance here, in America. She needs . . . she needs a family."

I slid my phone from my pocket and read the last paragraph to him, the description of her "imaginative and thoughtful" personality and the side note about her love of music and singing.

And then . . . and then I showed him her picture, the one I couldn't blind my eyes or my heart to.

His curious expression morphed into confusion, and then confusion into disbelief. I knew that look well. I'd worn a similar this-can't-be-real expression at exactly 8:44 this morning.

"Is that . . . wait." He took the phone from my hand and

pinched the screen to zoom in on the picture. "Lauren." He glanced from me to the phone as if to double check whether the image of *Horton Hatches the Egg* was a figment of his imagination. That it was still there, still lying on top of a red knit blanket in a country far, far away.

Emotion edged my voice as I answered a question he hadn't yet asked. "Jenna is the only person I've ever told about what that children's book has meant to me, to my life's journey."

"That's . . . it's . . ." He scratched his head before a brief, impossible-sounding laugh pushed from his throat. "I mean, of all the books in the world . . . it's that one on her bed?"

"I know." My voice faltered. "I think God's trying to make a point."

"I'd say so, too." His eyes steadied on mine. "You're meant to be her mother, Lauren."

A bittersweet battle of celebration and sorrow waged war inside me. "I have less than forty-eight hours to give my agency an answer."

"But you already know your answer."

"It's not that easy."

"Why not? You've been waiting for months—years, even. And it would appear that she's been waiting, too, for you." A sudden enlightenment split his stoic timbre into a hearty laugh. "It's pretty incredible, actually. She's in *your* age group, the age you know best and have taught for what—ten years now?"

I bobbed my head once, my earlier nausea returning.

"So why aren't you . . ."

At his trailing question, my palms grew damp. "If I say yes to her . . ." I rubbed my lips together. "It means that . . . you and I can't . . . we won't be able to continue this." I gestured between the two of us, every part of me wanting to reject the statement I'd just spoken.

The instant comprehension dawned, Joshua the Problem Solver took over. "Lauren, those pre-adoption rules don't have to change anything between us. You can still abide by everything you signed and adopt her as a single woman, but they shouldn't have much bearing on what happens after you're back home with her. We'll take it slow, of course, but we can still be together."

"Joshua." I silenced him with a touch of my hand on his arm. "This little girl will require everything I have to give for *at least* the first year we're home. I won't have the extra emotional capacity for much else besides meeting her needs and helping her adjust to her new world, her new family." *Her new mommy.*

"But what about *your* needs?" He broke away from me, pacing the room much the way I'd done at Gail's. "What about the help you'll require during that first year? You won't be able to do everything by yourself. That's not how family is designed to work."

Oh, how I'd wrestled with that very argument on multiple occasions. "You're right, it's not. I can't do it alone, and I won't have to. God's provided me a network of support here, a community of extended family."

"And you don't want me to be a part of it?"

"Of course I do!" An unfiltered response.

"Then let me." He advanced again, taking my face in his hands, forcing my eyes to watch him speak the words my heart had yearned to hear. "Let me be a part of this with you."

"It's not that simple." Tears trickled out the corners of my eyes as I locked my lashes closed. "No part of me wants to give you up, but—"

"Then marry me."

My eyes flew open. "*What?*"

"Marry me, Lauren," he repeated, his thumbs wiping away my tears. "We'll do this together. You and me and this little girl. We'll be her family. I'll work out the details here, reserve the license and the judge, and we'll do it immediately after you get home from China."

His earnestness caused me to weep. "Joshua . . ."

"I'm in love with you." A frantic, imploring declaration. "I fell for you that very first day at school when I stumbled all over myself, trying to figure out how to get you to say yes to a date with me. Because I knew, even then, that you were someone special, someone worth being a fool for." He wiped another tear from my cheek. "Someone I knew I'd regret walking away from."

I'd convinced myself for years that words like that—passionately scripted lines spoken from the mouths of my favorite movie actors and book characters—would never be directed at me. That my specific journey wouldn't include a sweeping romantic gesture or a heart-stopping rescue. And I was okay with that—I was *prepared* for that.

Which meant that in no way was I prepared for this.

"Joshua." Gingerly, I wrapped my fingers around his wrists, needing to break his intimate caress of my face. I couldn't think with him this close, with his soul-stirring gaze examining the depths of my heart. "I love you, too." Only this profession of love—*my* profession of love—wasn't layered in hopeful anticipation of a future together but rather anchored in heartache and buried under a thick blanket of remorse.

The conviction I'd been fighting against for weeks had won.

Becoming Joshua's wife wasn't a difficult image to conjure up, nor would his last name be a difficult one to wear. He wasn't wrong in thinking we could *make it work*—a lightning-fast, justice-of-the-peace procedure in which we exchanged vows and rings, all while I held the hand of a frightened little girl who wouldn't have a clue what was going on around her. The significance of her new mother's wedding day would be lost on her in the moment, but the impact wouldn't. It would simply be one more decision made on her behalf that would have lasting implications on her future.

Making a marriage work just so we could avoid the hurt of

saying good-bye was a proposal I couldn't say yes to. Convenience and desperation weren't the ingredients for a healthy marriage or a healthy family life. I knew that better than most.

Though what Joshua and I shared *felt* right in so many ways, our timing was off.

"We can't get married."

"Sure we can. I'll manage the details so you can focus on the adoption. We can do both."

"Joshua." And this time, when I said his name, he heard me. The land of the double-minded where I'd pitched a tent and set up camp was now deserted. "Think about this for a minute. We've only known each other for seven weeks."

"My parents only knew each other for a month before they married."

"And was their first year of marriage dedicated to attaching to a child who once lived in an orphanage overseas?"

His determined gaze slipped from my face.

"No," I said, answering for him. "Your parents, like the majority of newly married couples, likely spent those first years figuring each other out. Learning what made the other smile and laugh, about what buttons triggered their partner's fears and past hurts. They were focused on their spouse, which is exactly how a marriage should be."

He reached for me, gripping my upper arms. "There are exceptions to every best-case scenario."

"But do you really think an exception should be applied to a *marriage*? Or to the adoption of a child who's experienced more life trauma than you and I can even imagine?"

He closed his eyes, his silence an unspoken answer.

I'd spent the better part of a month questioning my ability to hear and understand God's plan for my life. And while I didn't have all the answers, there was one I did have: God hadn't called me to be a wife before He'd called me to be a mother. It wasn't a sequence that followed the traditional model of a family, but

God had asked me to trust Him. And that was the one thing I hadn't done, not completely.

"There has to be another way." The defeat in his voice stabbed me with remorse.

"There was," I said. "Only, when that way got too hard, I chose my own."

My sister's opinion of me hadn't been wrong after all. I *was* a broken person, full of dysfunction and conflicting desires. I'd shifted blame, pointed fingers, and fueled the fire of my self-righteousness time and time again by justifying my actions . . . even at the cost of the people I loved most.

And nearly at the cost of an orphaned child in need of a mother.

Hollowed to the core, tears tripped down my cheeks. "I knew the sacrifices involved in saying yes to an adoption when I applied, but once I met you, *once I had you*, I didn't want to let you go. I've been so self-focused, blinded by my own desires and . . . I'm sorry." My throat barely scratched out the words, though I could have said them a million times over and it wouldn't have felt like enough. "I'm so, so sorry I've hurt you."

My rebellion had felt so right, so justified in the moment, and yet all it had managed to produce in the end was misguided hope and two shattered hearts. I covered my face with my hands, too ashamed to see the damage my willful disobedience had caused him.

I expected him to leave, to walk out the door and close it behind him without a single look back. I deserved worse. But instead, Joshua took me in his arms and allowed my shame to soak his shirt, offering me a mercy I could never repay.

And there, in that broken, repentant place, the missing *peace*—the one George Avery had spoken of in his kitchen when he said yes to his calling for the second time—washed over me, too, and granted me the courage to say *yes*, for the second time, to mine.

chapter twenty-nine

Five weeks later

My feet shuffled to a stop as Jenna's guiding hand tugged gently on my shoulder. "We're here." If my best friend were a balloon, she would have burst by now, confetti hearts exploding like rain. "You can take the blindfold off, Lauren."

I had absolutely zero idea where *here* was, but my fingers obeyed her suggestion, groping for the knot at the back of my head. She'd insisted I put the glittery bandanna over my eyes when she kidnapped me from my classroom and escorted me through the parking lot. Wherever she'd taken me, this destination had involved *a lot* of figure eights and sudden stops.

The knot loosened in my grasp, and slowly the bandanna fell away. Like a newly released prisoner seeing the sun for the first time in ages, I squinted as familiar fluorescent lights spilled over me. I blinked to adjust my vision, then gasped. Several dozen people—friends, colleagues, adoption group members—clapped and hollered with the enthusiasm of a live game show audience.

Their voices lifted in a unified "Surprise!"

My hand fluttered to my mouth. "Oh my goodness. What? What is—?"

"Happy surprise adoption shower, Lauren!" Gail emerged from the crowd and pulled me close.

"What? Are you serious? I can't believe you guys did this!" A few of my work friends hugged me, showing me how they'd captured my deer-in-the-headlights expression on their cameras. No doubt that face would be featured on the front page of the next Brighton newsletter.

One brief glance over their heads had confirmed my family wasn't in attendance. And while I felt the quick sting of disappointment at their absence, I wouldn't let it dim the progress we'd made recently with our baby-step interactions over the last few weeks. The acceptance of my daughter's match email had pushed my pride to the side, and I decided early on that I wasn't going to keep her a secret from my family this time around. No matter how distant we'd become, I'd soon have a daughter who would bear my name—and theirs, too. She was worth trying to bridge the gaps in our broken communication.

Lisa had replied back with a video message less than an hour after I'd sent them all an email with my daughter's picture and the bullet-point details about my upcoming trip to China. Iris jumped up and down over the news of a female cousin her age as she rattled on and on about all the things she'd teach her as soon as we were back home. The list included ballet, rock painting with real acrylic paints, and, of course, how to play "veterinarian" with Grandma's grumpy cat. I'd laughed, knowing Lisa's approval was hiding somewhere behind my niece's enthusiasm. True to my mother's lack of fanfare over most things in life, she simply replied to my email with a single question: *Can you do FD this Sun eve?*

To which I'd readily replied: *Yes, I'd love to come for family dinner. Thank you, Mom. I'm sorry I've been so distant.* The words that still remained unsaid I wanted to say to her in person: *And I'm sorry for hurting you.*

"You really had no idea, did you?" Jenna linked my arm through hers before turning her head in Gail's direction. "I literally drove her in circles around the parking lot for at least ten minutes. Even turned on my blinker and complained about the non-existent stoplight."

Gail laughed. "I knew you'd be the perfect one to distract her as the guests showed up. Good work, Jenna."

"Wait . . ." I began, looking between them, still flabbergasted they'd managed to pull this off without me knowing. There had to be at least . . . fifty, sixty people here? "How long have you been planning this?" They exchanged a mischievous grin. Obviously, the two had been in cahoots for some time.

I scanned the entirety of the room, overwhelmed by the detail of the color scheme—pinks, corals, teals, and accents of rose gold. The same cheerful colors in my daughter's bedroom.

Last weekend, Gail had organized a painting day at my house. A couple of the women from adoption group had showed up, paint rollers and blue tape in hand. We'd snacked on pizza, soda, and chips like teenage girls at a sleepover. Lighthearted conversation had been the perfect distraction as we'd rolled over every last inch of Cadet Blue with Sherbet Coral, an act that led to my heart's prayer for Noah and his new family: *Bond them quickly, Lord, and bless their home with love and laughter.*

"I think we started planning the shower about a month ago or so," Jenna answered, pulling me off the current track of my reflections and setting me on a different one, one that traveled the timeline of accepting a little girl as my daughter . . . and saying good-bye to a man I'd come to love.

For the first few weeks, I'd kept my phone in the junk drawer in my kitchen at night, replacing it with a dusty alarm clock I should have sold in a garage sale long ago. But leaving it on my nightstand would have made it way too easy to reach for in those uninhibited minutes between sleep and awake, dream and reality. The temptation to text him, to check in, to connect with him—even in the smallest of ways—had been nearly unbearable. But now, while the hollowed portion of my chest was still just as vacant, somehow, someway, I'd made peace with the phantom pangs left in my heart.

A flock of congratulating loved ones swarmed me at once, asking a million questions a minute about travel dates and work leave and meal train sign-ups and all the itinerary details surrounding Adoption Day. After repeating the same answers several times over, Gail came to my rescue, offering a conversational life raft.

"Hey everyone, let's give Lauren a chance to decompress for a moment while you help yourselves to refreshments. I'm sure she'll bless us all with the details of her upcoming adventure in April."

April seventh. Just over eight weeks from today.

I mouthed a silent *thank you* as Jenna whisked me to a chair decked out with so much bling and fabric it could have been featured on a tween girl's makeover show. Really, my friends had gone above and beyond. Their kindness would be stored in my heart for decades to come. Gail ushered the crowd toward the refreshments table under a massive metallic balloon banner, letting me know she'd save a glittery pink cupcake for me. At the end of the table, my gaze caught on a mountain of prettily wrapped gifts.

"Jenna." I yanked on her arm and pointed at the pile. "Those can't all be for—"

"Aria." Jenna smiled and nodded unashamedly, my heart tripping over itself at her use of my daughter's newly chosen American name. Every time I heard it, the memory of her sweet raspy voice singing on a video I'd watched a hundred-plus times hummed through me like the healing remedy for a weary soul—which was exactly what Aria meant: *Song.*

Her breathy rendition of "Jesus Loves Me" had provided the strength to lean into the hard and find the hope awaiting us both.

Aria Fei Bailey.

My daughter.

"This is all just so beautiful, Jen. Thank you for doing this."

She blew me a comical kiss. "Don't thank me quite yet."

The playfulness in her tone caused me to raise a suspecting eyebrow. "Jen . . . what does that mean?"

She shook her head. "Nothing. Just a gift I'm hoping might arrive."

"You've already given me the best gift I could ask for—you didn't need to do anything else for me." If I ever doubted Jenna's support of my adoption, I'd only have to recall the way she'd squealed when I asked her to consider traveling to China with me. Her *yes* had come without hesitation, even after I'd explained she'd have to take roughly two and a half weeks off from work. But like most things with Jenna, once she'd made a decision, there was no convincing her otherwise.

"Nope, you've got it all wrong. Going to China with you is *a gift to me*. I've already started making packing piles all around my house. Brian is going crazy." She shook her head and scanned the room. "Anyway, I kind of went out on a limb, and I'm honestly not even sure if . . ."

And then it was Jenna's turn to be at a loss for words. Staring at the double doors at the back of the room, she pressed her lips together, letting the tiniest curve of a smile pucker her cheeks.

I followed her gaze, and as if in slow motion, my mind worked to process what my eyes focused on. The instant comprehension took root, my feet were moving. Because my mother—*my mother,* who despised social gatherings of every kind and who hadn't even attended Lisa's baby shower for Iris—was standing at the back of the auditorium, my sister at her side, with a gift bag clutched in her hand.

On instinct, I wrapped my arms around her shoulders and

pulled her in for a brief but long-overdue hug. I'd spent a lifetime logging her lack of maternal characteristics and not nearly enough time on the unique qualities she did possess as my mother. Her absence had shifted and humbled my thinking, or perhaps I owed this shift in thinking to the many prayers God had been answering over the last few weeks. Whichever the case, I no longer wished her to be someone she wasn't; I simply wished her here.

In this room, and in my life.

"I'm so sorry, Mom," I whispered into her cropped, wiry hair. "For all the ugly things I said to you. Please forgive me."

The returned pressure of her hand on my upper back opened up a chasm of warmth inside my chest.

"We're family, Lauren," she said on the tail end of a firm pat. "We don't need to say all that to each other."

I stepped back, giving her the space I knew she needed. "No, Mom, I need to say it *because* we're family." Whether or not she'd ever admit it, my harsh words had wounded her. She deserved my apology, and even my gratitude. Was she a perfect mother? No. But I wouldn't be one, either. Not even my beloved Gail could live up to such a lofty title. Very soon I'd be in need of the same grace.

The look my sister offered revived something inside me. "I have a few bags of things to give you—for Aria. They're out in my trunk. Some fancy play dresses Iris grew out of a while back, some shoes, and some newer toys, too. It was the first time she didn't throw a fit about having to clean her room."

"Thank you," I said, hoping this was a new beginning in our relationship, too. I'd prayed for a second chance with them—a chance to live out my faith in a way that honored both my heavenly Father and my family. "That means a lot, Lisa."

"Sure, of course." She nodded and took in the room. "Please tell me there will be cupcakes at this party."

Chuckling, I pointed to Jenna, whose sparkling eyes were still trained on our trio. "Jenna would never throw a party without them."

Lisa touched Mom's shoulder before heading to the refreshment table. Jenna greeted her there, pointing out the array of treats she'd collected for today's events as Lisa filled her plate. Feeling my mother's heightening anxiety over a crowd of strangers, I gestured to a grouping of chairs near a back table, knowing that would be her preference, when she placed a hand on my forearm and stopped me.

In all my life, I couldn't remember a single time my mother's eyes had glistened with tears, outside of the day she'd told us about my father's accident. Yet even then, she'd swiped at them as if batting away an annoying gnat. But these tears were different. She made no effort to blot them out or whisk them away. She simply leveled her gaze on mine.

"I do care," she said. "Not only about the money you save for your future—but about your life, too. All of it."

I covered her hand with mine as a single tear trailed her cheek.

"I know, Mom. I know."

Her gaze drifted momentarily, and I wished I could pull back the cover on her practiced, veiled expression. "We're . . ." She swallowed. "We're excited to meet your daughter—both your father and me."

Your father and me. A phrase I'd so rarely heard, yet even at my age, the words filled me with a security I'd craved since childhood. "Thank you. That means a lot. I'm excited, too."

As Lisa set a plate at the back table, we moved toward it.

"And you'll send us updates? From China, I mean?" A question that sent a thrill through my entire nervous system.

"Yes," I said. "I promise I will."

A simple nod, along with the handing off of her gift bag, and then Mom was sitting with Lisa at the table, steering the conversation back to closet work. And for once, I was more than okay with that, because my mother had just given me a gift far more valuable than whatever present she'd purchased for my daughter.

"Lauren?" It was my principal, Mrs. Pendleton. "A few of us have to duck out early for a staff meeting, but we'd love to watch you open our gifts first. The faculty went in together on something for Aria."

"Oh," I said. "Of course, but honestly, Mrs. Pendleton, I wasn't expecting you to organize a gift for us. You've already spent so many hours helping me sort out my maternity leave and—"

She squeezed my shoulder. "And I'd gladly help you again. I've always had a heart to do what you're about to do, Lauren, just never had the courage. If there's anything more I can do to contribute to your adoption of this blessed little girl—it will be my pleasure. That's a standing offer."

"Thank you."

I didn't miss the way my mom and sister focused their attention on our conversation, nor did I miss the awed expression on their faces as Mrs. Pendleton continued to offer words of love and support. I silently prayed that they, too, would feel a similar kind of encouragement just by being in this room with so many precious people I loved.

Mrs. Pendleton led me to the designated gift-opening throne, where Jenna and Gail had already transported the first load of presents.

The experience of unwrapping so many hand-picked, thoughtful tokens of love for a child none of them had even met, a child who'd never be able to repay them for their generosity, overwhelmed me with a gratitude I'd never be able to express in words. No matter how many packages I opened, the stack beside my chair seemed never-ending. Art supplies, books, clothes, shoes, knitted blankets and hats, and even a rolling travel backpack—given to me by the faculty of Brighton Elementary—which included sensory toys and a tablet preloaded with Mandarin-language movies for the plane ride home.

I'd lost count of the hugs I'd given and the cheek-kisses I'd received in return. Never could I doubt the community of support God had created for me, for Aria. As the last guests said their good-byes, I turned back to the room to help with the cleanup, only to see Gail walking toward me with a small red box wrapped with a gold ribbon.

"Do you have it in you to open one more little gift?"

And something about the way her top lip curved told me this one hadn't been forgotten from the present pile; it had been held back on purpose. She placed it in my hands now, her humble smile revealing what I already knew.

"This is from you?"

"It's from my entire family," she said sincerely.

I slipped the gold cord away from the box, lifting off the lid and then a thin layer of white tissue. Inside lay two slipknot bracelets made of thin red thread. I linked one around my finger.

"There's an old Chinese proverb that those of us in the adoption community love to share with those new to the journey." Gail pointed to a scripted piece of beautiful rice paper inside the box.

I retrieved it and read it out loud: "'An invisible red thread connects those destined to meet, regardless of time, place, or circumstance. The thread may stretch or tangle, but it will never break.'"

Gail lifted the bracelet still inside the box and slipped it over my wrist. "There's one for you to wear and one for you to give Aria when you meet her. God's connected you both, Lauren, since before the beginning of time, and His provision has made a way for you to meet. We'll be praying His love encircles you both when you're finally united as family."

Overwhelmed by a redemption story only God himself could author, all the tears I'd managed to hold back during the party spilled onto my cheeks as I slipped both bracelets over my wrist in anticipation of the big day ahead.

chapter thirty

EIGHT WEEKS LATER
ADOPTION DAY
BEIJING, CHINA

I'd imagined this day a million times, prayed for every detail about the significant moment to come, and yet there was still a part of me that felt like I was observing somebody else's life, somebody else's adoption story.

Jenna had been uncharacteristically quiet all morning in our shared hotel room, as if sensing my unspoken need for introspection and reflection. She'd been a steady presence at my side since our arrival in Beijing three days ago, up for whatever task or errand needed to be run before the big day, and never once voicing a complaint over the lack of familiar comforts. I'd never been so grateful for my best friend.

We'd met Sue, the guide and interpreter my agency had hired for us, last night for an authentic Peking duck dinner and a walk through the night market—which was quite the adventure. The tight confines of a crowded street, paired with spicy, unidentified aromas, had my senses on overload. As we'd bumped shoulders with tourists and locals alike who feasted on skewers of fried scorpion and tarantula, I began crafting an imaginary text thread to Joshua in my mind—something I found myself doing often while in the midst of hard-to-believe life experiences. Imagining his running commentary and the excited way his eyes would have lit up at the delicacies all around me kept me smiling throughout the marketplace. No doubt he'd be encouraging me to try the octopus on a bed of rice or perhaps a taste of the fermented mung bean juice. He'd be relentless, of course, because knowing Joshua, he'd have chowed down on more than a few fried treats of his own if given the chance.

When we'd finished our stroll, Sue escorted us back to the hotel lounge to fill us in on the details she knew about the order of events to come today. Her wise insight and cheery demeanor had brought much-needed confidence to an otherwise fish-out-of-water experience.

Jet lag had woken us both well before the sun, but even if I'd been completely adjusted to the time change, the anticipation of the day's events would have roused me just the same. I had never prayed so fervently about any one thing than I had for Aria over these past weeks. I'd asked God for her protection and peace, for her comfort and courage, and for His wisdom in navigating all the unknowns to come for us both.

Sue's sing-song voice spoke in Mandarin to our driver. She gestured to a side street and then to an alley that opened into a rural area. Her instructions were the only sound in the car other than the muted shutter of Jenna's Nikon. Jenna faithfully snapped pictures of the world around us, documenting through the lens of her camera a story I knew I'd treasure in the weeks and years to come.

Few children on Adoption Day reacted with the same level of anticipation and excitement as their awaiting parents. I'd seen enough documentaries and had read enough blog posts to empathize with the fear and grief Aria would likely experience today.

Please be with her in this moment, Lord. Help her to see you in me.

Trust me.

The reassuring words eased the nerves clutching at my lower abdomen as we pulled up to an iron gate that wrapped around an unassuming concrete building. Bold Chinese characters, as well as English letters, spelled out *The Heart House* just above the entryway.

Sue twisted around in her seat, and her apple cheeks rounded with a smile. "We're here."

Jenna's hand covered mine, giving it a quick and comforting squeeze.

"You both follow me, okay? We first stop in the lobby for paperwork, and then we go to the meeting room."

Both Jenna and I nodded our agreement. We'd been over this several times with her, yet everything was clearer now. The fog of hypotheticals had lifted. This was it.

The day an orphaned child would become a daughter.

The day a childless woman would become a mother.

I carried Aria's travel backpack around my arm, the inside filled with small toys, sweet treats, and, of course, books.

Jenna remained a step behind me, the nonstop click of her camera shutter in sync with the spastic sputter of my heartbeat.

"Right through here." Sue's confidence carried us through a double set of metal doors and into what looked like a small administrative office with two desks, a couch, a coffee table, a water cooler, and several crimson-colored wall hangings scripted with Chinese characters. Sue spoke animatedly to a college-age woman who sat at one of the desks. A laptop and several piles of paperwork sat beside her computer. The young woman nodded expectantly at us before dipping her head low and responding to Sue in a language I wished I could understand.

As soon as she finished speaking, Sue promptly interpreted their exchange to us. "This is one of the nannies. She say your girl has been singing for two days. She show everybody your pretty picture from the photo book you send her. She know today she meet her mama."

Jenna clutched at her chest and made a sound somewhere between a laugh and a sob.

I worked to swallow back my own rising emotion and bowed my head, thankful for the young woman's kindness. "I'm excited to meet her, too." An understatement of the highest degree, yet there wasn't a word in any language that could possibly define the feelings coursing through me now.

Just like Sue had explained at dinner last night and again in the car this morning, I was asked to complete another round of paperwork, signing and dating wherever Sue instructed.

And then, finally, it was time.

Sue led us into a spacious room I recognized immediately as the backdrop to so many of Aria's pictures. I mentally connected the mural of cartoon animals that ran the length of the room together, like pieces of a puzzle. My glance stopped momentarily on one I'd never seen before—a large, kind-eyed Brachiosaurus painted in the corner above a row of desks. I smiled at the discovery. It was almost like a certain green-eyed dinosaur-lover himself were here to give me a wink of encouragement.

The red and yellow gym mats on the floor, along with the shelves that housed a handful of toys and books under a bay of barred windows, were all familiar, but I struggled to focus on any one object for too long—not when the doorway directly in front of me would soon reveal the child who had grown in my heart since before I'd known her face, since before I'd called her mine.

A nanny with a long, low ponytail in a knee-length white overcoat, much like those worn by nurses in American hospitals during the fifties and sixties, entered the room, holding the hand of a little girl I would recognize anywhere. I'd memorized her dainty features, her violet-tinged lips, her dark chocolate chin-length hair. Clothed in a peach dress dotted with miniature ice cream cones and wearing white canvas slip-on shoes, she peeked up at me under hooded lids, her expression one of timid curiosity.

On instinct, I lowered myself to the ground, my knees pressing against the squishy play mat as my floral maxi dress spilled around me. I knew from years of teaching that mirroring a child's height and posture reduced potential threat and gave them permission to test and explore their surroundings. Aria would need the chance to do that with me, too, in her own way and in her own time.

With whisper-soft steps and a firm grasp on her nanny's hand, Aria neared me, taking me in as she tilted her head this way and that. Sue and the nanny conversed with each other over Aria's head while her nanny prodded her encouragingly. But for once I was glad I couldn't understand the words being spoken. Because Aria and I were holding our own wordless conversation with each other. From my knees, I lowered myself even further to the ground, crisscrossing my legs in front of me. I set the backpack between us and unzipped it before I scooted it toward her.

My heart galloped at three hundred beats a minute as I waited for her response.

Help her to trust me, Lord.

Her nanny squatted down beside her and gestured to the pack and then back to me, speaking in a friendly tone.

Timidly, the beautiful brown-eyed girl nodded, her gaze still locked on my face. One by one, she released the fingers she'd been clinging to and gingerly moved toward my gift. My smile couldn't be tamed as she reached the pack and took out a hot pink heart-shaped sucker. She looked back at her nanny, who giggled and encouraged her to eat it. Aria didn't hesitate. After unwrapping it with impressive dexterity, she popped it into her mouth, and I chuckled over her obvious enjoyment of such a sweet treat.

Sue flashed me a thumbs-up as Jenna snapped a quick succession of pictures. For the briefest of moments, Aria glanced from me to Jenna, and Sue bent to offer an explanation of my best friend's presence before she made the switch back to English. "I told her you have a very nice friend who traveled a long way to take pictures of her new family."

Aria looked between Jenna's camera and me once again before framing her sweet little fingers around her face and snapping an invisible picture of her own, of me. Speaking around her sucker, she said, "Mama."

My heart squeezed as a million answered prayers exploded over us. I nodded and pointed to my chest. "Yes," I said, my voice suddenly hoarse. "I am your *mama*."

She turned back to her nanny, speaking melodically in Chinese.

The nanny giggled as Sue bent to make eye contact with me. "Your daughter wants to know if you are a princess. She said you have hair like Cinderella."

Watery joy slipped down my cheeks as I touched the top of my blond ponytail and laughed. "Please tell her that I think *she's* the one who looks like a princess."

Sue did so, and Aria's lips parted to reveal the first real smile I'd seen since she entered the room.

I pointed at the backpack and mimed that she should open it further. I'd taken my niece shopping for a few of the special gifts inside, convinced that toy preferences likely crossed cultural borders when it came to children of the same gender and age. From the look on Aria's face when she pulled out each of the miniature Disney Princess figurines—including my longtime personal favorite, Mulan—Iris's selections had been the perfect choice.

Aria dropped into a squat that showcased her flexibility as she set the miniature dolls on the floor between us, arranging them into a semicircle. She tapped the bottoms of their plastic full-length gowns against the floor to make them dance, speaking to them in an adorably mousy voice that sent something to flight in my chest. After a few minutes of watching her play, I reached my hand toward her princess entourage, asking without words if I might play, too. She agreed, bobbing her head and scooting several of the pastel-colored dolls in my direction. *An invitation.*

I'd never know how long we stayed there on that floor, tapping and smiling and humming songs from movies I hadn't seen in ages, but time was suddenly and completely irrelevant. As if all the minutes of all the hours of all the days of my life had added up to this one God-ordained moment. I could do nothing but sit in awe of the precious gift in front of me.

As I slid Princess Jasmine into a waltz next to the toe of Aria's shoe, she reached out and touched the red thread bracelets encircling my wrist. It was the only prompt I needed to slip off the one intended for her. The red thread lay unassuming in my outstretched palm, yet the significance of it, the meaning of unending love and connection, held a power neither of us could yet comprehend. Her sparkling eyes met mine before her fingers grazed the gift in a timid acceptance of a lifelong promise. I helped her slip it over her wrist and tightened the slipknots to secure the fit. She held her arm next to mine, as if to see the similarities of our two bracelets for herself.

I nodded at her unvoiced appraisal and spoke one of a handful of phrases I'd memorized in my daughter's birth language: "We are family."

chapter thirty-one

I tiptoed out of the sleeping quarters and into the connected living area of our hotel room like a professional mom who'd been putting children to sleep for ages. Sliding the pocket door halfway closed so as not to disturb my little Sleeping Beauty, my glance caught on Jenna, who was busy uploading pictures from the day onto her laptop. The last twelve hours had been packed with enough events and emotions to fill a solid week. Had it really only been this morning that we were getting ready to go to The Heart House for the first time?

"She asleep?" Jenna whispered through a yawn.

I slumped onto the sofa beside her and lolled my head in her direction. The sinking sensation of cushy pillows enveloping my body might finally allow my steady adrenaline to decrease. "We looked through several books after her bubble bath, and then she wanted to play another round of princesses and draw on her Etch A Sketch. But after about forty-five minutes of trying, I finally got her to lie down long enough to close her eyes. I just kept rubbing her back until she fell asleep with her face smashed into that stuffed panda you picked out."

"Ah, sweet. Good. I figured you'd let me know if you needed my help."

Jenna had been so great in that way, never wanting to interfere without being asked. Over the last few months, she'd read all the recommended books on how to promote healthy bonding and attachment between newly adopted children and their parents. She'd even come to a couple adoption groups with me, asking more questions in her first meeting than I had in a year. But her understanding of the process, of how critical it was to let me provide for all my daughter's needs—from bathing to hugging to adding food to her plate—was truly a gift. Every little thing mattered in these first few weeks and months.

I crossed my feet on the coffee table between us. "I wasn't sure what to expect. Her nannies said she was a deep sleeper, but . . ." I pressed my fingers to my throbbing temples. "She's never been in this situation before, so I'm trying to keep my expectations for the days and weeks to come to a minimum."

"You have a headache?" Jenna asked.

"Yeah, I think I just need some caffeine." Between Aria giving me a guided tour of the house she'd spent almost five years in and all the clarifying questions I'd asked her nannies about food preferences and known allergies, bathing and bedtime routines, and, of course, any pertinent medical information I'd need to relay to Brian once we got home . . . my brain felt close to combustion.

The good-byes to Aria's nannies and her Heart House brothers and sisters had been the truest definition of bittersweet I'd ever experienced. While her hand had remained firmly latched in mine, her emotions had been divided, grieving the only life she'd ever known and hoping for the one promised in pictures and stories. Her tears had been a silent stream down her cheeks as she buried herself into my side. I'd carried her fragile body to the waiting car and stroked her hair until she'd fallen asleep across my lap.

Our modern, westernized hotel, adorned with fancy amenities unlike the ones Aria had known at The Heart House, proved an energizing distraction upon our arrival. In a six-hour time period, we'd unpacked her entire suitcase of clothing, stacked and re-stacked all the books I'd brought for her, colored in two different coloring books, played with Play-Doh, painted our nails, and took her first-ever bubble bath. The communication barrier had gone better than I'd expected after Sue left us for the day—thanks to the use of Google's translator app. But once Aria had learned how to work it, she was quick to point to my phone whenever she wanted to ask a question, usually about having another candy from the backpack, which I rarely denied her.

"As soon as I get these uploaded, I'll run down to the store in the lobby and get us something to drink." Jenna scrolled through a group of pictures from dinner, stopping on one that made me laugh despite the pounding in my head. "I still can't believe how many of those dumplings she put away. She's so little, and yet she eats like a teenage boy."

I chuckled again, remembering how she'd gobbled up an entire dumpling, reaching for a second helping before she'd finished swallowing the first. "She definitely doesn't lack for appetite." Her wonder over the big and little things made it nearly impossible for me to eat my own dinner, because watching Aria experience the world had quickly become my favorite spectator sport.

"That's great, though she'll need her strength for surgery," Jenna added in a matter-of-fact tone that made my stomach roil. I knew she wasn't wrong; I'd gone over the medical records and scans with Brian a half dozen times before we left and met with his cardiology team about possible scenarios, but everything felt different now. Because now that I had her in my care, now that I'd rubbed her back and put her to sleep in my bed, I couldn't imagine handing her over to anyone ever again. Not even Dr. Brian Rosewood.

"Did you see her nails?" Jenna's question was soft, yet I felt the sting of it in every cell of my body. I had seen them, the bluish hue around her nail bed, and also the violet line around her plum-colored lips. "Brian told me to look for that. It's a sign of low oxygen."

I hugged a pillow to my chest. "Yeah, I'm pretty sure the surgery will need to be on the sooner-rather-than-later schedule Brian suggested." It didn't seem fair that she'd have to go through another traumatic life event in such a short period of time, but the evidence of her condition was impossible to ignore.

I sighed, ready to focus on one of the positive aspects about our miraculous day together. I scanned Jenna's laptop screen, where a hundred-plus images were slowly uploading. "Thank you, Jen. For taking all of those. I'm so glad you're here with me."

She clicked through several images, then paused on one of me holding Aria just outside her orphanage door as her tiny hand combed through my ponytail. My smile could have spanned the length of China. "*This*," she said, pointing to the image. "This is the one you need to send to friends and family. It's the sweetest thing I've ever witnessed. That child is obsessed with her pretty mama."

Again, the smile I hadn't taken off all day expanded. "I'm even more obsessed with her."

"She's precious, Lauren. Like seriously, seriously precious. I thought my heart was going to crack open so many times this morning. I don't know how I didn't start blubbering when she called you *Mama* for the first time."

My eyes filled with tears at the memory. "I don't know how I didn't, either. I was just so focused on not wanting to frighten her, on earning her trust."

Jenna scooted back on the sofa, her eyes misting. "You were phenomenal, by the way. I haven't had a minute to tell you that yet, but really. You handled that meeting beautifully, allowing Aria to take the lead and creating a safe place for her to interact with you. I've never been more proud to call you my friend."

The compliment was so sincere I had to reach out to her,

touch her arm. She grasped my hand. "Thank you for letting me be a part of this." She smiled as a tear nestled in the corner of her lips. "I'll never, ever forget it."

For a minute neither of us said anything more, as if we both recognized the need to decompress the high emotions of the day. Of the last several months.

She squeezed my hand before letting it go and opened her mouth as if to speak, then closed it again.

"What?" I gently prodded, bumping her sneakered foot with mine.

She puckered her lips, twisting them to the side. "It's just, I've had quite a few texts today—from people asking for updates on how everything went with the meeting. On how *you're* doing specifically."

And something about the way she'd said *people* revealed she wasn't just referring to the friends and family who'd requested to join my private Facebook page for Aria's adoption journey.

"Who?" My heart had already started picking up the pace, had already started down the warm-up track of a race I'd forbidden it to run months ago.

Her internal struggle reflected in the pinch between her eyebrows. "I've worked super hard to keep my promise to you, not to bring him up unless you . . . unless you asked about him first."

The urge to brace myself, to close my eyes and breathe through my nose like a practiced meditation guru, nearly betrayed my feigned nonchalance. "It's been months now, Jen. You can talk about him. I'm okay."

"All right . . . well, he's been asking about you a lot. Ever since we landed in China. He talks with Brian, of course, so he knows we're here and safe on the ground, but I just feel weird about giving him personal updates without your consent."

A ripple of well-known heartache swelled inside my chest, but I wouldn't allow it to reach me. Not here. Not on this day. I had no right to feel the slightest bit of sadness when I'd just watched my little girl say good-bye to her entire world in exchange for one her mind couldn't even fathom. My life was about her now. We were a team, joined together by God. And I wouldn't risk that for anything or anyone.

"What do you want me to do, Lauren? I'll tell him anything you want me to. Regardless of his position with the hospital or his friendship with Brian, you're my first priority. Always."

I'd been so lost in thought I hadn't realized Jenna was still awaiting my response, but my mind had snagged on a phrase I hadn't heard before now. "His position at the hospital?"

Again, Jenna looked torn. "I didn't tell you because it all happened on the day we got the travel itinerary, and you were so focused on booking our flights and . . ." She shrugged. "It didn't feel right to derail you."

"He got the hospital contract?" My question was so soft it was almost inaudible.

Jenna nodded. "The board was super impressed with him. Their decision was unanimous. They awarded him one of the pediatric grants to begin work on the prototype immediately."

My lungs filled with microscopic pinpricks. "Wow . . ."

"Yeah, I know. Brian tells him all the time that he's a genius with the fashion sense of a seven-year-old. I still can't believe he managed to get him into a suit for the big presentation."

I shook my head, slightly disheartened at the thought of Joshua presenting in anything other than his faded *Anything is Fossil-ble* T-shirt.

"He is, though," I said resolutely. "A genius." Before my mind could drift too far, I circled back to her original question. "You can update him, Jenna. I don't want him to worry. He deserves closure, too."

"Okay." My friend sat quietly for a few seconds more before she stretched her arms over her head and declared she was heading down to the convenience store in the lobby. "It's either eat or sleep, and I think the only way we're going to beat this jet lag thing is to hold out at least another hour or two before we crash. Want a Diet Coke?" She grabbed her purse and riffled through her wallet in search of the *yuan* we'd exchanged for a few hours ago.

"Sure, thanks."

She fanned several colorful bills out for display. "I'm also gonna grab whatever chips are *not* seafood flavor. And whatever looks like it could be dark chocolate."

I gave her a tired salute of approval and waited until the door latched closed before I lifted Jenna's computer to my lap. Before I tapped a single key, I paused to listen for any sound of stirring that might be coming from my bed. Nothing.

Okay, I thought. *Now what?*

But my fingers seemed to be answering that rhetorical question with a very non-rhetorical response.

I clicked through Jenna's browser, thankful to see our iffy Wi-Fi connection was holding steady—at least for the moment—then logged onto my Facebook account, searching for his profile the instant my page materialized. True to Joshua's nature, he hadn't utilized his page much; in fact, his most recent post was dated over a year ago. I scrolled through his feed, familiar with the handful of nerd-driven memes he'd shared with the public. Several were on fossil discoveries, another few on advances in technology, and one link about how science and intelligent design can coexist. But my favorite part of his page was his profile picture—a simple photograph taken with his niece on what looked to be an Easter egg hunt in years past. She was a toddler then, and she wore a headband with fuzzy bunny ears. Naturally, her uncle wore a matching set. As Joshua smiled for the picture-taker, his niece smiled at him, her expression one that punched me in the heart every time I looked it up, which I'd done on numerous occasions in the past three months. Because this was one of only two pictures I had of him.

It was hard to believe that in the course of our short-lived romance, we hadn't taken a single picture together other than the one Jenna had snapped after the Charlie Brown Thanksgiving event, where he was an undercooked turkey and I was a frumpy pilgrim. But there were no selfies of the two of us, not even a single hand-the-phone-off-to-a-stranger snapshot. Yet sometimes I wondered what I would have done with such a photo if one had existed. Would I have had the courage to delete it? And if so, what exactly would deleting it have proved?

My heart knew the answer—*nothing*. We may not have captured our affection for one another on camera, but he'd left an imprint on me just the same, like a handprint pressed into wet cement. The surface was still usable, still solid enough to walk on, but it was forever transformed, forever impressed by a moment in time.

When I reflected back on our months together, it wasn't the stolen kisses I missed the most or the way he'd search my face before offering a toe-tingling compliment or even the routine call he'd make to tell me good night. It was the absence of his friendship that pained me most. Because more than anything, that's what he'd been to me from the start—a loyal, selfless friend who'd traded in his desires for the sake of mine.

I stared at his picture now, at his honest eyes and goofy grin.

"Congratulations on your new contract, Joshua," I whispered. "I'm so, so proud of you."

Like an echo carried back on the wind, my soul seemed to hear his answering reply. "*Congratulations to you, too.*"

I glanced over my shoulder, thinking of the freshly bathed child who lay asleep just beyond the pocket door. "I hope you'll get to meet her someday." And I hoped even more that when he did, he'd understand what I'd only just begun to comprehend.

That Aria Fei Bailey had been worth it all—every tear, every trial, every heartrending sacrifice.

Releasing a long, contented sigh, I closed the laptop and stood to peer into the darkness at the sleeping form on the right side of my queen-size bed. We had a long road ahead of us: surgeries and recoveries, new languages and cultures, new adjustments to life as a mother-daughter duo. And yet one unshakable, God-fearing truth would remain through it all: Aria was mine, and I was hers.

Forever.

chapter thirty-two

The vibration of my phone against the knee-high ladybug table on my right silenced every side conversation in the pediatric waiting room. Aria's small army of support, made up of family and friends alike, all held their breath, awaiting the next text update from Brian's team.

Only it hadn't been a surgery update at all but rather another sign-up for the meal train Gail had organized for Aria's recovery week back home.

I shook my head, my nerves too frazzled to spell out the fact that I knew nothing more than I had three hours ago when they'd wheeled my daughter into the operating room for her five-hour surgery.

Lisa piped up then, twisting in her vinyl armchair to bring her knees up to her chin, as if that might make the seat more comfortable for the hours ahead. "She's fine. We'd know it if she wasn't. No news is good news. That's how these things work."

"Lisa." My mother shook her head in that exasperated way of hers.

"What?" My sister continued, "It's true. I've watched a lot of surgical procedures, and that's always how it goes. If something were really wrong, we'd be hearing about it over the pager system first. Probably as a code red. But in some cases, a code blue. It all depends on—"

"Those medical dramas you watch are not reality," Mom said as if she were reading a textbook.

"*Emergency Room* is a *reality* TV show, Mother. Not a drama. It's real life, with real people in medical crises."

My mother rolled her eyes and lifted the HGTV magazine she'd been reading as if it were a shield against my sister's poor conversational choices.

Gail, ever the peacekeeper, smiled at them as she patted my knee, though I barely registered her touch. My anxiety armor had grown thicker as each minute dragged into the next.

As Jenna came into the room holding a drink carrier filled with everyone's coffee and tea orders, I took a moment to stretch my legs and wander to the aquarium in the center of the waiting room. My small-talk abilities had expired around hour two, and frankly, I wasn't sure how I was gonna make it to hour five without doing bodily harm. I stared without seeing into a tank the size of a compact vehicle and tried not to think of my little girl unconscious on a surgical table.

On the other side of the glass, Jenna added a steaming to-go cup to the miniature homestead I'd set up on the ladybug side table: books I hadn't the capacity to read, a laptop I hadn't the desire to open, snacks I'd attempted to eat yet couldn't quite choke down, and a near-dead iPhone plugged into a sunshine-yellow wall.

A clown fish studied me for several seconds, gills expanding and contracting while his eyes tracked my movements. Perhaps he felt as stuck as I did at the moment, a spectacle trapped inside four suffocating walls. I pressed my finger to the glass and slid it to the right, and then to the left. He followed. "You're a smart one, Nemo," I muttered. "Too bad you're trapped in here for life." *Am I really talking to a fish? I've reached a new low.*

I shook my head and dropped my hand from the tank glass.

"I need some air." My announcement came out in a rush to no one in particular, yet all four women in the room stood, offering me their companionship. Their kindness wasn't unnoticed by any means, but I assured them that I would be okay taking a few minutes alone. To think. To pray. To fill my lungs with fresh oxygen.

Gail unplugged my phone from the wall and handed it to me.

"I won't be too long," I said, careful not to overpromise. I didn't know how long I would need, but I did know that I couldn't hold one more conversation about which containers worked best inside a pantry, or the ideal way to organize a laundry room. Nor could I discuss summer vacations, neglected hobbies of the past, or strange weather phenomena happening in the South Pacific. Truth was, the distraction of off-topic conversation had been nice for a time, but even distraction with the best of intentions would never equal comfort.

During the past several weeks since we'd arrived home, we'd become well acquainted with the hallways of Boise Pediatrics Hospital. We'd met with surgeons, specialists, anesthesiologists, and even a geneticist, since Aria's medical history was limited at best. We'd learned numerous terminologies like *syncope* and *regurgitation* and the most obvious of them all, *cyanotic*: the term for the bluish tint that outlined Aria's nail beds. Her low oxygen levels had remained steady since our arrival home—not ideal for the long-term, but not as critical as I'd feared during our weeks together in China.

When we'd set her surgery date for the end of June, I'd felt both a sense of relief for the extra adjustment time at home as well as dread for the coming unknown. But that, I'd learned, was adoption in a nutshell, a recipe for all things bittersweet. In the same mixing bowl were often heaping amounts of celebration and challenge, gratitude and grief, hope and heartache.

I pushed out the exit doors leading to the courtyard and immediately wrapped my arms around my chest. My thin pink hoodie was plenty sufficient for the sunny day, but my internal temperature would take some time to thaw, to feel the penetration of vitamin D.

The cobblestone path wrapped around a garden of several varieties of roses and assorted perennial flowers. For having no sure destination, my stride was anything but meandering, my mind everywhere but on the beauty surrounding me.

Instead, I focused on a succession of memories from earlier this morning: Aria's brave smile when we checked in at the nurses' station; the heavily glittered unicorn purse she carried—filled with lip balm, gum, and a mini notebook; the scent of her peach-vanilla shampoo that stirred my emotions as I readied her on the hospital bed, trading her My Little Pony pajamas for a plain indigo snap-back gown. And then there was Benny, who had woken up extra early on his second week of summer vacation to play three rounds of Connect Four with my girl, humoring her with funny faces and unpracticed Chinese phrases, while nurses buzzed around the room like honeybees.

My steps halted at the convergence of two cobblestone paths: a narrow bench made of concrete and stone to my left and the papery trunk of a cherry tree to my right. Delicate roses lined both walkways, their fragrance an overwhelming reminder of Aria's favorite bubble bath. And so right then and there, shrouded under graceful branches and manicured shrubs, I lifted my eyes to the parting clouds and spoke a prayer that resonated in the marrow of my bones. "Please, God, keep my baby safe. Make her heart whole again and send your comfort and peace to mine."

For several seconds my chin remained tipped skyward, my face soaking in the sun's transformative warmth, my soul lingering in the space between heaven and earth. Without conscious thought, my feet backtracked several steps as I sought the bench seat behind me. Because somehow, being in this sweet place, this tender spot where eternity felt close and peace felt tangible, was exactly what I'd been craving in that waiting room. Not an aimless walk around a rose garden, but a place to rest, reflect.

I closed my eyes and exhaled the breath I'd likely been holding since the moment I first took hold of Aria's hand in China. I tuned my ears to hear the flitting notes of a bird's song, the rustle of leaves somewhere overhead, and the hushed conversations of patients and their loved ones strolling through vivid blooms too beautiful to be associated with illness or suffering.

And then, after another deep exhale, I opened my eyes. And just like that, all the blood in my body warmed to a sight I hadn't laid eyes on in so, so long.

At first the figure in the distance was little more than a sun-spotted haze of long-legged strides and wind-tousled hair. But that one glance was enough to make me question, enough to make me stand, enough to make me exit my sanctuary of solitude and speak a name I thought often yet spoke rarely.

My lips pushed the three-syllable word out before the synapses in my brain had time to fire. "Joshua!"

Following a path I could see only through a slender gap in the hedges, he stopped, turned, and then simply stared.

I'd wondered about this day many times, wondered how it might feel to be near him again after so many months and a lifetime of events had passed us by. Wondered if time and circumstance would sever our once-strong connection.

Within a minute, he was there. Right in front of me, his face much the same and yet different somehow, too. His hair was trimmed, tailored to fit the professionalism of his business attire, yet his eyes were the same shade of kindness I remembered.

"Hi," I said, words suddenly eradicated from my vocabulary.

He shifted on his feet as if the ground beneath him was unsteady. "Hi."

A stiff breeze swept my hair across my face, and I worked to pin it back behind my ear, a move he silently tracked.

"I—" we both began at the same time.

We smiled and then tried again, only to stumble over each other's thoughts for a second time.

He laughed and gestured to me. "Go ahead. You first."

I nudged at a fallen flower with the toe of my shoe, hoping to sweep the awkwardness between us away just as easily. "My daughter—Aria—she's in surgery. Since this morning. Her heart." I didn't know why I couldn't form complete sentences, but he'd always been able to string together my disjointed thoughts. I hoped that hadn't changed.

He raked a hand through his hair and blew out a breath. "I didn't know that was happening today. I was told it was on the books for next week." He paused. "Jenna." Both a name and a statement—Jenna, the one to fill in all the gaps and connect all the missing links.

"They moved it up a few days due to a cancellation."

"How is she—Aria?" A tender question I wished I could answer in much more detail than a chance encounter on a hospital sidewalk allowed. In a different life, I'd tell him all about the *more* of motherhood, about bonding over sparkly nail polish and stick-on earrings, about the way my chest still constricted whenever she entered a room and called me *Mama*.

I'd tell him about the losses she'd already experienced at such a tender age, how she often wept before bedtime, clinging to me as if I might suddenly disappear, how she routinely spoke of children she missed from her orphanage, how she dreaded the dark and needed to be prepped before any lights were turned off, and how her hardest moments at home were often bathed in the struggle of needing to feel in control of something—anything—in her young life again. And then I'd tell him how God had broken my heart over and over and over, pruning away my limited views on love and grafting in His own.

I swallowed and slipped my phone from my pocket, glancing at the blank screen and rerouting my brain to current events only. "I'm waiting to hear still. They should be finishing up within the next hour or so. At least, that's my hope. Brian said it could take between five and six hours before she's back to her recovery room."

His eyes focused on mine, his expression so earnest and honed that I couldn't soften its impact on my pulse. "Lauren, I've started at least twenty texts to you since you've been back home. I just haven't known . . ." He allowed the sentence to fade into the breeze before he began a new one. "I've wanted to be sensitive to you. And to your daughter." He tugged on his left shirt cuff. "But if there's ever anything I can do, anything I can ever help you with after the surgery . . ."

"Thank you."

Another long pause as I noticed his laptop satchel and his crisp white button-down dress shirt for the first time. My gaze traveled from him to the path he'd been walking that led into the main building. "Oh—I haven't congratulated you yet! Congratulations!"

A fog of confusion shadowed his features.

"On your big hospital contract," I amended.

"A*h*," he said.

"It sounds like Brian and the entire board were so impressed with your presentation."

"It was a good day."

But the measured way he said it made a girlish voice inside me yearn to ask a trillion more questions, about all the days I'd missed—the good, the bad, the in-between. I cleared my throat, drowning her out with a mature voice of reason. "Does that mean the storyboard you created was a hit? You worked so hard on that. I bet your family was so proud to hear the news." I could easily imagine George slapping his son on the back, his smile bright and wide, while his mother's eyes glistened with unshed tears over her son's winning entrepreneurial spirit.

"Well, not to brag, but I did get a fancy dinner out of the deal."

"Oh yeah? Another Avery seafood extravaganza?"

"Better. My niece invited me over for a date. She cooked. I cleaned. We even had some extra guests join us last-minute—a few with well-loved fur, others with plastic scales. Oh, and one scantily clad Ken doll missing a leg."

I raised my eyebrows and stifled a laugh. "Well, now, that *does* sound like a fancy meal indeed. I didn't realize Emma had such an interest in culinary arts."

"Oh yes, she has quite the refined palate." He twisted his lips into a pondering smirk. "Let's see, I think her menu was mac and cheese from a box, a side of sliced hotdogs, and an applesauce pouch. Oh, and of course, hot Earl Grey tea."

I snickered at that. Emma and her obsession with all things England. "Sounds like a well-balanced meal."

"Exactly what I told her." A smile reminiscent of the ones lodged deep into the folds of my memories tugged at the corners of his lips.

I'd forgotten this, the banter that had come so naturally to us both, the common ground we shared, the satisfaction of being known. I'd missed it. Missed him, even more than I'd let myself realize.

"How are they—your family?" The humor had faded from my tone, replaced by a genuine need to hear about a family who had been so quick to take me in and show me kindness and care.

"As ornery as ever," he said. "But good just the same." For the briefest of moments, his glance skimmed the ground at our feet. "They still ask about you."

"They do?"

He nodded and tucked his hands into the pockets of his black slacks. "Emma especially. She thinks you moved to China to have a baby—no matter how many times I've tried to explain it to her, she still doesn't quite understand the concept of adoption." He shook his head. "But she hasn't forgotten your British accent. Whenever I attempt one of my own, she always says it's not as good as Miss Lauren's." He caught my gaze with his. "She's right."

My stomach dipped and knotted. "Tell her I said hello, will you? And that I haven't forgotten her, either. I haven't forgotten any of you."

An admission that bordered far too close to the truth.

The phone I'd tucked inside my sweatshirt pocket vibrated against my palm, sending all the blood in my body rushing to the space between my temples. I yanked out the device and shaded the glare of the screen with my hand, reading the update I'd been waiting on since our first appointment with the cardiology team at Boise Pediatrics two months ago.

The shorthand was separated into three digestible, bite-size phrases:

Surgery's over.

Better than expected.

Back in recovery room in thirty minutes.

The only words I could utter were "Thank you, God."

"Looks like a best-case scenario. Aria must be as brave as her mom."

"No." I shook my head. "No, she's much, much braver."

I raised my chin to find Joshua's cheek only a short distance away from my own. He'd been reading the update over my shoulder, right alongside me, and despite him never having met my Aria in person, and despite not being present for any of our major homecoming events, it felt absolutely right that he was here for this one. That he'd been the person with me when I received the good news. And for the first time, I wondered if running into him like this hadn't been happenstance at all, but something much more divine.

As if my feet had grown roots into the cobbled path, my body swayed slightly as new relief expanded in my lungs.

"She's good," he said firmly. "She's gonna be fine, Lauren."

His comforting words resounded in my heart on repeat. *She's gonna be fine. She's gonna be fine. She's gonna be fine.*

An arm fastened around my shoulders. It was the only encouragement my pounding head needed to nestle against a chest I'd sought comfort from before. We stayed that way for several minutes, joined together at the convergence of a divided path, a place that sought no apologies, or excuses, or any words at all.

Joshua escorted me inside the building and down the hallway where Aria's support team would be anxiously awaiting the good news. Steps away from the entrance to the waiting room with the giant fish tank and ladybug side tables, Joshua's stride broke. He stopped, as if there were a line drawn across the cold linoleum floor that prevented him from crossing the threshold.

He didn't reach out, didn't try to touch me at all. He just offered a smile that resurrected every emotion I'd filed away last January. "I'm happy for you, Lauren. For both you and Aria. It was really good to see you."

I cleared my thickening throat. "You too."

In lieu of a good-bye, he simply dipped his head once and strode away, back down the long, lonely hallway.

"Hey, Joshua!" I called after him, backtracking my steps at a near jog until he turned. His eyes locked on mine. "You should meet her—Aria," I exclaimed in a breathy sprint of words. "We'll be here for close to a week, so if you want to stop by in a few days, after she's in more of a routine, that would be nice. We're in Room 404."

For the longest time, his expression remained unreadable, completely transfixed, as if he were analyzing every possible angle of my spontaneous invitation, and perhaps, knowing Joshua, that was exactly what he was doing.

But when he finally blinked, finally opened his mouth to reply, his voice registered low and clear. "I'd love nothing more."

chapter thirty-three

In the eighth grade I went on my first-ever real camping trip to the mountains with a group from my school. We pitched our own tents, cooked our own food, and slept in sleeping bags that promised warmth in any weather and yet always felt cold and damp by the time the sun came up. After two long nights in the great outdoors, the highs of camping life had worn off, and I craved nothing more than the comfort of a soft mattress, walls that didn't shake from a light breeze, and a bedroom where nothing howled or screeched when the lights turned out.

In a way, extended hospital stays were much the same. Though my thirty-one-year-old body appreciated the fold-out recliner in arm's reach of Aria's hospital bed, both my daughter and I were ready for a full night's sleep without round-the-clock interruptions from beeping monitors and vital check-ups.

Today was day four of recovery, and Aria's moods had suffered even more than her REM sleep. My usually enthusiastic child had retreated into a worrisome shell of disinterest. And it seemed no matter how many times I tried to reassure her that these long days of recovery would not be the rest of our lives, the vortex of the hospital often felt a world away from reality.

"Mama." Aria's voice was a dry-sounding croak. She pointed

to her water bottle and mimed the action of drinking. I stood from my recliner—currently in the day position of a chair—and placed the ribbed straw into her mouth so she could sip. Her appetite had waned considerably since the surgery, but her thirst rarely seemed quenched.

"Are you hungry?" I set the jug of water back on the portable tray over her bed and reached for the slice of buttered toast she'd left on her breakfast plate. Along with ninety percent of her scrambled eggs and yogurt. Two things she had usually eaten with abandon since we arrived home from China.

"No." She shook her head and sighed against her pillow. Her once sparkly brown eyes looked dull and depressed, especially when compared to the bright *Get Well Soon* balloons and flowers that filled her room. I held up her Etch A Sketch and the colored pencil case my niece had brought her yesterday along with a sketchbook, but again she shook her head.

Although Brian assured me this response was normal, even expected after seventy-two hours in the hospital, the nagging sensation in the pit of my stomach wouldn't fade. It wasn't that I expected her to sing and dance and ask to be read to every few hours the way she had at home, but even the smallest light in her eyes would do my mommy heart good. Her heart, too.

Despite her low energy and even lower interest in the world around her, Aria's vitals had been excellent, ahead of schedule, with zero setbacks. I'd watched her sleep those first twenty-four hours, fearful to close my eyes for even the briefest of naps. But Gail had nudged me to put the recliner down when she'd visited the following day. And my body had sunk into a dreamless oblivion for nearly three hours without stirring.

Between Jenna, Gail, my mom, and my sister, I'd had plenty of opportunities to nap and shower and feel semi-human over the last few days. And while I longed to be home, longed to comfort my baby in her own room, I often wondered if my instincts would compare to those of a mother who'd worn the parenting badge for much longer than I had. Would I know what to do if something came up at home? I pushed the thoughts away and focused again on trying to find something—*anything*—that would spark some interest in my daughter's eyes.

I rummaged through the bag I'd packed with all her favorite toys the night before her surgery and passed on the digital book with vocabulary picture cards in both Mandarin and English. It was one of the best things I'd purchased for language development and a huge contributing factor to her English taking off so quickly over the last two and a half months. But while she'd loved using this tool inside our house, she hadn't been interested in it here at all, no matter how many times I'd presented it to her.

"Aria, look!" I'd just pulled my hand out of the bag, twisted around, and wiggled the five finger puppets I'd put on that I'd been saving for a day just like this one, when a knock sounded at the door.

"Come in." I expected a nurse to bustle inside, or whichever pediatric cardiologist was on call today, but it wasn't medical personnel standing on the other side of the door. It was Joshua.

My hand froze midair, all five members of Peppa Pig's family suspended in time.

"Hey, hi," I said dumbly, ripping the pigs off one by one and tossing them behind me. "You came. You're here."

"I hope I didn't miss the puppet show." He worked to smooth his hair to the side, but less than a half second later, it rumpled right back. "I texted you a couple hours ago. I wasn't sure if I should wait for a reply or try my luck and just show up."

I shot an anxious glance in Aria's direction. She was straining to catch a glimpse of the mystery man just outside her field of vision behind the door.

"No problem if it's not the best time for a visit, I can just—"

"No, no. It's a fine time. Perfectly fine. I just . . ."—*have no earthly idea how I should be feeling right now or how exactly I should introduce you to my daughter or if I even remembered to run a comb through my hair after I brushed my teeth*—"I'm sorry I missed your text. I keep my phone on silent because I'm never sure when Aria might take a nap."

"Mama?" Aria pointed at the doorway and then lifted her hands in a shrug. "Doctor?" She could pick out several words in an English conversation now, even string three-word and sometimes four-word sentences together, but there was no way she'd comprehended any of my quick, disjointed replies. Her understanding of body language, though, was another thing entirely. Aria could read a person's mannerisms and tone better than most adults.

"No, not a doctor," I said, shaking my head and waving our guest inside.

Joshua stepped over the threshold and into the hospital room. His clothing choice of a faded orange T-shirt with the phrase *Got Nerd?* on it, paired with distressed denim, was a far more familiar sight than the business attire I'd seen him in a few days ago, though his laptop satchel was still slung across his chest.

"Aria." I touched Joshua's upper arm as my daughter's gaze connected with the man who'd once loved me enough to let me go. "This is mama's *pengyou*." The Mandarin word for friend. "Joshua." I said his name slowly, emphasizing the consonants and vowels and giving her a few seconds to absorb it.

"Jo-shu-a." Aria tracked my pronunciation well, mouthing and repeating his name. "Pengyou. Friend," she translated on her own.

"Yes," I encouraged. "Good job, Aria."

Joshua stood at the foot of her bed, gripping the thick railing while a smile spread across his entire face. "Wow." He looked from her to me, clearly impressed, and perhaps a little stunned for words, too. I'd come to recognize that response from people when they encountered her for the first time.

He turned his attention fully back to Aria. "You're very smart." He tapped his temple, stretching the words out slowly.

Though she'd heard that particular phrase from me many times, she squinted and tilted her head to the side now, as if processing it anew. From him. I was reaching for my phone to pull up the translation app when she surprised us by saying a sincere "Thank you."

Again, his eyes widened in awe. I'd grown so accustomed to her picking up on new words and phrases over the last couple of months that the shock of how quickly she caught on to English had worn off a bit. And yet it ratcheted up again every time her social circle widened.

Joshua opened his mouth. Closed it again. And then chuckled as if he wasn't exactly sure what to do next.

I tossed him a life raft.

"Here, why don't you sit down? Take the recliner. It's the only semi-comfortable choice for a guy your height. That rocking chair in the corner is brutal."

He glanced around the room. "But where will you sit?"

"All I've done for the last few days is sit. I'd like to stand and stretch my legs a bit."

Aria glanced between us, our words too rapid for her to catch, and yet I could tell her brain was processing something regardless. She pointed to the phone in my hand and then tapped her chin twice, our sign for needing the translator app.

I handed it over to her and then scooted out of the way, making room for Joshua to sit. And as he did, he picked up the sketchbook Aria had disregarded days ago on the side table. "Do you like to draw?" He mimed the action as he spoke, and she nodded once, studying him in earnest.

He flattened a hand to his chest. "Me too."

She gestured at the sketchbook and then made a scribbling motion. "Jo-shu-a, draw?"

"Oh, um, sure." His eyes shifted to mine, and I nodded, my

heart expanding ten times inside my rib cage as I observed their exchange. Aria was often shy around new people, especially men, but whatever she saw in Joshua had lowered her usual caution to a minimum. Perhaps it was due to my close proximity to them, but perhaps it was something else. Something innately Joshua.

He flipped a few pages in her book, giving her previous artwork several compliments and a thumbs-up before stopping a moment on the sketch she'd drawn of us holding hands underneath a thick rainbow.

"Aria?" he asked, pointing to the shorter, dark-haired girl she'd drawn in a crimson dress and shiny black shoes with bows on the toes. She nodded in answer.

His finger trailed right, to the woman with the goldenrod hair and pale blue gown suited for a royal ball. "And this must be your mama?"

Aria nodded. "Pret-ty."

"Yes, she is." And though his focus never left the page, my neck prickled under his admiration.

He reached into the art tin and picked out an ebony-colored pencil. With short, quick strokes, he drew a shape on a new page, then spent the next few seconds shading in some of the white space. Aria kept trying to peek at the paper, but he'd pull the notebook higher and hold up a single finger, indicating she had to wait.

She beamed at me, giggling as if art peekaboo was her new favorite game. Anything that involved her smiling like that was my favorite.

At last Joshua flipped the picture around and she *oohed* and *aahed* over it, pointing for him to show it to me, as well.

"Panda," he said, tapping the cute, plump panda bear he'd sketched for her.

"Pan-da," she repeated, the *da* too soft to be heard.

"Hmm. What's *panda* in Chinese?" he asked.

She tilted her head again, giving me a look that said she wasn't sure what he'd asked. I tapped my chin, encouraging her to use the app she'd grown quite proficient with.

As soon as she held it out to him, Joshua spoke directly into the phone's microphone. Within half a second, the translation was given and Aria was nodding in understanding.

"*Xiongmao*," she said, answering his question about the Mandarin word for panda.

He tried it. "Xiongmao."

She giggled and said it again for him. Slower.

He practiced three more times until his inflections matched hers exactly.

She gave him a delighted double clap, which was the most energy she'd expended since her surgery.

He bowed low. "Thank you. Thank you."

After a few more rounds of playing Mandarin Pictionary on Aria's sketchbook, where Joshua drew pictures and then asked her the corresponding word, he seemed to remember something he needed in his satchel. He opened the worn leather flap, reached inside, and plucked out a mini iPad. He powered it on, tapped the screen, and pulled up an app I didn't recognize. All the while, Aria's eyes never strayed from him once.

"I made something," he said as if he were admitting something he wasn't quite sure he should be admitting. Briefly, his glance flickered to me, before focusing once again on the screen. "It's for Aria, but I can show it to you first if—"

"No, that's okay. Go ahead, I trust you." And I did trust him. Implicitly.

"Technically speaking, it's still full of glitches and not even close to being ready for mass market, but I hoped it might brighten her remaining days at the hospital. One advantage is, it doesn't require language to play."

Curious, I leaned over his shoulder as he typed in the ID and passcode.

A white firework exploded on the dark screen, melting away the passcode page. Aria *oohed* as the screen shifted to an image of a hospital room and bed, much like the one my daughter lay in now. On the far left side of the screen was a column with every kind of wardrobe accessory imaginable. Wands, tiaras, fancy shoes, superhero shields, tool belts, etc. And standing in the middle of it all was an avatar that perfectly resembled my little warrior princess.

"What?" I breathed. "Is this the app you've been building for the hospital?"

He nodded. "The basics of it, yes. Aria will be our first official user."

He turned the tablet to show her fully, and she immediately gasped and pointed to her healing chest. "Aria?"

A sob-like laugh escaped me. "Yes, sweetie. That's you."

"May I show her how it works?"

"Of course, yes."

He wheeled the bed tray aside and handed Aria the device, stooping over her to tap on the screen and show how to move her avatar around the room, dress her in costume, and venture out into the obstacle course of a hospital she'd come to know too well for a child of nearly six. Every time her avatar leapt over a new hurdle to gather gems, coins, or diamonds to add to the treasure chest in her room, she exclaimed as if she were winning them in real life. But it was the sound effects of the game she seemed to enjoy the most—repeating certain actions over and over again and giggling to herself.

Joshua chuckled, obviously delighted by her responses.

After slipping my phone from the folds of blankets on Aria's bed, I leaned against the counter at the back of the small room. I took several pictures of them together and immediately sent them to Joshua's phone. Some moments were too precious not to capture. And as they sent, I saw Joshua's missed text message for the first time.

Wow. This is the first text I've sent to you in five months. That doesn't seem possible. But here we are, and it feels right that my first text to you should be about meeting your daughter. I'm glad to hear her recovery is better than expected. How are you doing? Is today a good day to visit? I'm free any time today until 2:00 p.m.

Yes, I thought, listening to a beautiful blend of laughter in the background. *Here we are indeed. Five months later.*

And though I had absolutely no clue where *here* was, or even if there would ever be a *we* to speak of again, I couldn't help but smile as I watched two of my favorite people interact together, their only common language a unique connection they'd discovered all on their own. As Joshua tapped an icon that made a squirting sound, Aria melted into a fit of giggles I wouldn't have imagined possible earlier this morning, and yet lately it seemed my entire life could be summed up in the impossible becoming possible.

"Knock, knock," Dr. Brian said, pushing into the room, a weighty clipboard in hand. "Ah, I wondered who was causing all those belly laughs. Makes total sense now."

"Hey," Joshua said, straightening. "I was just showing your patient a few gaming tricks on the new app."

"Seriously?" In a matter of seconds, Brian dropped his doctorly status and hightailed it to Aria's bedside with the eagerness of a teenage boy. "You haven't even shown this to *me* yet."

"Well, you're not even half as cute as little Aria is, so—"

"Whoa," Brian said, ignoring Joshua's comment and focusing on whatever Aria was causing her avatar to do. "This is seriously cool! Even better than you said it would be." Brian popped his head up and spoke to me. "It's hard to believe something so ingenious can come from a guy who dresses like that, right?" He hitched his thumb toward Joshua.

"Hey," I said, pushing away from the counter. "Stop picking

on his shirts. They're a creative expression. Nobody tells you how to dress."

Joshua's eyebrows hiked at my defensive jab, and immediately my cheeks were aflame.

"Uh, have you met my wife? She threw out eighty percent of my wardrobe while we were still dating. I don't even remember the last time I bought myself an article of clothing."

We all laughed, and Joshua gave me a wink—a signature Joshua action, like his taste in apparel.

He glanced at his watch and surprise hitched his eyebrows skyward. "Oh, wow, it's almost two already. I actually have to get going. I'm headed out of town for a quick trip." He rotated to speak to Aria. "It was sure good to meet you, Aria Fei. And you should know, you have the best mama around." Joshua laid a gentle hand atop Aria's head, her uncomprehending eyes staring at him unblinkingly. "Good-bye, sweetheart."

Joshua swept his satchel off the floor, slung it over his chest, and then tenderly gripped my elbow, leaning in close enough for our cheeks to graze. "She's incredible, Lauren. Thank you for letting me meet her."

Before I had time to respond, he pressed a soft kiss to my cheek and moved toward the exit.

Aria's face grew concerned. "Jo-shu-a bye?"

"Yes," I assured her as he paused at the door. "He has to go bye-bye, but we'll see him again soon." The instant the words were out, I hoped they'd come true. "I mean, I hope we will."

Hope knocked hard against my chest as his eyes lingered on mine for a second more before Brian blocked our line of sight and began his review of Aria's latest scan reports, forcing my mind to switch gears entirely.

I never even heard the door close behind him.

"Got to admit," Brian said, putting his clipboard down for a second time and adjusting Aria's bed with the remote so it lay nearly flat. "I'll miss seeing that guy around the hospital."

"What? " I asked, confused. "Who?"

As if the answer was as obvious as the reports he'd been reading from on his clipboard. "Joshua." He pointed to the ties at the back of Aria's neck. This was our routine, my job as mother-of-the-patient: untying her gown so he could check the sutures on her chest and update me on her healing progress. Only now my body moved stiffly, almost robotically, as my mind stumbled to process what he could possibly mean.

"Where's he going?"

He loosened her collar enough for me to hold up the fabric as she laid her head back on the pillow, her eyes watching me intently.

"Dallas," he said.

My insides twisted into one giant knot at his matter-of-fact pronouncement.

Aria whimpered a bit as he touched the inflamed skin around her healing scar, and I bent to kiss her forehead. "He's almost done, baby. Just a minute more. You're doing great."

Brian let the gown settle back over her tender skin, and I tied the loose strings into a bow.

"What's in Dallas?"

"A massive tech job," he said while jotting some notes down. "With our mothership hospital. Pretty sure that's where he's headed now, for a final meeting to work out contract agreements. I told him not to forget the little people as he climbs up the nerd ladder. But really, an opportunity like that can be life-changing for a career like his. Couldn't be happier for him. His brand of genius ought to be shared with the world."

Brian retracted his pen and dropped his clipboard to his side, flowing easily from one subject to the next while I reeled over the idea of Joshua moving half a country away. "She's looking great, Lauren. I'm really pleased with how her body's healing. Another two to three days in here, and we'll send her home with those recovery instructions we discussed." He flashed Aria a thumbs-up on his way out of the room as if he hadn't just plucked out a seedling of hope that had only just been planted thirty minutes ago. "Keep up the good work, champ."

Aria returned his gesture, then pointed to the paused iPad Joshua had left for her on the bed. "More?"

"Yes, that's fine." I kneaded the area at the base of my throat and watched my daughter play on the creation Joshua had made especially for her.

Joshua is moving to Dallas.

Moving. To. Dallas.

The news diminished my hope that maybe what I'd witnessed between him and Aria could bloom with time. That maybe there was a possibility for us to . . . to start over, to begin a different type of friendship. But those possibilities were simply not meant to be, and I needed to be okay with that.

We'd only spent two hours together in the last five months. I had no right to feel disappointed or to question his life choices. Joshua deserved better than that from me. He deserved to be supported, championed, encouraged to chase after his dreams without any reason to look back. Hadn't he given me the same gift when I'd needed it most?

I forced a smile on my face and snuggled up to my little girl, who was giddily waving a magical wand around her virtual hospital room. I kissed the top of her head and made a promise to love Joshua the same way he'd so selflessly loved us.

By letting him go.

chapter thirty-four

Before this week, I hadn't known what a blessing Meal Train could be, especially after five days of eating mass-produced hospital food. The online dinner delivery schedule Gail had organized within our small community had been a tremendous help, and one less thing I had to think about as we made the transition back home. However, the serving sizes delivered each night had more than exceeded what any woman-and-child duo could consume in a week, much less in a single evening. I'd run out of places to store 9x12 lasagna pans, porcelain casserole dishes, and all of the snap-lid containers once filled with salads, pastas, and every kind of loaf bread known to Pinterest.

Whenever possible, I gave away the leftovers—to neighbors, to friends, to the mail carrier who didn't blink twice when I handed him a paper plate of blueberry muffins in exchange for my daily mail. But while my kitchen counter resembled the aftermath of a cooking competition on the Food Network, it was impossible to see the extra dishes as anything other than a reminder of God's promised provision for my little family. He'd asked me to trust Him, and when I had, He'd given back tenfold what He'd asked of me.

I peeked under the lid of a steaming pot of dumplings. The aroma filled my kitchen and my heart as I thought of the hands that had prepared such a kindness for my little girl: Melanie and Peter Garrett, the couple I'd met at the adoption group last fall.

I'd been surprised to receive the text alert when the Garretts had signed up to bring a meal over tonight, but even more surprising was that the Melanie I'd encountered last November and again around Christmas, the one who once shot ice daggers from her eyes and bolted from the support group mid-discussion, was not the same Melanie who showed up on my front porch with my daughter's favorite meal tonight. Gone was the bitter edge to her voice and the air of resentment that had once encircled her. In their place was an empathic woman who'd been reformed from hardship and refined by love. She thanked me again for folding their laundry that day in December and gave me an update that brought tears to my eyes. Their adoption had finalized the same month I'd been with Aria in China, although she didn't credit the adoption certificate for the massive changes in their home; she credited their new church community and the Cartwright family in particular.

I'd given her a hug and asked if we could stay in touch, get our kids together for a playdate once Aria was fully recovered, and she had readily agreed. God was full of surprises.

I secured the lid on the steel pot once more and rose up on my tiptoes to glance over the counter at a snoozing Aria. She'd fallen asleep on the sofa while I was visiting with Melanie at the front door. My daughter's arm was draped over her eyes like an aristocrat on a fainting couch. She hadn't eaten dinner, but her tummy was likely still full of animal crackers from all our errand running today. I sighed and contemplated how I was going to get her upstairs to her room. Aria was a petite child, but sleeping weight was difficult to manage no matter the child's size when it meant hiking a full flight of stairs.

Skye bolted upright, leaping off the sofa from her place at

Aria's feet. She pressed her nose against the narrow window next to my front door, whining and scratching and carrying on. *Odd.* She never acted like that.

"What's up, girl?" I crossed the living room. "What do you see out . . ." But my words trailed off as soon as my gaze registered what—*or who*—had provoked such a spontaneous bout of excitement from her. Joshua had mentioned he had something to give Aria from his family, so perhaps whatever he was hefting out of his trunk was just that—a gift delivery. Only I knew it wouldn't be his only reason for coming tonight.

Though I hadn't seen him since the hospital room last week, he'd texted twice, once to thank me for the pictures I'd sent of him and Aria, and once three days ago to see if we'd settled in at home okay. He'd asked if there was anything he could bring us from the grocery store, but I hadn't taken him up on the offer. It wasn't fair to him, not when I knew what he was planning to do in just a few weeks' time. Or maybe I simply hadn't been ready for the inevitable conversation that would come along with a delivery of Pop-Tarts and fresh produce.

But I'd had ten days to prepare for this moment, and I was ready now. I could have this hard conversation. Not because I wanted to, but because Joshua needed me to. And I could—*would*—do it without tears. He deserved nothing less than the same unshakable support he'd offered to me.

I ducked behind my closed front door for a full five seconds to fix my two-day-old messy bun, exhale the static populating in my chest, and repeat a prayer I'd spoken often. "Please be with me, God."

As he started up my walkway, backlit by a nearly full moon, I opened my front door to greet him. Only Skye charged ahead of me, whirling around his legs and nearly causing him to stumble.

"Oops! Sorry!" Barefoot, I trekked to the edge of my front porch and called for my spastic dog to come back inside.

"Hello to you, too, Skye," Joshua said, trying not to step on her as he lumbered up the walkway, his arms overloaded.

After my third scolding, Skye finally obeyed, her tail between her legs. I gripped her collar so she couldn't break away again. "I didn't think about her being a tripping hazard when I opened the door. Can I help you with . . . whatever that is you're carrying there?"

Joshua peeked his head around the bulging basket. "Maybe just tell me when to step up? I can't see where I'm walking."

"Oh, okay, sure." I told Skye to go to her bed and then touched Joshua's elbow, guiding him to the edge of the porch step. Whatever he carried inside the basket was heavy enough to strain all the veins in his forearms and leave a glistening sheen on his forehead.

"Ready, step. Now one more. Okay, you're good."

A warm breeze whipped stray hair from my messy bun as he neared my open doorway.

"Thanks. Do you mind if I set this down inside?"

"Of course not, come in." Did he really think he wasn't welcome inside? I ushered him into the living room, where he set the armload on the ground with a grunt.

My eyes widened at the sight of the treasures in the belly of the enormous basket.

Books. So many, many books. Hundreds.

Immediately, I lowered myself to the floor. "Joshua . . . what are all these?" But it was obvious as I began pawing my way through a variety of children's books—board books, early readers, chapter books. A collection of handpicked masterpieces I knew by heart.

"According to my dad, they're the top recommended beginner books for ESL students. He pulled a few strings, and of course he threw in a few of his favorites, too, for good measure."

With my jaw completely unhinged, I looked from the books to him and back again several times. "I'm speechless. Thank you, and please, please thank your father for us. This is one of the kindest, most thoughtful gifts I've ever received. Aria will absolutely love these." I glanced behind Joshua at the sofa where Sleeping Beauty rested. "When she's awake."

His gaze held on Aria's sleeping form on the far side of the living room. "How's she doing? How's the recovery been going?"

"Really well overall." I stretched tall again, which meant Joshua still dwarfed me by at least six inches. "But she's been pretty exhausted today. We had her first round of check-up appointments this afternoon, and although everything's on target medically, she's pretty maxed out on waiting rooms and doctors. She cried all the way home, and I figured she'd fall asleep on the car ride, but nope. That girl might have been born with an imperfect heart, but I assure you her vocal chords are in great working order." I shook my head and chuckled. "She played with Skye for almost an hour before she finally gave in and passed out on the couch there. Honestly, you'd never guess she just had heart surgery. Her only real limitation now is getting to the top of the stairs on her own. But Jenna always tells me I should be working out more, so . . ." I flexed my puny biceps and drew his attention back to me.

The second his gaze met mine, all the oxygen leaked from my lungs. Because I *knew*. Joshua was going to tell me right now. Like this. With one foot on the way out the door, and suddenly I needed a bit more time. Just a few more minutes. Not to avoid the obvious, but to embrace it for the sake of closure. For the sake of everything we once shared together.

He rubbed the back of his neck, exhaled, and opened his mouth to—

"Do you like pork dumplings?" I asked, my voice a bit too high and crackly.

He blinked hard and shook his head as if working to transition his brain to a new track. "What?"

"Pork dumplings," I said, trying to slow down the anxious

spike in my pulse. "We have a huge pot of dumplings, and I have some noodles as well. I'd love to feed you dinner if you're able to stay a little longer." *So we can say a proper good-bye.*

My eyes pleaded for him to say yes, for him to spare another few minutes, for him to say all that he needed to say over a nice meal in a familiar kitchen.

Again, he glanced back at Aria. "But what if she wakes up? Will it be okay if I'm here? I don't want to intrude on your plans this evening."

The concern in his voice was the first rolling rock of an avalanche in my chest.

"You're not intruding at all. I'm inviting you to stay. She's only been asleep for about thirty minutes, and after the day we've had, I wouldn't be surprised if she slept right on through the night."

He gave a hesitant nod. "Okay, then. Thank you."

The smile I wore cramped my cheeks, but I refused to let it drop a single centimeter as we trailed through the living room and into the kitchen, where so many memories, including those of our last day together in my home, replayed in my mind.

I'd just set two plates next to the stove when he launched in, his resolute tone turning my stomach inside out.

"Lauren, I need to be honest. I didn't stop by tonight just to deliver those books. I've actually had that basket in my trunk for over a month now."

My hand froze on the lid, and I forced myself to look directly into his eyes, to give him the same kind of courtesy and respect he'd given me on a day not so long ago, standing in a Cadet Blue nursery just one floor away.

"I'd planned to wait a while to say this. I'd hoped to give you a bit more time to adjust and settle in after the surgery, but I'm afraid Brian might have forced my hand when he . . ." His pained expression tugged at my empathy.

"Joshua, I know. And I'm happy for you." The words escaped my mouth before I could tell myself to stay quiet, before I could play along and pretend I didn't know what was coming next. But I loved him too much to put him through that, to make him suffer a single second more than necessary.

He paused. "You're *happy* for me?"

"Yes." I nodded as encouragingly as I could. "I think Dallas sounds like an incredible opportunity." Severing our connection, I placed a huge helping of fried noodles onto the plate nearest him and stacked a tower of dumplings on top of it for good measure. "I'm really, really happy for you."

"You are?" His voice held a note of confusion, and maybe something else as well, but I didn't have time to sort it out. Not when I was committed to making this the happiest good-bye in the history of farewells.

"Absolutely." Though according to the mountain of noodles I was serving myself, I was about to consume roughly ten years' worth of repressed feelings. "And I want to hear all about it. What Texas is like, what you're looking forward to the most. Everything."

Without taking his eyes off me, he slid his hand onto my wrist, making my plight of carrying two twenty-pound plates to the dining room table an impossibility.

His voice was close, and far, far too gentle, as if tenderness alone could call my bluff. "So you're telling me you'd be fine with it? Me moving out of state? Taking a job one thousand, six-hundred and thirty miles away from here?"

I remained completely still, unsure if I could will my body to betray me in such an epic way by agreeing to such a blatant mistruth. *Fine* with it? No, not even close. But this decision wasn't about me this time. It was about him, what was best for Joshua. Hadn't he done the same for me? For Aria?

I blinked up at him as a genuine smile replaced the one I'd been forcing since this conversation began. "I'm happy about what makes you happy, even if that means that happiness has to stretch one thousand, six-hundred and thirty miles away from here."

"And what if it doesn't?"

I crimped my brow. "Doesn't what?"

"Have to stretch. What if my happiness is everything within a twenty-foot radius of where I'm standing right now?"

My breathing became shallow. "What are you saying?"

"I turned down the job, Lauren. I'm not moving."

A sharp twist in my gut forced me back a step. "But why? Brian said it was a life-changing career opportunity."

He seemed to filter his next thoughts carefully. "At first I did consider taking it. I prayed about leaving town for weeks, questioned if that would be the best option in light of everything that had happened. Because even though I gave you the space you asked for, there wasn't a single day I didn't think about you or wonder how things were going. In China, at home, at the hospital." He paused, his eyes softening even more. "Nobody told me Aria's surgery had been rescheduled, Lauren. I'd actually planned to avoid the hospital that entire next week so our paths wouldn't accidentally cross. But weirdly enough, on my drive to the hospital that day I felt increasingly unsettled. I was frustrated that God hadn't made the answer clear about taking the job in Dallas. As I parked, I told Him I needed something concrete, something that would either set or change my course one way or another." The emotional charge in his voice stole my ability to inhale. "And then I saw you in the courtyard not two minutes later."

Tears clouded my vision, but no words formed on my tongue. Everything I'd planned to say, every emotion I'd planned to feign, was now completely irrelevant.

"I knew then that I wasn't supposed to leave, and I also knew that I'd do whatever it took to stay in your life. To stay in Aria's life." He slid a finger down my cheek, wiping away moisture I hadn't even known was there. "When I told Brian tonight that I'd recommended one of my partners for the job instead, and then about my plan to be a steady presence in the background of your lives, he confessed that he might have messed things up when he announced I was moving to Texas after my visit with Aria."

"That may have put a bit of a damper on things," I whispered through a broken laugh while I reached for his hand, held it, squeezed it.

Joshua steadied his gaze on me and exhaled. "I should have offered to wait, Lauren. That day in the nursery when you told me about Aria. I should have told you that no matter how much time you and Aria needed to adjust and attach, that I'd be here, waiting for you both in the background and cheering you on." With his free hand he smoothed the wisps of hair around my face that had broken free from my tired bun. "It was irresponsible to propose marriage, reckless even. I realize that now. Love isn't about instant gratification, it's about showing up for the journey and riding out all the twists and turns along the way . . . together." He brought our joined hands to his mouth and kissed my knuckles. "I'm not suggesting we need to figure anything out tonight, but I am hoping we can take it a day at a time, even if that means I'm your goofy friend who comes around once a month to draw panda sketches in a notebook with Aria."

"I have zero objections to that plan," I added, choking back tears.

"Our story is an original, Lauren. And I'm more than okay with waiting on the next chapters to be written." Joshua moved in and pressed his lips against my forehead. "I love you. More now than I did six months ago. And there is not a doubt in my mind that I will love your daughter just as fiercely."

"I love you, too. So, so much." I wrapped my arms around his middle and nestled my head against him. I needed to hear his heartbeat. To feel the rise and fall of his chest. To convince myself this was how our story would continue, not how it would end. "This is really happening? You're really staying?"

He held me tighter. "I don't want to be anywhere else."

Not far from where we embraced, Aria stirred on the couch.

We rotated to face the living room just in time to see her twist and press her nose into the back sofa cushion. Nothing about her position looked even remotely comfortable.

Joshua eyed me. "Do you think she'd be happier in her own bed?"

"Probably." I had a monitor in the kitchen and one on the nightstand in my bedroom, but the thought of trying to hike those stairs with her limp frame in my arms again was—

"I'll get her if you can get her blankets."

"You'll carry her up?"

"Of course," he said with a slight tease in his voice. "I wouldn't want to strain those puny biceps of yours."

I punched his arm, and he chuckled.

He started toward the sofa, then hesitated. "Wait—if she wakes, I don't want to freak her out."

"I really don't think she will." At least she hadn't any of the times I'd attempted and failed such a maneuver.

"Well, you better stay close behind us, Mama. Just in case."

"I will."

He bent to one knee and slid his arms underneath her slumbering form, as if he'd been doing such a maneuver for years. She curled into him, mumbling incoherently before falling back into her deep breathing pattern once more.

As the three of us moved up the staircase together, my daughter cradled in Joshua's strong arms and her favorite blanket and stuffed panda cradled in mine, I couldn't help but think of how much our lives had changed since that first day in Mrs. Walker's classroom, back when Joshua pretended to be a T-Rex for a room of children while I pretended to have my entire future figured out.

Neither one of us could have imagined this.

I shuffled in front of him to pull Aria's bedcovers back and turn on her princess night-light. He gently laid her down, then backed away to allow me space to tuck the blankets in around her body and kiss her forehead.

Back in the hallway, Joshua reached for my hand, saying nothing as we gazed into Aria's dimly lit bedroom through a doorway I once doubted would ever be open.

"When's her birthday?" Joshua asked.

"September twenty-seventh. Why?"

Joshua shook his head as if he'd just made a discovery.

"What?"

"Didn't you tell me you started feeling the nudge to adopt about five years ago, when Benny came into your classroom?"

"Actually, it will be . . ." I stared up at him, my eyes rounding as the calculation unfolded. "Six years. This September."

"The same age as Aria," we said at the same time.

Awe overwhelmed me at the thought of God's intricate and grand design. Six years ago, when Aria's birth mother made the heartbreaking sacrifice to surrender her sickly daughter over to the Chinese welfare system for reasons I'd never judge, and likely never know this side of heaven, God was already at work, preparing my heart and growing my faith for the call to adopt one of His precious children as my daughter.

Six years before I called her mine.

Joshua squeezed my hand. "We can trust His plan and His timing, Lauren."

"Yes." I nodded, tears shimmering in my eyes. "And we'll take it one day at a time."

For Aria.

For each other.

And for the much greater story at work within us all.

Acknowledgments

To my God, the Ultimate Storyteller: I pray my life will always reflect your deep, abiding love and grace. Thank you for loving me enough to show me where I'm weak so that you may be strong. I am nothing without you.

To my husband, Tim: Four years ago, on our twelfth anniversary, all I wanted was to finish eating my molten lava cake and enjoy the beautiful lakefront scenery . . . and yet you had something else in mind when you carefully and kindly brought up a conversation about stewardship in reference to orphan care. Though we had sought adoption together several times, the timing, for one reason or another, was never right. Thank you for being sensitive to the Holy Spirit's prompting after I'd closed (and locked) that particular door. Thank you for your tremendous patience as I wrestled my frustrations and fears out with Jesus, and for your grace to withstand my many, MANY freak-outs along our adoption journey. Once again, you saw *the more* I was too scared to believe in, and yet here we are, with a daughter who has expanded our heart and family in ways unimagined. You continue to lead our family well, and I am *so* *proud* to be your wife and adventure partner. You have always been my number-one fan, and I will always be yours.

To my kiddos, Preston, Lincoln, and Lucy: I am so proud to be your mama and even prouder to watch God at work in all of your lives. You are all passionate, kind, and dream-oriented, and I pray you always continue to press in to Jesus.

To my family: Thank you for opening your hearts to the idea of adoption even when it was little more than an item on our prayer list. Your faithfulness, encouragement, and support of our God-given calling was often what kept us going in the hard moments. We are blessed beyond measure to have parents and families who honor and uphold the heart of Christ. I (we) love you.

To Tammy Gray and Connilyn Cossette: You are my secret weapons, and I never ever want to write a story without either of you. I'm SO grateful that God joined our paths together when He did. Thank you for your MANY read-throughs of this book and for believing in the heart of my premise even before I put a single word on the page. You both challenge me to be the best version of me I can be, and yet you love me just the same. Here's to many more books together and many more years of friendship.

To Coast to Coast Plotter's Society: Christy Barritt, Connilyn Cossette, Amy Matayo, Tammy Gray. Five years! WOW! Now that's something awesome to celebrate! Thank you for the many hours you've dedicated to brainstorming this story with me and for all your enthusiasm and support. Can't wait for May!

To Jessica Kirkland: I vividly recall our phone conversation when I told you we were pursuing international adoption. I'd worried that you'd be concerned about the future of my career since adopting would mean a big break in my production schedule, but instead you so selflessly assured me that writing could wait and that Lucy could not. Thank you for your wisdom and guidance, in both my profession and personal life, and for being the best agent I could ever hope for!

To Raela Schoenherr, Acquisitions Editor: Thank you for saying yes to an early breakfast date one September morning and for ultimately saying yes to me. I'm honored to call you my editor.

To the dedicated team members at Bethany House Publishers: You've made my dreams for this story come true . . . and then some. Thank you for all the hours you've spent bringing Lauren's story to life and for cheering me on along the way. You're all awesome!

To Santha Yinger: I'm pretty sure by now I owe you somewhere in the ballpark of three million dollars for all the therapy and spiritual mentorship you've given me over the years. But here's hoping a yummy meal at Fire Pizza and a signed book might keep me in the black for another year. I cannot express how much your listening ear, prayer, and sound biblical advice have meant to me. You are my real-life Gail Cartwright (times ten), and I wouldn't want to do life without you. Thank you for leading well and for loving like Jesus.

To Daryla Collodi: For the COUNTLESS number of prayers you offered up for my little Lucy Mei during our journey . . . and especially the ones you offered up for her anxiety-ridden mother. You took such amazing care of us during our transition home, and we will never forget your MANY dinner deliveries (my boys still talk about your homemade cinnamon rolls)! Thank you, also, for giving me a nonjudgmental shoulder to cry on when I needed it most and for always, always directing me back to the feet of Jesus. I love you and miss you dearly, friend.

To my Life Group at RLM: You gals and guys rock! You've prayed with me, cried with me, laughed with me, and eaten way too much dessert with me. And I'm so grateful for the many seasons of life we've shared together.

To my early readers and influencers: Amy Matayo, Ashley Espinoza, Becky Wade, Bobbi Deitz, Carrie Schmidt, Carmen Hendewerk, Jessica Wardell, Joanie Schultz, Kacy Gourley,

Kara Isaac, Kedron Annotti, Kristin Avila, Lara Arkin, Laurie Tomlinson, Renee Deese, Susie May Warren, and my entire tribe at Nicole's Book Nook. Thank you for your ongoing support of Contemporary Christian Fiction and for your faithfulness in sharing your love of reading with friends, family, and abroad. You make it possible for me to live my dreams.

To Rel Mollet: Thank you for being the best author assistant an unorganized gal like me could hope for, and thank you for sending me timely, encouraging emails from across the world exactly when I needed them most. You are my favorite Australian. (*Shhh*, don't tell the others.)

To Holt International Adoption Agency and their awesome social worker Amy Castle: Not only do I need to thank you for verifying my facts and going over my story premise and conflict, but also for the dedicated service you and your fellow staff members provide to families all across the country every single day. It is no wonder Holt has such a highly esteemed reputation . . . it's because of social workers like you, Amy. You helped us every step of the way when we adopted our precious Lucy Mei, and we are forever in your debt.

Author's Note

From the moment I started writing Lauren's story, I knew at some point I would need to put down my author pen (or my MacBook—yet that never sounds quite as romantic) and share a different kind of story with you. Not one I've written, but one God has been authoring in my life since August 4th of . . . an undisclosed year in the early 1980s. *Before I Called You Mine* is my tenth novel. And while I'm usually partial to my most recent manuscript, there is something vastly different about this story's hold on my heart. Because so much of the journey found in these pages—of this struggle to live out the kind of faith that often calls us to the edges of ourselves—is my story, too.

In the summer of 2017, my husband and I flew to China to adopt our daughter, Lucy Mei, after eleven long months of prayer, paperwork, and only a handful of pictures of a tiny girl living in an orphanage far, far away. Lucy was just shy of seven years old at the time, spoke only Mandarin, and knew very little of what living in a family—with a father and mother and two older brothers—would be like. And yet her courage to trust us (which I assure you took longer than the reading of this novel) and allow us to guide her into a world where nothing felt familiar, easy, or comfortable is a testimony of faith that continues to challenge and convict me often.

And while saying *yes* to God's call to partner with Him and adopt Lucy into our family has radically transformed our lives, my prayer and intention for this story has never been about persuading my reader to adopt a child from overseas. (Though if that's what God is calling you to do, then w-o-n-d-e-r-f-u-l!!! Consider this my hug to you!) But my ultimate hope for this story isn't about the events of the climax at all; it's about *you*. Specifically, it's about a question I hope you'll ask yourself: *What is the hard that God's asking me to partner with Him in?*

Sure, it could be something involving a social justice matter, or maybe it's an investment of time or money in a ministry organization God keeps impressing upon your heart. Or maybe it's something closer to home, like committing to love and pursue that one cranky neighbor who yells at you to *slow down!* even when you're driving at a snail's pace. Or maybe it's something far more personal that He's asking you to trust Him in—a difficult relationship in need of loving boundaries, a broken marriage in need of forgiveness, a struggling child in need of extra grace.

God doesn't look for perfect people to share in His redemptive story (you only have to read the first three chapters of Genesis for proof of that). Instead, He searches the earth, looking to "strengthen those whose hearts are fully committed to him" (2 Chronicles 16:9).

The character of Lauren Bailey isn't perfect, either—she was insecure, anxious, avoidant, doubtful, fearful, and failed often. Yet her story, much like my own—and perhaps much like your own, too—is marked by the redemptive power of Christ and His love for us all, His chosen children.

Now, nearly three years post-adoption, when I look at our beautiful, healthy nine-year-old daughter, the fog of forgetfulness often hovers close. The hard that God has taken us through is a little further away, yet I will myself to remember where we've been and where He's taken us. Because God's best for us rarely comes without the stretching, and it's in those stretching seasons, those periods of complete and utter dependence on God's faithfulness, that He holds our hearts and molds them into a shape that only He can fill.

Wherever you're at on your partnership journey with Christ today, please know you can trust Him. You can trust Him to take your doubts, your fears, and your ten thousand reasons of why you couldn't possibly be the right candidate for His calling on your life, and allow Him to create the kind of story only heaven can script.

In His perfect love,
Nicole Deese

Nicole Deese's (www.nicoledeese.com) humorous, heartfelt, and hope-filled novels include the 2017 Carol Award–winning *A Season to Love*. Her 2018 release, *A New Shade of Summer*, was a finalist in the RITA Awards, Carol Awards, and INSPY Awards. Both of these books are from her bestselling LOVE IN LENOX series. When she's not working on her next contemporary romance, she can usually be found reading one by a window overlooking the inspiring beauty of the Pacific Northwest. She lives in small-town Idaho with her happily-ever-after hubby, her two wildly inventive and entrepreneurial sons, and her princess daughter with the heart of a warrior.

Sign Up for Nicole's Newsletter!

Keep up to date with Nicole's latest news on book releases and events by signing up for her email list at nicoledeese.com.

You May Also Like . . .

In an effort to restore the elegant house her grandmother grew up in, Kate finds herself being drawn to Matt, an ex-hockey player hired to help her renovate. When their stilted, uncomfortable interactions shift into something more, is God answering the longing of her heart—or asking her to give up more than she ever dreamed?

My Stubborn Heart by Becky Wade
beckywade.com

BETHANYHOUSE

Stay up to date on your favorite books and authors with our free e-newsletters. Sign up today at bethanyhouse.com.

facebook.com/bethanyhousepublishers

@bethanyhousefiction

Free exclusive resources for your book group at bethanyhouseopenbook.com

More from Bethany House

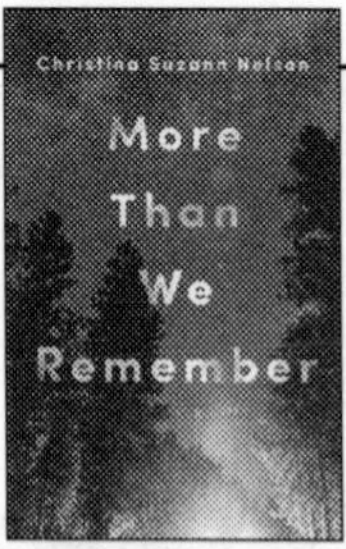

After a life-altering car accident, one night changes everything for three women. As their lives intersect, they can no longer dwell in the memory of who they've been. Can they rise from the wreck of the worst moments of their lives to become who they were meant to be?

More Than We Remember by Christina Suzann Nelson
christinasuzannnelson.com

Famous author Josephine Bourdillon is in a coma, her memories surfacing as her body fights to survive. But those around her are facing their own battles: Henry Hughes, who agreed to kill her for hire out of desperation, is uncertain how to finish the job now, and her teenage daughter, Paige, is overwhelmed by fear. Can grace bring them all into the light?

When I Close My Eyes by Elizabeth Musser
elizabethmusser.com

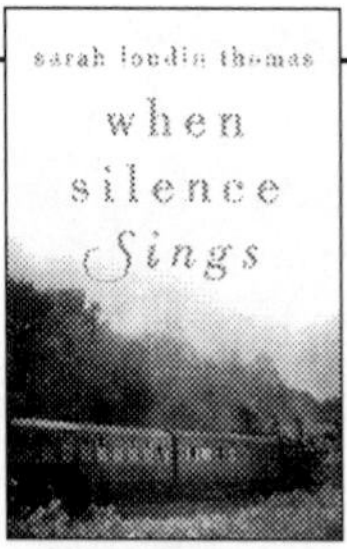

After the rival McLean clan guns down his cousin, Colman Harpe chooses peace over seeking revenge with his family. But when he hears God tell him to preach to the McLeans, he attempts to run away—and fails—leaving him sick and suffering in their territory. He soon learns that appearances can be deceiving, and the face of evil doesn't look like he expected.

When Silence Sings by Sarah Loudin Thomas
sarahloudinthomas.com